Eleanor's heart gave a jolt when she looked up to find Damon's face at her open bedroom window.

Her jaw dropping, she watched in disbelief as he eased his broad shoulders through the window and hauled himself inside, then lowered his feet to the carpet.

He was still dressed in formal evening wear, Eleanor noted distractedly, but that wasn't what held her speechless. It was the fact that he had climbed up two stories to a lady's bedchamber, after midnight, bold as you please.

"Damon!" she exclaimed, her voice a high, breathless rasp. "What the devil are you doing here?"

"I believe we left our conversation unfinished," he said coolly, crossing the room toward her bed.

"*To Romance A Charming Rogue* is Nicole Jordan at her finest! Sexy, sensual, and sparkling with wit, this book is a complete charmer!"
—KAREN HAWKINS,
New York Times bestselling author of
To Catch a Highlander

By Nicole Jordan

The Courtship Wars
To Pleasure a Lady
To Bed a Beauty
To Seduce a Bride
To Romance a Charming Rogue

Paradise Series
Master of Temptation
Lord of Seduction
Wicked Fantasy
Fever Dreams

Notorious Series
The Seduction
The Passion
Desire
Ecstasy
The Prince of Pleasure

Other Novels
The Lover
The Warrior
Touch Me with Fire

A Novel

TO ROMANCE A CHARMING ROGUE

Nicole Jordan

BALLANTINE BOOKS · NEW YORK

A Ballantine Books Mass Market Original

Copyright © 2009 by Anne Bushyhead

Published in the United States by Ballantine Books, an imprint of The Random House Publishing Group, a division of Random House, Inc., New York.

BALLANTINE and colophon are registered trademarks of Random House, Inc.

ISBN 978-0-345-51010-5

Printed in the United States of America

www.ballantinebooks.com

OPM   9   8   7   6   5   4   3   2   1

With heartfelt thanks to my readers—
the best inspiration a writer could have.
This one's for you.

Chapter One

*Never appear to be too captivated by a gentleman,
particularly if it is true. Revealing your weakness for
him will give him the upper hand, and a woman needs
all the power she can muster if she is to triumph.*

—An Anonymous Lady,
Advice to Young Ladies on Capturing a Husband

London, September 1817

"Eleanor, my dear, the worst has happened! Wrexham is *here*."

Her heart leaping at her aunt's disconcerting news, Lady Eleanor Pierce froze on the sidelines of the crowded hall. "Here? Tonight? At Carlton House?"

"Indeed. His arrival was just announced." Eleanor's proper aunt and chaperone, Lady Beldon, made a sour face. "The nerve of him! He should have the decency to respect your sensibilities."

Eleanor agreed that Damon Stafford, Viscount Wrexham, had a great deal of nerve. In truth, Damon was the boldest man of her acquaintance. But she had braced her sensibilities against the impact of seeing him again—or so she'd believed until just this moment.

Eleanor smiled in an effort to pretend composure and to slow her all too rapid heartbeat. "I daresay Lord Wrexham has a right to attend Prinny's fete,

Aunt Beatrix. No doubt he was invited, just as we were."

George, Prince of Wales and currently England's Regent, regularly entertained at Carlton House, his garishly grand London residence. And Lady Beldon was sometimes included on the guest list, since her late husband had been an intimate of the pleasure-loving Regent's set.

Tonight the overheated mansion was filled with a crush of elegant gentry and aristocrats. Yet a surreptitious glance around the thronged hall told Eleanor that the charming rake who had once won her heart and then trampled on it was nowhere in sight.

"You make too much of the matter," Eleanor murmured, hiding her relief. "Wrexham is perfectly at liberty to move about society as he pleases."

Her Aunt Beatrix gave her a piercing stare. "Surely you do not mean to defend him? After he treated you so abominably?"

"No, certainly not. But I am resigned to meeting him again. It must happen eventually. He has been in London for a sennight, and we move in similar circles."

Lady Beldon shook her head in disgust, then studied her niece more closely. "Perhaps we *should* take our leave, Eleanor. I will tender our excuses to Prinny—"

"I have no intention of running from Lord Wrexham, dearest Aunt."

"Then you must prepare yourself. He may appear at any moment."

Nodding distractedly, Eleanor drew a deep breath. She was as prepared as she would ever be to encounter the wickedly charming nobleman who had been her betrothed.

She'd had several days' warning that Damon had returned to London after a two-year absence, since Lady Beldon's friends were eager to keep her abreast of society gossip. Eleanor had carefully planned what she would say to him, and how she would act. She would be gracious and cool and completely indifferent, showing him common politeness but no more.

"I am capable of facing him with equanimity," she avowed, her calm assertion belying the butterflies rioting in her stomach.

Aunt Beatrix, however, was neither convinced nor willing to excuse his lordship's past sins. "You should not be compelled to face that scoundrel. Were he a true gentleman, he would have the good manners to stay away."

"He has stayed away," Eleanor said with a dry edge to her tone. "For two years."

"Even so, his absence was not long enough! Indeed, I think he should be banned from polite society entirely."

Regrettably, Damon's crime against her didn't quite justify so severe a punishment, Eleanor reflected. "I suspect banishment might be a bit too harsh, darling Auntie."

"Not in the least. And I will never forgive myself for introducing you to that wicked rogue."

"You are not to blame. You did not actually introduce us, if you will recall."

The elder woman waved an elegant hand in dismissal. "Wrexham met you at my annual house party, which amounts to the same thing as an introduction.

Had I not welcomed him into our home, you would never have been exposed to heartbreak and ridicule. But he was a friend of Marcus's. How could we know he would turn out to be such a libertine?"

How indeed? Eleanor wondered silently.

Her beloved older brother Marcus had thought very highly of Damon until the eventful dissolution of her betrothal—as had *she*. With his stirring good looks and his reckless, devil-may-care charm, Damon was every young lady's illicit fantasy, and every matron's worry.

As far as motherly natures went, Beatrix Attree, Viscountess Beldon, harbored very few nurturing instincts. Yet she'd taken in Eleanor after her parents' deaths when she was but ten years old, and had been her chaperone ever since. And Beatrix loved Eleanor as much as she was capable of loving anyone.

Her ladyship was an aristocrat to the core, and she had strict notions of what was proper for the nobility. In the beginning she'd made allowances for Lord Wrexham, despite his rather wild reputation, because he held an illustrious title that went back several hundred years and a fortune that was even larger than Eleanor's.

For her own part, Eleanor had cared little for Damon's title or wealth. It was the nobleman himself who inspired her ardor. The first moment they met, she'd felt a lightning bolt of attraction for him, as well as a connection she rarely experienced with any other man.

Falling in love with him had been ridiculously easy.

Of course, her foolishness in succumbing to his irresistible allure could possibly be excused by her relative youth at the time. She was only nineteen then, and in her girlish heart she had yearned for a wildly romantic love. A suitor who made her burn, who made her feel feverish and desired, just as Damon did.

She'd been spellbound for those few short weeks of their whirlwind courtship and engagement, believing they were ideally matched, that Damon was the man of her dreams. She had expected—*hoped*—to live with him happily ever after as his wife. Until that fateful morning two years ago when she spied him driving in Hyde Park with his beautiful mistress, not only not bothering to hide his affair but actually *flaunting* it.

Feeling grievously hurt and betrayed, Eleanor had immediately terminated their engagement and vowed to have nothing more to do with Damon. He had broken her heart as well as severely embarrassing her and savaging her pride. Even now, she couldn't quell her lingering resentment. Yet she refused to cower at the thought of facing him—

"Well," Lady Beldon announced, breaking into her niece's thoughts, "if you insist on staying tonight, you would do well to keep Prince Lazzara by your side in the event Wrexham has the gall to approach you."

"I shall, Aunt. His highness only stepped away to fetch some refreshments for us."

An Italian nobleman, Principe Antonio Lazzara di Terrasini had come to England in the company of his elder distant cousin, il Signor Umberto Vecchi, who was a diplomat to the British court. Reportedly the prince was in the market for a bride and was considering Lady Eleanor for the position.

Eleanor well knew that her chief attractions had little to do with her character or intellect. She was a notable heiress in her own right, due to the extensive fortune left to her by her mother. She was also the daughter of a baron, and now the sister of an earl, since her elder brother Marcus had recently inherited the Danvers earldom from his own distant relation.

However, she hadn't yet decided how seriously she wished to be considered as Prince Lazzara's future princess. Admittedly she was attracted to him. His sensual voice and melting dark eyes were the very essence of romance. He was also handsome, engaging, charming, and witty—and from all reports, as much of a rake as Damon had ever been.

And after her disastrous betrothal to Damon—followed by a second, even briefer betrothal to another nobleman shortly afterward—Eleanor was adamant that the next time she became engaged, it would be for good. More crucially, she would *only* marry a man whom she loved and who loved her in return.

Just then a hush fell over one end of the hall. Eleanor suspected that Prinny had entered with his entourage. But when her aunt stiffened and muttered "Speak of the devil" under her breath, Eleanor realized that it was not only His Royal Highness who had attracted attention.

Damon Stafford, Viscount Wrexham, stood beside the Regent, drawing all eyes, including hers.

The company began bowing and scraping fawningly to Prinny, while Lord Wrexham casually surveyed the elite gathering—and the gathering returned the favor.

In some vague corner of her mind, Eleanor was

aware of the excited murmur of feminine voices remarking on the noble newcomer, yet in truth all she could register was Damon . . . his height, his muscular vitality, his charisma. He seemed to fill the hall with his presence.

His features, which boasted strong brow, cheekbones, and jawline, were rawly masculine and just as striking as she remembered, although his complexion *was* more sun-bronzed now by his travels in Europe. His hair was the rich color of sable, without the blue-black hue of her own ebony. His eyes, set off by heavy eyebrows and thickly fringed lashes, were still dark as midnight and just as bold—

Eleanor's wits abruptly scattered when those penetrating eyes found hers in the crowd.

Despite all her self-warnings, she simply froze as Damon locked gazes with her. It was peculiar, how one could experience heated flashes and cold chills at the very same time. How the air could be drawn from one's lungs so swiftly, making it difficult to breathe.

The impact of seeing him again was like being struck by a lightning bolt; that same sizzling jolt she had experienced when she first laid eyes on Damon just over two years ago.

Her hand stole to her breastbone in a futile effort to calm her heart, which was somersaulting painfully in her chest. Her heart was not the sole victim, either. Her palms had grown damp and her knees felt absurdly weak.

But of course, she was foolish to expect any other response. No man had ever fired her blood or touched her deepest emotions the way Damon had. . . .

Suddenly scolding herself, Eleanor straightened her spine. *I will not make a scene,* she vowed silently. Not with so many denizens of the ton watching.

The hall was currently abuzz with speculation as the crowd's gazes shifted to her. All society knew that she had jilted Viscount Wrexham because of his rakish ways, and clearly the guests present were eagerly waiting to see how she would deal with him now.

"I have brought you champagne, Donna Eleanora, as you see."

When the deep, velvety, Italian-accented voice broke into her chaotic thoughts, Eleanor had never been more glad for a distraction in her life.

Tearing her gaze from Damon's, she turned her back on him and flashed Prince Lazzara a brilliant smile. She refused to let her former betrothed's arrival spoil the evening for her.

For tonight, at least, she was fiercely determined to ignore the bittersweet memories of her hapless romance and the wicked rake who had caused them.

Eleanor's determination lasted the better part of two hours, until Prince Lazzara invited her to take a turn outside in the gardens. Glad to have a moment's respite from the warmth and the genteel din of Carlton House, Eleanor left her aunt in the charming company of the distinguished Signor Vecchi and took the younger Italian's royal arm to stroll along the gravel paths.

Prinny's taste in decor was considered questionable at best by most of the haut ton, but Chinese lanterns hanging at intervals lent the gardens a fairy-tale aura. The flickering golden light reflected in various fountains and pools, bringing to Eleanor's mind a memory of another glittering evening—and another shimmering fountain that had played a unique role in her brief engagement to Damon the first time he'd kissed her.

It was only when the prince called her attention to her distraction that Eleanor recalled her companion. "Why do you keep staring at that fountain, *mia signorina*?"

Why indeed? Eleanor wondered, scolding herself silently even as her cheeks flushed. She had no business remembering Damon's stolen kiss or its aftermath, when she'd pushed him into the nearby fountain for his bold impertinence.

"The sight is lovely, don't you agree?" she equivocated.

Prince Lazzara nodded. "My palace at home boasts many beautiful fountains. Perhaps you will have the opportunity to see them one day."

His teasing smile hinted at the reason she might have for visiting—as his bride—but Eleanor could not put too much stock in his suggestive remark, since the prince was known for his skillful ability to flatter and entice the fair sex.

"Will you tell me about your home, highness? I have never been to Italy, but I hear there are many spectacular sights."

To her relief, Don Antonio launched into a warm recitation about the southern half of his country— which recently had been designated the Kingdom of the Two Sicilies by Europe's ruling powers—and the principality he ruled over near the Mediterranean.

Eleanor listened politely, although with only half

an ear. Much to her dismay, she couldn't stop herself from dwelling on her past memories of Damon.

Barely a few days after meeting him at her aunt's annual house party, he'd taken more liberties than she could even have dreamed of from a gentleman, stealing a kiss and earning himself a thorough drenching. Inexplicably, her unconventional response to his seduction had only intrigued him more.

A fortnight later they were engaged to be married.

Eleanor had lost her heart to him, not because he was wealthy, titled, and sinfully handsome. Nor was it even due to Damon's charm, his wit, or his effortless ability to make her believe she was the most desirable woman in the world. It was because he challenged her and made her feel alive. Because he eased her loneliness, the sense of aloneness she had felt since childhood.

Her attraction went beyond the physical, with an almost instant meeting of minds. She could talk to him about her yearnings, her dreams. Could tell him her innermost thoughts and secrets.

Damon, however, was far more reticent about sharing his feelings. It was as if he kept part of himself hidden from the world—and specifically from her.

She'd been so confident that she could eventually break through the walls he erected. And since they seemed to be so ideally matched in spirit, wit, and passion, she was certain Damon would eventually come to love her, despite his reputation as a heartbreaker.

Then she discovered that he hadn't given up his long-term mistress as he'd led her to believe. He had broken her trust irrevocably. Trampled her pride, crushed her vulnerable young heart.

The pain had subsided over time. Now Eleanor felt only a bittersweet ache—or at least she had until tonight when she realized she would have to meet Damon face-to-face.

It should be a matter of sublime indifference to her whether or not he'd returned to London. She still harbored a measure of resentment and anger toward him, true, but little thought of revenge or violence or serious ill will. In fact, she had braced herself to meet him with equanimity.

All the same, as she strolled the garden paths with Prince Lazzara, Eleanor kept an eye out for the particular English nobleman who had thrown her composure into such chaos with his unwanted appearance this evening.

Perhaps that was why she gave a start when a figure emerged from the shadows along another path.

It was only one of Carlton House's liveried footmen, Eleanor saw with relief. The servant had been sent to search for Prince Lazzara, since his countryman, Signor Vecchi, wished to introduce him to some important personages.

When Don Antonio offered Eleanor his arm to escort her back to the great hall, she declined with a smile. She had no desire to return to the house where she might encounter Damon. "I think perhaps I will remain here in the gardens for a moment longer, your highness. I see several of my friends just over there. I will join them."

She would not be alone, since there were small groups of strollers enjoying the lovely evening, including several ladies whom she recognized. And her aunt knew where she was after all, Eleanor reasoned.

Thankfully the prince did not try to press her or take her to task for remaining unchaperoned in the gardens, but merely bowed gallantly and promised to return shortly. Eleanor watched him disappear down the path, then turned in the opposite direction, toward her friends.

Her heart gave a leap, however, when another tall figure stepped out from the shadows. She recognized those broad shoulders in an instant; that sense of power, of vitality, of danger about him.

She knew those bold dark eyes and the low voice that stroked her nerve-endings like velvet when he spoke, as he did now.

"Elle," Damon said simply.

An arrow of pain pierced Eleanor at his casual form of address. The French word for "she" had been his pet name for her.

She tried to catch her breath but couldn't manage it just then. Nor could she speak. Her throat had gone dry and she felt a trifle faint. Damon had rendered her paralyzed and tongue-tied—she who was never at a loss for words. *Devil take him!*

Deploring her weakness for him, Eleanor squared her shoulders and found her voice. "My Lord Wrexham," she murmured with a regal nod.

In response, Damon cocked his head, studying her. "So you mean to treat me with distant formality? I confess relief."

"Relief? What did you expect from me, my lord? That I would box your ears?"

His mouth curved with a hint of humor. "You did so the last time we met, as I recall."

Eleanor flushed. That last time she had been a woman scorned, and she'd taken her fury out on Damon's handsome face when she ended their betrothal.

"I admit," he said, lightly rubbing his left cheek as if in remembrance, "I deserved your scorn then."

"You did indeed," Eleanor agreed, only slightly mollified. "But you may rest assured I will do nothing so unseemly tonight. Now, if you will please excuse me . . ."

She made to pass him, but Damon reached out and touched her arm. "Pray, stay a moment. I went to some trouble to get you alone so we could speak in private before we must meet in public."

Her eyes widened in comprehension as she stared up at him. "You contrived to get me alone here in the gardens? *You* had Prince Lazzara called away by that footman?" Realizing her voice had risen unbecomingly, Eleanor lowered it to a tart whisper. "What Machiavellian gall!"

Damon's faint smile was a bit rueful. "I am guilty of manipulation, true, but I thought we should attempt to clear the air between us, and I didn't trust what you might do if I approached you in a crowd. Hopefully you will not shove me into a fountain or worse just now."

Eleanor arched a skeptical eyebrow. "No? There are several fountains nearby."

She thought she saw humor spark in his dark eyes at her veiled threat. "At least suppress your urge for retribution until you hear me out."

Suppressing that urge would be harder than she'd thought. Yet Eleanor held her tongue as Damon continued more slowly. "I doubt you will readily forgive me for what happened two years ago—"

"Whatever gave you *that* impression?" she interrupted sweetly. "Merely because you turned me into a laughingstock and a figure of pity in front of the entire ton, you think my magnanimity would be in short supply?"

"No one would ever think you a figure of pity, Elle."

She stiffened this time at his soubriquet. "I prefer you not call me that silly name. The proper form of address now is 'Lady Eleanor.' "

"Ah, yes. I had heard Marcus petitioned the Crown to raise your precedence from a baron's sister to an earl's. Very well, then, my Lady Eleanor . . . will you grant me a brief audience?"

Damon's cordiality was beginning to wear on her nerves. "What do you wish to say to me, Lord Wrexham? You needn't apologize for your despicable behavior so long ago. It is over and done with and I scarcely ever think of it anymore."

At her lie, his expression remained enigmatic, even as his gaze searched her face. "I regret hurting you, Eleanor, but I did not seek you out tonight in order to apologize."

"Then why did you employ such machinations?"

"I hoped we could declare a truce. For your sake more than mine."

"*My* sake? How so?"

"I don't want your reputation to suffer for my past sins, so I hoped we could avoid any awkwardness when we are seen in public together for the first time. Even if you were merely to cut me, it would provide more fodder for the tongue-waggers."

"I agree. We can behave civilly toward one another when we officially meet."

"I thought we could go one step further tonight. Perhaps I could request your hand for a set. A simple country dance, nothing more," Damon added when her eyes narrowed.

"Why on earth would I wish to dance with you?"

"To put any gossip to rest."

"On the contrary, my dancing with you would only inflame the gossip by making it appear as if we were on familiar terms again. No, there is no need for such intimacy, Damon. But I will not cut you dead whenever I see you. Now, if that is all . . . ?"

"Don't go just yet."

His low remark was neither a command nor an entreaty, yet it made Eleanor pause. The temptation to stay with Damon was overwhelming, even if she didn't like being in such close proximity to him, particularly all alone at night. "I don't wish to be seen alone with you," she began.

"We can remedy that."

Startling her, Damon took her elbow and drew her a few yards off the gravel path, behind a topiary yew and deeper into the shadows.

Eleanor didn't protest, even though she knew she should. Perhaps it *was* better to get their first meeting over in private, so there would be no awkward moments when they met in public. But understandably, she was not in a generous mood.

"I cannot fathom what you hope to accomplish,"

she said rather peevishly. "We can have little to say to each other."

"We can catch up on the past two years."

But she didn't wish to catch up, Eleanor thought. She didn't want to dwell on what Damon had been doing all the time he was away—what women he had been with—or to recall how lonely and abandoned she had felt when he left. Even so, she managed a polite response.

"I understand you have been traveling on the Continent?"

"For much of my absence, yes. Chiefly in Italy."

"And you have returned to England to stay?"

"For a time, at least. I enjoyed my travels but found myself longing for home."

Eleanor felt a twinge of envy since she had always wanted to travel. A single young lady, however, jaunting all over the globe was considered highly improper, particularly by her aunt. Moreover, Europe had been extremely unsafe until the defeat of Napoleon's armies three years ago. But someday she hoped to fulfill her dream to see more of the world than her own country.

Then Damon surprised her again by reaching up to touch a curling tendril on her forehead. For a moment she thought he meant to straighten the narrow silk bandeau she wore, which was adorned with blue ostrich plumes to match her empire-waisted gown of pale blue lustring and overskirt of silver net.

"Your glorious hair . . . Why the devil did you cut it off?"

The question took Eleanor aback. She wore her raven hair in short curls now. The style was quite fashionable, but in truth she'd cut it severely two years ago in an act of defiance, since Damon had professed to cherish her long hair.

"What does it matter to you, my lord?" she retorted archly. "You haven't the right to care how I wear my hair."

"True."

Giving a casual shrug of his broad shoulders, he unexpectedly changed the subject again. "How is Marcus faring?"

Eleanor breathed more easily. She could relax a measure if Damon would only speak of such mundane matters as her brother. "He is faring very well, as it happens."

"I understand he married this past summer."

"Yes . . . Marcus wed Miss Arabella Loring of Chiswick. They are in France at the moment, visiting Arabella's mother in Brittany, along with her two younger sisters, who also recently wed. I believe you know her sisters' husbands, the Duke of Arden and the Marquess of Claybourne?"

"I know them well." Damon paused. "It surprises me they all three succumbed to matrimony so suddenly. I thought them confirmed bachelors."

"Matrimony is not catching, if that worries you."

Her wry quip elicited a quick smile from Damon. "I am cured of any desire to wed, believe me."

Eleanor bit her lip at his implication that *she* was the one who had cured him of his momentary madness.

A long pause followed as Damon grimaced, appearing to regret his careless remark. And his tone was more serious when he said, "I heard that you were betrothed shortly after I left England, but that it did not last long."

Eleanor raised her chin, once more feeling defensive. "No, it did not." She had quickly broken her second engagement, a betrothal she had made out of defiance and pain and had regretted almost instantly. "I decided I was not willing to settle for a marriage of convenience after all. I was not in love with him, nor he with me."

I still loved you, Damon, she thought with a wistful ache.

Damon's voice lowered another register. "It is just as well that you broke off our betrothal. I could not have given you my heart."

"You could not, or would not?"

His expression was unreadable. "I see little difference. And you deserved better for your husband."

"Yes, I did."

"And now you are being courted by Prince Lazzara," Damon observed, his tone prodding.

Eleanor hesitated. "I would not say he is *courting* me, precisely. The prince came to England to see the sights."

"And to look for a bride?"

"So rumor says."

"I am not surprised that he is showing a marked interest in a beautiful heiress."

Not inexplicably, Damon's observation stung. "You think my fortune is all he sees in me?"

"Certainly not." The corner of his mouth curved. "But you don't need me to flatter you by cataloguing your many appealing attributes. Nor, I suspect, does

Lazzara. The man would have to be a fool not to be attracted to you as well as your fortune."

But you feel no such attraction any longer? Eleanor wondered, feeling the ache increase. Aloud, she said in an offhanded tone, "It can be of no import to you if he thinks to woo me."

"Even so, I am concerned. He would be fortunate to claim you for his wife, Eleanor, but you could do better for a husband. He is not good enough for you."

She frowned at Damon. "How can you possibly know that?"

"Because I know *you*. You deserve better."

Eleanor truly did not know what to think of his remark, so finally she shrugged. "It is exceedingly presumptuous of you to set yourself to judge my suitors, Lord Wrexham."

"But then you know how presumptuous I can be."

She did indeed, she thought, as Damon unexpectedly stepped closer.

He halted barely a foot away and stood looking down at her for a long moment. When his dark gaze held her transfixed, Eleanor's heart suddenly began wildly somersaulting again. Dear heaven, did Damon intend to kiss her? She would never forget the thrill of his kisses, never forget the taste of that firm, sensual mouth, which was moving slowly toward hers. . . .

Eleanor's breath faltered altogether when Damon reached up and traced a fingertip over her cheekbone. She felt overwhelmed by his nearness, his warmth, his scent. Then, as if he could not help himself, he slid one hand behind her nape and lowered his head, letting his warm lips cover hers.

The delicious shock of it held her completely immobile; any thought of struggle melted at the softness of his kiss. His lips drifted, lingered, melded with hers, making her shiver.

At her involuntary response, Damon angled his head and pressed deeper, as if refamiliarizing himself with her taste, relearning her texture, his tongue probing her inner recesses, exploring.

Suddenly she was tumbling headlong into his kiss, falling. Myriad sensations poured through Eleanor at the magic of his mouth, while a rush of feeling blossomed in the depths of her body. She had no thought of escape. Damon had captured her completely. And the sweetness, the tenderness, the heat, all combined to rouse a trembling ache inside her.

When a soft whimper lodged in her throat, Damon drew her even closer, bringing her breasts against his chest, her thighs against his sinewed ones. Her body reacted helplessly; her spine arched and her limbs weakened. Eleanor strained toward him with hungry yearning as his tongue continued stroking, tangling, mating with hers in a bewitching rhythm.

When his hand rose to cup her breast, a fission of fiery sensation sparked within her—a stark reminder of how easily he could arouse her yearning.

An even starker reminder of the pain he could bring her.

Suddenly recollecting their circumstances, Eleanor fought the searing wash of desire that was flooding her. She'd let Damon beguile her with his sensual caresses once before, and he had broken her heart.

The realization gave her strength to renew her struggle for control. Striving for willpower, she brought her hands up between them and pressed, trying to break free of his seductive embrace.

When Damon didn't immediately release her, Eleanor shoved at his chest, thinking to push him into the yew hedge. Apparently he was prepared for just that response, for he braced himself against her force as he lightly grasped her upper arms.

When he continued to claim her lips, Eleanor drew back her slippered foot and kicked Damon hard in the shin, striking the white silk stocking below his formal satin knee breeches.

Thankfully her violence had the immediate result of prying loose his grasp—and even elicited a muffled sound of pain from him.

Stifling her own whimper of pain, Eleanor freed herself completely and backed away.

Breathing hard, her pulse leaping in fits and starts, she tried to regain her dazed senses as she stared up at Damon.

His features had turned enigmatic again. To her surprise, there was no triumph in his expression. Instead, she glimpsed regret in the shadows that darkened his eyes.

"Forgive me, I became carried away," he said, his voice a husky rasp.

So had she, much to her chagrin, Eleanor acknowledged unwillingly. She was furious at Damon for enchanting her so that she had actually returned his kisses, and yet she felt oddly bereft now that they had ended.

"Donna Eleanora?" a deep masculine voice called out softly.

She went rigid upon realizing Prince Lazzara had come in search of her.

Hoping her lips were not too wet and swollen, Eleanor scurried out from behind the hedge. "Yes, your highness?"

Don Antonio smiled charmingly when he spied her, although his smile faltered when Damon stepped out behind her.

Heat staining her cheeks, Eleanor hastened to explain. "I encountered an old acquaintance, you see. In fact, I was just telling Lord Wrexham about my brother's recent marriage."

"Lord Wrexham?" Prince Lazzara repeated slowly as his gaze sharpened on Damon.

Damon, however, made an easy reply. "Will you introduce us, Lady Eleanor?"

When she reluctantly complied, the prince raked Damon from head to toe, obviously not liking what he saw. Bowing stiffly then, he dismissed Damon and pointedly held out his arm to Eleanor. "Shall we resume our stroll in the garden, *cara mia*?"

She gratefully took the prince's arm and murmured a polite "Good evening, my lord" to Damon as she turned away.

Admittedly Eleanor felt a vast measure of relief as she let Prince Lazzara lead her away. The wild thud of her pulse had calmed somewhat, yet she was enraged at herself for yearning for Damon's kisses, particularly since she still harbored more than a little residual anger and hurt from his betrayal two years ago. It had felt good to kick his shin, despite the pain her toes had suffered.

At least she had survived their first encounter, even if she *had* acquitted herself poorly.

Just then her princely escort broke into her distracted thoughts. "Lord Wrexham is the gentleman who was once your betrothed, is he not?"

His tone held more than curiosity; a note of masculine jealousy tinged the question.

"For a very brief while." She offered the prince a bright smile. "My feelings for Wrexham cooled shortly, I assure you. He is nothing to me now, and I am quite over him. He is merely a friend of my brother's, no more."

And yet Eleanor couldn't help but note that the conviction in her declaration sounded weak to her own ears. She was *not* over Damon, if her reaction to him a moment ago was any indication.

Of course, any woman would have been affected by his sensual assault. Damon's kisses were magical, passionate, swoonworthy. . . . Worse, the sparks between them still flared in full force.

Damn and blast him.

I should have kicked him harder, Eleanor muttered silently to herself. The pain would make her remember just how dangerous Damon still was to her.

Now she could only hope she had no more intimate encounters with him. She didn't trust herself not to behave in that same wanton manner if he ever attempted to kiss her again.

And if he did? Well, she feared she was likely to succumb to Damon's wicked charm all over again, and she most certainly would not let that happen!

Chapter Two

Play the damsel in distress upon occasion. Your apparent helplessness will allow him to feel superior—and gentlemen greatly relish feeling superior.

—An Anonymous Lady,
Advice to Young Ladies on Capturing a Husband

A distracted frown shadowed Damon's brow as he left Carlton House to climb into his town carriage. He had fully expected to see Eleanor again this evening. He'd even planned to speak privately with her—and had gone to great lengths to arrange it. But he sure as the devil hadn't intended to kiss her.

On the contrary, he'd simply wanted to try to mitigate any hard feelings Eleanor bore him so they could put the discomfiting past behind them. That, and to ascertain how serious her feelings for Prince Lazzara were.

So why in hell did you succumb to the fierce urge to taste her lips again? Damon wondered dryly. *You should know better than to play with live coals.*

Yet despite the risk of being burned, he couldn't regret kissing her. Her mouth was everything he remembered and more. *She* was everything he remembered: vibrant, lush, alive with a warm radiance that still had the power to captivate him.

Eleanor Pierce fired his blood more than any woman ever had, and possibly ever would. She had intoxicated him tonight, just as she had two years ago—

Damon felt the carriage rock as his portly friend, Mr. Otto Geary, settled heavily on the leather squabs beside him.

"Thank the saints that ostentatious display is over and done with," Otto declared with a relieved sigh as the carriage pulled away from Carlton House. "I beg you never to drag me to another of these tedious, priggish affairs ever again."

Forcibly shifting his thoughts away from Eleanor, Damon curved his mouth wryly at his friend's complaint. "You know very well why I 'dragged' you here tonight. To get you away from your hospital for a few waking moments. Otherwise you would bury yourself there with your patients. No doubt you did so for the entire two years I was away."

When Otto tugged at the swaths of his formal cravat, a shock of bright red hair fell into his eyes. "I am perfectly content to bury myself with my patients. The ton, on the other hand . . . I don't know how you bear it, Damon. I fancied you had little fondness for Prinny."

"You fancy correctly, but His Royal Highness can provide you with advantages I cannot. And since he covets my support in financing his many pleasures, he is willing to lend his patronage to your endeavors as a favor to me."

Otto sighed again. " 'Tis a blasted shame it takes a bloody fortune to run a hospital."

Damon understood quite well how expensive operating a private hospital could be, since he had supplied a significant portion of his own fortune to first fund Otto's medical studies and then help him to establish the Marlebone Hospital in northern London some half dozen years ago.

Through hard work, dedication, and sheer brilliance, Otto Geary had become one of England's most respected physicians. But the Regent's patronage could garner him even more respect—and more crucially, support and charitable contributions from wealthy British society.

"I doubt, however," Otto said leadingly, "that securing the Regent's patronage for me was the only reason you came tonight."

In the light of the carriage lamp, Damon saw his friend studying him. "What other reason could there be?" he hedged.

"Because you are enamored of a particular genteel young lady, perhaps?"

"When have I ever been enamored of a young lady?"

"Two years ago, in fact." When Damon sent him a penetrating glance, Otto went on with amusement. "You have been uncommonly restless and irritable for the past four days, my good man. I can see it, even if you pretend otherwise. If I had to make a diagnosis, I would say your symptoms were due to the anticipation of seeing Lady Eleanor again."

An ironic smile pulled at Damon's lips. "How the devil did you guess?"

Otto laughed. "You forget I know you too well, old chap."

Damon couldn't deny the statement. They had met long ago under grim circumstances, when Otto had taken over the deathbed care of Damon's sixteen-year-old twin brother, Joshua.

"Lady Eleanor is exceptionally beautiful, I must say," Otto probed. "Did you manage to speak to her tonight?"

"Yes."

"And? Is that all you mean to tell me?"

"There is nothing more to tell." Damon had no intention of explaining his feelings for Eleanor, particularly when he wasn't certain exactly *what* he felt for her now.

"You cannot be happy that Prince Lazzara is courting her," Otto stated.

That was emphatically true. Upon hearing that Eleanor was being wooed by the Italian prince, Damon had returned to England a week sooner than originally planned. He'd rightly wanted to protect her from being hurt by Lazzara's libertine propensities . . . although he was hard-pressed to justify the savage surge of jealousy he'd felt at seeing her together with the handsome noble tonight, since he had absolutely no claim on her any longer.

"No, I am not happy about it," he acknowledged in a low voice.

Otto pursed his lips in a frown. "You should take care, Damon. You would do well to keep away from the lady entirely. You do not want to give her or anyone else a false impression about your intentions by showing too much interest in her."

"I bow to your superior wisdom," Damon returned, making light of the moment. Yet he was in full agreement with his friend's advice.

Eleanor was compelling, dangerous, addictive. She

had left a deep mark on him, so deep that for the past two years he hadn't been able to get her out of his mind. Indeed, since those few exhilarating weeks of their brief courtship ended, his life had seemed as bland as blancmange pudding, despite the excitement of his travels and the satisfaction of achieving several long-held ambitions.

Damon's frown returned as he averted his head to gaze out the carriage window at the dark streets of London. Until tonight, he'd convinced himself he had conquered his feelings of ardor for Elle. Perhaps that was partly why he had kissed her, because he'd had some vague notion of proving to himself that he was over her. Yet his ill-advised experiment had confirmed just the opposite.

The sparks between them still burned as hot as ever—which made her supremely dangerous to his resolution to keep away from her.

It was probably fortunate that Eleanor was still furious at him for the way he'd treated her. She was unlikely ever to forgive him for his transgressions during their betrothal.

He deeply regretted hurting her and knew he was fully to blame for the entire painful affair. He also knew he never should have proposed marriage to her in the first place, since he couldn't give her what she wanted.

Admittedly, he'd been bowled over by the high-spirited raven-haired beauty with the quick wit and warm laugh. Eleanor had totally set him on his ear when they first met. She'd made him feel truly alive again for one of the first times since his family's deaths. What was more inexplicable was the uncanny bond he felt with her, a closeness almost as powerful as the one he'd shared with his twin.

Which was the prime reason, Damon conceded, that he'd impulsively asked for her hand in marriage. That and the fact that he had wanted her so badly, he was afraid he might take his desire beyond mere kisses and dishonor her if he didn't legitimize his passion with matrimony.

Her shy, sweet declaration of love the next week, however, had stunned him. As soon as he realized how ardent Eleanor's feelings for him had grown—and comprehended how perilously intense his own attraction to her had become—he'd taken steps to end their relationship. He hadn't wanted to compound her pain any further by letting her fall in love with him more deeply, rationalizing that the sooner he made her break off, the sooner she would recover.

You should let the past be a warning to you, an insistent voice in his head admonished. Otto was right, Damon knew; he ought to keep far away from Eleanor. And practically speaking, now that he had seen her again, he should be able to move on with his life.

Except that he felt uneasy leaving her as a target for Prince Lazzara, a charming Lothario who was possibly a fortune hunter and most certainly a rake. In Italy, Lazzara had not only left a trail of broken hearts, he'd ruined a woman of good family and refused to take responsibility.

Damon didn't think Lazzara would actually besmirch Eleanor, since her family and social connections were so powerful. He *was* worried, however, that the prince could hurt Eleanor just as he himself had done—that she would fall in love and wed Lazzara and then be devastated by his infidelities.

Damon's mouth curled at the corner. He suspected that in addition to protecting Eleanor, he wanted to salve his own conscience, to absolve his guilt in some measure.

Wishing to take his mind off her, he was glad when Otto changed the subject to speak about his pet topic, his precious hospital. Nor did Damon regret being left to himself when the carriage set the preeminent physician down at his lodgings in Marlebone near the hospital and then proceeded on to the Wrexham mansion in Cavendish Square in Mayfair, London's most fashionable district and home of many of the aristocracy.

The house had been in Damon's family for several generations, but the empty quiet that greeted him as he entered bore little resemblance to the memories of his childhood. The corridors had rung with laughter when he and Joshua were boys.

Now those corridors seemed painfully empty and only echoed the grief he'd felt at age sixteen when he lost his beloved twin brother to consumption, a ravaging lung disease with no cure.

His twin's death had dealt Damon a powerful blow, since the two of them had been as close as shadows. Losing his parents to a violent storm at sea a short time afterward had left Damon bereft of immediate family and purposefully devoid of feeling. From that moment on, he'd buried his emotions so deep, he would allow no one close enough to matter to him. Instead, he had pushed people away.

He'd turned reckless as well, certain he had nothing more to lose. For the next decade, he defied fate at every opportunity and earned himself a wicked reputation.

A reputation that had never concerned him until he met lively, beautiful heiress Eleanor Pierce during her first Season, when she made her social debut under the auspices of her high-stickler aunt, Lady Beldon.

Accepting a lamp from the footman who admitted him, Damon mounted the sweeping staircase and made his way down the hall on the right, to the master's quarters. Entering his bedchamber, he went straight to the windows to throw them wide open.

For two years now the house had been closed and shuttered, the furnishings shrouded in Holland covers. The musty odor that still permeated the rooms even after thorough airings came not from death and sickness—the foulness that normally pervaded hospitals and sickrooms—but from disuse. Yet Damon still couldn't abide the smell.

Turning, he shed his brocade evening coat, loosened his cravat, and poured himself a stiff brandy. His mind was still far away as he sank into a wing chair before the hearth, where a small fire burned cheerfully.

A respectful rap on the door, however, eventually brought him out of his reverie.

When Damon bid entrance, his elderly valet stepped into the bedchamber. "May I be of service, my lord?"

Damon frowned at his longtime servant. "It is late, Cornby. I believe I told you not to wait up for me."

"So you did, sir."

"But then you rarely heed my orders, do you?"

"Not in this instance, my lord. What kind of

proper servant would I be if I shirked my duty whenever I felt the urge?"

Damon couldn't hide a smile at the impossible notion of the gray-haired Cornby shirking his duty. The old man had been in the Stafford family's employ for many years, long before Joshua took sick, and he'd cared diligently for the dying boy. In gratitude for such loyal service, Damon had kept the manservant on well past the time he should have retired.

Yet Cornby refused to accept anything resembling charity and so acted as Damon's valet and general factotum. Despite his advanced age, he'd accompanied Viscount Wrexham on his travels in foreign lands. Admittedly, there was many a time when Damon was glad to have Cornby's familiar presence at hand. The two of them shared the easy camaraderie of long acquaintances, with far less formality than usual for a nobleman and his manservant.

"Did your attire this evening meet your satisfaction, my lord, if I may ask?" Cornby inquired.

"Yes, it was quite satisfactory."

Just then Cornby spied Damon's coat draped over a chair, and he gave a small moan of dismay. "My lord, you should not be so careless! That coat cost more than a pretty penny."

Gently picking up the garment—a superbly tailored new evening coat fitted by Weston—he carefully smoothed the rich brocade. "Truly, your lordship, I am astonished. But then perhaps it has served its purpose. Attending the Regent's fete was a special occasion, was it not? This evening you primped in front of the cheval glass longer than I have ever seen you do."

Damon shot the old man a glance. Granted, he had

dressed carefully this evening in anticipation of seeing Eleanor, but he hadn't expected his efforts to be so obvious. "I beg to differ. I did not 'primp.' "

"If you say so, sir."

Biting back amusement, Damon fixed the manservant with a stern stare. "You do realize, Cornby, that I do not pay you to make observations on my behavior?"

"Yes, my lord."

"One can only hope that sometime in the next decade or two you might learn to show a modicum of respect for your employer."

"I expect that is highly unlikely, my lord. You know the saying—that it is difficult for an old dog to learn new tricks."

Damon shook his head sadly. "I shall have to reconsider your employment. Remind me to terminate your post in the morning, Cornby."

"You fired me a fortnight ago, before we left Italy, sir. Have you forgotten?"

"Then why are you still here?"

"Because you need me. You have very little staff to see to your welfare."

"That is no longer the case," Damon responded. "We hired an appropriate staff when we returned to London."

"But none of them know just how you like things, my lord."

That was certainly true, Damon silently admitted.

"My lord, if you will pray excuse me for a moment," Cornby added, "while I hang your coat properly . . . ?"

"Yes, of course."

He took a long swallow of brandy as Cornby left to hang the coat in the suite's dressing room.

Upon returning to the bedchamber, the manservant glanced pointedly at the brandy snifter in Damon's hand. "Are we beginning early this year, my lord?"

"No, *we* are not beginning early. I merely decided to have a nightcap."

"I have ordered you a cask of prime brandy as you requested."

"Good."

Damon rarely overindulged in spirits, but once a year, on the anniversary of his brother's death, he got thoroughly soused in a futile effort to drown out the sorrow he still felt. The fateful date loomed just ahead, in less than a fortnight, but he hadn't yet begun to observe his yearly ritual of grief. Even so, he didn't care to be reminded of it, even by a faithful servant.

"Cornby?" Damon said, glancing at the old man over the rim of his glass.

"Yes, my lord?"

"I will raise your salary considerably if you will leave me in peace."

"You pay me exceedingly well now, my lord. If it is all the same to you, I will forgo further monetary remuneration for the pleasure of needling you now and then."

"If it were only now and then, I could bear it with more equanimity," Damon muttered in exasperation, even though they both knew he was jesting. He would not have enjoyed the fawning subservience most servants showed their aristocratic masters.

With polite dispassion, Cornby stood awaiting the

viscount's orders, and when none were forthcoming, he prodded mildly, "Are you certain there is nothing more I may do for you, my lord?"

"Actually, there is one thing. You can have my riding clothes ready by seven in the morning."

Eleanor was likely to be in Hyde Park early tomorrow, Damon suspected. A superb horsewoman, Elle relished a brisk morning gallop. And if she was riding with that Italian royal . . . Rightly or wrongly, Damon felt obliged to make certain she was not getting in over her head.

"Very well, sir. Will it be another special occasion—"

"Pray, go to bed, Cornby," Damon said, not giving the valet a chance to quiz him more about Lady Eleanor. "You look fatigued enough to keel over, and I don't want your demise on my conscience."

"Aye, my lord. As you wish." The old man went to the door, then paused. "I must say, it is good to be home and to be privileged to sleep in a good English bed. Those foreign contraptions that pass for mattresses are scarcely fit for livestock. Sleep well, my lord."

Damon acknowledged the servant's adieu with a slight nod of his head. It was indeed good to be in his own bed after living for so long on foreign soil. Yet he knew it would be damned hard to sleep after kissing Elle tonight. Too many memories had been stirred up, both good and bad.

He had never let himself become emotionally involved with any woman until Eleanor. After enduring so much grief, he'd refused to let himself care for anyone, never wanting to again risk the pain of losing someone he loved.

But her joie de vivre had enchanted him so utterly that he'd ignored the warning signs of their growing intimacy until her fateful admission of love.

The danger she presented had only been underscored by yet another death—when his distant cousin, Tess Blanchard, had lost her betrothed in the Battle of Waterloo. Seeing Tess's shock and devastation savagely reminded Damon of the grief he risked if he went through with his marriage to Eleanor.

It was why he had driven her away. He knew the anguish and emptiness he'd felt at his brother's tragic death and his parents' untimely demise would be even greater if he lost Eleanor after the incipient bond between them had strengthened and deepened.

Damon had resolved to make her call off their betrothal, however, since a gentleman could not honorably jilt a lady. And so he'd arranged a public scene where she was sure to see him with his former mistress.

He had not actually been unfaithful to Eleanor; he'd merely let her believe him so—and therefore think him the lowest cad in nature.

To spare her further pain and humiliation, Damon had left England the following week.

Fortunately, during his travels on the Continent he had a mission for his pent-up passion and disillusionment, a larger purpose for himself. Perhaps it was because his family's senseless deaths had left him with a fierce need to control fate, but with Otto's guidance and connections, Damon had spent the past several years trying to save some of the unfortunate innocents who were struck by the devastating malady that had taken his brother.

The success of his endeavors was a source of, if not pride, then certainly satisfaction. He had accomplished what he'd set out to do, beyond his greatest hopes, in fact.

Not surprisingly, though, Damon had found himself yearning for England of late. A few short weeks ago, he'd decided he had wandered long enough, that it was time to return home and resume his former life. The rumors about Lazzara courting Eleanor had only hastened his departure.

Which brought him to this evening and the question of what to do about Elle.

He wouldn't repeat history by growing too close to her and then hurting her again when he walked away. Yet he couldn't just abandon her now. Not when she was being pursued by a rake who would make her a deplorable husband and only cause her misery. She deserved far better.

He wanted Eleanor to be happy, to be able to fulfill her dreams of marriage, love, children. The very future he had shunned when he'd deliberately and publicly betrayed her. If someday he married in order to carry on his title, it would be purely a union of convenience for him.

Still, he was certain Prince Lazzara was *not* the man of her dreams. Therefore, Damon thought darkly as he drained the last of his brandy, he intended to be in the park tomorrow morning on the chance he would encounter Eleanor there with her royal suitor.

Specifically so he could protect her from the profligate philanderer who was wooing the lovely, lively woman he had once thought to make his own wife.

* * *

Upon returning to their home in Portman Place, Eleanor accompanied her aunt upstairs and paused outside Lady Beldon's bedchamber to say good night.

"I am glad you enjoyed the evening, Aunt," Eleanor said sincerely. "Signor Vecchi is quite agreeable, is he not?"

"He is indeed," Beatrix answered with a slight blush at the mention of Prince Lazzara's elder relation. "The Signor is the epitome of charm. I suspect charm must be an inherent trait of Italian gentlemen, regardless of age."

"You may be right."

It warmed Eleanor's heart to think she could be witnessing a budding romance between her patrician aunt and the distinguished Italian diplomat. Since being widowed a half dozen years ago, Beatrix had shown no interest in any gentleman of any kind. But clearly her attention was engaged now by Signor Vecchi, who was likewise widowed. Moreover, he seemed to be attracted to her in return.

Aunt Beatrix's blush faded, however, as she gave Eleanor a careful scrutiny. "Did *you* enjoy the evening, my dear? You are not overly distressed by Wrexham's return, are you?"

"Certainly not," Eleanor prevaricated. "He may go to the devil for all I care."

"He already *has* gone to the devil, no doubt," Beatrix replied tartly, "although you know very well that ladies do not use such coarse language as 'devil.' "

"Yes, Aunt," she murmured, hiding a smile. Her noble relative was fastidious about proper behavior, yet Eleanor wanted to please her aunt whenever possible, to repay her kindness for taking her in so long ago.

"I trust Wrexham's return will not interfere with Prince Lazzara's courtship of you," her ladyship observed.

"I cannot imagine why it should. Wrexham has no interest in me any longer, nor I in him." Under no circumstances would she divulge that Damon had kissed her witless in the gardens barely four hours ago, or that for an enchanted moment, she had returned his wonderful kiss with a shameful eagerness.

"Do you mean to drive with Don Antonio in the morning, Eleanor?"

"Yes, at ten o'clock."

Beatrix raised an eyebrow. "That is rather late for you, is it not?"

"It is, but the prince claims to be a late riser."

"In any event, be sure to take one of our own grooms with you, for appearances' sake, you know."

"I shall," Eleanor replied without argument.

"Then sleep well, dear."

"And you, Aunt," she responded, although certain sleep wouldn't come easily to her tonight. She was infinitely glad her initial meeting with Damon was done with, yet he had only roused painful, poignant feelings of regret and desire inside her.

She did not kiss the older woman's cheek or even press her hand before turning away, since Lady Beldon considered such demonstrations of affection ill-bred.

Perhaps, Eleanor reflected as she made for her own bedchamber in the adjacent wing of the house, her aunt's strict reserve was why she had responded so readily to Damon's warmth when he first started wooing her.

She'd had a rather lonely upbringing, growing up in the care of stern, very proper governesses. Her parents, Baron and Baroness Pierce, had a cold marriage of convenience and held little affection for each other or their children. And since Eleanor's beloved brother Marcus was almost a dozen years her senior, for most of her childhood he was away at boarding school and university.

Upon her parents' deaths in a fatal carriage accident, Marcus became her legal guardian, yet Eleanor went to live with their mother's sister, Viscountess Beldon, since her ladyship was a far more suitable chaperone for a ten-year-old girl.

Supremely aware of her breeding and consequence, Aunt Beatrix refused to allow Eleanor to attend boarding school where she might have made close friends. And even now, despite her current popularity among the ton, she had few truly dear friends except for Drew Moncrief, the Duke of Arden, and Heath Griffin, the Marquess of Claybourne, who were both like older brothers to her.

Oh, Eleanor remembered wryly, she had attracted numerous suitors during her comeout at eighteen. Once she reached marriageable age, her fortune and lineage had made her highly sought after.

Marcus had worried that she might fall victim to a fortune hunter, while Aunt Beatrix had wanted her to make the brilliant marriage expected of most heiresses—a union of bloodlines and fortune—even if there was no chance for mutual affection. Eleanor, however, had a crystal clear vision for her future. She planned to hold out for a love match.

Then, barely six months after her debut, she met the wickedly charming rogue, Lord Wrexham.

She had initially resisted Damon on sheer principle. Every woman wanted him, so *she* was determined she would not. But even she had quickly fallen under his spell. He was unlike any man she'd ever known, virile and vital, with a sense of intensity, of danger about him that was exhilarating.

She would never forget that first unexpected kiss between them. They were strolling in the gardens of the Beldon country estate near Brighton, at the beginning of her aunt's annual house party, when he struck up an easy flirtation with her, one that challenged her wits and undermined all her defenses.

"You are too seductive for your own good," Eleanor finally told him with a laugh. *"It could lead you into trouble."*

His half smile was enchanting. *"It already has upon occasion. But the potential rewards are worth the risk."*

Then and there Damon leaned toward her and boldly captured her lips, giving her a stunning taste of heat and arousal and pure captivation.

After a long, dazed moment, however, Eleanor reacted sheerly on principle, determined to show him that she was not to be trifled with. She pushed at his chest, catching him completely off guard and sending him tripping backward over the ledge of the nearby fountain.

With a splash, Damon sat down hard in the pool

and sprawled there, staring up at her, his formal evening attire soaking through.

"*I trust that cooled your ardor, my lord,*" Eleanor said sweetly, trying to hide her breathlessness.

After a stunned moment, he started laughing. "If you think that, Miss Pierce, you don't know me very well."

Her unconventional response had *not* cooled Damon's ardor in the least. It had merely made him more subtle in employing his powers of seduction.

That beguiling, enthralling kiss had been the first of many during their courtship, even though Damon had never allowed their passion to go beyond a few forbidden caresses. Remembering now, Eleanor lifted her fingers to gently touch her lips.

It had been a grave mistake to succumb to Damon's sensual allure and offer him her heart, she'd learned. It was an even bigger mistake to hope that he would end her loneliness by coming to love her. Their short romance had held fireworks that flamed and burned out at the first test of fidelity.

If she had any regrets about terminating their betrothal, they were fleeting and usually haunted her in the small, lonely hours of the night. And regrets were easier to quell when she recalled that those few amazing weeks of joy and elation Damon had given her were followed by months of pain—and when she contemplated how much greater the pain would have been if she'd discovered his penchant for infidelity *after* she wed him.

No, Eleanor thought as she reached the door to her bedchamber, she would marry someday, but it would be on *her* terms, when she could be certain her husband bore her a true, undying, mutual love.

Her abigail was awaiting her and helped her undress and prepare for bed. After dismissing the cheerful girl, Eleanor climbed into bed, although she didn't immediately extinguish the lamp flame. Instead, she picked up the small, leatherbound book that lay on her bedside table.

Recently published, *Advice to Young Ladies on Capturing a Husband* had been penned by "An Anonymous Lady." Yet Eleanor knew firsthand that the author was actually the Loring sisters' close friend from their girlhood, Fanny Irwin, who had left home at sixteen to become one of London's most renowned Cyprians.

In her book, Fanny shared her secrets not only for landing a husband, but for infatuating him once he was locked in matrimony.

In short, making a man fall madly in love.

Eleanor had told a number of her friends about the book, mainly as a favor to Arabella, her new sister by marriage. Word had spread quickly, though, and now the entire female half of the ton was talking about *Advice* with great excitement.

Even though most of Eleanor's peers—the young ladies who had made their comeouts with her during her first Season—had already married, they were eager to try out the Anonymous Lady's wisdom on their husbands. And of course, the new crop of debutantes and their matchmaking mamas were even more eager to use it to capture a coveted husband. For them, *Advice* was like catnip to cats.

Eleanor had little patience for such social intrigue,

which seemed to smack of dishonesty in luring a man to his doom. Yet she was fiercely determined to fall in love and marry a man who loved her deeply in return. She would *not* end up a lonely spinster who led a solitary, barren life. She would not end up like her Aunt Beatrix, either, a widow who had never experienced the joys of love.

Therefore, Eleanor had concluded, if she meant to rule her own destiny, she would have to take her romantic future into her own hands, starting with Prince Lazzara.

Undeniably she was attracted to the handsome, passionate, Italian nobleman, yet she wasn't convinced he could ever love her as she yearned to be loved, or that he would be faithful to her in marriage.

Which is why she had resolved to allow the prince to court her while she attempted to win his love by employing the secrets of Fanny's book.

However, she certainly had not counted on Damon coming back into her life again just when she was beginning to make progress with Prince Lazzara!

Oh, why could Damon not have stayed away for just a few more months? Eleanor wondered with more than a little vexation. Even if she could manage to ignore his unwanted presence in town, she knew her mind would insist on making comparisons between him and any other suitors—and few would likely measure up to him.

There was so much about Damon that she had treasured. His sharp wit, for one. The way he'd challenged her, indeed, dared her to be her own woman. The way he never patronized her or treated her as a fragile blossom, as too many of her other beaux did.

He didn't treat her as an heiress whose fortune he coveted, either. Instead he ragged her and teased her—sometimes enough to rouse her ire—the way her brother did, the way Marcus's two close friends, Heath and Drew, did.

Realizing how her thoughts had wandered to Damon, Eleanor snapped the book shut, put out the lamp, pulled up the covers, and shut her eyes.

To her utter dismay, Damon had made her lose her head tonight. But she would never let it happen again.

She would not think about that charming devil, either. She simply would not!

She dreamed about him, however. A vivid, captivating fantasy that overwhelmed her with desire and yearning. Damon's embrace was demanding and passionate, yet tender enough to draw the very soul from her body . . . and stirring enough to make her weep.

Eleanor woke in the night with tears on her face and a savage ache in her heart.

For a moment she lay there in the dark, pining for what she had lost when she'd repudiated Damon. It was not only the sweet promise of first love, but their blossoming friendship also. She had lost a friend as well as the ideal husband.

She wondered if Damon ever thought of her, ever dreamed of her, as she still did of him. She had felt as if he were her soulmate—

But quite obviously he had not felt the same way about *her,* Eleanor thought with a growl of self-disgust. Rolling over in bed and punching her pillow, she renewed her vow to forget all about him.

However, she was very glad to have a goal to distract her and occupy her attention just now. Practicing the techniques laid out in Fanny's book to make Prince Lazzara fall madly in love with her should offer an antidote to her deplorable tendency to dwell far too much on her lost dreams and the heartless rogue who had shattered them.

When Eleanor woke again in the early morning, she reiterated her plan in her mind as she dressed and breakfasted and prepared for her drive with the prince.

And even though she felt somewhat restless and out of sorts, she managed a bright smile when his highness called on her promptly at ten. Once she had settled in his elegant high-perch phaeton—with a young Beldon groom mounted on the tiger's stand behind—Eleanor kept up a cheerful conversation as they bowled along the crowded streets to Hyde Park.

She kept an eye on the prince's driving, however, and his high-strung pair of gray Thoroughbreds.

"Your pair is very spirited," Eleanor observed, wincing as he jabbed at his horses' mouths.

"Yes, indeed. Spirit is a prime requirement in my horses. I purchased these at Tattersall's."

Marcus would have called Lazzara ham-handed or worse. Suspecting she would handle the ribbons far better than the prince, Eleanor wished she could take over the reins. But she held her tongue and did not offer to drive as she recalled Fanny's specific advice. No gentleman would be flattered to think a female was more accomplished at any task, and she wanted to earn the prince's admiration, not affront his pride.

Eleanor was grateful when they reached the park entrance and turned onto the wide, tree-lined avenue of Rotten Row, since the restless grays seemed less fitful here.

Her heart skipped a beat, however, when she saw a rider approaching the prince's phaeton and recognized Damon.

Of all the ill luck, Eleanor thought in vexation.

When Damon slowed his mount and, out of politeness, raised his tall beaver hat in greeting, Lazzara was compelled to halt his vehicle and return the bow.

Eleanor managed a graceful nod as well, even though her feminine sensibilities couldn't help but admire how Damon's broad shoulders filled out his elegant burgundy coat and the way he sat on his magnificent black horse. Damon always was a splendid rider, which was one more thing they'd had in common. Another pang of regret twisted her heart when she recalled the glorious rides in the countryside they had shared during the early days of their betrothal.

"Lady Eleanor, what a pleasant surprise," was the first thing Damon said. "It is quite unexpected to encounter you here just now."

Eleanor's eyes narrowed slightly. Damon knew very well she enjoyed coming to the park every morning, rain or shine. "Unexpected, my lord? How so?"

"I know you would much rather ride than drive—and furthermore, your outings usually begin two hours earlier than this."

Ignoring Damon's reminder that he had intimate

knowledge of her habits, she offered him a bland smile. "But I enjoy driving quite well, my lord. Particularly with an escort so agreeable as Prince Lazzara," she added pointedly, not so much to flatter the prince as to remind Damon of the gentleman sitting beside her.

"No doubt," Damon returned, "Prince Lazzara is delighted with such a charming companion as yourself."

"Indeed," the prince said, finally joining the conversation.

Damon's gaze shifted to him. "Your highness," he said with an amiable nod. "I recently spent many pleasant months in your country."

"Oh?" the Italian replied courteously. "Did you visit our magnificent cities? Rome? Florence? Naples?"

"Yes, but mainly I was in the south. . . ."

Eleanor sat there silently while the two noblemen conversed, all the while wishing Damon would move on. Couldn't he tell that she wanted nothing more to do with him?

She was in full accord when Prince Lazzara eventually ended the discussion of his country and bowed again, then snapped the reins and sent his grays trotting off at a brisk pace.

Eleanor resisted the urge to look behind her to see if Damon was watching their departure, yet she felt his gaze following her as they picked up speed.

She clutched at the side rail when the grays broke into a canter—but then suddenly the phaeton gave a lurch, followed by a violent jolt.

Thrown sideways against the prince, Eleanor gasped,

while behind her, the tiger gave a yelp as he was tossed off his perch. It took her another shocked moment for her to realize that a rear wheel had come off the phaeton.

Startled, the frightened horses bolted into a gallop and went careening down the Row, heedless of the carriages and riders directly in their path. Prince Lazzara not only had lost complete control of his pair but had dropped the reins and was clinging to the rail with both hands.

Desperately struggling for balance herself, Eleanor lunged for the reins and managed to grab the left ones, which sent the team veering off the avenue onto the grass, heading directly toward a stand of elms. Her heart pounding, she hauled with all her might, yet she feared she would have no success in stopping the frenzied horses in time to prevent a catastrophic wreck.

She was only vaguely aware of the sound of hoofbeats beside her and the flash of black as Damon charged past the phaeton. When he came alongside the nearest gray, he strove to catch the bridle. To her amazement and awe, he was able to guide the frightened pair a few degrees off their disastrous course.

Together they eventually slowed the carriage and brought it to a shuddering halt. For a moment Damon stayed where he was, calming the trembling grays in a low, soothing tone. But his dark eyes found Eleanor's blue ones with penetrating force.

"God, Elle, are you all right?" he demanded, worry making his voice sharp.

Her heart racing, she nodded. "Yes," she said

breathlessly as she sat upright—an awkward task considering that the leather seat was canted at an unnatural angle. "Thank you for saving us."

He stared at her another long moment. Then to her surprise, Damon's eyebrow lifted, while his mouth curved at the corner. "Oh, I suspect expressions of gratitude are premature. With your quick reflexes, you might have managed it all on your own."

It was deplorable, how her heart warmed at his praise, and so was the flush that heated her cheeks.

"*Si,*" an unsteady Italian voice broke in. "That was quite courageous of you, Donna Eleanora."

She had actually forgotten her companion, Eleanor realized, chiding her thoughtlessness as she tore her gaze from Damon's.

Don Antonio looked rather shaken as he righted himself. "I am in your debt, Lord Wrexham," he added, not sounding happy about it.

"You lost a wheel, your highness—"

"An unnecessary observation, my lord," the prince muttered rather stiffly.

The Beldon groom came running up then and went to the horses' heads, all the while apologizing profusely and begging his mistress's pardon for being thrown off.

Eleanor hastened to reassure first the lad and then soothe the prince's wounded pride, certain that Fanny would advise her to do so quickly. "Of course you would have easily saved us had the reins not been torn from your hands, your highness."

"Indeed, I would have done so," Antonio answered with a measurable decrease in frostiness at the encouraging smile Eleanor gave him.

Watching from his position on his horse, Damon felt his jaw clench. Seeing Elle favor that rake with such a sweet, alluring smile set his teeth on edge. Especially since his heart was still lodged in his throat from the sight of her possibly being dragged to her death.

Edging his mount closer to her, he held out his hand. "Allow me to take you home, Lady Eleanor."

Her eyebrows arched up in surprise. "You do not actually think I would be so improper as to ride tandem with you?"

It was on the tip of Damon's tongue to reply that she had done so before, but he doubted Eleanor would want to advertise their former intimacy to her companion. Instead, he merely murmured, "It may be some time before a wheelwright can be found to repair Prince Lazzara's phaeton."

"Perhaps," she replied. "But we should have no difficulty finding someone with a carriage to come to our aid. Ah, there is the Dowager Countess Haviland in her barouche." Eleanor turned to the Italian nobleman. "Lady Haviland is a bosom friend of my aunt's, your highness. I have no doubt she will offer to carry us home in her carriage once she has finished her morning promenade of the park."

"That should suffice admirably, *mia signorina*," he replied in a charming tone as he raised her gloved hand to his lips. "I regret that I have put you to such trouble."

"Truly, it is no trouble," Eleanor said, letting her hand linger in the prince's grasp far longer than was warranted, to Damon's mind.

"But this mishap endangered your very life. My servants will hear of this outrage, you may be sure."

"Your servants may not be to blame, your highness, and you most certainly are not. It is not uncommon for a carriage wheel to come off. Besides, a little excitement can enliven the day."

The prince looked dubious, yet he smiled. "You are too generous, Donna Eleanora."

"No, not at all. If you wish," Eleanor added, "my groom can unharness your grays and lead them back to their stable. It is not very far. And then you may make arrangements for the repair of your carriage without fear for your horses' welfare."

Damon doubted the royal would concern himself much with his livestock, no matter how superb their breeding. But the prince nodded in approval of Eleanor's plan and waved a permissive hand at the lad—a wise move, Damon knew, since she would never have abandoned either servant or animals in such dire straits.

When Eleanor glanced around her, as if searching for the best way down from her precarious seat, Damon dismounted and went to help her.

Eleanor refused his assistance, however. "Thank you, Lord Wrexham, but I am not helpless," she announced as she scrambled down on her own.

"Of course you are not," Damon couldn't help but murmur, amused by her understatement. "You are the least helpless female I know."

He'd lost a year off his life, seeing her in such danger, but he should have known Eleanor could be depended upon to save herself and her milksop prince. Pride and admiration flooded Damon now at her bravery, since perhaps one woman in a thousand would have the presence of mind to try to halt the runaway pair.

Eleanor did not appear pleased by his compliment, though, if he were to judge by the darkling look she shot him as she waited attentively for the prince to climb down. Evidently she didn't care to be praised for her heroics since she didn't want to show up her companion.

The nobleman did not appear any happier for the unwanted interference, either. And when Eleanor took the prince's arm, he cast a smug glance at Damon, a look of sheer male triumph. He might have suffered the indignity of appearing weak in the lady's eyes by remaining helpless in the face of danger. But in the end, he had claimed the prize: her warm smile.

Damon watched with narrowed eyes as they moved off toward the barouche that reportedly belonged to Lady Haviland. Eleanor was correct, he thought irritably. It was not uncommon for a carriage wheel to come off. Just extremely poor luck—or in the prince's case, extremely *good* luck to be able to see Eleanor home.

Damon muttered an oath as he made to remount his horse. His plan to ascertain just how serious Elle's feelings were for her Italian suitor had gone nowhere, he conceded.

Although now he was even more convinced that his instincts were valid: Lazzara would make a disastrous husband for her.

Warning her outright about the prince's womanizing, though, might not have the desired effect, Damon suspected. Coming from him, she was unlikely to believe it, since his concern would smack of sour grapes and male rivalry.

Even so, Damon mused with a thoughtful frown, he ought to actively try to separate Eleanor from her noble courtier. Of course, she would not thank him for his unwanted interference, but raising her ire was a small price to pay for keeping her safe from hurt.

Chapter Three

It is unlikely that a gentleman will fall in love without proper encouragement. Often a lady must take her fate—and his also—into her own hands.

—An Anonymous Lady,
Advice to Young Ladies on Capturing a Husband

Bringing her jaunty lady's phaeton to a halt before Fanny Irwin's elegant residence in Crawford Place, Eleanor handed the reins to her groom and stepped down without assistance.

"I shall be no more than an hour, Billy, if you will walk the horses and return for me then."

"Aye, milady," he replied, seeming particularly eager to please after the carriage accident this morning.

The genteel neighborhood was situated only a short distance north of Hyde Park and boasted a dozen row houses that appeared refined and tastefully expensive. Number Eleven was Fanny's private home, not her usual London residence where she conducted business and entertained her elite male clientele. Yet Eleanor didn't wish to advertise the fact that she was visiting one of London's leading Cyprians by leaving her phaeton out in front.

She didn't have the luxury of openly befriending a notorious courtesan, since she was living under her aunt's roof and felt obliged to honor Lady Beldon's dictates. But she valued her blossoming friendship with Fanny, whom she had met just last month at Lily Loring's wedding.

Eleanor could understand why the Loring sisters refused to shun their childhood companion, regardless of the social consequences. The beautiful Fanny was delightful and charming and full of life, in addition to having a shrewd head on her graceful shoulders. Eleanor envied the women's closeness and hoped to become an intimate member of their circle someday.

Knowing Billy would keep her confidences, Eleanor left the young groom to see to her horses and mounted the short flight of steps to the house. She was admitted by a very proper-looking older footman, who showed her to an elegant parlor, where Fanny was hard at work at her writing desk.

"Ah, welcome, Lady Eleanor," Fanny exclaimed with a warm smile over her shoulder at her visitor. "I promise I will only be another moment. Please make yourself at home. Then Thomas will bring us tea so that we may have a comfortable coze."

As the footman bowed himself out, Eleanor obliged, settling on a rose velvet settee.

Eventually Fanny set down her quill pen, blew gently on the page to dry the wet ink, then rose to join Eleanor.

"Forgive me," she said, sinking into an opposing wing chair. "I was completing a scene in chapter seventeen. I believe I finally struck on the right course for my plot, and I needed to write it down while it was still fresh in my mind."

"Your plot?" Eleanor asked curiously. "Are you writing another book?"

Fanny smiled as if harboring a secret. "Yes, although I have been reluctant to tell anyone until I know for certain if I can manage it. I am trying my hand at writing a Gothic novel, you see."

"How intriguing," Eleanor said with all sincerity. "I should think writing fiction would be very different from your first endeavor in publishing."

"Indeed—and much more difficult than sharing advice on how to deal with the male sex. But my publisher says Gothic novels by female authors are in great demand just now, and are highly lucrative as well. Ann Radcliffe developed a wide audience in past years, and Elizabeth Helme and Regina Roche, among others, followed in Radcliff's footsteps."

"I know," Eleanor responded. "I have read works by all three ladies."

Fanny's expression intensifying, she leaned forward in her chair. "And did you enjoy them?"

"Well . . ." Eleanor pursed her lips. "The stories definitely held my interest, although I found some of the actions exaggerated to the point of disbelief. I doubt such melodrama happens often in real life—" She broke off with a smile. "But then I suppose that is why novels are deemed 'fiction.' "

The footman returned just then with a laden tea tray, which he deposited on the table before his mistress. After dismissing the servant and pouring her guest a steaming cup, Fanny continued. "It would seem your tastes are similar to Tess's."

"Miss Blanchard's?"

"Yes. Since Arabella and Roslyn and Lily are away in France, Tess has been reading my manuscript and giving me her criticisms."

Miss Tess Blanchard, Eleanor knew, was also a good friend of the Loring sisters, and a fellow teacher at their Academy for Young Ladies. Additionally she was a distant relation of Damon's—third or fourth cousins on their mothers' side, Eleanor recalled.

Fanny paused to sip her tea, then went on. "As it happens, I would value another opinion, Lady Eleanor. Would you possibly consider reading my draft when I am finished?"

"Of course. I would be honored."

"But you must tell me honestly what you think, with no attempts to spare my feelings."

Eleanor smiled. "Surely you know by now that I am known for my frankness, Fanny."

"True, but you are also quite kind, and you might feel obliged to soften your criticisms. If I am to continue with this career, I want my work to sell well. To be truthful . . . I hope that I may eventually earn enough from my writing so that I may marry where I choose."

It had surprised Eleanor to learn that Fanny intended to leave the demimonde. But she was looking to the future, since the life of a Cyprian was uncertain, and beauty and youth were fleeting. And recently, a most unlikely romance had developed between Fanny and her longtime friend and former Hampshire neighbor, Basil Eddowes—a serious, scholarly sort of gentleman who earned his living as a law clerk.

"I have heard that Mr. Eddowes has a great fondness for you," Eleanor said, "but I didn't realize it had grown so serious as to contemplate marriage."

Fanny's perfect ivory complexion warmed with a becoming blush. "The thing is . . . he has not proposed yet, and he may never do so. But I hope to persuade him to eventually. Yet practicalities stand in the way of our marrying. Naturally Basil doesn't wish me to continue in my profession, and neither do I. And we must be sensible about finances. Thanks to the generosity of Lord Claybourne, Basil has obtained a post as a nobleman's secretary, which will provide him a significantly greater income, but I must do my part to support us. You have been extremely generous to promote my *Advice* book, Lady Eleanor."

"It was my pleasure, truly. And many of your readers are grateful to you now since they are having remarkable success employing your techniques. Several of my friends say their husbands have never paid them such devoted attention as now."

"I am glad to have aided their cause," Fanny said. "Females have too little power with men—and in marriage particularly. It does my heart good to think I can help wives be a bit happier."

"My unmarried acquaintances," Eleanor added, "have expressed relief with your advice that they needn't rely solely on beauty or fortune to engage a gentleman's interest."

Fanny nodded sagely. "Beauty and fortune might attract a man initially, but disposition and manner will *keep* him attracted. So," she said, redirecting the subject, "how is your romance with Prince Lazzara faring, if I may ask?"

The question was no surprise to Eleanor, since during her last visit here she had sought Fanny's counsel regarding the prince. But her efforts had not quite gone according to plan, Eleanor remembered, wrinkling her nose with wry humor. "In truth, I thought it was going well until this morning. . . ."

Briefly she told Fanny about the morning's disastrous carriage accident and how Lord Wrexham had come to their rescue—and how she had done her best to soothe the prince's ruffled pride.

Fanny saw the difficulty at once, and her eyes danced with amusement. "It is fortunate that no one was injured, but *un*fortunate that the prince was shown to such poor advantage, having your former betrothed act so heroically. I would say you did well to minimize his pique. I hope, however, that you have no more encounters with Lord Wrexham when you are supposed to be showering all your attention on another gentleman."

"As do I," Eleanor said feelingly.

Fanny hesitated. "I also hope Wrexham does not cause you undue pain by his return to England."

With pretended ease, Eleanor waved a dismissive hand. "Not in the least. Wrexham's reappearance just now is untimely, nothing more."

No doubt Fanny had heard the tale of the dissolution her betrothal, Eleanor mused as she raised her teacup to her lips to hide her frown. It occurred to her that Fanny might be acquainted with Damon's former mistress, the beautiful widow, Mrs. Lydia Newling, who was occasionally mentioned in the society gossip columns. In Fanny's profession, the two women might have easily crossed paths.

But Eleanor quelled the urge to introduce so utterly inappropriate a topic. Besides, it mattered not a whit to her if Damon kept a dozen mistresses, then or now.

She cared nothing for him any longer, so whatever dalliances he enjoyed were none of her affair.

And if she still harbored any remaining feelings of attraction or tenderness or love for him . . . well, Eleanor vowed fiercely to herself, she intended to conquer them immediately, once and for all!

The trouble was, forgetting about Damon was much easier said than done. Eleanor left Fanny's house in good spirits, having further discussed her strategy for appealing to Prince Lazzara. She was disappointed, however, that she saw no sign of the prince that evening when she attended a musical concert with her aunt.

And she was exceedingly vexed when fantasies of Damon intruded on her sleep for the second night in a row. Even worse, she dreamed about the time shortly after they became betrothed, when she'd taken Damon to see her special place—the rose garden that her brother had given her—and foolishly confessed her love to him. . . .

Writhing with humiliation at the remembrance, Eleanor woke early the following morning, furious at herself for not having better control over her mind and her heart. Damon was no longer the man of her dreams—so why the devil would he not leave them now?

Yet she was actually startled when the object of her vexation was announced by the Beldon butler just after she finished a solitary breakfast and repaired to the morning parlor to reread a chapter in Fanny's advice book.

Damon strode into the room as casually as he'd done during their betrothal, when he'd had the right to share her company.

Her gaze flying to him, Eleanor nearly dropped her book. He was dressed for riding this morning, and he looked incredibly handsome in a blue coat and buff buckskin breeches that molded his athletic form to perfection.

Deploring how her heart leapt at his unexpected appearance, Eleanor started to rise from the sofa where she was seated, but Damon held up a hand to forestall her.

"Pray, don't trouble yourself on my account, Lady Eleanor. I shan't be long."

"My l-lord . . ." she stammered. "Whatever are you doing here?"

"I thought to catch you at home before you set out on your morning ride."

She didn't intend to disclose that she would not be riding this morning—Eleanor abruptly cut off that thought when she recalled that they were not alone.

"That will be all, thank you, Peters," she said to Lady Beldon's august butler, who was hovering protectively at the parlor entrance.

Peters's expression showed the slightest measure of disapproval, but at Eleanor's dismissal, he bowed and retreated from the room.

Setting aside her book, she frowned at her noble visitor. "You should not be here, my lord."

Damon raised an eyebrow as he moved closer to stand before her. "Is it a crime to pay you a morning call?"

"Not a crime perhaps, but definitely a social transgression. You have no business here."

"I wanted to make certain you were unharmed after the carriage accident yesterday."

Eleanor's brows drew together uncertainly. "As you see, I am quite well. Did you expect the incident to overset my sensibilities?"

"Hardly. I know you too well."

When Damon flashed her an amused smile, Eleanor did her best to hide her involuntary physical response. Yet she couldn't repress the dizzy pleasure she felt when he smiled at her that way, or control the flush of warmth that suffused her body when his gaze drifted over her morning gown of jonquil muslin.

"You do look the picture of health," Damon observed.

Not having a ready reply, Eleanor stirred in her seat and kept silent.

"I gather the Dragon has not yet risen this morning," he said, casting a glance up at the ceiling toward the second floor where Lady Beldon was still abed.

Eleanor stiffened at the unappealing sobriquet. Her Aunt Beatrix had been more of a mother to her than her own mother, so Eleanor felt compelled to defend her. "You only consider her a dragon because she championed me two years ago when our betrothal ended."

Damon gave a mock wince. "My ears are still ringing from the tongue-lashing she gave me."

"You deserved it, you know very well."

"True. But Lady Beldon never approved of me from the start."

"Because of your wicked reputation. My aunt does not care for rakes or rebels."

Damon laughed softly as he settled on the sofa beside Eleanor. "Or anyone who fails to bow to her notion of proper behavior or grovel suitably before society's dictators. It amazes me that she tolerated our betrothal at all."

"Your title and fortune were significant points in your favor," Eleanor said dryly.

"But now they cannot compensate for my faults."

"No, they cannot. She wants me to have nothing more to do with you. My aunt believes a lady can never be too careful of her reputation."

"And you mean to be the good niece and do exactly as she decrees."

"Precisely."

Damon shook his head sadly. "I thought better of your revolutionary spirit, Elle. As long as we are speaking of what is proper, however . . . I suppose I should pay my respects to Lady Beldon."

"She would not welcome it after what happened between us," Eleanor pointed out.

"I take it she will never forgive me?"

"I sincerely doubt it."

"And you, Elle?" His voice dropped a register while his dark eyes searched her face. "Will you forgive me?"

Eleanor swallowed against the sudden ache in her throat. "I believe I mentioned, Lord Wrexham, I have put that unpleasant incident from my mind. I scarcely think about our betrothal, or you for that matter."

"I thought of you often while I was away," he said in a low voice.

She was about to remonstrate with him when his eye was drawn to Fanny's book lying beside her. Damon reached for it before she could think to stop him.

His eyebrows shot up as he recited the title aloud. "*Advice to Young Ladies on Capturing a Husband.* Are you actually reading this?"

"Yes, I am," Eleanor replied, feeling her cheeks turning red.

She tried to snatch the book from him, but Damon held it away until she gave up.

His eyebrows remained high as he thumbed through the pages. And his handsome mouth curved in a small grin when he came to one passage. " 'Offer him subtle flattery,' " Damon quoted, " 'that holds at least a grain of truth. Exaggerate his pleasant attributes, ignore the rest.' " He raised his gaze to Eleanor. "I suppose that is wise advice, but I would never have expected you to stoop so low."

Her flush deepened at his ribbing. "I am hardly *stooping* by following an author's practical guidance."

"You are honest and forthright, not coy and deceptive. This goes against your very nature, using an instruction manual to try to ensnare a husband."

"There is nothing deceptive about it! It is merely applying an understanding of the male temperament."

"Can you not succeed in capturing a man on your own?" Damon asked, his eyes dancing.

"Of *course* I could," Eleanor retorted. "But I do not want just any husband. I want one who loves me, and this book may help me win his affection."

Damon's amusement suddenly faded. "Have you set your sights on Lazzara, then?"

"What if I have? A union between us would be unexceptional."

"You would make an admirable princess, I'll grant you that. You were born to the role."

Hearing his dubious tone, Eleanor narrowed her gaze. "But you don't think I could bring the prince up to scratch?"

"Of course he will be drawn to you. You are lively, warm, passionate. Everyone adores you. And certainly he will appreciate your beauty and wit."

"You needn't try to flatter me," she replied irritably. "Your irresistible charm won't work on me any longer."

"A pity," Damon murmured. "It is not flattery, however, to say that his highness will be attracted to your fortune."

"He is hardly a fortune hunter. He has three palaces—indeed, his own kingdom."

"Anyone who spends his wealth the way Lazzara does would welcome an heiress bride to help fund his penchant for high living." When Eleanor started to object, Damon raised his hand. "But regardless of his motives for courting you, I have to question your choice. You would be bored to flinders with a milquetoast. You need a man who will challenge you as much as you challenge him."

Eleanor bit back a retort, finding too much delight in her exchange of words with Damon. But then, he had always been the most enlivening, stimulating, provocative man of her acquaintance. Even when they argued, she felt a delicious tingle at the challenge of matching wits with him.

"Prince Lazzara is most certainly not a milquetoast," Eleanor finally protested.

"Perhaps. But I know his sort—a charming pleasure-seeker with little genuine substance. In his country, Lazzara is known for breaking hearts. I don't want to see him hurt you, Elle."

"Isn't that like the pot calling the kettle black?" she asked with exaggerated sweetness.

Damon's wince this time looked real, but he continued with an edge of determination in his voice. "Your prince not only is royalty but he was raised in a country where women are shown little respect and rarely seen as equals to men. Lazzara demands subservience and submission from his subjects now. I'd wager that once the courtship is over, he will expect you to do his bidding and obey his every word. You are hardly a biddable female, Elle."

Eleanor hesitated, knowing Damon had a point. Currently Prince Lazzara was all charm and affability with her, although she knew he could be forceful in getting his way with his servants and even his elder relative, Signor Vecchi.

"If you expect," Damon said, "to lead the prince around by his nose after the wedding, as you do all your swains now, you will likely have a rude awakening."

"I do no such thing," she objected. "I certainly never led *you*."

"Which is a prime reason you enjoyed our courtship, because you were not able to rule me."

That much was true, Eleanor had to agree, even though she was not about to tell *him* so.

"You would not enjoy being ruled, Elle," Damon observed. "And you are in for a great mismatch if you wed Lazzara."

Eleanor grimaced, knowing he was calling her Elle just to rile her. "I am not interested in your opinion in the least, Lord Wrexham."

He sighed. "Why do you insist on addressing me by my title, as if we are strangers?"

"We *are* strangers now."

"I beg to differ, love. We still know each other very well."

Eleanor had difficultly controlling her response to Damon's smile. That slow, lazy smile was his most potent weapon. "You are wrong, my lord. I don't know you at all. It seems I never did."

"You don't know Lazzara either."

"But what I do know of him, I like very much. He is extremely considerate and yes, charming. What is more, he has the Italian flair for romance, which is a strong point in his favor."

"Because you want a passionate lover for your husband."

Indeed, she wanted a man who made her feverish, who made her burn, the way Damon had once done. "Perhaps, but I also want more than passion. I have not given up on finding love in marriage."

Damon's gaze turned shadowed. "So you believe your Romeo is passionate. Has he kissed you yet?"

Eleanor's chin lifted. "I beg your pardon? That is hardly any of your concern."

"He must not have," Damon said with satisfaction,

"or you would not be so prickly in coming to his defense."

"I am not prickly!"

"Do you intend to dunk him in a fountain if he dares to take liberties with you?"

Taking a deep breath, Eleanor tried to regain control of their conversation. "I have no intention of dunking him. He is a prince, after all. And I doubt he would take liberties in any case. *He* is a gentleman."

"Meaning that I am not?"

Eleanor returned an arch smile. "You may divine whatever meaning you choose, Lord Wrexham."

"Very well . . ." Damon leaned toward her, pausing with his mouth barely inches from hers.

She froze, feeling stupidly breathless and dizzy at his proximity. "What do you think you are doing?" she managed to rasp.

"It's called kissing, Eleanor. You have done it before—with me, in fact. Several times . . ."

He bent his head before she could protest. The pressure was light, only the barest touch of his warm mouth to hers, but it promised so much more—which doubtless explained the shock of desire that jolted through her.

Her heart suddenly pounding, Eleanor drew back sharply, even though all her senses were alive with awareness and alertness and excitement.

"Damon!" she declared tartly. "You cannot just kiss me whenever you feel the urge."

"No, but I want to prove a point."

When she made to rise, though, he grasped her shoulders to keep her from fleeing. "Let me try again. . . ."

Eleanor's entire body went rigid, yet she found it impossible to struggle against Damon's light hold.

What was it about this devilish rogue that demolished all her common sense? Eleanor wondered, cursing her weakness for him. She should push him away, but he was so enchantingly close. His virile warmth spoke to some primal feminine instinct in her, while that beautiful, wicked mouth enticed her. . . .

She watched, paralyzed, as his mouth moved even closer. When his breath fanned against her lips, she inhaled raggedly. Then Damon's lips caressed hers again, alluring, whisper soft.

His mouth was as delicious as she remembered, his taste as heady. Warmth spreading through her, Eleanor felt herself melting as his lips slowly twisted and pulled at hers.

When his hands slid from her shoulders to her upper arms, sensation skittered up her nerve endings and danced over her skin. Then Damon deepened the pressure of his kiss, settling his mouth more fully on hers while drawing her against his hard body.

When his tongue penetrated her lips in a sensual invasion, a heated rush of feeling assaulted Eleanor. His taste was incredibly arousing. She shivered at the warm stroke of his rough-silk tongue inside her mouth.

Of their own accord, her hands rose to clutch Damon's shoulders, and she could feel the hardness of his corded muscles beneath her fingertips.

At the same time his fingertips drifted to her bodice to skim the underside of her breasts. When his strong hands cupped the swells beneath the muslin, Eleanor shuddered at the riveting sensation.

A helpless sigh whispered from deep in her throat

as he began to stroke her with stunning sensuality. His long fingers shaped her breasts, his palms molding the weight, while his thumbs coaxed her nipples, making the sensitive tips engorge painfully under his light touch.

Eleanor gave a breathless whimper—a sound that Damon evidently heard, for his caresses slowed before he finally ended their embrace.

She was dazed and trembling when he drew back.

His eyes smoldered with heat as he stared back at her. "You felt that, didn't you?" he murmured, his voice hoarse and deep.

"Felt w-what?"

"The sparks between us."

Oh, yes. Heaven help her. The sparks were still there between them, running along her nerve endings, over her skin, flaring inside her. Eleanor couldn't believe how powerful, how searing they were.

Unable to look away from the dark intensity of Damon's gaze, she swallowed mutely.

"Do you feel those same sparks with your prince?" he prodded.

She had only one answer to give: *No.* Damon still sparked a fire inside her that she had never felt with any other man, including Prince Lazzara. *Damn him.*

Eleanor abruptly gave herself a fierce mental shake. Damon was weaving the exact same spell over her as he had two years ago, and like a fool, she was allowing it, despite all the pain he had caused her then.

With effort, she rose unsteadily to her feet, ignoring how weak her knees were. It was dismaying—appalling even—to find herself just as attracted to her former betrothed as she'd once been. It was galling, her inability to resist Damon. And it was frustrating in the extreme, knowing he had deliberately kissed her to prove a point—that she still wanted him and that her new suitor couldn't compare to him in terms of passion.

Her ire rose along with her dismay, but Eleanor clamped it down, knowing she would get further with Damon if she remained cool and composed.

"Lord Wrexham, you may take your leave now," she announced, proud that her voice sounded almost even. "You have outstayed your welcome."

When he didn't respond at once but merely sat there staring up at her, as if he too had been rendered spellbound by their kiss, Eleanor turned toward the bellpull to ring for the butler. But Peters miraculously appeared in the doorway, as if knowing she needed him.

"Lord Wrexham wishes to leave, Peters," she said in relief. "But he is having difficulty finding the front entrance on his own. Will you please show him out?"

"Very well, my lady. But you have another visitor. Prince Lazzara has called."

Chapter Four

*Regularly permit him to make a show of gallantry
and manly strength. He will be happy to preen his
feathers for your admiration.*

—An Anonymous Lady, *Advice . . .*

Eleanor muttered a silent oath. This was all she
needed, having the prince call a half hour earlier than
expected, just when Damon had been kissing her witless. Thank heaven his highness hadn't arrived two
minutes sooner.

"Do you wish to receive him here in the morning
parlor, my lady?" the butler asked.

"Yes, Peters. Please ask Prince Lazzara to join me
here."

When the illustrious servant exited to follow her orders, Eleanor distractedly raised her hands to her hair
to make certain her curls weren't too disheveled. No
doubt she looked like a wanton with her cheeks
flushed and her mouth wet and swollen from Damon's
kisses.

And the culprit showed no signs of remorse, she
realized when she sent him a resentful glance. Damon
lounged back on the sofa, looking comfortably settled, evidently prepared to remain there for the dura-
tion of the prince's visit.

"This should be priceless," Damon murmured with

obvious enjoyment, "watching you work your new-found wiles on Lazzara."

Eleanor had no time to remonstrate, however, before her second handsome caller of the morning appeared.

"I beg a million pardons for my early arrival, Donna Eleanora," the prince said as he bowed gallantly over her hand and then kissed her fingers. "It is my great hope that you will forgive me. I was eager to see you again and to begin our outing. And as they say in your language, the bird who is early catches the worm. The shops are waiting for your patronage."

Eleanor managed a smile. "Certainly I will forgive you, your highness. I am eager to begin as well."

Lazzara's brow furrowed when Damon caught his attention by rising from the sofa. "Ah, I did not realize you had another caller."

"His lordship was just leaving," she said hastily.

But Damon offered her a bland smile. "In truth, I am in no hurry. What is this outing you speak of, your highness?"

Prince Lazzara replied in a rather indulgent tone, "I mean to escort Donna Eleanora shopping at the Pantheon Bazaar on Oxford Street. She wishes to search for a gift for the birthday of her aunt. And I will be intrigued to see a bazaar. We have no such things in my country, merely markets and shops."

"How gallant of you, your highness," Damon said mildly. "Lady Eleanor must be impressed by your magnanimity."

The prince narrowed his gaze, as if uncertain whether he was being roasted.

Eleanor hastened to intervene. "I am exceedingly

impressed—and appreciative that Don Antonio is willing to give so generously of his time and attention."

"Would it inconvenience you greatly if I tagged along, your highness?" Damon asked. "My valet has been after me to show better style in my appearance and to take an interest in the fashions that have come into vogue during my absence from London."

When the prince hesitated, obviously debating how discourteous it would be to refuse the English nobleman's request, Eleanor answered for him, alarmed at the notion of Damon accompanying them. "Surely, Lord Wrexham, you have better things to do with your own time."

"Not at the moment. I can think of nothing more enjoyable than assisting a beautiful lady to achieve her heart's desire."

At the mischief glittering in his eyes, Eleanor pressed her lips together. Just now her heart's desire was to be rid of Damon. But he was the same wicked rogue he had always been. She should know better than to expect him to observe proper rules of etiquette.

She also knew better than to fight him overtly. He was not above using his formidable powers of persuasion to gain whatever he wanted, but conducting a battle of wills in front of the prince would not help her win Lazzara's admiration. Thus, she left it to his highness to give his approval or not.

"You may ride with us in my barouche, my lord," he said with evident reluctance.

"You are all kindness, sir." Damon turned to Eleanor. "Do you mean to leave at once?"

"I must fetch my pelisse and reticule and alert my abigail that we are leaving sooner than expected." For propriety's sake, her lady's maid would attend her during her shopping expedition with the prince.

"Then why don't you proceed? I will keep his highness entertained in your absence," Damon asserted.

Entertained? That possibility worried her exceedingly, Eleanor thought, experiencing a fierce urge to tell Damon to go to the devil. He was clearly amused by her struggle to hold her tongue.

Annoyed that she amused him, she smiled graciously at Don Antonio and said aloud, "If you will excuse me for a moment, your highness . . . ?"

"Naturally, *mia signorina.*"

Yet Eleanor felt a strong measure of trepidation when she left the parlor and went upstairs in search of her maid, Jenny. She didn't particularly trust Damon alone with the prince. Not after his gibes about her using Fanny's book to attract her royal suitor.

The remembrance made her want to squirm. Yet who was *he* to judge her attempts at romance? Eleanor muttered to herself, still piqued that she was required to defend her actions to Damon.

Somehow he had known that the sparks were missing from her current courtship. She felt a physical attraction to Prince Lazzara, true, but nothing whatsoever like what she had felt for Damon. At least not yet. Then again, it was still early in their courtship. She hadn't had much opportunity to apply Fanny's sage advice.

She meant to remedy that very shortly. She intended to rouse Lazzara's ardor—and increase her own ardor for him at the same time.

It would be far more difficult with her former betrothed underfoot, but she would manage, Eleanor vowed. Moreover, she reminded herself with a determined surge of optimism, wooing another nobleman should go a long way in helping her crush her continued foolish captivation with the provoking rake who had once meant so much to her.

Keeping his hands clasped over his lap as he settled again on the sofa, Damon crossed one booted leg over the other and surreptitiously arranged his breeches to hide his swollen arousal. Kissing Elle had left him woefully hot and painfully hard.

A rather unseemly state, given that he was face-to-face now with her royal courtier.

Damon was glad to have this opportunity, however. All his instincts shouted that Lazzara wasn't the right match for Eleanor. She was not precisely gullible where men were concerned, but she genuinely liked most people. As a result, she would be too willing to overlook Lazzara's faults and fail to examine his character closely enough in favor of his more superficial qualities of charm and physical appeal.

Especially since she was set on using that damned advice primer to help her win his affection.

Damon felt a muscle flex in his jaw. He had pretended amusement at Eleanor's professed determination to entice the prince into marriage, but there was nothing amusing about it.

Of course, he admitted rather grudgingly, jealousy

was possibly driving him in addition to his determination to protect her.

And from Lazzara's expression as he took a seat opposite, the prince was feeling a strong measure of jealousy himself. They were like two bucks sizing up each other before battle, fighting over the same doe.

However, the prince's next words surprised him. "I understood, Lord Wrexham, that you no longer have any claim to Donna Eleanora. Was I mistaken? Shall I consider you a rival for her hand?"

Although appreciating that Lazzara had come straight to the heart of the matter, Damon sidestepped a direct reply. "I gave up my claim to Lady Eleanor some time ago, as she will attest. But that does not mean that I am not concerned for her." His regard intensified. "What are your intentions toward Lady Eleanor, your highness?"

Lazzara lifted his chin with royal hauteur, as if wondering how anyone dared to ask him such a thing.

Damon held back a tight smile. It was ironic that he was questioning Eleanor's latest suitor just as Marcus had questioned *him* two years ago when he'd sought her hand in marriage.

"You presume a great deal, sir," the prince finally said.

"Her elder brother, Lord Danvers, is a friend of mine," Damon replied, shading the truth a little. "In his absence, I feel obliged to keep an eye out for her."

Which was only partly accurate. His callous treatment of Marcus's sister had cost Damon their longtime friendship. Indeed, Marcus had threatened to carve out his liver if he didn't leave London immediately so the sensation could die down. It was fortunate that the warning had coincided with Damon's need to pursue his own goals in the warm, dry climate of the Mediterranean.

A hint of anger flashed in Lazzara's eyes, while his reply was dismissive of Damon's concern. "My courtship of Donna Eleanora is my own affair, my lord. I need not explain my intentions to you or anyone else."

Damon felt his jaw clench at that unsatisfactory answer, but he settled for a warning of his own. "It would be a mistake," he said in a silken tone, "to think you could escape retribution from Lady Eleanor's family and friends were you to hurt her in any way, even unintentionally."

Lazzara hesitated, evidently reconsidering sparring with Damon. His scowl disappearing, he instead offered a smile meant to charm. "I promise you, my lord, she is quite safe with me."

Damon put no trust in such a pledge, though. Nor would he be deterred by it.

He intended to observe Lazzara's courtship of Eleanor closely and would act to end any serious romance between them. It would be a challenge, devising ways to interfere without earning her scorn. But he meant to keep Eleanor from making an irrevocable mistake, even if it meant going against her express desires.

The Pantheon Bazaar, situated between Oxford and Marlborough Streets, offered a wide assortment of wares by mercers, milliners, hatters, tobacconists, and perfumeries, among many others.

This was Damon's first visit to the Bazaar, since it had opened barely a year before he'd left London. The large, airy building, he noted when their small party entered, was furnished with numerous stalls on the ground floors and with galleries above.

Much of the time Damon hung back a little, observing Eleanor and her chosen suitor as they wandered through the crowds and perused the stalls, examining clothing and accessories, jewelry, furs, gloves, fans, and expensive novelties such as ornamental clocks. Eleanor's abigail, Jenny, followed close behind her, gaping at the sights, while the prince's two footmen hastened ahead, clearing a path for his royal highness.

After more than an hour, Eleanor settled on a gilt ormolu clock as a birthday gift for her aunt, asking for it to be wrapped and delivered to their home at Portman Place. Prince Lazzara purchased several items also and turned them over to his footmen to carry out to his barouche, which awaited them on the street.

As she effortlessly charmed the prince with her sparkling laugh and quick repartee, Damon tried to stifle the jealous pangs he felt. Yet he couldn't wholly dismiss the prodding voice in his head that reminded him *he* could have been the one escorting Eleanor to the fashionable shopping districts, bantering with her and enjoying an easy camaraderie rather than the prickly tension that existed between them now.

When they reached the end of the building, they viewed the waxwork exhibition and then strolled through the conservatory, which boasted a display of rare plants and evergreen shrubs as well as a menagerie of chattering animals, including parrots and monkeys.

For the most part, Damon was aware, Eleanor seemed to be ignoring him, except once when they passed a fountain and basin filled with goldfish.

A wry smile curved his mouth at the image that entered his mind—of her pushing her royal suitor into the water if he made so bold as to try to kiss her. And when Damon caught Elle's eye, he knew she was envisioning the same image.

For a fleeting moment as their gazes locked with shared humor, they were in complete accord. But then Eleanor quickly quelled her amusement and turned a shoulder to him as she took her Italian escort's proffered arm.

Shortly they returned to a particular watchmaker's stall where previously the prince had spied an ornate gold watch fob that appealed to him. While his highness discussed a possible purchase with the merchant, Damon waited to one side with Eleanor.

Somewhat to his surprise, she chose the opportunity to take him to task for his intrusion on her romance, although she did it in an undertone that couldn't be heard over the cheerful din of the bazaar.

"You have some nerve, Lord Wrexham, inviting yourself along on our outing."

Damon raised an eyebrow at Eleanor, pretending surprise. "You did not want me to accompany you?"

"Of course not. Not when you are obviously set on making mischief."

"Whatever gave you that impression?" he queried innocently.

Eleanor grimaced in exasperation. "I can tell from the devilish gleam in your eyes."

He tried to keep his expression bland, even though he was indeed provoking her on purpose, attempting to open her eyes to the prince's shortcomings. "You wound me, love. Do you honestly think I would try to come between you and your Romeo?"

"Will you *please* cease calling him that?" Eleanor exclaimed in a whisper.

"Very well, if you insist—although in Italy he earned that reputation in his own right. I confess, I cannot quite understand what you see in him."

She made a visible effort at composure. "To begin with, Prince Lazzara is very much the opposite of you in several respects."

"I would say so," Damon said dryly. "He likes fancy clothing and gewgaws and whatnot, and spends money as if it were water."

Eleanor shot Damon a quelling glance but refrained from comment, perhaps because she saw some truth in his charge.

"It surprises me," he continued, "that you've allowed yourself to be so blindly attracted to a pretty face. But I suppose I cannot fault you. You always were the idealist."

"You mean that I am naive."

"Perhaps you are. Isn't it naive to think you can win a gentleman's affection because some tome tells you so?"

Her chin rose. "I won't dignify that remark with a reply."

Damon chuckled at her expression of disdain.

"Look at it this way, Elle. I am actually aiding your cause."

Her blue eyes widened in mock amazement, while her tone turned sweetly skeptical. "Pray tell, just how are you aiding my cause?"

"If Lazzara thinks I am his competition, he will make a greater effort to cut me out. Indeed, he already is trying."

That theory gave Eleanor pause. "So you are bedeviling me for *my* sake?"

"You could put it that way. I told you, I don't want him hurting you. Therefore, I am appointing myself your personal protector."

As if praying for patience, she raised her gaze to the high ceiling overhead, then fixed Damon with an exasperated glance. "Well, I wish you would stop."

"I don't intend to reveal your secrets to your prince, if that worries you."

"What secrets?" Eleanor demanded warily. "I have no secrets."

"What of your plan to capture Lazzara for your husband by using that advice manual?"

"Don't you dare tell him about that!" she ground out.

"And what of the fact that you were kissing me two minutes before he walked into your parlor?"

Her cheeks flushed becomingly. "That was a grave mistake, one that will not be repeated. And I trust you will not tattle to him."

"In all honor, my lips are sealed."

Eleanor regarded Damon with suspicion. "I would be much more reassured if you would return to the Continent and spend another two years there."

"But I am enjoying myself here."

"At my expense, it seems," she said tartly. "Cannot you just leave me in peace?"

"I'm afraid I can't promise that," he said, although trying to keep his tone conciliatory.

In response, Eleanor pasted an arch smile on her mouth. "At least I have only to endure your interference for another week."

Damon didn't much care for *her* tone—satisfaction tinged with a note of triumph. "How so?"

"My aunt's annual house party begins on Friday of next week, and Prince Lazzara has accepted her invitation to attend."

Damon's brows drew together sharply. He didn't like the implication of her announcement in the least. If Lazzara attended Lady Beldon's private house party, then Elle would be at even greater risk than now.

As if realizing she had struck a nerve with *him*, Eleanor broadened her smile and continued with a casual air. "I'm quite eager for the opportunity to become better acquainted with the prince. I will have an entire fortnight to apply the advice in my book."

Damon felt his gut clench. A great deal could happen in a fortnight. Indeed, it was ample time for Eleanor to fall in love with a Lothario who would make her miserable.

"So it is that serious, is it?" he asked. "Your aunt has given Lazzara's courtship her approval?"

"Indeed. My aunt thinks very highly of him. And of his relative, Signor Vecchi, as well. The signor will be attending also."

Wishing he could make her see reason, Damon

held her gaze as he shook his head. "I believe you would be making a grave mistake, Elle, wedding a man like Lazzara. You are full of mettle and zest for life. You don't want all that spirit stifled by a husband who cannot appreciate the very qualities that make you so unique and rare."

She parted her mouth to speak, then shut it again, before finally saying, "Why can you not merely let me handle my own affairs, Damon?"

"Because I don't want to see you throwing your life away by marrying the wrong man."

Her eyes flashed. "You don't know that he is the wrong man!"

"In my opinion, he is."

Eleanor drew a deep breath. "Loath as I am to disappoint you, Lord Wrexham, I don't care a whit about your opinion. I suggest that you see to your own future and leave me to mine."

Perceiving that the prince had nearly finished with his purchase, she turned and went to join him at the stall counter, leaving Damon where he stood.

Her admonition to see to his own future was not bad advice, Damon reflected, watching her stiff back. He had returned home to England, knowing it was time to take stock of his life and determine what to do with the rest of it.

The prospect gave him little pleasure, however. The years stretched out before him with barren monotony. A solitary path, purposely devoid of feeling, where he kept to himself and allowed no one else to touch his heart with joy or pain or any emotion in between.

But that was precisely how he'd planned it, Damon

reminded himself as the old emptiness echoed inside him.

Yet the hollowness he'd felt since his twin's death was a stark contrast to what he was experiencing just now after his spirited contention with Eleanor. The sparks in her blue eyes alone had made him keenly aware of the difference.

He hadn't felt this alive in two years.

The regrettable truth was, he liked flustering Elle and ruffling her feathers, although he would much rather win her laughter. He relished making her laugh, the way she once had during their courtship.

A memory suddenly surfaced from the enchanting fortnight he'd spent with her at her aunt's house party. Of Elle laughing after having won an impulsive horse race between them. Of her breathless, passionate response when he'd bestowed a fervored kiss upon her as her reward.

At the unwanted recollection, tenderness nagged at him—a dangerous sentiment, Damon knew very well. So was desire, he reflected, remembering that brief moment this morning when Eleanor had melted in his arms. He couldn't deny his powerful desire for her, or his feeling of triumph at her surrender.

She had tried to pretend disinterest, but she had enjoyed his kisses, he was certain of it. Even now there was an undeniable fire between them—

Which was also exceedingly dangerous.

If he was wise, Damon sternly warned himself, he would quell every ounce of attraction he felt for her and concentrate solely on spoiling her budding romance with her hedonist prince.

* * *

It soon became clear to Damon that Eleanor was determined to avoid any further conversation with him during the remainder of their excursion. In contrast, she maintained a delightful exchange with Prince Lazzara, praising his gallantry when he declared his intention of escorting her to London's premiere confectioners, Gunter's Teashop in Berkeley Square, to enjoy their famous ices and sorbets.

But when their party exited the bazaar to return to his highness's carriage, they soon discovered there was a problem with retrieving the vehicle. Further down the street, the barouche was mired in a snarl of traffic. Apparently a dray had spilled part of its cargo of turnips and was blocking most of the street, resulting in an altercation between drivers, merchants, and coachmen.

Grimacing impatiently, Prince Lazzara begged Donna Eleanora's indulgence while he went to investigate.

"Of course, your highness," she said quickly, smiling with reassurance.

Yet she was obviously *not* delighted at being required to wait on the sidewalk with Damon, even with the protection of her maid. Eleanor maintained a cool silence, while Damon surveyed the growing dispute, wondering if he would need to intervene to forestall a brawl.

It was pure chance that he happened to see the incident that befell Lazzara while crossing the street. A small, dark-haired man darted after the prince and collided with unmistakable deliberation, pushing him to the cobblestones. Then, with one smooth slight of hand, the miscreant reached inside the nobleman's coat and drew out an object . . . a leather purse by the looks of it.

It was over in an instant; Lazzara lay sprawled there inelegantly, his features twisted in shock and anger, while the pickpocket fled.

Reacting instinctively, Damon sprinted after the thief while Eleanor gave a small cry of alarm and hurried to assist the prince.

When Damon eventually lost the pickpocket in the crowd, he returned to find her kneeling at Lazzara's side, her worry evident as she helped him to sit upright.

"Were you harmed, your highness?" Damon asked with a sincere measure of concern.

"No!" the Italian snapped. "My purse . . . that devil stole my purse." He broke into a flood of Italian, spouting invectives that Damon knew meant devil and blackguard and several more pithy terms describing the vile scoundrel's parentage.

Then evidently recalling his audience, the prince ended his tirade abruptly. "Ah, a million pardons, *mia signorina.* I am ashamed to have used such language. It is improper for your tender ears."

At the reference to her tender ears, Eleanor bit back a smile, although when her gaze accidently met Damon's, he could see the glint of humor dancing in her blue eyes. But she quickly erased any traces of amusement.

"It is no matter, your highness. Since you spoke in your language, I missed most of what you said. And in any event, I have doubtless heard worse from my brother and his friends. I have not lived as sheltered a life as the women of your country."

Despite her conciliatory tone, Lazzara's face was rather red as he stood and dusted himself off, then helped Eleanor to rise. Clearly he was embarrassed at once again having been shown at a disadvantage in her eyes.

He seemed further embarrassed as he muttered, "I regret, Donna Eleanora, that we shall not proceed to Gunter's to fulfil your desire to partake of ices. I have no means to pay."

Eleanor barely hesitated before giving him an easy smile while brushing at her skirts. "But I have the means, your highness. I would be happy to pay for tea and ices."

When Lazzara stiffened, Damon could see that Eleanor immediately realized her mistake. She had obviously wounded the nobleman's pride, however inadvertently.

"Pray, allow it to be my treat, your highness," Damon interrupted smoothly. "You were generous enough to permit me to intrude on your shopping expedition. The least I can do is repay the favor."

He could see Lazzara warring with his conscience, whether to let his offended pride take precedence or claim the chance to bask in Eleanor's company for another hour.

He chose the latter, nodding brusquely and offering his arm to her.

Damon followed them to the barouche, for which the footmen had somehow miraculously cleared a path. As he climbed in and took his seat opposite them, however, he felt himself frowning at a sudden realization. The pickpocket had had the olive complexion of the peoples of the Mediterranean.

It seemed a stretch to suspect one of Lazzara's own countrymen of perpetrating the theft, although someone acquainted with the prince and familiar with his habits, including where he kept his purse, would have an advantage over the average thief.

More likely, though, the pickpocket was a stranger who'd carefully observed the foreign nobleman shopping at the stalls and targeted him as an easy mark, using the traffic tangle as a distraction.

It still seemed an odd coincidence, however—not to mention remarkably ill luck for Lazzara to have suffered two hazardous mishaps in as many days.

Damon's frown deepened when he saw Eleanor and the prince laughing with their heads close together. Apparently his highness had recovered enough from his embarrassment to reopen his spigot of charm.

The sight elicited the same strong reaction in Damon as a few moments ago, when Eleanor had knelt protectively beside the supine prince. She was far too solicitous for his peace of mind, and much too susceptible to the Italian Lothario's blandishments.

Silently voicing an oath, Damon acknowledged the fierce emotion spearing through him: possessiveness. There was no point in trying to deny his condition any longer.

Indeed, he was quickly coming to the conclusion that he didn't want Elle wedding Lazzara—but not only because he didn't want her to be hurt by making such a wretched choice for her husband.

No, Damon realized, tightening his jaw, he didn't want her wedding any other man at all.

Chapter Five

When discussing even mundane matters, allow a gentleman to show off his knowledge and expertise, even if you know far more about a subject than he does.

—An Anonymous Lady, *Advice . . .*

Damon had difficulty stifling his impatience the following evening as he lounged in the upper gallery of the Theatre Royal, Covent Garden, waiting for Eleanor to arrive. He had no intention of letting her surreptitiously woo her prince without impediment, certainly not if her pursuit might lead to marriage.

He had no intention, either, of hieing himself back to the Continent, as Elle had so tartly suggested. He'd had enough of foreign lands for a while. And although he wasn't clear precisely what he wanted for his future, he was certain that whatever he wanted was here in England—and that his chief goal just now was to spike the wheels of Eleanor's romance with Prince Lazzara.

Therefore, yesterday at Gunter's, when his highness had mentioned escorting Eleanor and her aunt to the benefit concert here tonight, Damon had scrambled to arrange the seating to his liking. There were no private boxes in the Theatre Royal, but his party had been allocated a prime section of the gallery close to the stage, thanks to his distant cousin, Tess Blanchard.

As one of the organizers, Tess had hired the theater and constructed the program to offer a variety of theatrical amusements, including opera arias and choruses in English and Italian, skits, dramatic recitations, and a pantomime by the marvelous pantomime clown, Joseph Grimaldi.

The event was considered so exclusive that the denizens of the ton had fought to put down their money for tickets. Prinny himself was scheduled to attend, a coup for Tess, who spent much of her time advocating for charities such as the Families of Fallen Soldiers as well as several orphanages and hospitals. Recently she had joined the youngest Loring sister, Lily—who was now the Marchioness of Claybourne—in starting a home to provide shelter and education for unfortunate women.

Tonight Damon's friend, renowned physician Otto Geary, had been given a seat of honor, since the proceeds of the evening would go to his beloved Marlebone Hospital. Thus, it had been relatively easy for Damon to drag him here. Even though Otto disliked opera, he'd had no choice but to leave his patients for a few hours.

Damon was seated next to Otto now, awaiting Eleanor and Prince Lazzara's arrival.

"I wish they would hurry things along," Otto muttered, tugging on his cravat. "I have too much work to do to be lazing about in this indolent fashion."

"It won't be long now," Damon assured him. "And you owe Miss Blanchard a show of gratitude, so pray cease your fidgeting."

The physician scowled briefly before his eyes began twinkling at Damon. "I suspect you are a bit restless yourself, old friend, given how closely you have been watching the door these past ten minutes. And I fathom that gratitude to Miss Blanchard has nothing to do with your insistence on my presence here tonight. You only wanted me here for your protection."

Damon bit back a wry smile. "That is not the sole reason."

"But a reason nonetheless." Otto's amusement broke out into a grin. "In truth, I don't know if I care to be anywhere near you once Lady Eleanor discovers what you have contrived. And in any case, I'm certain Miss Blanchard is more capable than I of shielding you."

"Perhaps. But there is safety in numbers."

Tess planned to join them shortly—a fortunate situation, Damon judged, since he hoped his cousin might be able to smooth over troubled waters, as it were. Eleanor would not be happy to discover that she and her prince and aunt would be seated so close to him.

He wasn't mistaken. When Elle finally made an appearance, he only had eyes for her, so he didn't miss the narrowing of her gaze when she realized how he had manipulated matters to suit his purpose.

In a similar reaction, Lazzara stiffened with suspicion, while Eleanor's aunt went rigid with disapproval.

Lady Beldon had never forgiven Damon for his rift with her niece two years ago. Accordingly, she was at her haughtiest when he politely rose and began the introductions, although at least she didn't overtly cut him.

Prince Lazzara was then compelled to make known his relative, Signor Umberto Vecchi, a tall, silver-haired gentleman. A diplomat from the Kingdom of the Two Sicilies assigned to the Court of England, Vecchi had responsibility for commercial dealings, chiefly the lucrative trade of Marsala wine. And only he seemed unaware of the sudden chill in the air as they all stood for a moment making genteel but awkward conversation.

Fortunately the tension was relieved when the elderly Dowager Countess Haviland joined them, escorted by her grandson, Rayne Kenyon, the new Earl of Haviland.

The earl was well known to Damon from their salad days at university. Haviland had been an unapologetic rebel then, and the black sheep of his illustrious family, so it was no surprise that he'd spent many of the intervening years attempting to thwart Napoleon's aim of world domination—reputedly, it was whispered, as a brilliant spymaster for British intelligence.

Clearly his grandmother and Lady Beldon were fast friends. But when another round of introductions followed, Damon noted with some surprise that Lady Beldon seemed to harbor a decided fondness for the handsome Italian diplomat, and that she lost a good deal of her aristocratic starch when speaking to him, almost to the point of coy flirtation.

However, it did *not* surprise Damon when Eleanor made use of the diversion to take him to task under her breath. "Your machinations are beginning to annoy me excessively, Lord Wrexham. I wish you would stop hounding me in this absurd way."

Damon raised an innocent eyebrow. "I am hardly hounding you."

"No? What do you call *this*?" She waved a hand, indicating the seating arrangements. "You intruded on our excursion yesterday, and now this."

"I should think you would be pleased to have such a choice view of the performers. Miss Blanchard went to great trouble to accommodate my request. But if you wish, I can ask her to move your party elsewhere."

With an exasperated huff, Eleanor sent him a quelling look. "You know it is much too late now to relocate. I don't wish to make a scene. But take warning. I will not allow you to spoil my prospects with Prince Lazzara."

Her words were a challenge, while her flashing eyes pinned him. But wisely, Damon refrained from responding and provoking her further. Then Tess arrived with her spinster friend, Miss Jane Caruthers. Tess greeted him warmly before turning to the others to welcome them to the concert.

Eventually they all took their seats. Tess sat next to Damon, who had settled behind Eleanor and her suitor.

Damon was glad for the opportunity to share Tess's company. A dark-haired beauty with a gracious and serene air about her, she was only a fourth cousin or so, but one of his few relatives and someone he cherished. Tess had been so busy with her various charities, however, they'd had no time for any private conversations since his return to England.

"It is so good to see you again, Damon," she murmured, leaning closer to be heard over the din of the audience.

"And you, love. You have outdone yourself this evening."

Her smile was tinged with relief and pride. "I do hope it goes well. If the Prince Regent will only arrive soon, we may begin before the audience becomes too restless."

The entire theater was resplendent with the cream of society present. The glittering crowd wore their richest finery, and the display of silks and satins and jewels shimmered in the glow of gaslight flame.

Damon had a good view of Eleanor's bare nape and graceful shoulders as she leaned closer to her own companion to discuss the program.

The opening performance would be in English, a chorus from Mozart's *Don Giovanni,* followed by an aria in Italian from Italy's Gioacchino Rossini, then selections from George Fredric Handel and the Irish composer Thomas Cooke.

He could hear Eleanor questioning Prince Lazzara about opera music—no doubt following the advice of that damned book on how to capture a husband. Her encouragement allowed his highness to boast about the superior nature of his country's contribution to world culture.

"I confess astonishment," the prince eventually lamented, "that some of your operas are sung in English. The effect will be ruinous."

Leaning forward, Damon interjected himself into their discussion. "On the contrary, your highness," he said mildly. "Being able to understand the words makes opera more appealing to the common Englishman."

Lazzara glanced dismissively over his shoulder at Damon. "What would you know of it, sir? You do not strike me as the sort who would appreciate good opera."

"You would be mistaken. I enjoy opera greatly. As it happens, I had the pleasure of hearing Rossini's debut of *Barbiere di Siviglia* in Rome last year."

Lazzara's eyebrows rose in surprise. "Indeed?"

Damon smiled. "Yes, and since it is just the sort of comedy we English enjoy, I would not be surprised if it were soon to be performed here in London in our language."

Lazzara gave a delicate shudder, clearly looking down his royal nose at this violation to his sensibilities, while Eleanor frowned at Damon.

He caught her reproving glance, but sat back satisfied that he had at least made her think about the vast divide between their two cultures.

Beside him, Tess watched him with curiosity, but then her attention was diverted by the commotion across the theater in the opposite gallery. The audience was rising to acknowledge the arrival of His Royal Highness, the Prince Regent. Damon could almost feel his cousin breathe more easily once Prinny's entourage was finally settled and the performance began.

On her part, Eleanor sat stewing during the first performance, deploring her powerful physical awareness of Damon behind her. Mercy, he looked stunning in a black evening coat, with the crisp white lace of his cravat a perfect foil for his sun-bronzed skin. It had required a valiant effort to tear her gaze away from him.

At least her efforts to ignore him were helped by her frustration. The vexing rogue kept appearing during her outings with the prince, making an utter nuisance of himself and driving her to distraction.

Yet she couldn't deny that his very presence set all her nerves and senses humming. Admittedly, Damon was the most enlivening, stimulating man of her acquaintance, if one admired clever, well-informed minds, which unfortunately she did. She would have liked to ask him about his recent travels on the Continent . . . but under no circumstances would she encourage such familiarity between them.

She was genuinely glad, however, to meet Damon's friend, the preeminent physician, Mr. Geary. She'd heard much about Geary's successes in bringing patients with serious illnesses back from death's door. Reportedly, his hospital was unique in that he insisted on immaculate cleanliness—a demand that was scoffed at by many of his peers but that was gaining credibility in the medical field. Eleanor admired scientific genius, particularly anyone who succeeded in going against the grain of society.

She also admired Damon's cousin for her charitable works. Eleanor had met Tess Blanchard several times during the past few months, due primarily to the lady's close friendship with the three Loring sisters. They all taught classes at the sisters' Academy for Young Ladies, along with Jane Caruthers, who managed the school's daily operations.

And just recently Eleanor had approached Miss Blanchard to ask how she might contribute to her valiant efforts at reducing the poverty and misery of the less fortunate.

Thankfully Eleanor was better able to ignore Damon when Madame Giuditta Pasta stepped onto the stage to sing an aria from Rossini's *Barber of Seville,* "Una voce poca fa."

The Italian soprano had recently made her London debut, and although the reviews thus far had not been particularly favorable, from the first liquid notes Eleanor found herself spellbound. She sat rapt as Madame Pasta's voice soared with exquisite brilliance, and when the last beautiful note faded, Eleanor had tears in her eyes. Then when she wiped surreptitiously at the moisture, Damon reached over her shoulder and silently handed her his handkerchief.

As Eleanor glanced back instinctively in gratitude and murmured "Thank you," she made the mistake of meeting Damon's eyes. Her heart gave a small leap at the hint of tenderness she saw in the dark depths. A tenderness that was reminiscent of the private moments they had shared during their betrothal.

He had been watching her enjoyment, Eleanor realized, flustered and dismayed at the thought.

Quickly, she averted her gaze and faced forward. She had difficulty paying attention to the music that followed, yet eventually she rallied to applaud the dramatic readings, to smile at the comedic skits, and to laugh with delight at the antics of the pantomime.

When the concert ended, Eleanor's composure had steadied somewhat, and she felt as if she could actually face Damon with equanimity.

That is, until they exited the gallery with the large crowd of theatergoers. Lady Beldon had insisted upon leaving at once, not wishing to wait until last for their carriages to be brought around.

As their party made its way along the corridor and down the wide staircase, Prince Lazzara shielded Eleanor from the jostling while Signor Vecchi saw to her aunt's defense.

They had nearly reached the lower landing when suddenly the prince lurched forward into the throng below. With a surprised cry, he tumbled down the final three steps, nearly dragging Eleanor with him.

She was only saved because Damon caught her arm and hauled her back to safety.

"Merciful heavens!" Lady Beldon exclaimed in alarm while Eleanor gasped.

After a stunned moment, she broke free of Damon's grasp and rushed down the last steps to kneel beside the prince, who lay prone on the carpet, his breathing harsh.

"Your highness—are you hurt?"

His answer was a groan as he rolled onto his side and clutched his left knee in obvious pain.

However, when he followed with an obvious epithet in Italian, Signor Vecchi said something sharply to him in the same language, and the prince looked chastised.

"A million pardons," he said, grimacing up at the ladies.

A space had cleared around him, while the crowd had quieted at the spectacle of a splendidly dressed foreign nobleman sprawled on the floor. Thus, Eleanor had no difficulty hearing Damon when he turned to his physician friend.

"Otto, can you be of assistance?"

"I will do my best."

While Prince Lazzara's injured limb was being examined, his elder relative shook his silvered head sadly. "I fear Don Antonio has extremely ill luck," Signor Vecchi commented.

"It was not ill luck, Don Umberto!" Lazzara retorted rather peevishly. "I was *pushed,* most definitely."

Eleanor gave a start at the revelation, and her gaze immediately went to Damon. Was it possible he had precipitated the fall? He had been directly behind them, after all, with Signor Vecchi adjacent to him. It would have taken only a slight shove to topple the prince. . . .

She moved to Damon's side, frowning up at him. "Did you cause his highness to fall just now?" she asked in a grim whisper.

Damon stared at her for a moment. "I beg your pardon?"

"He could have been badly hurt, being pushed down a flight of stairs."

A muscle flexed in Damon's jaw. "Indeed. And you could have been hurt as well, since you were clinging to his arm. But no, I did not cause his fall," he stated, fixing her with a stern look.

Eleanor's frown deepened. "It seems strange that the prince is beset by mishaps whenever you are around."

Damon emitted a low, incredulous laugh. "You don't honestly believe I had anything to do with this one?"

"Why not? His troubles did not begin until you returned to London. And you have been present for all three incidents thus far."

"As have you," Damon pointed out coolly. "You could have orchestrated his misadventures yourself so that you could come to his rescue and prove your resourcefulness and compassion. Isn't that what your book tells you to do?"

"No," Eleanor snapped, longing to set him back on his heels. "In fact it advises just the opposite. I am supposed to appear helpless whenever possible."

His mouth curling, Damon glanced down at the injured man. "Lazzara is the one who seems helpless just now."

"A state that you obviously relish."

His jaw hardened. "So you think I sabotaged his carriage and risked your safety—even your very life— the day you drove with him in the park?"

Judging from his tone, she had obviously roused his ire with her accusations, but Eleanor didn't back down since her own ire had escalated. "Perhaps you did. You seem determined to interfere in our courtship."

"What of yesterday? I was nowhere near Lazzara when he was pushed into the street."

"You could have hired a pickpocket to assault him. And you were in a prime position just now to cause his fall."

Damon returned the dagger-eyed look she was giving him with steel in his own. "There is only one problem, sweeting. I had nothing to do with any of his mishaps. You will have to look elsewhere for the culprit."

Eleanor could see that he was angry. But she was

furious herself to think Damon might be so set on spoiling her courtship that he'd deliberately endangered the prince.

"Of course you would deny it," she returned in a fierce undertone, "even if you are guilty."

When Damon pinned her with his gaze, she could feel the air crackling between them.

"Are you actually questioning my word?" he asked in a dangerous voice.

Realizing they were attracting attention from various bystanders, Eleanor lowered her own voice. "I don't know if I am or not. But clearly I cannot trust you to tell me the truth."

"Eleanor," her aunt suddenly interrupted. "Come, my dear, we should be going home."

Damon was still regarding Eleanor with smoldering eyes. "This is not the place to be arguing," he bit out. "We should continue this discussion in private."

"We should not be speaking at all!" Eleanor practically hissed in return. She stepped away from him just as Mr. Geary concluded his examination.

"I do not believe any bones are broken, your highness," the physician announced, "but you require care since you appear to have badly sprained your knee. You should be taken home at once and put to bed. I shall attend you if you wish."

Lady Beldon spoke up immediately. "I will send for my own physician, Mr. Geary. You need not trouble yourself any further."

The physician looked dubious, but he nodded. "You would do well to put cold compresses on your knee, your highness. And of course you must keep it immobile for a time."

"We will see to his welfare, Mr. Geary," Lady Beldon insisted.

Signor Vecchi helped the prince to rise then and lent his shoulder for support. Still in severe pain, the injured nobleman limped onward with the aid of his relative.

"You came in Prince Lazzara's carriage, did you not?" Damon said tersely to Eleanor. "If need be, I will take you and your aunt home."

She glanced sharply at him. "It is *not* necessary, my lord. You have done more than enough this evening. Indeed, I would be quite pleased if you would keep away from us all for the distant future."

With that, Eleanor turned and followed the injured prince, feeling Damon's eyes boring into her back all the while.

Her frustration with Damon did not abate as she entered the prince's carriage with her aunt, although by the time the barouche had carried them to Portman Place and deposited them on their doorstep, Eleanor's anger had calmed the slightest measure.

Perhaps she'd been mistaken to accuse Damon of such nefarious deeds, she reflected grudgingly as she followed her aunt upstairs to the viscountess's elegant suite of rooms. He might be a rake and a rogue, but that was a far cry from wishing to harm an innocent man merely for courting her, particularly when he himself had no claim to her.

The moment Eleanor was alone with her aunt in the sitting room, however, Lady Beldon made clear her own opinion of Damon.

"I dislike seeing you speaking to that wicked Wrexham, Eleanor," Beatrix complained. "You needn't acknowledge him beyond the dictates of mere politeness."

"You are right, of course, Aunt. I shall do my best to avoid all contact with him in the future."

"Good. You do not want to give the prince any reason to think less of you. You should be encouraging his attentions whenever possible, and Wrexham's presence could very well hinder your courtship."

"I am well aware of that, Aunt."

Eyeing Eleanor, Beatrix pursed her lips in a thoughtful frown. "I expect it is only fair to tell you what Signor Vecchi says."

"What does the signor say?"

The elder lady grimaced. "That the prince is something of a rake himself when it comes to women. Signor Vecchi hinted rather strongly that his highness might not make you a good husband. But then I put little store in such warnings. Prince Lazzara's birth and breeding are impeccable, and his fortune is magnificent. And as far as his personal affairs . . . well, he is likely no worse than many noblemen."

Eleanor hid her own grimace. She had heard the gossip before, about the prince's reputation for profligacy, yet she had chosen to overlook it for now. Not, however, merely because she wanted to give him the benefit of the doubt. According to Fanny Irwin, some rakes could be redeemed by true love, so Eleanor was not ready to condemn the prince as a hopeless cause solely for his past. It might just be a matter of his meeting the right woman, one who could win his heart.

Herself, possibly? Eleanor wondered. If she could

make Prince Lazzara love her, he might change his wicked ways for her sake. Even Damon might have done so two years ago, she reflected. If Damon had really loved her, surely he would not have turned to his mistress so shortly after becoming betrothed to *her*—

That painful thought was interrupted as her aunt continued briskly. "At least you will be able to advance your suit next week at my house party. And it will be good to repair to Rosemont where Wrexham cannot follow you."

Eleanor had to agree wholeheartedly with that sentiment.

"I do so want it to go well," Beatrix added with an odd note of wistfulness.

"I am certain it will. Your house parties are always splendid."

"Signor Vecchi says he is anticipating the event with great relish."

When Eleanor smiled at her aunt, Beatrix's cheeks turned a pretty shade of pink. She looked years younger when she spoke of the Italian gentleman, Eleanor thought fondly.

"Do you think I am wrong to encourage his advances?" Beatrix asked uncertainly.

"No, dearest aunt," Eleanor said softly. "I think you are very right to do so."

"He has quite a gentle way about him. Unlike Beldon, who was an insufferable bear when crossed . . ." Beatrix suddenly stiffened. "But enough of my late husband. Ring for my maid, Eleanor, if you please. I vow I am fagged half to death after all that drama of the prince's accident."

Realizing that Aunt Beatrix was suffering a touch of embarrassment at having shared her innermost thoughts, Eleanor obeyed and bid good night, then made her way to her own bedchamber in the east wing.

Her aunt was lonely, although she rarely let herself show it, Eleanor suspected. It would be heartwarming to see the aloof, unemotional viscountess fall in love for the first time, or at the very least, find a gentleman whose friendship and companionship she could enjoy.

Whatever happened, Eleanor added to herself as she shut her chamber door behind her, she hoped her aunt could find happiness, regardless of her own relationship with the prince.

Deciding against summoning Jenny since the hour was so late, Eleanor changed out of her gown and put away her undergarments. Yet as she performed her ablutions and prepared for bed, her thoughts returned to the evening at the theater and her ire started to rise again. It dismayed her that Damon seemed determined to spoil her opportunity for love.

But she would *not* allow him to interfere, Eleanor vowed as she donned her nightdress. She would proceed with her subtle pursuit of Prince Lazzara, and if Damon dared to intrude again . . . well, she would simply have to devise a plan to discourage him once and for all.

She had settled in bed to review another chapter of Fanny's advice book when she heard a slight noise from across the room.

Her heart gave a jolt when she looked up to find Damon's face at her open bedroom window.

Her jaw dropping, Eleanor watched in disbelief as he eased his broad shoulders through the window and hauled himself inside, then lowered his feet to the carpet.

He was still dressed in formal evening wear, she noted distractedly, but that wasn't what held her speechless. It was the fact that he had climbed up two stories to a lady's bedchamber, after midnight, bold as you please.

"Damon!" she exclaimed, her voice a high, breathless rasp. "What the devil are you doing here?"

"I believe we left our conversation unfinished," he said coolly, crossing the room toward her bed.

Chapter Six

Throwing off the covers, Eleanor sprang out of bed so quickly, she felt lightheaded. Or perhaps her weakness was simply the result of having her tall, handsome, former betrothed stalking her when she was so scantily clad.

"You know very well you shouldn't be in my bedchamber!" she declared as she backed away toward the door.

A hard smile touched Damon's mouth. "At the theater you refused my offer to continue our discussion elsewhere."

"Because there is nothing to discuss!" When Damon kept advancing, Eleanor held up her hands as if to ward him off. "Damon—stop right there!"

Thankfully, he obeyed her command, coming to halt a half dozen steps from her. But there he stood, looking as immovable as granite, his dark eyes piercing in the glow of the bedside lamp.

"You need to leave this minute," she insisted.

"Not until we set a few matters straight."

He was still angry at her, obviously, but then, so

was she. "I mean it, Damon! Get out, or I will call for Peters to throw you out."

"No, you won't. You don't want your servants to find me here."

Eleanor clenched her teeth in frustration, knowing full well she couldn't make good on her threat. Summoning the servants to her rescue might very well result in scandal. At the very least her Aunt Beatrix would be appalled and dismayed to learn that she had gotten herself in such a fix.

Eleanor wanted badly to send Damon to the devil, but it was clear he intended to have it out with her, despite the fact that he was flouting propriety with a vengeance.

Realizing she had no choice but to listen to him, she gave a huff of resignation and crossed her arms under her bosom—which had the unwanted effect of attracting Damon's gaze to her breasts.

When his dark eyes raked her, taking in her delicate nightdress of white lawn, she quickly dropped her arms to her sides and retreated another step. "Very well, what do you want to discuss?"

"The situation with Lazzara. I want you to listen to me, Eleanor."

"Will you please keep your voice down then? Someone might hear you."

Damon obliged, but his tone still held a hard note when he continued. "I can't fathom why you think me guilty of some sinister purpose toward your prince, but you not only accused me of trying to injure him, but of lying."

Eleanor lifted her chin. "You cannot claim that you have never lied to me before. After we became engaged, you said you had given up your mistress, but you most certainly had not."

He returned an enigmatic look as he slowly moved around the foot of the bed. "I won't argue with you on that score, but you are far off the mark if you think I had anything to do with Lazzara's mishaps. That makes as much sense as you causing his accidents yourself."

Eleanor gave him a measuring stare. "Whyever would I cause his accidents?"

"Perhaps to maneuver him into a position where your reputation would be compromised . . . to compel him to wed you."

Her mouth dropped open. "That is a perfectly revolting accusation."

"So is your accusing me of deliberately attempting to harm him. I don't take kindly to having my honor questioned."

"I would imagine not," Eleanor retorted. "But you must admit it looks highly suspicious when you were present for all three incidents. And you were directly behind us this evening."

Pinning her with his gaze, Damon took a step closer. "There is one major factor you are forgetting, sweetheart. I would never put your safety at risk. Since you were clinging to his arm, you could easily have fallen tonight and been injured yourself. Even had I wanted to shove him down a flight of stairs, I would have waited until you were clear of him."

She had to admit that Damon had acted swiftly to save her from the prince's fate. Eleanor nodded slowly. "I remember that you caught my arm to prevent me from being dragged down by him."

"I did indeed."

"So you think he merely tripped?"

"Perhaps, but to my mind he has suffered too many recent mishaps for it to be mere coincidence. It's possible that someone actually may want to harm him."

"Who, then?"

"I haven't the foggiest idea." Looking thoughtful, Damon moved over to her bed and settled one hip on the mattress. Before Eleanor could protest, he went on as if musing aloud. "I did note that the pickpocket looked as if he could have been a countryman of Lazzara's. They shared the same olive complexion. At the theater this evening, however, there was no one of that appearance near him other than Signor Vecchi."

"But Signor Vecchi would not push his own relative down the stairs," Eleanor said, frowning in puzzlement.

"I shouldn't think so."

Her frown deepened. "If some unknown assailant *is* trying to do the prince harm, I would very much like to discover the culprit so he can be stopped. Lazzara could be seriously hurt."

"I would like to know as well," Damon declared. "As long as he is courting you, you could be in danger."

Her eyes widened a little. "You are worried for *my* safety?"

"Is that so incomprehensible, Elle?"

His tone had softened a measure, and Eleanor felt her own defenses slacken. "No, I suppose not."

"I dislike you associating so closely with Lazzara," Damon said. "If these attacks keep up, you could be hurt. And I won't stand idly by and let that happen, Eleanor."

He held her gaze, making her suddenly aware of her near state of undress and the tangled covers on the bed.

"Thank you for your concern, my lord," Eleanor hastened to say, "but you should go. You shouldn't be here," she repeated.

Showing no signs of preparing to leave, Damon smiled crookedly. "You must at least give me credit for resourcefulness. You wouldn't allow me a moment of privacy with you, so I was forced to take drastic measures. It wasn't easy, climbing that damned oak tree outside your window."

Eleanor was surprised to hear herself laugh softly. It was deplorable how Damon could make her laugh when she should be irate at him for risking her reputation.

"See," he said casually, "you admire a man who can keep you on your toes."

She tried to hide a smile. "If you are fishing for compliments, you will grow old and gray before I add to your conceit."

Damon shook his head as he drawled in a wry tone, "I may not have the opportunity to grow any older after tonight. My valet will have my head if I have ruined my new coat. Cornby sets great store in turning me out as a gentleman of fashion."

He looked little the worse for wear, she thought, other than his sable hair was more tousled than usual.

"Then again," Damon continued more affably, "you might rejoice at my demise."

"Of course I would not rejoice." Her desire to

smile vanished. She certainly did not wish for Damon's demise. She just didn't want him anywhere near her, especially when she was at such a disadvantage.

"Seriously, Damon, you must leave. You said you didn't want to put me at risk, and your simply being in my bedchamber could cause a scandal."

"True, it could." Yet instead of acceding to her request, Damon shifted his weight so he was sitting on the edge of her bed, looking as if he intended to stay put. "But I believe you owe me an apology first for accusing me so unjustly."

"Very well, I apologize. Now, will you please go?"

"I fancy I deserve a better one than that."

"What do you mean?"

"I mean that you need to kiss me."

Eleanor's heart missed a beat. He was demanding a kiss as an apology?

"Come here, Elle," he murmured when she stood rooted to the floor.

At the husky note in his voice, her mouth went dry. She absently licked her lips, and when his gaze instantly fixed on her mouth, Eleanor recalled the particular advice in Fanny's book about licking her lips to appear kissable.

She most certainly did not want to appear kissable to Damon!

"I am not about to kiss you," she stated emphatically.

"If not, you should be prepared for the consequences. I am willing to wait all night if need be." Damon cocked his head. "What will your aunt say in the morning if she discovers I have spent the entire night with you?"

"You are a complete and utter rake," Eleanor said feelingly.

"I won't deny it," Damon replied, unchastened.

Her exasperation rose. She should have known that getting rid of him would be difficult. Damon was the very definition of "trouble"—and the most provoking man alive.

"I believe I have changed my mind," she muttered. "Your demise might indeed be welcome after all."

"Now *that* is the Elle I know and love."

The amusement in his voice made her ball her hands into fists. "You do not love me! You never have!"

Strangely, his expression sobered . . . softened even. Yet he didn't relent. "A kiss, Eleanor. That is my price for leaving."

Still resisting, she refused to budge. "You do realize how shameless it is to insist on kissing a woman against her will?"

Damon's features softened even further. "It isn't shameless of me, merely tactical. I mean to remind you again of the sparks that are missing between you and your prince."

So *that* was his purpose, Eleanor thought, torn between frustration and understanding. Damon was still determined to prove how weak her attraction was for her royal suitor. And again, he was giving her no choice but to comply.

What vexed her more, though, was how tempting she found the prospect of kissing him.

Even worse, Damon seemed to know how she felt.

He was watching her, his eyes bright with purpose, while the silence between them suddenly felt charged with magnetic currents.

A tremor ran down Eleanor's spine as she felt the dizzying pull of him.

"I am waiting, Elle," he murmured.

Hearing that low, sensual, velvet-edged voice only weakened her resistance further.

Eleanor dragged in a breath. When she reluctantly moved forward, Damon took her hand and drew her between his spread legs, flush against his upper body.

She was quiveringly aware of him . . . the heat of his powerful torso, the feel of her breasts pressed against his hard chest. Her nipples were pebbled and sensitive, and she had difficulty catching her breath as her heart began lurching against her ribs.

Then he cupped her derriere, drawing her even closer, so close that his breath caressed her mouth, brushing sparks across the surface.

But there he stopped. "Well?" Damon asked.

"Well, what?"

"You are to kiss me, remember?"

He tugged her arm with enough pressure to bring her down into his lap so that she sat sideways on his hard thigh.

Knowing he wouldn't give up until she capitulated, Eleanor pressed her lips to Damon's quickly. Even that brief contact fluttered her insides, but he frowned in disappointment.

"As an apology, that tiny peck is hardly adequate. My wounded vanity needs soothing. It still stings something fierce."

"Then it will continue to sting. I wouldn't have the faintest notion how to soothe your oversized vanity."

His eyes gleamed. "Allow me to show you how it is properly done. . . ."

His hands closing on her shoulders, Damon laid Eleanor back so that she was sprawled on the bed with her lower legs still draped over his thigh.

Caught by the mesmerizing intensity of his gaze, her pulse beating wildly in her throat, Eleanor held her breath as he slowly bent down to her and bestowed a probing kiss against her lips. When his tongue slid inside her mouth in a slow and thorough invasion, she very nearly moaned.

Breaking off eventually, Damon lifted his head enough that he could see her face.

"Just as I said . . . sparks," he murmured, his voice decidedly more husky.

She felt them, too . . . the embers exploding wildly inside her.

Then he stopped speaking altogether and bent his head again to resume his delectable attentions.

It was sheer madness to respond, Eleanor knew, yet she opened to him fully. How could she resist the aching need he aroused in her? How could she fight the dizzying rush she only knew with Damon? He was kissing her into submission, succeeding with each caress of his warm mouth, inciting all her yearnings all over again.

This was every woman's fantasy, being kissed so passionately by a lover, with such devastating thoroughness. And being kissed by Damon was her own personal heaven. His lips stroked hers, playing, seducing, enticing as his tongue danced in her mouth.

When he shifted their positions on the bed and pulled her closer against his body, she could feel him—his power and strength, the sinewed length of his legs, the breadth of his chest, the hardness of him—and she had to fight the urge to melt into a liquid puddle. Her breasts felt heavy and sensitive, while a sweet, foreign ache blossomed between her thighs.

Then Damon deepened the pressure, kissing her as if he was determined to know every secret she held. Her pulse throbbed even harder at the feel of him, the scent of him, the taste of him.

At the same time, he reached between their bodies and curved his long fingers over her breast, sending sensation streaking through her.

Eleanor inhaled a sharp breath and pulled back from his magical kiss. His hand was warm and possessive on her breast, and she grasped his wrist in order to stay him.

"Damon, that is far enough," she said unevenly.

He raised an eyebrow. "Is it? You like having me touch you, Elle."

"No, I do *not*."

"Then why can I see the points of your nipples through the lawn of your nightdress? Methinks your body is betraying you, darling."

She glanced down at herself. In the spill of lamplight pouring across the bed, her nipples were clearly, visibly aroused. A flush of heat rose in her cheeks. "You shouldn't be seeing me in my nightdress."

His mouth curved at one corner. "I would rather see you wearing nothing at all."

He reached for the small buttons on the front of

her bodice and undid them one by one. Eleanor deplored her excitement at his brazenness, yet she couldn't make herself stop him. Not even when he moved his hand to the neckline. It was rash, it was reckless, it was thrilling, to have Damon free her breasts to his heated gaze.

His dark eyes caressed the pale swells as his fingers captured one pouting crest, teasing the furled bud with expert skill. Her eyelids drifted shut as a low moan escaped her . . . which only seemed to encourage him. He stroked and fondled her until she was aching. Yet apparently, that was not enough for him.

"I want to taste you," he murmured, his voice a husky rasp as he bent down to her.

Eleanor made a last valiant effort to regain control of her dazed senses. "To taste me?"

His soft breath whispered against her skin. "I am hungry for you, Elle. I'll wager nothing tastes as good as you do."

She pressed her palms against his shoulders to hold him away. "I cannot credit that, since you have a highly skilled chef."

Damon left off his seductive ministrations to glance up at her. "How do you know what kind of chef I have?"

"Gossip."

"You listen to the wags gossip about me?"

Avidly, Eleanor thought to herself. "I can scarcely help hearing when all London has been talking about you."

A faint smile wreathed his mouth. "Are you truly interested in discussing my chef just now?"

"I told you I don't want to discuss anything with you."

"Good, then be quiet for now, love. . . ."

He filled both his hands with her naked breasts and lowered his head. Eleanor suddenly forgot to breathe. Damon had never taken such liberties before. . . .

His warm lips sent a sweep of sensation surging over her skin, but when he grazed her nipples with his tongue, the sweet shock made her gasp.

Then he closed his lips over one taut bud and drew it into his mouth. Her back arched off the mattress at the delicious spasm that arrowed down to her loins.

"Damon . . . you have to stop," she rasped.

"In another moment . . ."

She didn't think she could bear another moment of his delicious torment. But he went on laving her nipple with his tongue, drawing the swollen flesh between his teeth, pulling at it with a hard sucking motion.

Eleanor gave up trying to fight him. He was seducing her, and she didn't care. Urgent longing had gathered inside her, pulsing to vibrant life in that secret place between her thighs.

She found herself clutching his head to her breast, trying to draw his tantalizing, relentless mouth closer. Desire rose even higher when she felt his leg move so that his knee rode intimately between her thighs.

She shifted helplessly at the erotic pressure, but when slowly he drew up the hem of her nightdress, she was startled enough to summon the will to protest. "Damon . . . you cannot . . ."

With one last kiss to her breast, he raised his head. His eyes dark with heat, he gazed down at her.

"Aren't you curious about the pleasure I could show you?"

"Yes, no . . . I don't know."

"I don't intend to take your virtue if that worries you."

She winced. "I pray not. It is scandalous enough, what you are doing now."

His slow smile warmed her even more than his eyes. "What is the saying? I might as well be hanged for a sheep as a lamb?"

"I am most certainly not a lamb, and you are a *wolf*."

Quiet laughter was his only answer as he slid his fingers downward, between her thighs, to lightly rest on her woman's mound.

Eleanor's breath faltered.

Those eyes held her spellbound. Those intense, beautiful, dark-fringed eyes . . .

A lock of dark hair fell over Damon's forehead as he stared down at her, waiting. His gaze delved into hers, shattering any resistance she had left.

"Hush and let me pleasure you, Elle."

"Yes . . ." she whispered.

His searching fingers unerringly finding her feminine folds, he parted her slick flesh and touched her there.

Every nerve in Eleanor's body flared and tightened, while her breath fled. Damon had aroused her desire before with his kisses, but he had never gone further than fondling her breasts through her clothing. Until now.

His fingers moved maddeningly in light caresses over the heart of her, rimming the sleek cleft of her sex, teasing the damp bud he found hidden there. Arching against him, she shut her eyes.

When a whimper rippled from her throat, he captured the sound by kissing her again, more gently this time. His mouth shaped itself to hers, hot silk, while his warm, thrusting tongue plied with a slow, sensual rhythm, intensifying the brazen heat that was coiling inside her, centered between her thighs.

At length, her hands rose to Damon's hair and clenched in the silky thickness as she returned his kisses fervently. Her senses seemed imprinted with the scent and feel of him, with the relentless ache he made her feel. Her skin had grown hot and keenly sensitive, as if she had a fever.

A fever that only heightened as an overwhelming wave of fire began building inside her.

In desperation, Eleanor loosened her grasp on his hair and clutched at his shoulders, anchoring herself against his sinewed body. But her growing frenzy only drove Damon to increase his efforts.

He stroked her harder, more urgently, evoking a hunger in her she couldn't believe possible. She had never felt such intense sensations, such uncontrollable desire—

Then suddenly, she burst into flame—a fiery eruption that sent shuddering shocks of pleasure through every single part of her body.

When she let out a wild cry, though, his kiss deepened to drown out the ragged sounds she made.

The incredible bliss faded eventually. Stunned, Eleanor lay there a long moment, her breathing harsh and rapid. Finally she opened her eyes to stare up at Damon.

He was smiling faintly at her dazed expression, his gaze lingering on her flushed face.

Eleanor licked her dry lips and tried to find her voice. "So that is what all the fuss is about," she uttered in a thready rasp. "I never realized. . . ."

"Realized what, love?"

"That lovemaking could be so . . . amazing."

Tenderly he bent to kiss her forehead. "Yes, it *can* be amazing. Although there is much more I have yet to show you."

As if to match deeds to words, Damon eased himself between her spread thighs and covered her body with his. When their hips met, Eleanor could feel the hardness and detail of him beneath his satin breeches.

He let his weight sink lower, fitting her more fluidly against his rigid arousal. . . .

But then suddenly he stopped.

Quite unexpectedly, it was Damon himself who ended his seduction, to her startlement and dismay and relief.

He squeezed his eyes shut as if in pain, and his voice was hoarse when he whispered, "I would like nothing more than to spend the night making passionate love to you, Elle, but it wouldn't be honorable."

"No," she agreed, her own voice ragged. "We cannot make love, Damon. You know I am saving myself for marriage."

A sense of loss filled her when he took her at her word. Shifting again, he rolled to one side. Yet he did not go far.

Instead, he supported his weight on one elbow and

gazed down at her. "That is a problem that can be remedied," he said slowly.

"What do you mean?" she asked, puzzled.

He hesitated a long moment before finally answering. "I think you should marry *me*, Elle, not your precious prince."

Chapter Seven

Never let him think that a marriage shackle is your chief aim, else you may frighten him into fleeing in the opposite direction!

—An Anonymous Lady, *Advice* . . .

For the space of a several heartbeats, Eleanor lay there without moving, certain she had misheard Damon.

"You are jesting, of course," she finally said in a high, uneven voice.

"On the contrary. I am quite serious. I think you should marry me, Elle."

For the second time that night Eleanor sprang from her bed. Whirling to face Damon, she stared at him, first in stunned disbelief, then in narrow-eyed suspicion as she wondered what machinations he was plotting this time.

"What game are you playing, Damon?" she demanded in a warning tone.

"It is no game, I assure you."

Highly distrustful, Eleanor remained standing there, trying to gauge his purpose—until she realized that his gaze had dropped from her face to her brazenly exposed breasts.

"If you think for one minute that I would ever agree to wed you," she muttered while hastening to button up her nightdress, "then you are clearly suffering a fever of the brain."

Damon gave a mock wince. "Your estimation of my mental faculties wounds me deeply, love."

"Not deeply enough, to my mind!"

He cast a glance at the door. "I suggest you keep your voice down unless you wish to have your servants investigating why you have secreted a gentleman in your bedchamber."

"I have *not* secreted you," Eleanor retorted, although she did lower her voice somewhat. "You have secreted yourself—and I wish you would leave."

When he showed no signs of complying, she stalked across the bedchamber to her armoire and retrieved a dressing gown, which she quickly donned. At least she could face Damon with more equanimity when she was more modestly dressed.

Tucking her bare feet out of sight, Eleanor shook her head in continued disbelief. "You *must* be touched in the head, Damon. I can fathom no other explanation for why you would renew your offer of marriage after what happened the last time."

His enigmatic, shuttered look did not increase her faith that he held any enthusiasm for his astonishing proposal. Watching his expression, she was even more certain he couldn't truly mean it.

"You don't have any desire to wed me, any more than I wish to wed you," she said more calmly, determined to sound rational instead of letting Damon rile her as he was so expert at doing.

He pushed himself up to a sitting position. "That isn't true. I do want you for my wife."

"Why?"

"Various reasons. We are well matched, for one. We could make a good marriage."

At his unexpected prediction, Eleanor couldn't repress the sharp ache that wrenched her heart. "I once thought so, but no longer. You are not the marrying kind, Damon. I suspected it when I first met you, but I foolishly convinced myself otherwise. No, when it comes to marriage, I would say we are greatly *mis*-matched."

"You cannot deny that we are physically compatible."

"Perhaps. But there is little between us other than the vexing question of lust."

His mouth curled wryly. "Lust can be a powerful force." His hand briefly touched the bulge in his satin knee breeches, evidence of his still-swollen arousal.

"Which only proves my point," Eleanor declared. "You are acting in the heat of the moment, just as you did the last time you proposed. You let passion get the better of you then, impulsively overriding your own deep-seated objections to marriage, and look how *that* ended. You came to regret our betrothal almost at once."

Damon didn't respond directly to that argument, instead saying in a reasonable tone, "I want you in my bed, Elle. But the only honorable way to have you is with the sanction of matrimony."

She had to hide a wince. She was well aware that men wanted her for her physical beauty in addition to her breeding and wealth, and now Damon was stating it quite baldly. It was ridiculous, how he had touched a raw, deep-rooted insecurity of hers. Appealing to male carnal desires didn't mean she could attract them in ways that truly counted: in their hearts. She'd feared she might never find a man to love her for herself, and Damon's renouncement two years ago had only bolstered that fear.

She bit her lower lip. "I still think you are playing some kind of cruel game with me."

His expression instantly softened. "I promise you it is no game, Eleanor."

"Then why are you suggesting something so absurd? I would say you are trying to distract me from pursuing Prince Lazzara, but offering for me yourself is too drastic a measure merely to prevent his courtship."

"It isn't too drastic. I want to protect you from him, but so far I've been unable to make you see reason."

She frowned. "So you are proposing because you feel obliged to protect me?"

"In large part. I don't want you wedding Lazzara. He isn't nearly good enough for you."

"That is not for you to decide."

"He will only hurt you." Damon's dark eyes searched her face. "If you are so set on marriage, then you should wed me. I am a much better alternative than your prince."

Her thoughts in chaos, Eleanor raised a hand to her temple. Perhaps Damon truly did want to protect her from being hurt—and if so, she had to concede it was admirable of him. But wedding him would leave her far too vulnerable. She would only fall in love with him all over again, and he would hurt her even more than before.

"Thank you for your concern," she said at last,

"but I don't require your chivalry. I don't want you sacrificing yourself for my sake."

"It wouldn't be a sacrifice, Elle." When she made no reply, Damon swung his legs around and sat back against the headboard among her pillows. "Your Romeo won't make you happy," he insisted.

"And you would?"

"I would like to try."

The siren call of his extraordinary assertion beckoned to her. Yet she should know better than to listen to Damon's blandishments.

"You forfeited that right two years ago," she finally replied.

His gaze seemed to darken for a moment. "I won't deny that, but my particular failing doesn't mean your prince would treat you any better." Damon canted his head. "Do you actually think Lazzara will care anything about your happiness? Your pleasure? That he would trouble himself to see you satisfied? I suspect you would enjoy the marriage bed far more with me. In fact, I believe we just proved it—and that was only a taste of what you can expect from our lovemaking once we are wed."

Eleanor flushed at the reminder of the stunning experience Damon had just given her. She had suspected pleasure with him would be incredible, and indeed it had been.

"Perhaps so," she conceded, "but simply because you are a marvelous lover doesn't mean you would make a good husband. Marriage should be based on more than carnal pleasure."

"Ours would be."

"It would be nothing more than a union of convenience."

"What is wrong with that? Many members of our class marry to carry on bloodlines."

That gave Eleanor pause. "Do you care that much about continuing your bloodlines? You never said so before."

To her surprise, she glimpsed a fleeting impression of sadness in Damon's eyes before he answered with what sounded like honest sincerity. "I've always accepted that I have a duty to my title. And the years are passing. It's time for me to consider fulfilling my obligation."

She pursed her lips in an unyielding line. "If you seriously want to marry to carry on your title, any number of gentlewomen would suit your purposes."

His gaze held hers. "I want you, Elle, no one else."

She badly wanted to believe him, yet she couldn't risk it.

"Well, I do *not* want a mere union of convenience," she responded. "If I did, I could have been married several times over. I have had over a dozen proposals, but I turned most of them down."

"Most of them?" Damon contemplated her curiously. "I knew you were betrothed a second time, but were there more?"

Eleanor hesitated. Her second brief engagement had been a wildly impulsive response to Damon's defection. After he had humiliated her by publicly turning to a lightskirt for his pleasures, she had wanted to feel wanted, desired, worthy of affection. But thankfully she had quickly come to her senses and withdrawn her acceptance of Baron Morley's offer.

Her third, even briefer betrothal to a nobleman, however, had been a total ruse. She'd never had any intention of following through with it, nor had her third fiancé.

"I was betrothed to Lord Claybourne for a few hours this past summer," Eleanor admitted reluctantly.

Damon's eyebrow shot up. "To Claybourne? For a few hours? I should like to hear an explanation for *that.*"

Eleanor waved her hand. "It is a long story. Suffice it to say that Heath asked me for a favor to help him win Lily Loring, and I willingly obliged. Our betrothal didn't really count, though, since it was a pretense and very few people knew about it. But that doesn't mean I want to risk any more broken engagements. If I were to agree to marry you, who is to say we would actually go through with the wedding this time? I am in danger of developing a reputation as a jilt as it is."

"We would wed this time," Damon assured her.

She managed an indifferent shrug, even though she was not feeling *at all* indifferent. "Well, it is pointless to speculate, since I don't intend to marry you."

"Why not?"

Eleanor glanced away, hiding the vulnerability that she knew shone in her eyes. The undeniable truth was that Damon could never love her as she wanted— *needed*—to be loved. A marriage where affection was so profoundly one-sided would be even more painful than a cold contract of convenience.

"Because I am a romantic at heart," she answered. "*That* is the chief difference between us, Damon . . .

why we would never make a good match. I want true love in my marriage. I want my husband to love me."

It was a long while before Damon responded—and then his tone was rather curt. "You are putting too much store in the notion of true love, Eleanor."

"Perhaps. But I know it is possible. Marcus found that kind of love with Arabella. And I won't settle for anything less for myself." She took a step closer to Damon, her hands unconsciously reaching out to him in an imploring gesture. "You know about my childhood before my parents died. How lonely I was then, and afterward, when I went to live with a widowed aunt who never wanted to be saddled with a child."

Her voice lowered even further. "I don't want that same loneliness in my marriage, Damon. I want to matter to my husband. I want to matter *deeply*. I want to matter to my family. I want to bestow on my children the love I never knew from my own parents. The kind of familial love Marcus and I shared as children. That is not something you can give me."

Damon's brow had grown clouded, and she knew he was recalling her confession that day in the rose garden when she'd bared her soul to him. It was humiliating now for her to even think of it, or to remember how hopeful and happy she'd been then.

"I doubt Lazzara will give you his heart," he finally said.

"How will I know if I never try? I mean to try to make him love me, Damon."

She saw a muscle flex in Damon's jaw as he struggled to maintain his patience. "Lazzara is not the right husband for you," he repeated. "I would make a better one."

That twisting ache in her heart assaulted Eleanor again. Some vulnerable part of her couldn't help but be torn by his proposal. Yet the thrilling hope she'd once felt at the chance of becoming Damon's wife was offset by the fear of being badly hurt by him once more. She never again wanted to feel the doubt and pain of such a betrayal.

"I don't believe you would make me a better husband, Damon," she said quietly, "because you don't love me. That was the real problem before—you never really loved me. If you had, you would never have turned to a mistress."

Rather than look away, Damon returned her gaze steadily. "I regret hurting you, Elle. I assure you, it won't happen again."

She took a deep breath. "Indeed it won't, since I won't be idiotic enough to put myself in that position again."

Damon roughly ran a hand though his hair, as if striving for control. "I am not keeping a mistress now. I haven't for some time."

"No doubt because you haven't had the chance to secure one since you returned to England."

His mouth curled. "I have had ample opportunities, trust me. But I don't want a mistress. I want you—as my wife."

Eleanor determinedly shook her head. "What about after we are wed? You told me when I broke off our engagement that you would not promise me fidelity."

"I can promise that now. I am willing to take a vow of celibacy if you like."

Taken aback, she stared at him. "For how long?"

"For as long as it takes to convince you to wed me."

"You wouldn't last a month."

"I would, Elle."

The certainty shimmering in his dark eyes made her want to believe him, but she was a fool if she succumbed to Damon's velvet promises.

Stiffening her spine, Eleanor pointed at the window where he had entered her bedchamber. "I am sorry, Damon, but there is no possible way I could ever trust you again. Now would you please get off my bed and take your leave? This argument is pointless."

He hesitated another long moment. "Very well, but this is not the end of our discussion."

"Yes, it is."

"I beg to differ."

He levered himself off her bed as ordered, but instead of making for the window, he moved slowly toward her. Eleanor stood her ground—which was a mistake, she quickly realized. Before she could fathom his intent, Damon drew her into his embrace, flush against his hard body.

"I won't let you wed Lazzara, Elle."

"You cannot stop me," she declared, raising her chin.

His eyes sparked at her defiance. "Then you leave me no choice," he murmured in that low, husky voice. "I will have to persuade you one kiss at a time."

Her heart leapt as his wicked mouth came closer, yet Eleanor found herself riveted in place, unable to utter a protest. His palms framing her face, Damon stole her lips—and her breath as well—in a deep, intimate, caressing kiss.

Her pulse was pounding in her ears, her body trembling with renewed heat, when at last he released her. Eleanor drew away, dazed and flustered . . . which clearly was his aim. Damon seemed to derive great satisfaction from keeping her off balance, if his expression was anything to judge by.

"It is sneaky and underhanded of you," she complained with a touch of bitterness, "using physical arousal to turn my own body against me. You know I have difficulty resisting your seduction."

"I am counting on it." There was a distinct challenge in his gaze. "You should not underestimate my determination, Elle."

He bent to kiss her again, but this time she summoned the last ounce of her willpower and jerked away. "Blast you, Damon, keep away from me! If you do not, I won't be responsible for the consequences."

His lips twisted with faint humor. "Your wish is my command, my lady," he replied, giving her a bow before crossing the room to the open window.

There he hesitated and glanced back at her. "Promise me you will keep on your guard when you are with Lazzara, Eleanor. His continued mishaps could put you in danger, and you need to take the potential threat seriously."

"Right now the only threat I see comes from you," she declared irritably.

"Promise me, Elle," Damon repeated, his tone stern.

"Very well, I promise! *Now* will you go?"

He sat on the sill, then eased himself through and

onto a limb of the oak tree outside. Right then Eleanor decided to have her aunt's gardeners trim those branches first thing in the morning, to deny Damon access to her bedchamber in the future.

She watched warily as he disappeared from sight and then latched the window shut and drew the draperies. Crossing to her bed, Eleanor climbed in and sank back among the pillows, utterly dismayed by the turn of events.

She had behaved like a total wanton, allowing Damon to take scandalous liberties with her body. Involuntarily, she reached up and touched her swollen lips, remembering the incredible pleasure he had shown her . . . pleasure he had promised was only a small measure of what she could expect in their marriage bed.

Yet not only had he breached her defenses, even worse, he'd actually had the audacity to propose marriage so he could prevent her from pursuing a relationship with Prince Lazzara.

The very nerve of him! She couldn't fault his concern for her safety, but she couldn't give his proposal any serious credence either. Moreover, she had little doubt that once the prince's courtship ended, Damon would find some way to elude any marriage shackles.

And in the unlikely event that he actually was sincere about his proposal?

She most certainly would not marry him, Eleanor swore. She was fiercely determined to move on with her life. Of course, she would first have to overcome her deplorable infatuation with Damon. The vexing scoundrel challenged her, infuriated her, captivated her—and worried her to no end.

Damon had the enchanting ability to gain whatever he wanted, and he professed to want *her*.

Eleanor caught her lower lip between her teeth. She wanted to curse and pray at the same time: to curse Damon and to pray for her own deliverance.

Blast you, blast you, she thought, turning over to bury her face in the pillows.

He did not want her for his wife, no matter what he claimed. And even if he did, he was not getting her!

Did he truly want Eleanor for his wife? Damon wondered as he carefully negotiated the oak tree outside her window. Admittedly, he was not as sanguine about his impulsive offer of marriage as he'd let on. In fact, he'd astonished himself almost as much as he had Elle.

Certainly he wanted to protect her from Lazzara. He'd been frustrated as bloody hell by Eleanor's determined pursuit of the prince, as well as by her romanticized ideals of love and marriage.

Damon couldn't deny, either, that one of her accusations had hit uncannily close to the truth. Once more he'd acted in the heat of the moment; his hunger for her had sent blood streaming from his brain to his loins, along with any vestiges of wisdom he should have learned from his original experience at proposing. He was sporting a raging arousal now that made descending the tree rather painful at times.

"Which is what you deserve for nearly seducing her in her own bed, you sorry blighter," Damon murmured to himself.

His mouth curved with self-deprecation. The lust-induced madness that had infected him two years ago had struck him within mere days of encountering Eleanor again. He was climbing trees in the pitch dark, inviting scandal by visiting a genteel young lady's bedchamber late at night, and plotting how to pry her away from her princely suitor.

But at least his placid, boring life was no longer dull. Even more notably, the restlessness that had festered inside him in recent months was absent for the moment.

Dropping to the ground, Damon dusted off his hands and made his way to his carriage, which awaited him around the corner of Portman Place.

Still, he reminded himself, he'd had a sound rationalization for his irrational proposal besides sheer madness or lust or even protectiveness. It wasn't primal male possessiveness driving him, either, or the fact that he didn't want to give Eleanor up to any other man.

It was that he couldn't allow her to leave his life so irrevocably. He didn't want to think of his world without Elle in it.

Granted, Damon reflected, while he had always intended to marry eventually, he'd planned on making a union typical of the British aristocracy, with a genteel female who would never engage his heart. Yet he would lose Eleanor for good if she married her prince—and that he couldn't bring himself to accept.

Despite her arguments, though, a marriage of convenience between them was not so illogical, Damon reasoned. If he was to marry, Eleanor would be his best choice by far. He would never find another woman who was so ideally suited to him.

And he could say the same about his own suitability for her. Most definitely he would make her a better husband than her prince or anyone else. He would make certain of it.

He would never purposely hurt her again, he was willing to swear his life on that. Eleanor's happiness was important to him. He would see that she had everything she desired . . . except for love, of course.

And that really was the crux of the matter—

Damon was glad that his reflections were interrupted as he reached his carriage.

"Home, my lord?" his coachman asked respectfully.

"Yes, Cavendish Square," he answered, before settling on the squabs inside.

As the carriage drew away from the curb, he heard the echo of Eleanor's low voice. *I want true love in my marriage. I want my husband to love me.*

Turning, Damon gazed unseeingly out at the darkened streets of Mayfair. He couldn't give Eleanor the love she yearned for. He wouldn't allow himself. Not when he knew the devastation of losing his loved ones.

It had been twelve years, but he still felt the aching loss of his twin's death, still remembered the agonizing helplessness of watching his vital, fun-loving brother waste away from the cruel ravages of consumption.

Those last, bleak, heartbreaking images would be forever burned into his consciousness: Joshua's skin gray and mottled. His body shrunken by fever and racking coughs and drenching night sweats. His agony while spitting up blood from between his cracked lips as his tortured lungs struggled to draw breath.

Damon clenched his jaw as he fought to drive back the savage memories. In the last stages of the disease, little could be done to relieve a consumptive's terrible suffering, except to administer heavy doses of laudanum to provide oblivion for a few blessed hours at a time.

When the end had finally, mercifully come—when his brother was buried in the cold earth decades before his time—Damon was left with a soul-deep rage, along with a stark, soul-numbing loneliness. And then his brother's tragedy had been swiftly followed by his parents' senseless deaths. . . .

His grief had hardened him, Damon knew. He would do anything to avoid that pain again—the anguish of losing his very best friend, his shadow, and the parents he'd cherished.

Emptiness was preferable to feeling, so he'd purposely turned his heart to stone.

There was danger in wedding Elle, of course. Two years ago he'd allowed her to assume too much importance in his life. He'd let himself become enthralled with her—with her charm, her liveliness, her vitality.

Yet he was older and wiser now, Damon told himself. He could keep his emotional distance from Eleanor now that he was forewarned. They could have passion in their marriage without any real closeness or intimacy. A simple union of convenience, nothing more.

He could offer her friendship at least. She would

never be lonely as his wife, he could promise her that much.

And he could and would vow fidelity in their marriage. Eleanor's accusation that he couldn't control his lustful urges and remain faithful to her was far off the mark. He'd been celibate for a while now, certainly since returning to England.

He hadn't kept a mistress either, not since dismissing his former paramour.

In truth, he'd decided to end his arrangement with Mrs. Lydia Newling the moment he met Eleanor.

He didn't miss the beautiful widow, even though their affair had lasted three years. There had been no emotional intimacy between them, because Damon had always taken care to keep their relationship strictly business. In that respect, Lydia was the perfect mistress for him. They'd had a mutually satisfying agreement. Damon paid her lavishly, and Lydia skillfully accommodated him when he sought refuge in sexual release.

He hadn't seen her since using her to help break off his betrothal to Eleanor, although he knew Lydia had a new protector. Otto Geary had mentioned her just the other day. Reportedly Lydia's sister was ill, so she had recently sought Otto's medical counsel.

Damon's grim expression turned sardonic as he recognized the irony of his thinking. The relationship he proposed to have with Elle was much the same as he'd had with Lydia: a strictly physical connection. He could understand why Eleanor would not be enamored of the idea.

He also understood why she would refuse to trust him after the way he had treated her.

He would have to prove himself deserving of her faith, Damon was well aware. And with patience, he might eventually win her acceptance.

Yet even if he wasn't able to convince her to wed *him,* Damon reflected, he would use any means necessary to prevent her from wedding her prince.

He couldn't save Joshua, but he would keep Eleanor safe.

Chapter Eight

To Eleanor's dismay, she dreamed of Damon that night. As he roused her with his breath-stealing kisses and his tender, caressing hands, myriad emotions assaulted her—spellbinding intimacy, spiraling heat, stunning pleasure.

Her body dissolved beneath his skilled touches . . . but then somehow her dream changed from sensual fantasy to poignant memory.

The rose garden was small and secluded, her own private sanctuary at her aunt's enormous country estate. She was still in a daze of happiness since her betrothal to Damon was so brand new, only four days old. The house party had just ended, and this was their first chance to be alone together since the guests departed.

Making their escape from the manor, Eleanor brought Damon here to show him her special place, a part of her past that she never shared with anyone.

"This garden was Marcus's gift to me after our parents died when I was ten years old," Eleanor explained. "He planned to return to university, and

when I pleaded with him not to leave me here, he planted a rose bush for me. Then each year on my birthday, he has given me one more."

She followed the gravel path where ten large bushes of lush pink roses spiraled out in a pattern. Leading Damon to the very heart of the spiral, Eleanor bent to lovingly stroke a velvet rose petal. "This plant was the first one." Her voice dropped. "Marcus said he would be with me in spirit as long as I had my roses. And I would have something to remind me of his love. I am never lonely when I come here."

Her heart filled with joy, she turned to gaze up at Damon, drinking in the sight of him. "Love vanquishes loneliness, and now that I am to be your wife, I know I will never be lonely again."

At first she didn't notice how still Damon had become. "Love?" he asked quietly.

She smiled shyly up at him. "Yes. I love you, Damon. More than I ever thought to love anyone." Bending again, she plucked a bud and held it to his lips. "I know you don't return my love yet. After all, it has not even been three weeks since we first met. But I hope that will soon change."

After a long hesitation, he reached up to touch her cheek gently. "I don't want to hurt you, Elle."

She shivered, wondering at the shadows in his eyes. His response was not the one she wanted, but she would not give up hope. "You could never hurt me, Damon. You would never . . ."

Eleanor started awake in the darkness, hearing the echo of her naive, trusting words, remembering her utter devastation the following week after they returned to London, when she'd spied Damon with his beautiful mistress.

Even two years later, the ache still burned inside her. Squeezing her eyes shut, she buried her face in her pillow to hold back the tears.

When she woke again, it was morning. The ache had diminished, but Eleanor was left with a feeling of great sadness, along with an even-greater restlessness. Yet after Damon's vexing visit to her bedchamber last evening, she was more determined than ever to persevere with her plan to employ Fanny's book, *Advice to Young Ladies on Capturing a Husband,* on Prince Lazzara.

She would redouble her efforts to win his affections, Eleanor vowed, and to elicit a proposal of marriage from him. More crucially, she would do her utmost to fall in love with him. What better way to forget the alluring Lord Wrexham than to bestow her heart on someone else?

The major impediment to her plan, however, was that the target of her designs was missing. Eleanor saw nothing of Prince Lazzara that day, although she received a short note of apology from him, explaining that regrettably he would have to forgo their planned afternoon drive in the park, since he was resting his sprained knee.

Her spirits a little deflated, Eleanor spent a quiet evening at home with her aunt. She was heartened during dinner, though, when they discussed the ball that Beatrix's good friend, the Dowager Countess of Haviland, would be giving the following evening.

"Mary has not held a ball in over a decade," Beatrix remarked, "since her health is not robust. But she is eager to get Haviland married off, so she is leaving no stone unturned in her effort to introduce him to eligible prospects."

Lady Haviland's handsome grandson, Rayne Kenyon, had come into the title the previous year upon the death of his father, Eleanor knew. His name had been linked with Roslyn Loring's for a time during the summer, but obviously their suspected romance had come to naught since Roslyn had wed the Duke of Arden.

"The cream of society will be attending Mary's ball, you may be sure," Beatrix added, "along with a horde of debutantes. . . . At least the ones who did not manage to secure husbands this past Season."

Eleanor suspected her aunt was correct. Before the wars ended, Haviland had frequently been out of the country. And more recently, he'd been in mourning for his father. But he was available now. And since a wealthy, unattached earl was a prime catch on the Marriage Mart, there undoubtedly would be numerous young ladies trying out their wiles on Lord Haviland—the very sort of audience that Fanny's book was intended for, although Eleanor kept that amusing observation to herself. She did not wish her aunt to think she was interested in pursuing Haviland. One nobleman at a time was ample.

And in any event, Beatrix was too focused on Prince Lazzara at the moment to think of pushing Eleanor into any other match.

"Signor Vecchi assures me that he and the prince will be at the ball," Beatrix said with satisfaction. "It is a pity that his highness cannot dance with his injury, but even if he cannot, he may watch from the sidelines. We will take care to secure seats beside him, Eleanor, so that you may carry on a conversation with him throughout the evening. It could prove an excellent opportunity for you."

Eleanor eyed her aunt with curiosity. Having no fondness for dancing, Beatrix usually escaped to the cardroom to play whist with her cronies as soon as the orchestra struck up the opening tune. "Do you mean to sit with us to act as chaperone, Aunt?"

"No, no, you hardly need a chaperone, and my presence could impede your progress with Prince Lazzara. But I intend to remain in the ballroom. It has been a long while since I have actually enjoyed a ball, and Signor Vecchi has asked me for the first set of dances."

"Ahh," Eleanor replied lightly. It was the lure of the distinguished Italian diplomat that would divert her aunt from her long-held habits.

Surprisingly, Beatrix flushed. "I suppose it is absurd at my age to be cavorting like an ingenue, but I confess I feel like a young girl again."

Eleanor smiled with affection. "I think it is perfectly lovely. Age is not always the best indicator of how young at heart you feel."

"It is fortunate that we commissioned new gowns for my house party. I had thought to save the lavender satin until then, but I think I will wear it tomorrow instead. And you should take special care with your appearance as well, my dear. You want to look your very best for the prince."

"I intend to, aunt," Eleanor said with all seriousness.

*   *   *

Like her aunt, Eleanor chose to wear one of her new ball gowns the following evening, a stylish confection of rose-hued mousseline de soie that boasted an Empire-waisted bodice seeded with tiny pearls. She dressed carefully and had her hair artfully coiffed by her aunt's dresser, so that her short raven curls were threaded with rose ribbons and pearls.

They would not arrive fashionably late to the ball as was Lady Beldon's custom. Instead, they would strive for promptness, since Beatrix wished to influence the seating arrangements and also to be prepared to dance the first set with the signor.

The event would likely prove a crush if the receiving line was any indication, Eleanor decided as she and her aunt slowly made their way into the ballroom. They had to wait for nearly ten minutes to be greeted by the silver-haired Lady Haviland and the tall, raven-haired nobleman standing beside her.

Lord Haviland's features were more rugged than Damon's, although perhaps not as intense, Eleanor thought, unconsciously comparing the two men. But like Damon, the dangerous edge of Haviland's appeal was enough to make every female head turn.

His smile, too, was just as arresting, and his eyes were rimmed by heavy lashes like Damon's, although the earl's eyes were a vivid blue, nearly the same color as her own, rather than midnight brown as Damon's were.

As her aunt had predicted, Lady Haviland was intent on matchmaking for her grandson.

"I am delighted you have come, Lady Eleanor," the elderly dame pronounced. "You will make Haviland an exceptional dance partner . . . will she not, my dear?"

"Indeed," his lordship responded easily. "I would be honored if you would oblige me with a set, Lady Eleanor."

"It would be my pleasure," she answered in the same vein. Haviland seemed prepared to take his relative's scheming with good grace, and the appealing glimmer of amusement in his eyes made Eleanor like him all the more.

Once they were through the receiving line, however, she shifted her attention to the swelling crowd and began searching for one particular guest. Her aunt spied Prince Lazzara and his distinguished older cousin first—in the far corner of the ballroom, seated before a cluster of potted palms—and led Eleanor over at once.

The prince rose with the aid of a cane and bestowed a fond smile and a deep bow on her. "I deeply regret I cannot dance with the most beautiful lady in the room, Donna Eleanora," he murmured once the salutations were made. "But you would do me a great kindness to keep me company for a short while."

"Of course, your highness. I would be very pleased," Eleanor replied, taking the chair beside him while her aunt stood conversing with Signor Vecchi. "I am sorry your injury is so severe."

Prince Lazzara's mouth turned down in a woeful expression. "It causes me no little pain, but now that you are here, it will all be forgotten. And since you mean to sacrifice on my behalf . . . permit me to provide you with refreshment."

He waved a hand imperiously at a footman, who

brought her a cup of punch similar to the one the prince was drinking. Eleanor politely sipped hers and made small talk with the Italian royal, and yet she found her mind wandering as she surveyed the assembly. She was thankful she saw no sign of Damon and held out hope that perhaps he would not attend tonight's ball.

Lamentably, her hope was short-lived.

She became aware of Damon within seconds of his entrance. But what else did she expect from a bold, dynamic nobleman who always commanded attention? Garbed in formal attire—charcoal gray coat, silver brocade waistcoat, and white satin knee breeches—he was taller, more vital, more striking than any man in the room except for perhaps Prince Lazzara and Lord Haviland.

His physician friend, Mr. Geary, was with him, Eleanor noted. They made an odd pair, since Mr. Geary was short and portly and more plainly dressed, with bright red hair and a freckled complexion.

A moment later Damon glanced around the ballroom and found her in the crowd. Eleanor stiffened, cursing the irritating response her heart made whenever he merely looked at her.

His regard was more intent than usual, however . . . drifting over her gown, lingering on her bodice. Somehow she knew he was not merely admiring the rich design of the seed pearls. No, he was recalling what had happened between them two nights ago, the wanton way she had responded to his scandalous caresses . . . devil take him.

Eleanor felt her skin flush with heat, even before Damon's gaze lifted and met hers. When their eyes locked, she experienced that same idiotic, overwhelming feeling she always had around him . . . breathless, spellbound, captivated.

For the space of several heartbeats, the noise and bustle of the ballroom faded away, and it seemed as if she and Damon were the only two people in the room, enveloped in their own private world.

The spell was suddenly broken as several young ladies hurried toward him, yet Eleanor couldn't help watching in resentful fascination as Damon greeted them with his alluring brand of male charm.

She was not the only one watching, either. Beside her, the prince muttered a low oath in his own language, having spied Damon.

"Must he appear every time I have you to myself? His ubiquitous presence is growing tiresome."

"I agree," Eleanor murmured wholeheartedly.

Lazzara's brooding gaze was still fixed on Damon. "He seems to be pursuing you, Donna Eleanora."

"If so, it is completely against my wishes, I assure you."

Tearing his gaze from across the ballroom, his highness gave her a considering look. "Wrexham is a wild and reckless sort. Not the ideal a young lady such as yourself would wish for in a suitor."

The comment was posed more as a question than a statement, and when Eleanor responded, "Most certainly not," the prince seemed satisfied with her answer and turned the conversation to less controversial topics than her choice of suitors.

After perhaps another quarter hour had passed—during which a number of their acquaintances came up to greet them and sympathize with the prince over his injury—the orchestra began playing the opening minuet. When Signor Vecchi led Lady Beldon onto the ballroom floor, Eleanor was left alone with Prince Lazzara.

"It is quite warm here, is it not?" he asked after a moment.

To Eleanor's surprise, his face appeared abnormally flushed and a sheen of perspiration covered his forehead.

The ballroom did indeed feel rather oppressive with the heat from myriad chandeliers and the press of so many elegantly clad bodies, but no more than usual, she judged.

"Perhaps you will take a turn with me outside, where the air is cooler," the prince suggested.

"Should you be walking, Don Antonio?"

"I may walk with my cane, even though I cannot dance. And I would very much like to have your attention all to myself."

Eleanor did not have to feign a smile. The prince was offering an opportunity for them to be alone, and she intended to take full advantage of it. "I would like that as well, your highness."

He took her punch cup and set it on the floor beside her chair, along with his own half-empty one. Then rising, he lightly grasped her elbow and guided her behind the bank of potted palms, through an open French door.

"This is significantly better," he remarked when they stepped out onto a balcony overlooking the side gardens. "The night air is much cooler here."

Eleanor murmured her agreement. She was comfortable in her short-sleeved ball gown, in part because she wore long kidskin gloves that covered her arms, but also because the mid-September evening was unseasonably mild.

"In my country our young ladies are not permitted to be alone with a man," Lazzara observed. "It makes courting rather difficult."

His voice had dropped a level and held a husky undertone, she realized. Eleanor glanced up at him, seeing that his handsome features were illuminated by dim moonlight.

"In my country, the rules are not quite as strict," she replied, wondering if he intended to kiss her. He had a rakish reputation after all. But reluctant to leave the outcome solely to him, she lifted her face slightly, offering silent encouragement.

He did not seem to need further invitation. Bending his head, Lazzara pressed his mouth to hers.

His lips were full and soft and unaccountably . . . tame, Eleanor thought, unable to suppress her disappointment. She had expected the prince to be more assertive, at least. He was treating her like a fragile blossom, nothing like the way Damon treated her when he kissed her—

Irked that she would be thinking of Damon when she was being embraced by another man—and even more irked that she was not enjoying the prince's kiss as she should—she raised her hands to his shoulders and offered her mouth more fully. . . .

Just then she heard a throat being cleared behind them, her first indication that someone else had joined them on the balcony. The prince broke off abruptly at the intrusion, while Eleanor tried to keep hold of her composure.

She would have known it was Damon by the way her senses reacted to his lazy drawl, even before she comprehended his actual words. "So this is the latest utilization of your advice book on capturing a husband, Lady Eleanor? What chapter does a romantic tryst belong in?"

Her cheeks flushing with embarrassment, she turned to find Damon leaning one broad shoulder against the door frame.

"Tsk, tsk, my lady," he added, his tone lightly admonishing. "Whatever would your proper aunt say?"

Her aunt would likely be delighted, Eleanor reflected with frustration, although she could not possibly say so in front of the prince.

At a loss for words, she settled for giving Damon a quelling frown. But he went on just as if he were not interfering where he most certainly wasn't wanted. "Fortunately I discovered you first. You would not wish to be caught in a compromising position with Prince Lazzara, or you might be forced into a union you both might regret."

Although the prince had stiffened, he recovered before Eleanor did. As if to shield her, he stepped toward Damon—then grimaced as his weight landed on his injured leg. Making use of his cane, he raised himself to his full height and tried to stare down his nose regally at Damon.

The effect was not quite as imposing as the prince wished, since he was not as tall as the Englishman. But there was no mistaking the tension in the air when he announced curtly, "I doubt I would regret such a union. It would not be a hardship, being wed to so lovely a lady."

Damon's gaze shifted to the prince, looking him up and down. "Perhaps you weren't aware, your highness, that I have a prior claim to Lady Eleanor."

Eleanor drew a sharp breath at that patent falsehood, while Lazzara's jaw hardened. "The signorina seems to disagree."

"Indeed I do," she said quickly. "Lord Wrexham has no claim to me whatsoever." She fixed Damon with a censorious stare of her own. "Pray oblige us by taking your leave, my lord."

He looked at her a long moment while Eleanor glowered at him. "Very well, love, but don't tarry out here too long. You don't want to give the wags cause for gossip."

With that, Damon turned on his heel and exited the balcony, leaving Eleanor mortified and fuming.

Before she could think of what to say, however, the prince spoke first.

"Forgive me, I should not have taken advantage of you as I did," he offered.

For some absurd reason, his apology only vexed her further. Damon would not have apologized for that limp effort at lovemaking, nor claimed to be taking advantage of her when she had willingly participated. But then the prince's manners clearly were far more gentlemanly. She should not take her ire out on him when the real culprit at arousing her temper was an interfering rogue.

Eleanor managed a smile. "There is nothing to forgive, your highness. But perhaps we should return to the ball before our absence is noted."

Prince Lazzara nodded in agreement. "Yes. Please go ahead without me, however. I believe I will remain here for a while longer to enjoy the cooler temperatures."

He still looked flushed, she noted with sympathy.

With a polite curtsy, Eleanor left him on the balcony and stepped through the doors, into the ballroom. Not to her surprise, Damon awaited her inside in the shadow of the potted palms. Far from resenting his presence, though, she welcomed it, since she was eager to do battle with him.

"What the devil do you mean, embarrassing me in that horrid fashion?" Eleanor hissed in a fierce undertone.

Damon seemed unrepentant. "Did you honestly expect me to stand idly by, knowing you were trying your hand at seducing him?"

"I was not attempting to seduce him."

"But you were kissing him."

"Even so, it is no concern of yours! You have no claim to me."

"One could argue that point," Damon drawled. "I feel a certain measure of protectiveness because of our past history, if nothing else. And you overestimate my powers of restraint if you think I can control my jealousy."

Eleanor's scowl deepened. "You have no right to be jealous."

"Then perhaps you should thank me for arousing *his* jealousy. What better way to kindle his desire for you?"

"I most *certainly* will not thank you," Eleanor retorted. "I am not a bone for two dogs to fight over."

She stood there glaring daggers at him. Yet Damon

met her gaze without flinching, his own eyes full of heat and challenge.

Just then the strains of a waltz filled the ballroom. Before she could utter a word of protest, he stepped closer and took her in his arms.

"I may not be able to claim your hand in marriage, but I am claiming this dance."

Even though Eleanor tried to pull back, Damon would not release her. The very air was crackling between them, but she had no choice but to allow him to sweep her past the palms and onto the ballroom floor among the other dancers.

"I wish you would go to Hades," she said through gritted teeth.

"I will take your wishes under consideration, but you know I don't take well to being dismissed."

Eleanor clamped her lips shut. Damon riled her to no end, which was doubtless his intent. Therefore, she resolved to deny him the satisfaction of getting any further under her skin.

When she refused to respond to his taunt, his own expression became milder. "Smile, love. You don't wish the company to see us at loggerheads."

"I don't wish them to see us dancing together, either."

"But short of causing a scene, you cannot stalk off the floor."

"Your effrontery is boundless," she grated, forgetting her resolve.

"I won't contradict you. For now I will simply relish the pleasure of dancing with the most beautiful woman in the room."

"If you are trying to mollify me, you infuriating scoundrel, I promise you it will not work."

For a moment she lapsed into simmering silence. Then growing more conscious of the countless pairs of eyes watching them, Eleanor focused her attention on the steps of the waltz and tried not to admire Damon's natural grace as he swung her to the rhythm of the lilting music.

"Come, admit it," he said after a time. "You enjoy sparring with me."

"You are laboring under a serious misapprehension, my lord," Eleanor retorted, even though she knew her reply for a lie. There was nothing more exhilarating than sparring with Damon, except perhaps kissing him.

He drew back a little to survey her face. "I'll wager your conversations with your prince are not nearly as enjoyable as ours. You did not seem to be very enthusiastic earlier when you were relegated to the sidelines with him. In truth, you looked rather bored."

"I was having a perfectly delightful time before you appeared."

"Is that so?" Damon looked dubious. "I confess I don't understand his appeal. I would not have expected you to be attracted to that tame man-milliner."

"Prince Lazzara is nothing of the kind," Eleanor asserted firmly, even though she was beginning to have her own doubts.

"Then what do you see in him?"

"He is charming and intelligent for one thing, not boring in the least. Moreover he has exquisite manners, unlike certain *other* noblemen of my acquaintance," she added pointedly, staring at Damon.

"Are you physically attracted to him?"

"Yes, of course."

"Why?"

"He is quite handsome."

"In a pretty sort of way, I'll grant you."

"He has beautiful eyes."

"So do I."

Although amusement tinged his voice, it was said without a modicum of modesty—yet Eleanor could not refute him. Damon's piercing dark eyes, with their heavy fringe of lashes, were an attribute that keenly appealed to her. The prince's eyes were more soulful, but they couldn't fire her blood the way a mere look from Damon could do.

And when it came to comparing the two men's physical appeal, there was no contest; Damon won hands down. His vitality, his sheer masculinity, melted her. The mere sound of his voice excited her, for it reminded her of those heady days and nights of their courtship.

Even so, Eleanor arched an eyebrow. "You do not need me to fan the flames of your conceit, Lord Wrexham."

He flashed her a charming smile. "True. I know very well how my charms attract you."

Ignoring the scoffing sound she made, Damon guided her expertly through a knot of dancers, which proved to be a tight squeeze. For a brief moment they came together so that they pressed against each other. When Eleanor felt Damon's body hard and warm against hers, her heart missed a beat, while a shiver of raw sensation ran down her spine.

As if he knew exactly the effect he was having on her, his eyes turned heavy-lidded, and he bent closer to murmur in her ear, "I doubt your prince arouses you the way I do."

His suggestive tone made Eleanor instantly recall two nights ago in her bedchamber, how Damon's wicked mouth had lovingly teased and fondled her nipples. Just thinking about him kissing her bare breasts again was enough to make her knees weak.

Eleanor silently muttered an invective. How she resented him for making her feel this way! With her past beaux, she had always felt in control, but she never had the slightest control with Damon.

She pressed her lips together, then said stiffly, "I know you are deliberately trying to fluster me."

"Am I succeeding? Are you flustered, sweet Elle?"

"You are utterly impossible."

With a disgusted sigh, she stopped dancing, intending to break away from him, but Damon inexorably urged her back into the movement of the dance. "Remember, love, you do not want to create a spectacle."

Eleanor forced herself to take a calming breath, realizing the wisdom of his reminder. "You needn't worry. A lady does not do a gentleman bodily harm in public, no matter how galling the provocation."

"You have no desire to be a lady all the time."

His comment gave her pause as a sudden thought struck her. She paused for a long moment before saying slowly, "Perhaps you are right."

"About what?"

"About my desire to be a lady."

When Damon glanced down at her quizzically, Eleanor savored the feeling of having puzzled him.

Perhaps she had been going about this all wrong, she realized. Whenever she became flustered and riled, Damon only used her weakness to his advantage. But she was weary of always allowing him the upper hand, of constantly being on the defensive.

It was time she took the reins back into her own hands, Eleanor decided.

"If I recall correctly," she mused aloud in a thoughtful tone, "Lady Haviland's library is on the floor below, at the rear of the house. No one will be occupying it during a ball."

"So?" Damon asked somewhat cautiously as the waltz came to an end.

"So, I think you should meet me in the library ten minutes from now."

Chapter Nine

Although naturally a lady must remain within the bounds of propriety, rousing his desire for you should be one of your chief aims.

—An Anonymous Lady, *Advice . . .*

The lower floor of Lady Haviland's mansion appeared deserted to Eleanor as she made her way down a corridor to the library. But that was to be expected since the ball guests were occupied with enjoying the entertainments offered upstairs, while the servants were busy seeing to the company or preparing the late supper that would be served in a few hours.

Damon was waiting for her as promised, she saw when she stepped into the room. The draperies had been drawn, and he had lit a lamp so that the library was bathed in a warm glow.

Quietly Eleanor shut the door and pressed her back against it, deploring how her pulse leapt at the sight of him. Damon was standing before the cold hearth, one hand casually resting on the mantel as he watched her with deceptive idleness. Yet she expected he was feeling far from casual.

At least *she* was feeling far from casual. For a moment she stood there unmoving, willing the giddy, fluttering sensation in her stomach to dissolve while questioning the prudence of her impulsive decision to go on the offensive. He thought he could end her pursuit of Prince Lazzara by sheer force of his seductive personality, but she intended to foil Damon's machinations and give him a taste of his own medicine at the same time. She would fluster and arouse him while she remained in control and completely unaffected—which might prove difficult, judging by her body's reaction to his mere perusal. She felt his gaze like heat on her skin as he waited for her to speak first.

"So what is the purpose of your invitation, sweeting?" he asked when she remained silent.

"I told you, I am weary of always acting the lady. I intend to behave a little scandalously for a change."

His slashing black eyebrows rose a measure. "There are three hundred guests in the house in addition to an army of servants."

Eleanor nodded. She could hear the refrains of music and the far-off din of voices chattering and laughing, yet she was completely alone with Damon, and she meant to keep it that way.

Turning to lock the door, she glanced provocatively over her shoulder at him. "I doubt we will be discovered, but the risk we are taking only adds to the titillation. Of course, if you are afraid, we can call off the whole thing. . . ."

She let her voice trail away as her hand remained resting on the key, suggesting her willingness to unlock the door if he wished her to.

Damon's slow, enchanting smile made her heart jump. "I am not in the least afraid. I only thought you would be."

She couldn't let him affect her this way, Eleanor scolded herself. She needed to hold on to her resolve and her resentment if she had any hope of success just now.

With renewed determination, she crossed the library to Damon, standing so close that she could feel the heat of his skin through their clothing. Reaching up, she tangled her fingers in his silky mane of hair and lifted her face to his, letting her warm breath taunt his lips.

But when he started to draw her into his arms, Eleanor stepped back quickly, pressing a hand against his chest to forestall him.

"No, you cannot touch me," she said, keeping her tone light. "I cannot leave here with my hair or my gown disheveled."

Moreover, she wanted to be completely in charge. For once she wanted to unsettle *him,* to see him lose his legendary poise. He knew how to reduce her to trembling submission, and she meant to do the same to him—not to mention making him regret interfering in her romantic affairs.

She gestured at the brocade sofa at one side of the library. "Why don't you make yourself comfortable?"

When he obliged her by sitting down, she moved to stand before Damon, then knelt on the Aubusson carpet at his feet, to his evident surprise.

With a faint smile, she slipped off his silver-buckled evening pumps and set them aside, admiring his well-muscled calves covered by white silk stockings. Then she surprised him further by easing herself between his spread thighs.

"Just what do you have in mind, sweetheart?" he asked, his voice holding a husky edge.

"You will see all in good time," Eleanor replied. "You must cultivate a little patience."

When she lightly licked her lips, he followed the seductive movement avidly with his gaze. As he watched, she raised her hand and touched her fingers to *his* lips, then trailed them down his throat, along his lace cravat, then lower to the buttons of his coat. Unfastening those, she pushed aside the lapels and opened his waistcoat as well, exposing his fine cambric shirt.

Placing her hand on his chest, Eleanor could feel his heart pounding hard where her palm lay. Then, with her own heart thudding in nervous anticipation, she slowly grazed her hand downward to his flat abdomen to hover over his loins.

Damon was watching her with intent focus, no doubt wondering how far she would go.

"You make an alluring temptress, bright-eyes," he murmured when she hesitated, "but do you have any idea what you are about?"

Her mouth curled playfully. "Truthfully, no. I have learned some things from my friends who are married and from you yourself. I know you grow hard when we are kissing, and that it is painful for you when you cannot find relief—"

"Indeed, extremely painful," Damon supplied.

"—but otherwise, I have little experience in carnal matters. I suspect you will need to tell me what to do."

A glimmer of humor shone in his eyes. "Your book does not advise you?"

"Not specifically, no. My book is for ladies."

"What do your feminine instincts tell you then?"

"That I should try to arouse your desires. I thought I would begin by caressing you the way you caressed me two nights ago."

"That would be a good start. You can use your hands or your mouth to arouse me."

"My mouth?"

Damon smiled at her surprise. "Yes, darling. I told you, there is much about lovemaking that you have yet to learn."

A tremor of excitement ran through her. "Will you teach me, Damon?" Eleanor asked coyly, her tone belying her agitation. "Will you show me how I can give you the same pleasure you gave me?"

"Gladly."

The dark gleam in his eyes revealed his approval as he caught her hand and drew it against his loins. He was already greatly aroused, judging from the large bulge in his breeches. Eleanor could feel the thick ridge of his male member beneath the satin. She also felt how his body tensed at the slight pressure of her hand.

Hoping to increase his tension, she slowly slid her hand over the swollen hardness, stroking gently. A flare of heat sparked in Damon's dark eyes, giving her encouragement. But did she dare go further? Eleanor wondered, her entire body tightening at the forbidden thrill rushing through her.

Catching her lower lip between her teeth, she used both hands to unbutton the front placket of his breeches. Then drawing a slow breath, she opened his drawers and bared his naked loins to her gaze.

She stared, fascinated by his male anatomy and the long, dark phallus that jutted from the curling hair at his groin. He was every bit as virile as she had imagined him to be.

Reaching out tentatively, she brushed the surging, silky flesh with her knuckles. His rampant member jerked involuntarily, making her breath catch.

"Did I do something wrong?" Eleanor asked, drawing back her hand.

"No, not at all. Touch me again."

"Where?" she queried unevenly.

"My sacs. The head of my cock."

Obligingly, she cupped the heavy sacs beneath his arousal. His flesh was smooth and hot, she noted, savoring the feel of him. Moving upward, she traced her forefinger over the blunt, rounded head of his shaft.

At her light touch, Damon sucked in a breath. Emboldened by his response, she shifted her fingers lower to stroke the full length. Then letting her fingers curl around him, she cradled the rigid shaft with her palm.

The hot, granite thickness of his manhood felt strangely erotic and quivered in her hand. In response, something deep within Eleanor shivered in purely sensual reaction.

"Is this the way?" she asked.

"Yes," Damon replied, his voice suddenly hoarse. "But stroke me harder."

His hand moving over hers, he coaxed her to fondle his straining erection. When he gave a soft groan, Eleanor looked up and found herself caught in the smoldering heat of his gaze.

Ensnared, she was hard-pressed to breathe or to calm her own pounding pulse. A yearning filled her, a welling bubble of desire that threatened to burst inside her.

Struggling to gather her control, however, she reminded herself of her aim and offered Damon a smile that was both sweet and seductive, innocent and tantalizing, as she went on exploring the hardness and detail of him.

Damon was caught in her enchantment; his entire body clenched with the arousal that simple smile had awakened in him.

He had never seen Eleanor quite like this. She was vibrant and intoxicatingly alive, a sparkling-eyed beauty who radiated temptation.

When another groan escaped him, she asked almost tauntingly, "Does that hurt?"

"It's pure torment," he answered truthfully.

"Good. I like making you feel the same torment you have made me feel."

She was succeeding utterly, Damon decided. He felt as if he might burst. His primal impulse was to draw Elle beneath him and make violent love to her; he wanted it more than his next breath. And yet he knew he had to go slowly out of respect for her virginal state. . . .

Then suddenly, she left off arousing him.

"I have a surprise for you," Eleanor murmured, her voice husky.

"What surprise?"

Her eyes, vividly blue and fringed with black lashes, met his. Those eyes had a suspicious glimmer in them, Damon noticed.

"You will see soon enough," she replied. "Close your eyes."

Damon thought about disobeying. He was so aroused, he felt feverish, so he was in no mood for any more teasing or seductive games. But when Eleanor repeated her command, he dutifully shut his eyes and clenched his jaw at the savage ache that continued to twist and tighten his loins.

"No peeking now, my lord," she added as he heard her rise from her kneeling position.

Something in her tone seemed off, which prompted Damon to ask, "Can I trust you, Elle?"

"Why certainly you may trust me. Just as much as I can trust you . . ."

Her voice had come from further away, from across the library. When he heard her unlock the door, Damon quickly opened his eyes. Eleanor had retreated across the room, carrying his shoes.

His gaze speared her when he guessed that her intent was to leave him. "Just where are you going, Eleanor?"

She smiled when she answered. "Back to the ballroom. I think I have exhibited enough unladylike behavior for one evening. And my aunt will doubtless be wondering what became of me."

"*Now* you are worried about your aunt?"

"Actually, I wished to prevent you from returning to the ball. I doubt even you would dare go before such distinguished company barefoot."

Damon half rose from the sofa, trying to judge whether or not he could reach her in time to rescue his shoes, then sank back down when he realized any attempt would be futile.

His lips twitched. "Elle, you little wretch. You meant all along to arouse me and leave me like this . . . in pain."

"Well, yes."

"That is not how I treated you the other night."

"No. But you delight in provoking and flustering me. Turnabout is fair play, Damon."

Reaching down, he tucked his still-swollen cock inside his drawers and closed the placket of his breeches. "I suppose this is your revenge for my interrupting your kiss with your prince," he grumbled.

"How perceptive of you."

Damon shook his head, a smile—half wry, half grim—curving his mouth. "I must commend your creativity. It was highly effective."

"Why, thank you. I also thought," Eleanor mused as he fastened the buttons of his breeches, "to put your vow of celibacy to the test . . . to make it more difficult for you to keep your pledge. Of course, if you find it too painful, you could always go to your mistress for relief."

"I told you," he retorted in exasperation, "I don't have a mistress."

"Perhaps you should employ one to see to your carnal needs," Eleanor said carelessly. "Then perhaps you won't continue to pester *me*."

Despite the lightness of her tone, Damon caught the small hitch in her voice that suggested she was not as nonchalant about the subject of his mistress as she tried to appear.

"That just shows how little you know about the male body, sweeting. I can soothe the pain myself. I don't require a woman to slake my carnal needs."

His remark made her hesitate and raise her eyebrows in curiosity. "Oh? How?"

"By stroking myself. It is not nearly as pleasurable or satisfying, bringing myself to climax that way, but effective for easing the pain."

Eleanor gazed at him a moment, as if trying to picture what he was describing. Then flushing, she shook her head quickly, evidently irritated with herself for allowing him to distract her. "Your carnal state is certainly no concern of mine, Damon, nor are my romantic affairs any concern of yours. I'll thank you not to interfere in the future."

She opened the door, then paused to say, "I will ask Lady Haviland's butler to summon your carriage for you so that you will not have to wait in the entrance hall for long. If you are swift enough, perhaps he won't notice that you are missing your shoes."

"I am not troubled about the Haviland butler," Damon said dryly. "It is my valet who worries me. Cornby will be highly distressed if I return home without my shoes."

Eleanor dimpled. "You can always tell him that I absconded with them."

As she slipped out the door, Damon couldn't help laughing softly.

Letting his head fall back, he shut his eyes, remembering the picture Elle had made as she delivered her parting shot . . . her eyes sparkling, her luscious mouth curved in an enchanting half smile. That image would haunt him for days.

And so would his physical ache from her outrageous trick. Damon shifted in his seat to ease the pressure caused by his raging arousal.

Yet he had probably deserved her retribution, he thought with a self-deprecating grin. And perhaps he had been mistaken to interfere so overtly in her romance. As it was, he seemed only to be driving her into the prince's arms, not to mention inflaming his own aching need for her.

He needed to cool his blood, although he was not about to turn to a mistress or any other woman. His vow of celibacy was real, even if it led to acute physical suffering. When he returned home, he would take care of his pain, Damon decided.

At the moment, however, his physical discomfort was not his chief problem.

For now he would have to determine how to obtain a pair of shoes that fit so he could leave the Haviland ball with his manhood figuratively intact.

Before Eleanor returned to the ball, she hid Damon's evening pumps where she doubted he would find them: in the music room two doors down from the library, behind the draperies of a window seat. Once in the entrance hall, she approached the Haviland butler and requested that he send for Lord Wrexham's carriage immediately.

As she made her way upstairs, Eleanor couldn't help feeling a twinge of satisfaction and triumph along with a measure of self-recognition. Despite her professions to the contrary, she had unconsciously wanted revenge on Damon for hurting her so deeply two years ago.

Even if her scandalous escapade tonight had been a bit spiteful, Eleanor decided stubbornly, she didn't regret it in the least, although she had discerned a wicked glint in Damon's eyes that had promised retribution. She had succeeded in both her aims—to discomfit him the way he had discomfited her of late, and to prevent him from returning to the ball and interfering further with her pursuit of Prince Lazzara.

When she arrived in the ballroom, the din of gaiety and laughter had increased from earlier in the evening, in part because a lively country dance was in progress.

She saw her Aunt Beatrix at once, speaking to their hostess, Lady Haviland, but she didn't immediately see Prince Lazzara or Signor Vecchi. Taking care to avoid the sprightly dancers, Eleanor threaded her way through the crowd and headed to the far corner where the prince had been seated earlier.

She discovered him still there, sitting in the same chair, except that this time, curiously, he was bent over at the waist, a handkerchief pressed to his forehead.

Concern seizing her, Eleanor leaned down to murmur in his ear, "Highness, are you feeling unwell?"

When he lifted his head, she could see that his olive complexion had paled, while the term "green around the gills" perfectly described his expression.

"I think . . . I might be sick . . . at any moment," he replied weakly before making a sound between a groan and a whimper.

"Come with me. . . ."

Quickly she took his elbow and made him stand. Then offering her shoulder to help support his weight and spare his injured knee, she led him over to the potted palms—and none too soon.

Releasing his grip on Eleanor, the prince lunged for

one of the large pots and used it as a basin to regurgitate the contents of his stomach.

As he endured the painful bout of retching, Eleanor spied a nearby footman and summoned him over to assist the ailing nobleman. While the sturdy servant was aiding the prince back to his chair, the dance ended and Signor Vecchi appeared.

"What is his trouble, Donna Eleanora?" he demanded when he saw his cousin's frail state.

"I don't know," she said worriedly, "but he just cast up his accounts. I think we should fetch a doctor."

To her surprise, the diplomat's face cleared as he studied the prince further. "I do not believe that will be necessary, since Prince Lazzara's illness is likely not serious. He has always had a weak stomach. Don Antonio, it is extremely unfortunate to end our evening so soon—I know you were anticipating this ball with eagerness. But we should take you home at once."

Prince Lazzara nodded as if grateful for the suggestion and wiped his mouth with the handkerchief.

At the diplomat's command, the footman enlisted another of his fellows and carefully helped the prince to his feet.

When the signor would have followed, Eleanor touched his arm to forestall him. "Signor Vecchi, I am growing concerned about his highness. He has suffered too many mishaps in recent days."

The Italian gentleman looked puzzled. "I suspect it is mere coincidence, Donna Eleanora. No doubt this illness was caused merely by something he ate. I will take him home so that he might rest and regain his strength. Pray give my apologies to your lovely aunt."

With an elegant bow, Signor Vecchi went after his cousin. Yet Eleanor was not satisfied with his casual dismissal of the threat to the prince. If someone was deliberately attempting to harm him, the culprit needed to be stopped immediately.

But first she needed to ascertain if there truly *was* a threat, as she was coming to believe.

Eleanor stood there frowning while she debated what to do, but then she recalled that Damon's physician friend, Mr. Geary, was present at the ball.

She found him a short while later conversing with several older ladies who were telling him of their physical complaints. Mr. Geary actually looked relieved when Eleanor requested a moment of his time.

When he stepped to one side with her, she explained what had occurred, finishing with her suspicions. "This last incident seems too much of a coincidence to me. Indeed, it seems rather sinister. Perhaps I am overreacting, but . . . is it possible someone tried to poison him?"

The physician's gaze sharpened at such a serious accusation. "Do you know if he ate or drank anything this evening, my lady?"

"He drank a cup of punch earlier. We both did."

"But you are feeling well?"

"Yes, perfectly well."

"When did his symptoms begin?"

"I am not certain," Eleanor replied, "but when I arrived tonight, Prince Lazzara was already flushed and perspiring and complaining of the heat."

Geary frowned. "There are a number of maladies and physics that may cause such symptoms. If he recovers fully, then we will know he was not poisoned."

"But what if he does not recover?" she asked in a troubled tone. "Is there nothing we may do now to investigate?"

"I do not see how . . . although if I were to examine the remains of what he ingested, I might be able to make a determination."

Eleanor's gaze arrested as a thought struck her. "Perhaps you can. Will you come with me, sir?"

She led the physician back to the corner of the ballroom where the prince had been seated. The punch cups were still resting on the floor beside his chair.

Picking them both up, Eleanor identified which one had belonged to the prince. When Geary peered into it, his frown deepened. "How odd. . . ."

Following his gaze, she could make out what had caught his attention: There were dregs of a powdered substance in the few remaining drops of liquid in the bottom.

Taking the cup from her, Geary first sniffed, then dipped his finger into the damp residue.

"This tastes very much like ipecac," he pronounced after a moment.

Eleanor looked at him in bewilderment, knowing ipecac was a powdered medication used to purge the stomach. "Are you certain?"

"Fairly so."

"So his cup was not poisoned?"

"I do not believe so, no. Ipecac is relatively harmless—or at least not life-threatening."

"But it could not have gotten there by accident."

"No, most certainly its introduction to his cup would have been deliberate."

Weakly, Eleanor sank down in one of the vacant

chairs. "But why in heaven's name would a medication have been added to Prince Lazzara's punch?"

"It is a puzzle," Mr. Geary agreed as he sat beside her. "Perhaps he is indeed the target of someone who wishes him ill, just as Wrexham suspected."

She glanced curiously at the physician. "Lord Wrexham mentioned the prince's mishaps to you, Mr. Geary?"

The physician nodded. "He said that his highness has been beset by several mysterious misadventures of late. Perhaps you should tell Wrexham of this latest one, Lady Eleanor."

Eleanor didn't reply at once. In the first place, she wanted nothing more to do with Damon tonight, or in the foreseeable future, for that matter. In the second, he had likely left the ball by now. And third, even if she had wanted to solicit his help, she doubted he would be interested in helping the nobleman whom he seemed to consider—quite mistakenly, to her mind—his rival.

"I suspect Lord Wrexham would not care to involve himself with the prince's misfortunes," she said finally.

"You might be surprised," Geary responded. "He has spent the last several years concerning himself with the misfortunes of others."

Her attention captured, Eleanor eyed him quizzically. "Misfortunes? What do you mean, Mr. Geary?"

"Well . . . perhaps the word 'misfortunes' is not quite accurate."

"Then what would be accurate?"

"Affliction would be a better term." When Eleanor's expression remained blank, Geary offered her a rueful smile of apology. "I mean the poor souls stricken by the scourge of consumption. Until now they have had little hope. But Wrexham has dedicated the last three years of his life to finding a cure, along with a significant portion of his fortune."

Chapter Ten

Predictability may bore him. Dare to be different, to stand out from every other lady competing for his attention and affections.

—An Anonymous Lady, *Advice . . .*

Eleanor's brow furrowed. "I never realized that Lord Wrexham had any interest in the field of medicine."

"You may have had no occasion to hear of his recent endeavors," Mr. Geary replied. "Especially since they took place in Italy."

"I thought he was taking a gentleman's tour of the Continent after the war's end."

"No, my lady. Pleasure most certainly was not his aim."

When the physician fell silent, Eleanor prodded him to explain. "Please continue, Mr. Geary. You have greatly piqued my curiosity."

He searched her face as if debating how much to say. "You were aware that Lord Wrexham's twin brother died of consumption when they were mere youths?"

"I knew he had a twin who died, but not the cause of his death."

"Well, Damon's brother Joshua contracted consumption when they were but sixteen."

"How very sad," Eleanor murmured.

"Indeed. What do you know of consumption, my lady?"

"It is a wasting illness of the lungs, is it not?"

"Yes, a disease that causes the slow death of lung tissue. Consumption is quite common in England and often fatal, but the cause is not known and no cure has been found as yet . . . although certain conditions improve the odds of surviving, including a warm, dry climate. That is why Damon chose the Mediterranean for his sanatorium."

"Sanatorium, Mr. Geary?"

"Yes, for the treatment of consumptives." At her inquisitive look, he smiled faintly. "I suppose I should explain how my relationship to Damon began. The thing is, my lady, I owe my entire career to him. I grew up in Harwich, near the Wrexham family seat in Suffolk. I was but a youth myself, two years older than Damon, but I had always shown a keen interest in the medical profession and was apprenticing with a local doctor when Joshua took ill. When it became clear there was no longer any hope for his recovery, I cared for Joshua on his deathbed."

"That must have been difficult for his family as well as yourself," Eleanor observed quietly and rather inadequately.

Geary nodded. "It was, my lady. To see such a handsome, vital boy wasting away while suffering great pain . . . And then as ill fortune would have it, Damon's parents—Viscount and Lady Wrexham—perished barely a few months later, when their ship sank during a storm while crossing the Irish Sea. They intended to pay a visit to some of her family there, but Damon refused to accompany them. Arguably, he is only alive due to the whims of Fate."

Eleanor felt her heart wrench at that disclosure. She could only imagine how agonizing it must have been for Damon to lose first his brother and then his parents so tragically. How devastated he must have felt. How starkly lonely. As an orphan, he would have had no one to grieve with, no one to share his anguish. . . .

The physician sighed in resignation before continuing. "In any event, after Damon inherited the title and fortune, in gratitude for my services to his brother, he provided the funds for me to attend university and to further my studies with the finest physicians in England. If not for him, I would likely be a country doctor instead of proprietor of my own hospital in London, which he also helped to finance."

Recalling what she had heard of Mr. Geary's remarkable achievements in the field of medicine, Eleanor perceived the significance of his admission: The world would have been deprived of a brilliant physician had not Damon intervened in his future.

"Naturally," Geary added, "you can see why I would go to any lengths for Damon. Thus, three years ago, when he came to me with the notion of advancing the quest for a remedy for consumption, I wrote to several renowned physicians on the Continent to enlist their aid. And with their patronage and involvement, Damon built an institution for the treatment of consumptives on the southern coast of Italy. It was an ambitious undertaking—their goals were to save as many lives as possible while attempting to discover a cure. And failing that, to relieve the suffering of the dying and to promote the swift recuperation of convalescents."

Eleanor gazed at Geary in surprise and not a little awe. "And did they succeed in their aims?" she asked.

"In many ways, yes. For the past year they have counted an impressive number of survivors. I myself sent more than a dozen of my patients there—at Damon's expense, I should say—and nine of them recovered fully."

She didn't doubt Damon's generosity in the least. She only wondered why he'd kept it hidden from her. During their betrothal he had never mentioned a single word to her about his desire to build a sanatorium, or about his late brother's death, either.

"It seems a disparity," Eleanor said finally, "that Damon has acted the philanthropist for so long, given his reputation as a rogue with a taste for wild living."

Geary smiled wryly. "It does strain the imagination, but I assure you, every word I told you is true." He hesitated for a moment. "I know that you and he have a past, Lady Eleanor, so I understand why you might be disinclined to think well of Damon, but I think perhaps you may have misjudged him—"

Geary's face suddenly turned ruddier with embarrassment. "Forgive me, that was impertinent to question your feelings for him. I should not have said such a thing. Truly, I meant no offense."

"I am not offended, Mr. Geary," Eleanor replied with rather automatic politeness since her mind was deep in reflections. "I think perhaps you are correct. I may have indeed misjudged him."

"Then you will not be averse to my telling him about this latest threat to Prince Lazzara?"

"No, I suppose there is no reason to keep this episode from him."

"Then I will inform him later, after the ball. Ah, there he is now. Perhaps you will wish to tell him yourself."

Eleanor was taken aback to see Damon moving toward them through the crowded ballroom.

After summoning a footman to dispose of both punch cups, Mr. Geary rose and bowed to her. "If you will excuse me, my lady, I will return to my gaggle of elderly ladies and resume my attempt to garner them as patrons of my hospital."

Nodding absently, Eleanor was only vaguely aware when the physician departed, since her entire attention was fixed on Damon as he approached. When eventually he reached her, she stared up at him in bemusement.

"Never tell me that I have surprised you, love," he remarked in a dry tone.

"You have indeed," she responded. "I presumed you had left the ball by now."

"I could not leave just yet. Geary accompanied me here in my carriage, and I must convey him home."

When Eleanor glanced down, she saw that Damon was wearing sturdy shoes of plain brown leather—a sore contrast to his elegant, expensive evening clothes.

"I purchased these from a Haviland footman," he explained about his new footwear. "They pinch a trifle, but beggars cannot be choosers." His expression was mild and amused rather than angry as she'd half expected.

"Don't you intend to upbraid me for the trick I played on you?" Eleanor asked.

"No." Damon settled beside her in the vacant chair. "In truth, I decided that you might have been justified in your reprisal. I should not have interfered in your attempts to romance your prince, much as I disliked seeing you kissing him."

His comment surprised Eleanor even more than the revelations about Damon's philanthropy, and she eyed him with suspicion. It was not like him to surrender so easily. But perhaps she didn't know him nearly as well as she had thought. . . .

"Mr. Geary told me how you occupied your time in Italy these past two years."

Damon seemed to go very still, as if all his muscles had tensed. "And what did he say?"

"That you have been championing the plight of consumptives because of how your brother died."

His dark eyes held an emotion that was impossible for her to read. Without answering, Damon shifted his gaze to look out over the crowded ballroom.

"Why did you never tell me?" Eleanor prompted when he was silent.

He shrugged. "What was there to tell?"

She studied his profile measuringly. "I might have concluded you were not the care-for-nothing rogue you led me to believe."

Damon's expression remained impassive, as if a mask had suddenly dropped over his face. And his drawl, when it came, sounded somewhat cool. "Does it matter what you think of me since we are no longer betrothed and you turned down my recent offer of matrimony?"

"I suppose not. But your compassion is extremely admirable."

His mouth twisted. "My efforts had little to do with compassion. I was acting out of anger."

"Why anger?"

"Better that than wallowing in maudlin sorrow. Building a sanatorium was my way of trying to control fate in some small measure."

"You could not save your brother so you became determined to save others."

"You might say that."

Eleanor fell silent, wondering if Damon had truly come to terms with his sorrow. She very much doubted it. She bit her lower lip, envisioning the grief he must have felt, the sheer desolation of losing his brother, then his parents. He would have been alone in the world. At least she'd had her brother Marcus to love and comfort her and ease her loneliness over the years.

"I am sorry I stole your shoes," she said softly. "I hid them in the music room, behind the curtains of the first window seat, if you want to retrieve them."

Apparently Damon saw through her attempt to apologize, for a hard note entered his voice when he replied. "I don't want your pity, Elle."

"It is not *pity*. It is sympathy. I can only imagine my grief were I to lose Marcus."

Damon's face remained closed, shuttered, yet for a fleeting moment, she could feel his vulnerability.

"It is hard without Joshua, isn't it?"

An old, savage pain flickered over his features but was gone just as quickly. Then Damon shot her a piercing glance. "You seem to have forgotten where we are, sweeting," he pointed out curtly. "My brother's wretched fate is inappropriate conversation for a ball." He rose just as abruptly. "You should be dancing with your prince."

This time it was Damon who walked away. Eleanor stared after him, yearning to follow and offer him comfort. She regretted that she had struck such a raw nerve in Damon. Obviously his brother's death was not something he liked to dwell on, but she had unwittingly laid his painful memories bare.

Regretting their conversation also, Damon found himself wishing that he had better deflected Eleanor's probing questions and unwanted observations. For the remainder of the evening, his chest felt tight, a circumstance that reminded him why he'd contrived to end his betrothal to her in the first place: Eleanor made him feel too much.

At least his attention was diverted for a time during the carriage ride home as Otto told him about finding traces of a stomach purge in Prince Lazzara's punch cup. But learning that his suspicions about the danger were correct couldn't curb the restless agitation Damon still felt when he arrived home.

Therefore, instead of repairing to his bedchamber to sleep, he went to his study, where he poured himself a very large brandy and sat drinking in the dark. An indulgence, Damon reflected, that was much like his ritual observance each year on the anniversary of his brother's death, which would occur next week. He was merely getting an early start.

When he could feel himself sinking into a stupor, Damon stretched out on the sofa and closed his eyes.

Sometime later he was dredged up out of an abyss of pain and darkness by a persistent voice urging him to awaken.

With a jerking shudder, Damon suddenly became aware of his surroundings. His valet was bent over him in the dim glow of candlelight, gently shaking his shoulders while he fought off the miasma of his bad dreams. Through his drugged senses, Damon could feel his heart pounding, while a sheen of sweat slicked his body.

"You were shouting, my lord," Cornby said quietly. "It appears you suffered the nightmare again."

Yes, of course. That was his trouble.

Sitting up slowly, Damon ran a hand roughly down his face. "Did I wake the entire household?"

"No, my lord. I had not yet retired, so I came here directly when I heard you."

"You should know better than to wait up for me, Cornby."

"It is no matter, sir."

Damon was in no mood to continue their ongoing argument about the valet's outsized sense of duty and protectiveness. "Thank you, then. You may go."

When the valet hesitated, Damon insisted gruffly, "I am all right, truly."

He was not all right, however, he reflected when his elderly servant had left him in peace, for he couldn't shake the savage tumult of his emotions.

He hadn't had the nightmare about his brother's death for a long while, although it had haunted him for years afterward.

Joshua lying there on his deathbed, struggling for

breath, the scattering of bloodstained handkerchiefs a macabre contrast to his ghostly pallor.

Joshua coughing harshly and grimacing in agony, then smiling with cracked lips, trying to offer reassurance to his family as they kept vigil during his last hours.

Their parents sat beside his bed, striving to keep up a brave front. Damon stood back, however, fighting tears of grief and rage.

Then Joshua slipped back into a drugged slumber, never to awaken. When finally his breath ceased and his ravaged body grew still, Damon's sobs had matched their mother's.

He felt as if he too had died that day, although his pain didn't dissipate readily, nor did his deep streak of anger. In the ensuing years, he had taunted death often, rebelling against fate, railing against life's injustice and the guilt assaulting him.

Why had *he* survived? Why had *he* not been the one stricken? Why had *he* inherited the title and fortune when he was no more deserving than his twin?

It wasn't even certain how Joshua had contracted consumption, except that he'd shown an amorous interest in a barmaid at a local tavern, who later was discovered to have the pernicious disease. But Joshua was the firstborn, the eldest by an hour. He should have been the one to live a full, joyful life.

Damon had never found the answers to his unanswerable questions. He'd merely learned to crush his emotions while relegating his memories of his brother's demise to his nightmares.

It was many years, however, before he'd begun channeling his anger toward a more productive course, using science and the latest innovations in medical thinking to make a difference in the lives of those stricken with consumption.

Eleanor was right, Damon acknowledged. He couldn't save his brother, but he'd come to hope that he could save others.

Yet even years later, it was little consolation for being the twin who had survived.

Lady Beldon was highly disappointed to learn that Signor Vecchi had left the ball early with Prince Lazzara and without even taking leave of her. She was also quite concerned that the prince had become ill, since it would hamper his courtship of her niece.

"Did they mention the alfresco picnic tomorrow at the Royal Gardens?" Beatrix asked Eleanor as they stood waiting for their carriage to reach the head of the long queue of equipages in front of the Haviland mansion.

"The prince may not be feeling well enough to attend a picnic, Aunt," Eleanor replied, deciding not to share the particular details about what had ailed him tonight. The probability that someone was threatening his health if not his life would only upset her aunt to no purpose.

"Of all the ill luck," the elder lady complained. "I believe our servants should arrange the picnic tomorrow. We can be certain to provide dishes that will tempt his highness's appetite, which he will appreciate if he still suffers from a sickly stomach. I shall write to Signor Vecchi first thing in the morning to propose my change in plan."

"You are very generous, Aunt," Eleanor murmured, thinking that it might indeed be wise to supply tomorrow's repast from their own kitchens. That way they could ensure the dishes and wine would be untainted.

Beatrix smiled. "Generosity has little to do with my motives, my dear. I am determined we should take every opportunity to encourage Prince Lazzara's attentions. He would make such a splendid match for you."

Eleanor refrained from replying, not certain that she agreed with her aunt's view any longer. In fact, she was seriously beginning to doubt that the prince would make her a good match at all.

The question continued to plague Eleanor after arriving home as she tried futilely to fall asleep, and later still as she tossed and turned in her bed much of the night.

When finally she dozed off, once again Damon featured prominently in her dreams, yet this time his bewitching lovemaking played no role, nor did memories of their courtship. Instead, she found herself struggling to reach him beyond a high stone wall overgrown with thick brambles. Damon had imprisoned himself inside, and she needed to scale the treacherous barrier in order to free him. . . .

The strange dream remained with Eleanor when she woke in the gray light of dawn. Feeling an inexplicable sadness, she lay in bed for a long while, contemplating the meaning.

Intuitively she had always sensed the emotional wall Damon had erected around himself. Perhaps now she knew why. The tragic loss of his family would explain his determined remoteness.

In the early days of their courtship, she had broken through that wall for fleeting moments at a time, Eleanor was certain of it. But during their betrothal Damon had become more and more distant, as if he were withdrawing from her. She'd been ready to give herself to him completely, heart and soul, but he had deliberately pulled back as she tried to grow closer.

And then their engagement had abruptly ended. No doubt Damon was vastly relieved that he no longer risked any possibility of her reaching him.

A sad smile touched Eleanor's lips when she recalled his claim last evening, that by building his sanatorium he had tried to control fate. She had undertaken a similar goal concerning her own matrimonial future, vowing to rule her destiny. They were very much alike in that respect. Yet there was one enormous difference. Damon did not want to find love as she did.

Her greatest fear had always been living a barren, lonely life without love, so she had been determined to fall in love with a man who loved her in return.

She'd hoped that Prince Lazzara would ideally fit her needs. And last week, when her former betrothed unexpectedly reentered her life, she'd escalated her efforts to attract his highness. Yet her burst of defiance, Eleanor could now admit, was driven more by hurt and wounded pride and anger against Damon. She would be cutting off her own nose to spite her face, as the saying went, if she continued her pursuit of Prince Lazzara.

More critically, the simple truth was, she could not possibly love him or any other man as long as she had unfinished business with Damon.

She didn't like to think of how vulnerable her new wisdom made her to Damon, yet that was not her most pressing problem at the moment.

She would have to end the prince's courtship, of course. It would be cruel to persist and thereby raise his expectations any further when she had no intention of fulfilling them. But she would gradually ease away so as not to wound *his* pride. . . .

Throwing off the covers, Eleanor rose and rang for her maid so she could bathe and dress and begin mentally preparing herself for their excursion to the Royal Botanic Gardens at Kew, if it was still on.

The question of what to do about Damon remained completely unsettled, but at least now she knew her mind regarding her noble Italian suitor.

Unfortunately, Eleanor had little time for private conversation with the prince that afternoon, since two of Signor Vecchi's fellow dignitaries and their wives joined their small party for the alfresco luncheon on the grounds of Kew Gardens.

Because Prince Lazzara could not walk easily, his servants spread quilts on a grassy stretch of lawn near the River Thames, in the shade of a large willow tree. The younger ladies willingly kept his highness company, while Signor Vecchi and his colleagues escorted Lady Beldon on a tour of the Botanic Gardens to view the exotic flora brought back by various scientific expeditions around the world.

Without privacy, Eleanor had no chance to discuss the events of last evening with Prince Lazzara, or to tell him her suspicions about the cause of his illness. His appetite had returned, however, judging by his apparent enjoyment of the delicacies provided by the Beldon chef. The repast was almost a feast, served formally on china and crystal and silver.

Nonetheless, his highness seemed eager to get her alone at the conclusion of the picnic. Standing with the aid of his cane, he offered Eleanor his arm so they could better view the swans swimming on the Thames.

As they slowly strolled the short distance to the river along a footpath flanked by willows and alders, she grew more confident in her decision to terminate their courtship. Prince Lazzara was not the right husband for her. She would never come to love him, no matter how valiantly she tried. One couldn't tell a heart what to feel or whom to love. And it was foolish to believe otherwise.

She would never be happy with so tame a gentleman, either, Eleanor decided as they reached the stone embankment overlooking the Thames. For all his attractive personal attributes and illustrious worldly advantages, Prince Lazzara was not only rather ordinary, he could not fire her blood the way a single look from Damon could.

"You are very quiet, Donna Eleanora," the prince observed as she stood watching the magnificent birds make lazy circles on the water's rippling surface.

Eleanor dragged herself from her contemplations to give him a faint smile. "To be truthful, your highness I was trying to determine the best way to broach a certain subject without sounding overly dramatic. You see, I am rather worried for your safety."

"Indeed?" Lazzara responded curiously. "And why is that?"

"Do you recall meeting the renowned physician, Mr. Geary, last evening?"

"Yes, I do. He is an intriguing gentleman."

"Well, after you became ill and left the ball, he discovered something very unusual about the punch you had been drinking."

Before she could say any more, however, Eleanor heard an odd whistling sound, followed by a soft thwack. Prince Lazzara gave a faint exclamation of pain before raising his hand and slapping the back of his neck behind his left ear.

Eleanor's first thought was that he had been stung by a bee, yet beneath his probing fingers, she could see a small brown object embedded in the skin above his high shirt collar.

At that same moment she heard a distracting rustle in the copse of willows behind them, but her attention was focused on whatever had struck the prince.

When he jerked it out and examined it, she realized the brown object appeared to be a feathered dart about one inch long, with a pointed metal tip that was needle-thin and sharp.

"*Che diavolo,*" the prince breathed in puzzled astonishment, which she took to mean the Italian equivalent of "What the devil?"

Then to Eleanor's startlement, Lazzara's eyelids drifted shut and his knees slumped. The dart slipping from his limp fingers, he slowly pitched forward into the river four feet below to land with a great splash.

Eleanor gave her own cry of dismay, yet she was held immobile by shock for an instant; to her horror, the prince had plunged headfirst into the water!

When he bobbed up again, he began struggling

lethargically to keep his head above the surface. Apparently he was not entirely unconscious, yet not only was he in danger of drowning, he was quickly floating downstream.

Regaining her senses, Eleanor shouted for help to the servants behind her, then threw herself feet first off the embankment after the prince. The impact as the cold water closed over her head was powerful enough to take her breath away, and her long skirts dragged her down. But once she fought her way to the surface, she desperately struck out after his highness using the currents to aid her pursuit.

It seemed to Eleanor like an eternity before she reached him. He was still flailing weakly, however, and when she tried to catch the sleeve of his frock coat, he fought against her with an urgency that resembled panic.

"For the love of God, your highness, *be still*!" Eleanor demanded. "I am trying to save you!"

Fortunately for them both, he didn't have the strength to continue resisting. When he surrendered, she rolled him onto his back and grasped his coat collar. Then with all her might, she towed him toward the stone embankment.

When they finally reached it, Eleanor was grateful to find a gnarled mass of willow roots they could cling to while waiting for help to arrive. The prince slumped there coughing and spitting up river water as she strove to catch her breath.

They had landed a dozen yards downstream from where he'd fallen in, but her shout had alerted the others in their party, and they all came running, guests and servants alike.

However, since apparently none of the footmen knew how to swim, it was some time before they were rescued with the aid of a leather rein purloined from a carriage. Eleanor insisted that the prince be hauled up first and so looped the rein under his armpits. When he had been dragged to safety, she followed to find him sprawled limply on his side.

Eleanor sank down beside him, wondering fearfully if he would survive—if he had been poisoned by the dart or merely drugged. But at least he was still breathing. And after a moment he shook his wet head and blinked up at her, as if trying to regain his bearings.

"What . . . happened?" he rasped in a hoarse voice.

"You fainted and fell into the river, your highness," Eleanor answered.

"I don't remember. . . . Ah, yes . . . you pulled me to shore. . . ."

He pushed himself up onto his elbow, still looking dazed and sluggish. But he seemed to be recovering. Perhaps the cold dousing had actually helped to clear his mind.

Just then she saw her aunt hurrying toward them, along with the signor.

"Good God, whatever happened?" Beatrix exclaimed in alarm upon seeing Eleanor's sopping wet gown and bedraggled bonnet.

When Eleanor repeated her explanation, Signor Vecchi grew visibly angry, but evidently not at her.

"We are grateful, Donna Eleanora," the diplomat said with a bow. "Your quick thinking very likely saved Don Antonio from drowning."

"It was no matter, signor, but I hope you will believe me now when I say that someone wishes him harm."

A worried frown darkened the prince's brow. "What do you mean, *mia signorina?*"

Eleanor would have reminded him about the dart that had struck his neck, but his elder cousin intervened. "Your highness, you have suffered a severe shock. We should take you home at once."

"Signor Vecchi," she protested, "it might be unwise to move Prince Lazzara just yet, since he still appears to be disoriented. And I think we should summon Mr. Geary to examine him and make certain he has suffered no ill effects—"

"He looks well enough to me, considering," the diplomat observed impatiently. "And he is likely to catch an ague if he remains here in his sodden clothing. Forgive me, Donna Eleanora, but I feel I must act to preserve his health. Come, your highness."

Apparently accustomed to obliging his countryman, the prince stood with the help of a footman and swayed dizzily before regaining his balance.

"This is becoming extremely vexing," he muttered, allowing himself to be led away.

Her Aunt Beatrix was of a similar mind as Signor Vecchi. "Eleanor, we must get you home and out of your wet clothing. And of course you must have a hot bath to warm you and"—she wrinkled her nose in distaste—"to remove that foul odor of the river."

Suddenly realizing that she was shivering in the September breeze, Eleanor decided not to protest further and accepted the quilt offered by one of the footmen. But she was not ready to leave just yet.

"Give me one moment, please, Aunt." She at least wanted Geary to examine the dart, if she could find it.

Wrapping the quilt around her shoulders, Eleanor quickly moved along the path to the spot beneath the willows where the prince had stood just before the accident. Searching the ground, she found the small dart half covered by leaves. It was clear proof that she hadn't imagined seeing him shot.

Upon returning to her aunt, she tucked the dart into her reticule, then allowed Beatrix to usher her into the Beldon carriage and whisk her home while the servants remained behind to clear the remnants of the picnic. But during the journey, Eleanor debated silently with herself about the best course to take regarding the prince's latest misadventure.

She wasn't certain where Mr. Geary lived, or if he would be working at his hospital, but she knew Damon could tell her. And although there was no love lost between the English and Italian noblemen, she trusted Damon to act honorably if the prince was in real danger.

Therefore, as soon as she reached the privacy of her own bedchamber and shed her wet gown in favor of a warm velvet wrapper, Eleanor wrote to Damon while waiting for her bathwater to be heated, asking him to call on her as soon as possible, and requested the Beldon butler to have her missive delivered without delay.

When the copper tub was filled, Eleanor washed her hair and scrubbed off all traces of the river. Then she sent her maid, Jenny, away and enjoyed a long soak.

She was drying her hair before the fire in her bedchamber when Jenny returned with word that Lord Wrexham was awaiting her in the blue salon.

Eleanor quickly dressed in a kerseymere afternoon gown. Then taking the dart with her, she went downstairs to the salon to find Damon standing at the window, frowning pensively. His eyebrows lifted, however, when she carefully shut the door behind her so they could be private.

"I am sorry to have kept you waiting," she began, but he brushed off her apology.

"Geary told me about the prince's punch being drugged last evening, and now you say that he has suffered another misfortune?"

"Yes, only this time I am certain it was no accident."

Crossing to Damon, she told him about the excursion to Kew Gardens and showed him the dart, recounting how it had struck the prince and likely caused him to faint and fall in the river, which resulted in her having to rescue him.

Eleanor was not surprised to see a scowl darken Damon's face at her account. What did surprise her, however, was that he barely glanced at the dart she held in her palm.

"What the devil do you mean," he demanded even before she concluded, "jumping in the Thames? Do you have any idea what treacherous undercurrents lurk in that river?"

Eleanor was taken aback by Damon's vehemence. "There was no help for it. I could not just let the prince drown."

"You could have drowned yourself!"

She felt her spine stiffen defensively. Yet not wishing to argue with him, she took a calming breath. "I did not ask you here so you could scold me, Damon. Rather, I hoped you would solicit Mr. Geary's opinion about this." She held out the dart for him to look at more closely.

Damon's ire seemed to cool a measure as he took it from her and examined it. "This could be a curare arrow. . . ." he said after a moment.

"What is that?" Eleanor asked.

"A hunting weapon used by certain Indian tribes in the southern Americas. The arrow's tip is coated with poison, then blown from a hollow stalk of bamboo."

Her eyes widened. "How in heaven's name do you know about poison arrows from the Americas?"

Damon smiled faintly. "I am interested in medical science. Sir Walter Raleigh described curare in his book on Guiana. And Sir Benjamin Brody experimented with the effect of curare on animals here in England several years ago."

"Is the poison fatal?"

"It can be. Chiefly, it paralyzes its target and prevents the ability to breathe. But Sir Benjamin proved that if the victim can be kept breathing by artificial means, it will recover and show no ill effects later."

Eleanor frowned as she tried to recall exactly how the prince had behaved after being struck. "This arrow caused him to faint," she said slowly, "but he seemed to be recovering."

"Perhaps curare was not used, or if so, the dose was so small, the result would not have been fatal."

"Do you think Mr. Geary can determine if the tip contains poison?"

"He could possibly analyze the chemical composition, although that's unlikely to garner any conclusive results."

"If poison *was* used, it means someone is trying to kill Prince Lazzara."

Damon's pensiveness returned. "Or Lazzara wants us to think so. Before this, I wondered if he might be causing these accidents himself."

Eleanor stared at him. "Whyever would he do such a thing?"

"To garner your sympathy. Perhaps he thinks you will find him more appealing if you must constantly fret over him."

"He wants me to think him a weakling?" If so, it was an absurd theory, Eleanor decided. She liked strong, capable men, not frail, impotent ones.

"Or perhaps," Damon added, "someone else merely wants to make the prince look weak in your eyes."

"That explanation seems more plausible to me," she said thoughtfully as she glanced down at the arrow in his hand. "And for the prince's sake, we must assume he is an innocent victim. In fact, I think he must be warned. I had no time to discuss my suspicions with him, either last evening or today. And Signor Vecchi was clearly not interested in hearing them."

She returned her gaze to Damon. "Will you help me, Damon? We must stop these attacks and determine who is behind them. The next time could end his life."

"Certainly I will help. It may be time to hire Bow Street to investigate and perhaps provide the prince personal protection."

The Bow Street Runners, Eleanor knew, were a private police force. "I think hiring them would be wise. Will you contact them, or shall I?"

"I will deal with it. Meanwhile you are to keep away from Lazzara."

His pronouncement gave her pause. "Keep away?"

"Yes, sweeting. I don't want you anywhere near him."

When Eleanor started to protest, Damon held up a hand, saying almost grimly, "Don't argue with me about this, Elle. I am not about to let you be hurt."

It made sense that Damon would want to protect her after losing his brother the way he had, yet his concern gave her a warm feeling. Even so, she was not pleased to have him dictating to her.

"I cannot keep away entirely. I am supposed to attend a balloon ascension with the prince tomorrow. One of his countrymen is an aeronaut and has promised to let us ride in his gas balloon. Even leaving aside the fact that I was greatly looking forward to the adventure, it would be rude to cancel at this late moment, since the prince went to so much trouble to arrange the treat for me."

Damon relented, although with evident reluctance. "Very well, you may go, but I intend to be there to keep an eye on you."

"You were not invited, Damon," Eleanor pointed out in exasperation.

"That hardly matters. You are not attending without me."

Instead of replying, she merely smiled pleasantly. "Thank you for coming so quickly, Lord Wrexham, but now I believe you have business with Bow

Street?" Moving to the salon door, she opened it and stepped aside, as if encouraging his departure.

Damon crossed his arms over his chest, however, and remained exactly where he stood.

"The ascension may be canceled in any case," Eleanor said finally. "After what happened today, the prince may not feel well enough to ride in a balloon."

Damon's jaw hardened. "That is not good enough, Elle. I want your promise that you will keep away from Lazzara unless I am present."

She pressed her lips together, remaining stubbornly silent. She had already decided to end the prince's courtship. In fact, the outing tomorrow would be the last invitation she accepted from him. But Damon was a trifle too highhanded for her to bare her soul to him about her plans for her romance.

Still, she knew he wouldn't leave until she conceded. "Oh, very well, I promise."

His grim expression relaxed a degree. "And you must swear that you will stop being such a damned heroine. Rescuing Lazzara could have been the death of you."

"You would have done the same in my place."

"That is different."

Eleanor rolled her eyes. "Pray don't tell me it is because you are a man."

"It is, in part. I am physically stronger than you. You would have been no match for Lazzara had he tried to drag you under the water."

His explanation mollified her a little. "I was not in much danger. Marcus taught me to swim when I was a girl, and I do it quite well."

Damon's mouth curved wryly. "I cannot say I am

surprised. You ride and shoot and fence with the best of them. And last evening you added thievery to your list of masculine accomplishments."

Eleanor couldn't help but laugh. "But you agreed that you deserved my retribution."

"I did." He crossed the salon and stood gazing down at her. "Don't mistake me, Eleanor. What you did was remarkable—and incredibly admirable. Perhaps one woman in a million would have had the presence of mind, not to mention the courage, to act as you did. You risked your life to save his. But I don't want any harm to come to you."

His dark gaze intent, Damon raised a finger to touch her cheek. It was a gentle caress, yet strangely tentative, almost as if he wanted to reassure himself that she was still there, alive and well.

Then his voice lowered to a rough whisper that was nearly inaudible. "I couldn't endure it if you came to harm."

Without another word, Damon turned and left the salon, leaving Eleanor bereft of words herself.

It was a long, long while before she could summon her vaunted presence of mind in order to follow.

Chapter Eleven

To Eleanor's gratification, the balloon ascension was not canceled. Yet even knowing of Damon's concern for her, she was surprised when he arrived in the Lazzara barouche the next morning to collect her and her aunt at Portman Place. As they were being assisted into the carriage, Eleanor sent Damon a quizzical glance, but he only returned an enigmatic smile.

Prince Lazzara did not look any worse for wear after his traumatic experience the previous afternoon, she noted with relief. Indeed, he appeared to have recovered fully, although he seemed a trifle embarrassed when he greeted her. He also seemed less effusive than normal as the barouche got underway, although Signor Vecchi was as charming and diplomatic as always when he again expressed gratitude for Eleanor's valiant action in rescuing his cousin yesterday.

The prince, however, recouped his spirits enough to display uncommon zeal as he explained to the ladies something of the history of ballooning.

"Various Frenchmen began experimenting with flying hot air balloons more than three decades ago,"

Lazzara asserted, "and soon succeeded in crossing the English Channel. But after several fatal flights where the paper-lined silk fabric of the balloons caught fire, aeronauts began using hydrogen gas developed by English scientist Henry Cavendish, since gas-filled balloons are safer and can travel further."

"The balloon today will be filled with gas?" Lady Beldon asked rather worriedly.

"But of course," the prince replied. "My country-man, Signor Pucinelli, is an eminent member of Italy's scientific establishment and an avid aeronaut. He has endeavored to bring the delights of his passion to the public, and is currently visiting England at the invitation of your Prince Regent."

Today's ascension, Lazzara added, would take place in an open meadow north of London, early in the day when the winds would likely be the weakest. Fortunately the weather boded to be fair. Bright sunshine warmed the cool morning air, while a scattering of puffy white clouds filled the blue sky above.

Eleanor felt an eager sense of anticipation as they drew closer. Even Beatrix, who had risen long before her usual hour for the occasion, seemed enthusiastic, since the outing afforded her more time in Signor Vecchi's company.

After a while, however, Eleanor couldn't help noticing that there were two rough-looking men trailing them on horseback. And when the barouche eventually turned off the main road onto a country lane, the riders followed.

"They are Bow Street Runners," Damon murmured to her in a low voice. "I hired them to protect the prince."

"Does he know?" Eleanor asked.

"Yes, I had a long discussion with him last evening."

She wanted to question Damon about his conversation with the prince, but there was no chance, since just then they reached their intended destination.

As the carriage turned into a large meadow and came to a halt, she could see the balloon in the near distance. The giant, gray-and-red-striped globe, which rose almost seventy feet into the air, bobbed gently in the morning sunlight.

The balloon was covered by a net of rope webbing and attached to a wickerwork basket below, which in turn was tethered to the ground by sturdy ropes. The basket was large, perhaps ten feet wide by fifteen feet long, and shaped somewhat like Eleanor's copper bathing tub at home.

A crowd had already gathered for the spectacle, and as Prince Lazzara led his party a short way across the meadow, Eleanor heard a dark-haired gentleman shouting orders in Italian to a crew of workmen who were hard at work amid a plethora of casks and bottles and metal tubes.

Upon spying the prince, the gentleman broke away and came to greet them. When the introductions were performed, Signor Pucinelli acknowledged Damon with a beaming smile and said a few words in Italian, which Eleanor interpreted to mean something on the order of, "Lord Wrexham, how good to see you again."

Apparently, the two men were acquainted, she realized, although that shouldn't surprise her, given that Damon had spent the past two years in Italy.

After another moment of conversing, the scientist

returned his attention to the entire party and proudly explained in broken English the principles of creating hydrogen fuel, mixing iron shavings and oil of vitriol—sulfuric acid, to be precise—and the complex contraption he had designed to inflate the silken orb with gas, chiefly a tin hose connected to the mouth of the balloon.

"We are nearly finished with the inflation," the balloonist said. "We can accommodate two passengers as well as myself."

"But you will not actually take flight beyond the meadow?" Damon asked, his tone serious.

"No, no, my lord," Pucinelli assured him. "My workers will keep hold of the gondola at all times, by means of long ropes. They will guide us around the field and then aid our descent as well. I expect to stay aloft for ten, perhaps twenty minutes. It is all quite safe."

"It is much like," the prince added, contributing his viewpoint, "towing a barge along the Thames, or piloting a gondola laden with goods along the canals in Venice. Except in this case, the men on the ground will prevent the balloon from flying away, thereby insuring a safe, open landing area." He turned to the aeronaut. "Donna Eleanora is eager to experience the joys of flight, signor."

Pucinelli beamed at her. "It is good to see such an intrepid young lady. If you will come this way . . ."

When he gestured toward the balloon, Eleanor moved closer, accompanied by Prince Lazzara and Damon, while her aunt and Signor Vecchi remained there to watch from a distance.

"Have you ridden in a balloon before?" she asked Damon curiously.

"Yes, with Pucinelli in fact, when I was last in Rome," he answered.

They stood for another short period while Pucinelli supervised his crew, who were busily unhooking hoses and closing flaps at the mouth of the balloon, then safely storing the casks and fueling machinery.

When the aeronaut eventually signaled they could board, Damon guided Eleanor forward to the wooden access steps. "Allow me, my lady," he murmured in warning.

Swinging her up into his arms, Damon mounted the four steps, then lifted her over the edge of the chest-high basket and set her on her feet inside. Then, to her puzzlement, he hoisted himself aboard.

"I thought Prince Lazzara was to be the other passenger," Eleanor said as his highness moved away to join their party.

"Not for this journey," Damon replied in a mild tone.

She recognized the glint he always got in his eyes when he was about to do something outrageous, and her own gaze darkened with suspicion. "Just what are you about, Damon?"

"I convinced Lazzara to stay behind."

"You convinced him. . . . ?"

"I told you, I have no intention of letting you go anywhere with him unless I accompany you. If someone wishes him harm, a balloon ascension could provide an ideal opportunity to target him."

A sudden breeze made the balloon tug at its moorings, which caused the basket to sway. Jostled, Eleanor clutched at the rim as she pressed her lips together in exasperation. Damon was obviously worried for her safety, but she wasn't certain his excuse could be fully trusted.

"Is that your only reason for taking the prince's place just now?" she asked. "Or are you still intent on spoiling our courtship?"

Damon's mouth quirked. "I confess that played a role in my rationale. I don't intend to let you wed him, Elle."

Miffed by his nonchalance, Eleanor eyed Damon reproachfully. "If Prince Lazzara is not coming, then you needn't be concerned for my safety, which means you needn't come either. In truth, I would rather go with Signor Pucinelli by myself."

Damon cocked his head. "The decision is not open for argument, sweeting. If you don't want my presence, then we will both remain here safely on the ground. I can lift you out as easily as I lifted you in."

She hesitated, aware that Damon could be even more stubborn than she. "That won't be necessary," she finally muttered. "I don't want to miss the chance to take a balloon flight."

"I suspected as much," Damon said wryly.

The basket rocked again, nearly making Eleanor lose her balance. Clinging to the rim, she decided that a gust of wind must have buffeted the balloon, causing it to rise a short distance. And yet the ground continued to fall away below them.

Then she heard Damon's low curse, followed shortly by Signor Pucinelli's startled shout from below. It took Eleanor a moment to realize what had happened: The basket had somehow been liberated from its tether and no one was holding the guide ropes. She and Damon were lifting off, just the two of them, with no one to pilot the balloon.

Pucinelli came running toward the rising gondola along with his crew, but they were too late. Although one man made a mad lunge for a dangling rope and managed to grasp it for an instant, after being dragged along the ground a dozen yards, he lost his purchase. When the rope was ripped from his hands, the balloon shot upward, sailing off into the blue.

From below, Eleanor heard shouts of surprise and horror, including what she thought was her aunt's frantic voice. Her own startlement at their abrupt ascent, however, was tempered by a sudden suspicion. "What is this, Damon, an abduction?"

His scowl dismissed her question as nonsense as he surveyed the scene below. "Why the devil would I risk your safety by arranging an abduction? I had nothing to do with this, Eleanor. My guess is that someone unfastened the moorings."

When he emitted another oath, Eleanor glanced down and became even more aware of the danger. They were at least a hundred feet above the earth by now, imprisoned in a weaving basket held aloft by a manufactured swath of fabric that would soon lose its buoyancy. Far below, the spectators looked like a milling colony of ants, while the meadow where they had launched was fast disappearing.

Eleanor suddenly felt light-headed, while her stomach lurched. When her knees were struck by a similar weakness, she sank down to the floor of the basket and leaned her forehead against her updrawn legs.

"You aren't turning vaporish on me, are you?"

Damon said bracingly as he went down on one knee beside her.

"Actually, I am," she mumbled.

"Well, buck up, Elle. You need to help me determine how to get out of this predicament."

She didn't have the strength to respond to his needling, yet it helped that the craft seemed to steady. When her stomach settled and her dizziness faded, Eleanor accepted Damon's aid and risked standing up again.

When she gingerly peered over the side of the basket, she could see the vast city of London behind them, with the River Thames meandering toward the sea like a winding ribbon. Ahead of them was a panorama of English countryside—a patchwork quilt of forests and fields and farmland stretching to the distant horizon.

"My heaven," she breathed in an almost reverent voice. "What a magnificent sight."

"Yes," Damon agreed.

Eleanor let out her breath slowly. The sensation of flying was not what she had expected. "It is so quiet," she observed. "It feels as if we are hanging perfectly still."

"We aren't. The air currents are carrying us north. We just cannot feel them since the balloon is keeping pace."

Relaxing her death grip a little, Eleanor took another slow breath. "Very well, what do you wish me to do?"

"Help me look for a place to set down."

"Can you land the balloon?"

"I think I can operate the vent valve. . . ." Looking

up, Damon reached overhead for one of two ropes that resembled bellpulls. "See these cords? They are attached to a flap at the top of the balloon so gas can escape. I'll open the flap to let air out, so we will gradually lose altitude. The danger is coming down too quickly, but that is what those sandbags are for. They serve as ballast." He pointed to the four corners of the basket, and for the first time, Eleanor noticed the small burlap bags piled there.

"How do you know so much about so many things?" she asked with a touch of wonder.

"I read a great deal. And as you know, this is not my first balloon flight."

"Still, I am exceedingly impressed with your wealth of knowledge."

Damon's mouth curved. "Save your praise until we are safely on the ground. I doubt the landing will be soft."

He didn't have to spell out the dangers any further to her. If he released too much gas, they could plummet to earth. And even if they managed to regulate the speed of their descent, they could still crash into a forest or some other obstacle such as a farmhouse.

His gaze searching the earth below, Damon tugged on one of the valve cords. Except for a slight whistling sound above them, his action initially seemed to result in no response. But then Eleanor realized that at least the balloon was no longer rising.

Damon pulled on the cord a fraction more. "If we begin to descend too rapidly, I want you to throw out a sandbag when I tell you to."

Nodding, Eleanor shifted her position by several feet so she could easily reach the ballast if necessary.

A long silence followed while Damon tried to gauge what effect the venting was having on their altitude. It seemed as if they were drifting lazily, Eleanor thought, but in reality, they were being carried along on a steady breeze. Still, the flight felt serene and peaceful, almost calming in fact—except that shortly Eleanor began to wonder how they had ended up in this quandary in the first place.

"Why would someone sabotage the launching?" she asked Damon after a moment. "The prince is not even here."

"An excellent question," he responded almost grimly. "I cannot imagine why, unless the saboteur thought I was Lazzara. I didn't see the perpetrator, but I would guess he was one of Pucinelli's crew. An outsider would have looked out of place and likely been spotted."

Eleanor winced inwardly at the thought of being trapped up here with the prince. With his extensive knowledge of ballooning, perhaps his highness would have proved to be as resourceful as Damon evidently was, but she felt far safer with Damon.

When she shivered, however, she realized she'd grown a little chilled, even though she wore a pelisse over her walking dress of jaconet muslin.

"Had I known we would be airborne for so long," she commented in a wry tone, "I would have worn a warmer pelisse."

Damon gestured with his head toward the floor. "There is a blanket for passengers in the corner behind you. Wrap it around your shoulders."

"No, I don't want to be encumbered if I must wrestle with sandbags."

Across the width of the basket, his gaze found hers. "Pucinelli was right. You are quite an intrepid young lady. Many women would have swooned or had an apoplectic fit by now."

"I am not normally the swooning sort, despite my bout of weakness a moment ago."

"I know."

When he flashed her a grin, Eleanor smiled back— and immediately felt a warmth that she was hard-pressed to justify, given the peril they were in.

It was easier to understand the tingle of excitement that surged through her blood. Naturally she was affected by the sheer exhilaration of flying. The danger was strangely exhilarating also, as was the beauty of the morning.

Yet the greatest cause of her sudden high spirits, she suspected—as well as the inexplicable sense of joy she was experiencing just now—was Damon's presence. He always made her feel so alive, so free . . . as if she could conquer the world with him at her side.

In spite of the threat they faced, this flight was a moment of a lifetime, and she was glad to be able to share it with him.

When he returned his attention to the valve cords, Eleanor continued to watch him. She had certainly never expected this unlikely turn of events. Damon was proving to be her knight in shining armor after all, just as he had seemed two years ago.

As a girl, she'd harbored romantic dreams of finding a knight who would sweep her off her feet and end her loneliness, and what could be more wildly romantic than sailing off into the skies with him?

Averting her gaze, Eleanor smiled to herself, even

while wondering how she could feel humor at a time like this.

"How far have we flown?" she asked to distract herself from worrying.

"It's hard to judge. I would guess ten miles or so, perhaps more."

Another few minutes passed as they sank lower and lower. When they came closer to the treetops, Damon shut the valve for good.

"There, Elle . . . there's a meadow beyond that line of elms. I want to try to set down there."

The grassy field was currently home to a small flock of grazing sheep, but Eleanor suspected Damon would attempt to maneuver past them. But then the balloon dropped so that they were barely skimming over the trees.

"We're too low—toss the ballast, Elle. . . ."

Obeying quickly, she hefted one of the bags over the side of the basket.

Their craft bobbed back up a short way and cleared the treeline before starting to sink again.

"Another one. We're going down too fast."

Again she did as she was bid, this time with better results. Their descent slowed to a safer speed.

"Now brace yourself, Elle," Damon ordered. "And when we hit, try to absorb the impact with your knees."

When she held tightly to the rim, he wrapped one arm around her from behind and grasped the basket's suspension ropes with his free hand.

The ground seemed to rush up at them, and Eleanor held her breath in apprehension.

It was indeed a hard, jarring landing, just as Damon

had predicted. The basket struck with a jolt, then tilted and bumped along the ground as the balloon dragged them another dozen yards. When a contrary breeze struck, however, the silken mass lifted once more, causing the basket to suddenly right itself and then come to an abrupt halt.

With their own continued momentum, Eleanor and Damon went sprawling sideways, although he purposely took the brunt of the impact as they fell together on the floor.

They lay there unmoving, his arms wrapped around her, while overhead, the balloon slowly grew limp.

For a moment Damon simply stared at her. Eleanor could feel his heartbeat thudding against her breast, could see the fierce relief on his face, yet as the haunted glimmer in his eyes began to fade, she knew his concern had been for her, not himself.

Her own pounding heartbeat beginning to quiet, Eleanor let out her breath slowly. They had faced danger and survived unscathed.

Neither of them spoke a word. Then Damon's arms folded around her more tightly and his lips came crashing down on hers.

His unexpected action took away the breath she'd just reclaimed and caused a sweet shock of response in every part of her body. His kiss was hard and frenzied, expressing the almost desperate relief she had seen in his eyes.

Damon filled her mouth with his tongue, taking, demanding, igniting a burst of heat inside her so powerful, she felt weak with it. She returned his kiss avidly, though, eagerly fusing her lips to his, drinking him in like a woman dying of thirst.

To her dismay, Damon was the one to end their frantic embrace, although with obvious reluctance. Breaking off the scalding kiss, he drew back, and when he spoke, his voice was husky and raw. "Much as I would like to continue this for an eternity, it wouldn't be honorable to ravish you, Elle."

"I suppose not," she murmured, her own voice low and ragged.

From the expression on his face—part grimace, part hungry desire—she concluded that he was as painfully aroused and bereft as she was, and that he had only stopped for her sake.

"We need to find a farm or a village, borrow a carriage to take us home."

"Yes," Eleanor agreed halfheartedly. She couldn't bear for him to leave her just now. She didn't want to return home. Instead, she wanted to beg Damon for more of his smoldering kisses, wanted him to ease the relentless ache he had created in her, to assuage the heart-deep longing inside her.

When a shadow descended over them, they both glanced up. The balloon had deflated significantly by now, and yards of heavy silk had settled over the basket, blocking out the sunlight and cocooning them in a private haven.

It seemed to Eleanor as if it were some kind of sign from Providence.

"Damon . . . can we not stay here a while longer?"

His eyes locked with hers, his gaze smoldering and intent. Her body responded to the possessive, hungry masculinity in his eyes.

A yearning welled up deep inside her, something utterly primitive and poignant and wild. Her chest ached. Her breasts grew heavy, while a hot throbbing kindled low in her belly, between her thighs.

Urged on by her longing, Eleanor lifted her face to brush her lips softly over his, once . . . twice. . . .

Damon responded just as she hoped; he groaned and covered her mouth again with his.

Their kiss was less fierce this time yet just as impassioned. Their tongues mated, sliding, stroking, dueling in a heated, urgent dance. In turn, Eleanor emitted a revealing whimper that spoke of desire and want and need. Emotion flooded her, the same heady joy she had once known with Damon so long ago. She ached for him feverishly, with a yearning that was too intense to bear.

The ravenous hunger for fulfillment had gone too long unsatisfied, but that would end here and now, Eleanor vowed. Her fingers reaching up to clutch at the dark waves of his hair, she eased away just enough to whisper against his lips.

"Damon . . . please." Her plea was hoarse and breathless. "Make love to me."

He pulled back to gaze solemnly at her, his eyes raptly searching her face.

Eleanor waited with bated breath, but Damon must have found whatever he was looking for in her expression, since a slow, soft smile spread across his lips.

That tantalizing smile warmed her like sunlight breaking through a storm cloud, and so did his reply.

"Yes," he said at last, his rasping voice ripe with promise.

Chapter Twelve

To be caught in a compromising position is perhaps
the surest way to capture a husband—although I
would not advise you to attempt employing so drastic a method.

—An Anonymous Lady, *Advice . . .*

Eleanor's heart turned over at Damon's answer. She
stared into his dark eyes, her body trembling. Time
seemed to halt as his tenderness enveloped her.

Helplessly drawn to him, she raised her mouth to
his once more. Yet this time his kiss was merely fleeting.

"There is no rush, love," he murmured in response
to her eagerness. "I want your first time to be unfor-
gettably pleasurable."

A quiet thrill coursed through Eleanor at his
avowal. She had little doubt Damon would give her
an experience to cherish.

Sitting up, he found the blanket and spread it out
to make a soft bed, then made her kneel upon on it,
facing him. Taking his time, he reached up to remove
her bonnet, then her pelisse. Next he undid the fas-
tenings at the back of her gown and drew down the
bodice to expose her undergarments. Making short
work of her chemise straps, he slowly stroked down
her throat to the swells of her breasts pushed up by
her corset. Another tremor ran through Eleanor, and

when he freed the peaks to his ardent gaze, a new ache spiraled hot and delicious throughout her body.

Damon was watching the rapid rise and fall of her bare breasts, but then he bent his head. She inhaled a sharp breath as he drew her nipple into his mouth, sucking softly. The lush, wet pressure sent a shower of heat rushing to her feminine center.

Her body clamoring for more, Eleanor tried to draw him even closer, yet Damon resisted.

"Slowly, Elle. You are not ready for me yet."

"Then make me ready," she urged.

"Gladly."

Her senses felt feverishly heightened as he lay her back on the blanket. Then raising her skirts above her knees, he lowered his mouth to a bare inner thigh and proceeded to kiss every inch of soft skin he found there. His touch was exquisite, his warm lips caressing, teasing, driving her slightly mad with yearning as he nudged her gown ever higher to her waist, revealing her most feminine secrets.

Eleanor shivered with heat as his mouth moved upward to her woman's mound covered by a thatch of ebony curls. When he stopped just short of the heart of her, though, she looked down. The sight of him poised between her spread thighs was enough to make her tremble. His dark hair was an erotic contrast to her pale skin as she felt the hot, taunting moisture of his breath brushing her cleft.

She whimpered when his tongue made its first sweep across her wetness. Then he tasted her fully, his lips enveloping the hidden bud of her sex. The sweet shock of it made her hips arch off the blanket, which only caused Damon to slide his hands under her buttocks to hold her steady.

Perhaps she should have been scandalized by his stunning passion, by her own wantonness, Eleanor thought in a dazed corner of her mind, but instead she welcomed the magical caresses of his mouth.

A moan sounded in her throat as he went on tonguing her, stroking the engorged, keenly sensitive nub. Eleanor clutched at his shoulders, not certain she could bear any more, but Damon continued his relentless assault, driving her on to greater heights until she was writhing beneath him, thrashing her head from side to side as the frantic fervor built and built. She thought she might shatter from the tormenting pleasure—and in only a few moments, she did just that.

She melted and exploded all at once.

The bright starburst that splintered within her left Eleanor weak and blissfully enervated in the aftermath. Her eyes remained closed as she strove to recover her dazed senses, but when she felt Damon ease to one side, she opened them again.

His expression was one of tender approval, she saw. Then to her surprise, he took her hand and brought it to the apex of her thighs, pressing her fingers against her feminine cleft, which was now slick with moisture.

"That is better," he said with satisfaction. "Your body has prepared itself for my entry. You're wet with your own honey."

Releasing her, he switched her attention to his own loins by reaching down and unbuttoning the front placket of his pantaloons. Her breath faltered when he opened his drawers and freed his long, swollen phallus, which jutted from the curling hair at his groin. Eleanor swallowed, fascinated by his male anatomy and the large, pulsing size of him.

Damon took her hand again and brought it to his blatant arousal, letting the surging warm flesh brush her palm. He inhaled a sharp breath when her fingers curled gently around the hard shaft, and shuddered with pleasure when she traced the firm, velvety sacs below.

"Enough of that, sweetheart," he said in a husky warning. "If you arouse me too keenly, I won't be able to control myself."

"I don't want you to control yourself," Eleanor murmured shyly, feeling brazen and joyously light-hearted.

"Yes, you do. We need to go slowly so I won't hurt you."

He stretched out beside her, bracing his weight on one elbow, and drew her close, letting her feel the swollen ridge of his erection against the softness of her thigh. When his hand rose to brush back a raven curl from her face, the tenderness and sensuality in his touch was unmistakable.

"I have dreamed of this," he murmured, gazing down at her.

She had dreamed of it as well, of Damon making love to her as he was doing now. Of Damon holding her and touching her and treasuring her.

His palm cradling her cheek, he bent again to feather kisses along her jaw and lower, down the column of her throat. At the same time, he reached out to cup her breast. The warmth from his palm seared her skin, and a moment later, his mouth joined in, grazing her nipples with arousing caresses.

When he shifted his position to cover her body, however, settling his weight between her thighs, Damon raised his head to look at her. His eyes shimmered with a hot, primal haze of desire, Eleanor saw with mingled excitement and elation.

Desire churned inside her as well, along with an exquisite heat that throbbed in time with her racing pulse. She wanted him with an intensity that frightened her.

Yet she wasn't afraid when his hard arousal found the wet haven between her legs and probed her entrance. Then slowly, ever so slowly, he began his careful penetration.

His intense, dark gaze never left hers the entire time. "Tell me if you want me to stop," he ordered softly.

"I will. . . ."

Yet she didn't want him to stop. His powerful thighs kept her own parted as he sank lower, pressing inexorably into her, yet her body was opening willingly for him, stretching, accepting his swollen maleness.

When at last he lay buried deep inside her, Eleanor felt overwhelmingly full of him, although she could not call the sensation painful. Her breathing had shallowed, however, and she was certain he could feel her pounding heart against the hard wall of his chest.

"Are you all right, Elle?"

The deep husk of his voice held a note of worry, but she reassured him with a faint smile.

"Yes," she whispered truthfully. Having their flesh

joined in the most intimate way possible seemed somehow right . . . perfect, even.

Careful and tender, Damon lay completely still, waiting for her to grow accustomed to his impalement, and after a while Eleanor realized that the coiled tension inside her was growing more urgent.

When her rigidness began to relax, Damon withdrew, then slowly slid upward once more, making her tremble, before pulling back again. He repeated his sensual action numerous times, stroking her with each gentle plunge and retreat, surging slowly, withdrawing rhythmically, coaxing her response, until instinctively her hips lifted and sought to match his pace in a dance of sweet abandon.

Her whimpers turned to moans as Damon stoked the bright flame of sensation at the center of her. His own breathing was rough as he moved inside her, yet he tempered the powerful thrust of his flesh into her, intent only on increasing her pleasure.

Eleanor was nearly sobbing now at the unbearable sweetness. Almost desperate, she strained and twisted under him as the incendiary sparks burgeoned into a conflagration. When the rush of fire crested and broke, her passion burst deep inside her in a delirium of joy and she arched against him, stunned, crying out.

He captured her wild moans with his mouth yet kept driving with the same compelling rhythm, expertly prolonging her ecstasy as wave after wave of rapture convulsed her.

Only then did Damon surrender to the same tumult that had swept Eleanor. A harsh groan ripping from his throat, he buried his face in the curve of her neck as his body wrenched and shuddered and finally went still.

Their ragged breaths quieting as the sensual reverberations waned, they clung together, weak and spent in the aftershocks of pleasure.

Damon recovered first. Raising his head, he kissed her flushed face again and again . . . slow, soothing, soft caresses of his lips that seared Eleanor's heart as much as his exquisite passion had done to her body.

"After all the fantasies I have had of you," he murmured against her lips, "reality was infinitely sweeter."

She hadn't the strength to reply, so she only smiled her agreement with her eyes still shut. Damon's weight was pressing down on her, but she had no desire to move. She only wanted to lie here, savoring his hard strength, relishing the feeling of being completely, achingly filled by him. She felt joined to Damon utterly, not just their bodies but their hearts. Their intimacy had been spectacular, hot and bold and thrilling, beyond her wildest imaginings. Yet the intense sweetness of it, the sheer enchantment, had flooded her with the same overwhelming, overpowering emotion she had known before. . . .

Eleanor froze at a sudden, shocking realization. The yearning pouring through her was love.

She still loved Damon. She had never stopped loving him—

The sound of voices and running feet seemed to come from far away, yet it was far too close to their cocoon of silk, Eleanor noted in one dazed part of her mind.

Damon went rigid, and so did she upon comprehending that they would not be alone for much longer.

He voiced a soft oath before carefully easing off her and fishing in his coat pocket for a handkerchief. "I was afraid this might happen."

Then offering her a rueful smile, he began to wipe away the traces of his seed from her thighs and his loins. "We had best repair our dishevelment, Elle, and quickly, since I suspect we are about to be interrupted by the local citizenry."

Eleanor was still reeling with the shock of her realization, but the awkwardness of being caught in flagrante delicto with Damon took precedence. They scrambled to right their clothing moments before several tenant farmers from the nearby fields came running to investigate the startling phenomenon from the skies.

Once the sagging balloon had been pulled off the basket and Damon calmly explained their predicament, the farmers offered to take them to the local squire's manor so they could borrow a carriage. But he declined, possibly, Eleanor surmised, because the fewer members of the gentry who saw them just now, the better.

Instead, Damon offered one farmer a substantial fee to convey them back to London in his cart and promised to pay another lavishly for returning the balloon.

Eleanor still had not recovered from her recent shock when they began the long drive to London. She was still in love with Damon, heaven help her. Since the moment he'd reappeared in her life, she had fought her emotions, struggled to crush any lingering feelings she still held for him, to no avail.

And she had just compounded her error by making love to him and giving him her innocence.

Eleanor squeezed her eyes shut, assailed by regrets and self-recriminations. Now that their enchanted lovers' spell was broken, she felt like an utter fool. She must have been mad to surrender to her yearning for Damon.

What in heavens name would she do now? She couldn't tell him how she felt, of course. It would be too hurtful when he rejected her love.

She had to get away from him, that much was certain. She was much too vulnerable to him now, loving him when her love wasn't returned.

Yet that wasn't the most urgent issue at the moment. Over a hundred people had watched them fly off into the skies together. They needed to decide how best to avert the possible negative repercussions. They couldn't discuss the matter just now in front of the farmer, however.

As for Damon, he remained mostly silent during the journey. Whenever Eleanor caught his eye, his enigmatic expression gave her no clue to what he was thinking or feeling, or if he was experiencing similar regrets.

Perhaps he was merely concocting a story to explain their long absence, she thought hopefully. By the time the farmer set them down in Portman Place in the early afternoon, they had been gone for nearly four hours.

"Damon," Eleanor began in a low voice as he escorted her up the front steps of the Beldon mansion. "My aunt will doubtless be unhappy about today's mishap, even though it was beyond our control. I think we should emphasize that we were discovered shortly after we landed."

Damon's expression remained inscrutable, although his tone was strangely nonchalant. "Allow me to deal with her, Elle."

As it turned out, Eleanor was given little chance to comply. When they were admitted by a footman, her Aunt Beatrix came rushing into the entrance hall from the nearest parlor, as if she'd been waiting on pins and needles for any news of the lost aeronauts.

"Thank God!" Beatrix exclaimed, flinging her arms around Eleanor. "Oh, my dear girl, I was frantic with worry. I feared you might have been killed."

Eleanor had never seen her aunt so agitated or so effusive in her display of affection, either. "The danger was not as grave as it might have been, Auntie. Lord Wrexham safely navigated the balloon to land in a field, and then we were rescued by some farmers."

At the mention of Damon's name, Beatrix stiffened and drew back, the profound relief on her face turning to disdain as she shifted her attention to him.

"I am grateful to you, sir," she said haughtily, "but I cannot forgive you. This calamity never would have happened had you not included yourself in our outing."

"It was hardly his lordship's fault," Eleanor hastened to point out. "Someone released the balloon's tether before Signor Pucinelli could join us in the gondola."

The elder lady frowned. "So I am told. Pucinelli was horrified that you were onboard and has apologized profusely. He believes one of his crew was the culprit, but the villain cannot be questioned since he has disappeared. Still, that does not excuse what Lord Wrexham did." She sent Damon a baleful glare. "This is the second time you have dragged my niece's good name through the muck, but this time she will be utterly ruined. Your disappearance together is already the talk of the ton."

Eleanor opened her mouth to defend Damon, but her aunt continued lamenting in despair. "This is beyond appalling, Lord Wrexham. Eleanor will be shunned from polite company, and I will never be able to hold up my head again—and *you* are to blame, sir. You are the worst sort of scoundrel. No lady is safe around you—"

"You are quite wrong, Lady Beldon," Damon interrupted her tirade coolly. "I assure you, Lady Eleanor is completely safe with me. And I am prepared to make amends at once."

"What do you mean, make amends?" Beatrix repeated, her tone scornful.

"I will wed her immediately, of course. We will be married by special license as soon as I can make the arrangements."

Eleanor felt her heart jolt. "I beg your pardon?" she rasped, gazing blankly at Damon.

Aunt Beatrix raised a hand to her temple, as if pained by even having to consider such an alternative. But after a long hesitation, she nodded grimly. "I fear he is right, Eleanor. As much as I dislike the idea of your taking this rogue for your husband, there is no hope for it. Marriage is the only way to salvage your reputation."

"No, Aunt," Eleanor exclaimed, her voice breathy

with panic. "Surely there is no need for such drastic measures."

"If I may, Lady Beldon," Damon said, "I would like to speak to your niece in private, to make her see reason."

Eleanor did indeed want to speak to Damon alone, but it was to make *him* see reason. Thus, when her aunt looked ready to object to a private tête-à-tête, Eleanor forestalled her. "A capital idea, my lord."

Turning without another word, she led him from the hall to the nearest parlor, and after shutting the door firmly, faced him.

"What do you mean, announcing your intention to wed me?" Eleanor said at once. "Is *that* your misguided notion of dealing with my aunt?"

"Yes," Damon replied mildly. "Your aunt is right, Elle. There is no hope for it. We must marry."

Eleanor stared at him. "How can you possibly treat this disaster so cavalierly?"

"I am not treating it cavalierly. But no amount of protesting will change the urgency of our circumstances."

Panic stabbing her, she lashed out at him. "My aunt is right. This would never have happened had you not insisted on spoiling the prince's courtship."

Damon held up a hand. "If you're going to tear a strip off me, you will have to wait until later. If I leave now, I will have time to apply for a special license, so we can hold the ceremony tomorrow morning."

Eleanor regarded Damon in disbelief. "We won't be holding a ceremony tomorrow morning or at any other time! I won't be forced into a holy union that will last for all of our days when there is no love between us."

"You have no choice, Elle. We went too far. Not only did I compromise you, I took your virginity." He cocked an eyebrow. "Your aunt would be even more appalled to learn that small detail, wouldn't you agree?"

She eyed him warily. "You wouldn't dare tell her."

"I might, since it would make her even more adamant about insisting upon our marriage to avert a scandal."

"I knew you were devious," she ground out between her teeth.

"Perhaps, but you *will* marry me."

Eleanor clenched her fists in frustration, fighting against acknowledging the truth of his argument.

She was angry at herself also for getting into this deplorable situation. She had wanted a love match, yet she'd totally destroyed that option now. If she hadn't made love to Damon this morning, she might have tried to weather the coming storm. But she could hardly claim that her reputation had been unfairly tarnished because nothing had happened when she was alone with him.

Dread filling her, Eleanor raised a hand to her brow. She would have a husband who didn't love her, a certain recipe for heartbreak. She was in love with Damon when he didn't return her affection in the least.

"I cannot believe you are so insistent about making amends for compromising me," she said weakly. "You don't give a fig about what society thinks about you—you never have."

"But I care what is thought about *you*. And I mean to protect you by making you my viscountess. You will be ruined otherwise."

"I could always move to the Continent and enter a convent," Eleanor muttered.

His quick smile indicated how absurd he considered her threat. "You are wholly unsuited for the existence of a nun, Elle. A woman with your passion, your hunger for life, shouldn't be locked away beyond the walls of a convent. We just proved that this morning."

When she stood there regarding him in dismay, Damon stepped closer. Reaching up, he curved his strong fingers gently about her cheek. "You could be carrying my child. Have you thought of that?"

Eleanor's hand stole to her abdomen. No, she hadn't thought of it, although she should have.

"We don't love each other," she repeated, grasping at straws.

"That makes no difference, Elle."

"It makes a difference that you are a rake."

Damon held her gaze. "I told you, I will be faithful to our marriage vows, even if I cannot love you."

Pain stabbed her anew at his assertion, yet Eleanor was determined to conceal it. "You also said you would remain celibate until I agreed to wed you, but you broke your vow in less than three days."

Damon's lips curved. "I don't believe that counts since I broke it with you."

"The *point* is," she said hurriedly, ignoring the temptation of his smile, "that I don't trust you, Damon."

His expression sobered at once while his dark eyes

seemed to soften. "I know, Elle. But I promise you, I have renounced my wicked ways. And I will do my utmost never to hurt you."

She couldn't believe him, yet she knew she was fighting a losing battle. She swallowed hard, trying to quell her panic as she repeated her objections. "There must be another way, Damon. I don't want to be forced to wed you simply because my reputation is in shreds."

"You want to spare your aunt a scandal, though, don't you?"

That consideration trumped all of Eleanor's protests. "Yes, of course." She owed her aunt immensely for opening her home to an orphaned girl. She couldn't repay Beatrix's kindness by miring her in scandal.

"Then there should be no question as to your decision," he pointed out.

While she stood there debating with herself, Damon closed the final distance between them. Without warning, he drew Eleanor into his arms, yet there was no passion in his embrace. He was offering her comfort instead.

"I know this is not what you wanted, Eleanor," he said softly, "but we have no choice."

She squeezed her eyes shut. His caressing voice had the power to daze and enchant her, but his tenderness made her want to cry. It wasn't fair that Damon made her heart melt with his tender concern.

Pressing her face into the warm curve of his shoulder, Eleanor gave a sigh of despair. "I suppose not."

He drew back slightly to regard her, although he kept his arms wrapped around her in a loose embrace. "Cheer up, sweetheart." His deep gaze became a dare. "If you had the courage to face the possibility of death in a balloon without flinching, you can face the prospect of marrying me."

Watching the uncertain emotion flickering in her vivid blue eyes, Damon knew the moment that she accepted the inevitable. He let out the breath he hadn't known he was holding.

"Will you tell your aunt, or shall I?" he asked.

"I will do it," Eleanor said with another heavy sigh.

He held her lithe body against him for a moment longer, then released her and stepped back. "I will get word to you as soon as I can secure a special license. And I will send Lady Beldon in to you on my way out. I suspect she is waiting anxiously to hear your verdict."

Lady Beldon was indeed hovering anxiously in the corridor when Damon exited the parlor.

"Your niece would like to speak with you, my lady," he informed her before bowing and making for the front door.

Upon leaving Portman Place, Damon hailed the first hack he saw. Intent on procuring a special license, he ordered the jarvey to convey him to the ecclesiastical courts at Doctor's Commons, then settled against the squabs, satisfied that he was taking the right course.

He'd known from the moment he made love to Eleanor that their carnal union would lead to marriage, even if she had not. He was honor-bound to wed her.

Yet he had no regrets, Damon realized. He had wanted Eleanor back in his life for good, and he had staked his claim on her today in the most permanent way possible.

Not that taking her body had been an entirely conscious decision. His wild physical response had been a reaction to the peril of the moment. He'd feared he might lose her, Damon admitted. His relief upon knowing that she was safe after their dangerous flight had left him weak—as had the passion they shared afterward. Eleanor's ardent, innocent sensuality had matched every fantasy he'd ever had of her. That, combined with her courage and her vibrant spirit, had awed and aroused and touched him.

He was extremely glad that their tender interlude had been interrupted, for it had allowed him to bring his emotions firmly back under control.

The incident should be a clear warning to him, Damon knew. He needed to keep his distance emotionally from Eleanor once they were wed. Yet he was quite expert at that by now. He'd spent most of his life cultivating dispassion in his relationships.

There would be no question of love between them, Damon promised himself. He knew the kind of devastating pain he risked if he let Eleanor into his heart. A pain that could be even worse than any he'd endured before.

He would not allow her to fall in love with him, either, because she would only be hurt when he couldn't reciprocate, and he was determined not to hurt her again.

He had to earn her trust, however. He had vowed

fidelity, but he would have to show her by deeds, not mere words.

No, Damon thought silently, he couldn't fulfill Eleanor's desire for love, but on his life, he would make every other possible effort to see that she was happy.

If Eleanor was stunned and dismayed by the necessity of marrying Damon, so was her aunt, judging from the elder lady's grim expression when she entered the parlor.

But when Beatrix heard of their plan to wed in the morning, she nodded in concurrence. "I agree, it is best to act quickly."

"I suppose so," Eleanor said quietly. "Although that means Marcus will miss my wedding. He and Arabella are not expected to return to England until early next week. And Drew and Heath won't be there, either."

"It cannot be helped, my dear. We need to stanch the brewing scandal as soon as possible. Indeed, I think we would be wise to leave for Brighton tomorrow afternoon, even though the house party is not scheduled to begin until Friday. Our guests can join us then as originally planned. The aspersions will die down sooner if we are away from town."

Since the prospect of leaving town to avoid facing the ton held great appeal, Eleanor made no objection.

Seeing her so dispirited, though, Beatrix tried to cheer her. "I regret that it has come to this, my dear, but the marriage need be in name only. And of course I will do my best to shield you from Wrexham whenever possible. I will ensure you have separate bedchambers at Rosemont at least . . . although as a newly wedded couple, it will not do for you to go your separate ways so soon after the ceremony. We don't want your union to look like a forced marriage, even if it is. We will put out word that you and Wrexham realized your affections are still engaged, so the gossipmongers will think it a love match. That should mitigate the scandal in some measure."

But it is not a love match, Eleanor's heart wanted to protest.

At her silence, Beatrix patted her hand briskly. "Now that our plan is settled, you should go upstairs and freshen up. Ring for Jenny to help you change and I will order our staff to begin packing at once. I will also ask Cook to prepare a large luncheon. Now that you are safe at home, I find that I am famished. I could not eat a single bite when your fate was so uncertain."

Eleanor smiled faintly at her aunt's surprising admission. Beatrix rarely allowed anything to interfere with her comfort. Nor did she often confess to caring about anyone else. Perhaps her budding romance with Signor Vecchi was softening her outlook on life to a small degree.

Eleanor dutifully went upstairs to her bedchamber, but she didn't ring for her abigail. Not only would she rather be alone with her thoughts, she wanted privacy in case the change in her virginal state was evident.

When she shed her pelisse and gown and undergarments, then surveyed her body in the cheval glass, Eleanor could see telltale signs of lovemaking—traces of Damon's dried seed on her thighs along with a pink tinge of blood. Her lips were redder than usual, as well, her breasts more sensitive. And she felt a distinct tenderness between her thighs when she washed herself at the basin.

What was more, the slightest touch made her vividly recall what had happened between them this morning—Damon kissing her and stroking her and moving inside her.

Eleanor shut her eyes, dismay filling her once again. At this time tomorrow she would likely be married to Damon, a fate that would have made her wildly happy two years ago. She had longed to become his wife then, but now. . . .

He claimed he didn't want to hurt her, that he would be faithful to their marriage vows, yet she couldn't bring herself to believe him. And if he betrayed her again? This time the devastation would be overwhelming.

Still, what future would she have if she refused to wed Damon? She couldn't hurt her aunt by bringing scandal down upon their heads. And even if she had cared nothing for Aunt Beatrix, a nunnery was out of the question. Nor could she flee to some quiet place in the country and secrete herself away in shame. She didn't want that kind of life, didn't want to be shunned by genteel society. She wanted to marry, to have children, a family. She wanted a husband who loved her.

That was the rub, Eleanor knew. Damon couldn't or wouldn't love her. She was beginning to understand why—because of the terrible hurt he'd experienced at losing his family. The knowledge made her incredibly sad, yet it also showed her what a powerful force she was up against.

A shiver racked Eleanor's body. She felt so terribly vulnerable, loving Damon when he didn't love her in return.

He could break her heart so easily. His power over her already was indisputable. When she was with him, he enchanted and vexed her and made all her senses come vividly alive. When she argued with him, he simply kissed the breath out of her. And when she made love to him, she felt on fire, wildly out of control.

It would be impossible to protect herself once they were wed, Eleanor suspected.

Drying herself off, she found a fresh chemise and began to dress again in a simple muslin afternoon gown as she resigned herself to her fate. The simple truth was, she had no choice but to accept Damon's proposal, especially if there was the slightest chance he could love her someday—

At the thought, Eleanor caught her breath. Would it be possible to make Damon fall in love with her?

That had been their chief problem during their courtship two years ago. He hadn't loved her, so he'd turned to another woman to fulfill his carnal desires.

But could he ever come to love her?

She was almost certain she'd seen more than simple lust in his eyes this morning, although she couldn't trust her judgment when it came to him.

For the first time since he'd announced his intention of marrying her, however, Eleanor felt a flicker of hope. She might never be able to win Damon's love, but she had to try. Her future, her entire happiness, depended upon it.

Perhaps she would be wise to ask Fanny Irwin for

advice. There was little in Fanny's book to suggest how to prevent heartbreak once a woman had captured a husband, but she might have suggestions on how to deal with Damon.

Coming to a decision, Eleanor let out her breath slowly. She intended to try to make Damon love her.

Even more crucially, she intended to make him love her enough to be faithful.

Chapter Thirteen

Because Eleanor penned a quick note to Fanny before luncheon and received an immediate reply, she was able to visit the courtesan's private home at Crawford Place later that very afternoon.

Fanny seemed delighted to see her and listened thoughtfully as Eleanor explained how the balloon ascension had unexpectedly led to her being compromised, which would result in her marrying Lord Wrexham on the morrow.

"I hoped," Eleanor concluded, "that you might advise me how to proceed now. Your book on capturing a husband mainly addresses the circumstances before wedlock, not afterward."

"I would be happy to offer you suggestions," Fanny replied before giving a wry grimace. "Sadly, you will be at a disadvantage once you are wed. Marriage changes a couple's balance of power significantly. A husband has the upper hand over a wife both legally and financially."

"I know." Eleanor hesitated. "But what concerns

me more is winning my husband's affection. The thing is . . . I love Wrexham."

"Ah, I see," the courtesan said slowly. "You know, of course, that loving him puts you at an even-greater disadvantage?"

"Yes," she responded, glad that Fanny understood her dilemma so quickly. "I need to know what to do, Fanny. How can I make him love me in return?"

Fanny's brow furrowed. "From what I know about Lord Wrexham, he will prove a significant challenge."

Her observation gave Eleanor pause. "Oh?" she asked with studied casualness. "Are you acquainted with him?"

"Somewhat." Fanny smiled, then sobered suddenly as if recalling her audience. "But *not* in the way you imagine, Lady Eleanor," she added quickly. "Lord Wrexham has never been a client of mine."

Eleanor knew her relief was showing.

"What I *meant*," Fanny continued, "is that he has proven highly elusive in the past, and he is likely to remain so. You will need all the ammunition you can muster in order to win your battle for his heart."

Unable to dispute that point, Eleanor sighed and responded with a question. "So what can I do?"

"The secret, I think, will be for you to increase his physical desire for you as much as possible."

"And how will I accomplish that?"

Fanny answered earnestly. "Most importantly, you should remember that even though you are wedded, you are still engaged in a mating dance with your husband. You cannot appear too eager for his attentions. You cannot surrender to his charms too readily, either. Instead you must resist his advances and give the impression of nonchalance. At the same time you will want to tease and titillate and arouse him subtly, just as I advised in my book. And once the consummation has taken place, you will be more knowledgeable about lovemaking and how to stimulate the male body."

Eleanor found herself flushing. "What if . . . the consummation has already taken place?"

Fanny did not seem surprised; on the contrary, she looked pleased. "Excellent. That will make my task of instructing you much easier. There are many techniques I never mentioned in my book so as to spare the innocent sensibilities of my readers, who are mainly ladies of the Quality. Fortunately, as a married woman, you can utilize your marital bed to your advantage without fear of scandal. You are at greater liberty to employ the arts of seduction. You can heighten your husband's anticipation and make him crave you all the more."

"So I should continue to follow the recommendations in your book but intensify my physical allurements?"

"Precisely," Fanny agreed. "The basic premise is still much the same for a married woman as for a single one, however. You must make *him* work to win you, not the other way around. In short, make him pursue you. Men like to be the hunters, not the quarry."

Fanny's counsel was welcome advice to Eleanor. She had treated her pursuit of the prince much like a game, but this was no game. The stakes were far, far higher now.

"It might help," Fanny interrupted her thoughts, "if I knew your immediate plans. I presume you will continue to live in London? Will you take a wedding trip?"

"I am not certain," Eleanor answered. "We have had no time to discuss any of the details, although the next fortnight is set. My aunt, Lady Beldon, is holding her annual house party at her country home near Brighton, beginning this weekend. She thinks it best to contain the gossip by absenting ourselves from London, so we are leaving early—tomorrow afternoon, in fact."

Fanny pursed her lips. "Repairing to the country with Wrexham could provide you some promising opportunities to win his affections. At least you may better control events to your own liking. Tell me, what occurs at these house parties of your aunt's?"

"Well, during the day, many of the guests enjoy riding and walking over the Downs. We also take driving excursions to various historical sites and at least one outing to the beach for sea bathing. In the evening there will be plays and poetry readings, and of course, cards and dinners and dancing, with a formal ball the last evening. Actually, Wrexham and I met there two years ago and became affianced the first time."

Fanny nodded happily. "Even better. You may be able to rekindle the intimacy you once knew there before your betrothal ended."

Recalling what had caused her falling out with Damon, Eleanor twisted her fingers in her lap. "The thing is, Fanny . . . I want very much for him to find me desirable as well as to love me, so he will not be interested in keeping a mistress as he did before."

The courtesan's gaze grew sympathetic. "I had heard that his mistress was the reason you broke off with him."

Despite the pain the memory caused her, Eleanor couldn't contain her interest. "I have wondered about her sometimes. Mrs. Lydia Newling was her name. Do you happen to know her?"

Fanny hesitated. "I am acquainted with her, yes."

"Does she still reside in London?"

"Yes, but she has a new patron, the last I heard. I doubt you have any cause for concern."

Eleanor's lips curved in a humorless smile. "To be truthful, I worry that Damon will not consider me as beautiful or desirable as he found Mrs. Newling."

Fanny shook her head firmly. "You know my opinion on that subject, Lady Eleanor. Beauty is not necessary to attract most gentlemen. But I cannot credit that Wrexham would think any such thing about you. You are far more beautiful than Lydia Newling."

"But she is highly skilled in her profession."

"So am I," Fanny replied. "All you need is a little private tutoring to add a few tricks of seduction to your arsenal, and you will be more than a rival for the Lydia Newlings of the world."

Eleanor felt a huge measure of relief at her offer. "I don't wish to impose any more than I already have, but if you have the time, I would be grateful for whatever you could teach me."

Her eyes sparkling, Fanny flashed a provocative smile that showed why she had become one of the most renowned Cyprians in England. "It would be my pleasure. And I have ample time at the moment since I finished the draft of my Gothic novel. In fact, I intended to write to you tomorrow to ask if you would read it and offer me your criticisms."

"Certainly, I would be delighted. If I may, I will take the manuscript with me to Brighton—" Eleanor paused before continuing dryly. "On second thought, I will begin reading it tonight. A good story will provide a welcome distraction to the terrifying realization that I am to be married tomorrow."

Her humor was met with soft laughter from Fanny. "I do hope you will find the story good, Lady Eleanor. Now then, if we may be perfectly frank . . . how much do you know about the male anatomy?"

Eleanor left an hour later, armed with a courtesan's perspective about techniques of seduction. She did not, however, feel overly embarrassed, since Fanny had been so practical and down-to-earth about carnal matters. Instead, her instructions and encouragement had left Eleanor feeling cautiously optimistic.

She could scarcely wait to put Fanny's advice into practice. Damon could make any woman yearn for his caresses, but she was determined to turn the tables on him now and make him yearn for *her.* It heartened her to remember how he'd responded to her sensual advances in the library the night of the Haviland ball.

Still, his seduction was not her chief aim. Her goal was to achieve a truly loving marriage with Damon. And if she followed Fanny's advice, Eleanor greatly hoped, she would eventually succeed.

And if not?

She wouldn't let herself think about the loneliness

and heartache she would face if she couldn't make Damon love her in return.

Eleanor had another reason to be grateful that evening, since Fanny's novel turned out to be highly engrossing and thus, for the most part, took her mind off her forthcoming marriage. Even more remarkably, she slept soundly that night, despite all that had happened in the past day to change her life, and all that would happen the next.

Her nerves were on edge the entire morning, however, as Jenny helped her bathe and dress in a long sleeved gown of rose-colored silk. Eleanor's agitation only grew as the moment neared—at least until Damon entered the drawing room at eleven o'clock, accompanied by his physician friend, Mr. Geary, and followed by a clergyman.

A sense of calm filled Eleanor then, even though the ceremony that ensued was nothing like what she had dreamed of. The bridegroom, who was dressed in a blue coat and pale gray pantaloons, was the same, stunningly handsome nobleman as in her dreams, yet she had planned to be married in a large church (St. George's, Hanover Square, to be precise) with her family and friends (Marcus and Heath and Drew, in particular) and half the ton in attendance (instead of a hurried wedding by special license with only a few guests present).

But her Aunt Beatrix had approached the challenge of lessening the social blemish to her reputation with Machiavellian efficiency. The elderly Countess of Haviland was there to lend her countenance to the proceedings and to proclaim her support for the niece of her bosom friend, Lady Beldon. Prince Lazzara and Signor Vecchi also attended for appearance's sake— to show society that his highness bore no ill feelings toward Eleanor now that his courtship of her had abruptly ended.

Damon raised an eyebrow at seeing the Italian gentlemen, as if wondering what the devil they were doing there, but he was given no opportunity to question Eleanor since her aunt conspired to keep them apart during the short interval before their vows were spoken.

At the conclusion of the ceremony, when Damon kissed her lightly on the lips to seal their union, Eleanor's heart quickened, and continued thudding in that same rapid rhythm as they signed the marriage lines.

They were irrevocably married now.

Then Beatrix stepped between them to discuss plans for the journey to Brighton.

"Of course you must ride with us in my carriage, Lord Wrexham," the viscountess said brusquely. "It would look odd for a newly wedded couple to be separated so shortly after the nuptials. But I warn you, sir, I mean to keep a close eye on you. I will not leave Eleanor at your mercy. Now, if you will excuse me a moment, I wish to say farewell to our guests and thank them for canceling their engagements so precipitously. They will join us at Rosemont tomorrow, a day earlier than planned."

Left alone with Eleanor for the first time since entering the drawing room, Damon regarded her with a frown. "The prince still means to attend the house party?"

"Yes, he was invited long ago, you will remember. He and Signor Vecchi will drive down in their own equipage tomorrow."

Eleanor saw Damon's jaw flex in disapproval. "The circumstances have not changed since yesterday," he pointed out. "If Lazzara is in danger, then your safety could be at risk whenever you are in his company."

"Perhaps," Eleanor replied, keeping her tone even. "But we cannot simply abandon him. If someone truly is trying to harm Prince Lazzara, he will be safer in the country at my aunt's estate. It will be harder for his unknown assailant to strike at him there, and you will be better able to protect him, as I am certain you are kind enough to do."

She smiled inwardly when Damon bit back a remark. He clearly was not happy to have the prince in such close proximity to her, or to be required to see to his protection.

Soothingly, she placed her hand on Damon's sleeve. "But in truth, I am not only thinking of the prince. I wish my aunt to be happy, Damon. She has become exceedingly fond of Signor Vecchi, but he is unlikely to attend the house party if the prince does not. And you must admit that their illustrious presence will help quiet the gossipmongers. Aunt Beatrix hopes to mend my reputation, and she believes that they, along with her high-stickler friends, will advance my cause better than anything else."

"I still don't like it," Damon said tersely.

Eleanor glanced up at him from beneath her lashes. "You are not jealous, by any chance?" she teased.

"Are you perhaps worried that his highness might tempt me to break our marital vows?"

"*No,*" Damon retorted with surprising conviction in his voice. "Given your beliefs about fidelity, I doubt I must worry about being cuckolded."

Yet he had not answered her question about jealousy, she noted. Before she could prod him on the subject, Prince Lazzara came up to them.

A doleful expression darkened his royal features as he bowed deeply over her hand and then kissed her fingertips. "I am quite grieved that matters have come to such a pass, Donna Eleanora. And I fear I bear much of the blame. Had I not escorted you to the ascension, you would not have been compelled to wed so suddenly."

Eleanor smiled. "You are not at fault, your highness. You could not know that the launching would be sabotaged."

The prince pressed his lips together, looking scornful. "Pucinelli has returned to Italy—I suspect because he feared being blamed for risking the deaths of an English peer and a highborn young lady." Lazzara turned to Damon. "You were generous to trouble yourself, milord, by having the balloon conveyed to my home. Pucinelli will be pleased to recover it, no doubt, although I am not certain he deserves your consideration."

"It was little trouble," Damon responded in a cool tone before changing the subject. "I understand you will be visiting Rosemont for the next fortnight, Don Antonio."

"Indeed. I am quite looking forward to the pleasure."

"I trust you will remember what we discussed earlier? That you will keep your distance from Lady Eleanor as much as possible, for the sake of her safety?"

"But of course," Lazzara said at once.

Eleanor doubted Damon was wholly satisfied with that answer, but he nodded in acknowledgment, then added some advice. "You would be wise to have the Runners accompany you. You might also consider leaving your entourage of servants here in London and relying on Lady Beldon's staff during your stay. Bow Street will find it easier to guard you if they can control anyone who has access to you."

The prince looked taken aback by the suggestion. "But I cannot manage without my servants. I will, however, make certain the Runners you hired continue in my service."

Just then Beatrix returned to Eleanor's side and proposed that they be on their way if they wished to make Rosemont in time to dine there this evening. After saying her own farewells to their guests and Mr. Geary, Eleanor followed her aunt out to the entrance hall, where she accepted her pelisse and bonnet from Peters.

A short while later, as she settled in the Beldon traveling chaise next to her aunt and across from her new husband, Eleanor decided she was pleased with how events were unfolding thus far.

Having the prince at Rosemont for a fortnight could prove advantageous, since it might serve to make Damon a little jealous. And she was comforted to know that she would be surrounded by allies. Being alone with Damon presented the greatest danger to implementing the stratagems she'd learned from Fanny, Eleanor knew.

She needed to maintain control of their relationship if her plan to win his love was to succeed. According to the courtesan, she had to remain elusive, all the while tempting and teasing Damon in hopes of driving him mad with desire. Yet he was so alluring and enticing—and her willpower so weak—that she was likely to surrender to her own desires before she could rouse his to the point that he would relinquish his heart.

And it was crucial that she follow Fanny's advice to the letter, since it was her only hope for happiness.

Damon was not happy when Lady Beldon contrived to keep him apart from his new bride, especially since he suspected she would likely continue her machinations during the entire house party. But he decided to endure her interference with good grace, at least until they arrived at Rosemont and he could be alone with Eleanor. It would be easier to elude her ladyship then.

In fact, Damon had asked Otto to accompany them, wanting a confederate to foil whatever designs Lady Beldon had planned, but the physician had pleaded duty, claiming he couldn't be absent from his hospital for so long.

"And you know," Otto added with a pretended shudder, "how much I loathe that sort of worthless social gathering. Besides, you are a noted expert with the ladies. Surely you can manage Lady Eleanor's dragon of an aunt for a fortnight."

"One would think so," Damon said dryly.

"It may turn out better than you think," Otto offered. "I am rather stunned that you actually wed Lady Eleanor after all this time, but I think she might make a good match for you. Then again, I am certainly no authority on matrimony, so I could be mistaken. In any event, I wish you the best of luck, old fellow."

Since Otto professed to be a confirmed bachelor, Damon had accepted his friend's prognostications with a grain of salt. But he still would have preferred to have the physician's company at Rosemont.

As was her ladyship's wont, her traveling chaise set a leisurely pace for the nearly fifty miles of good road leading south from London. They were followed by Damon's coach and a second, slower Beldon carriage filled with servants and luggage. Their cavalcade stopped at posting inns every hour to change horses, and once for a longer sojourn while they partook of a hearty luncheon.

Eleanor sat across from Damon, her expression serene but her eyes lively as she kept up a congenial conversation with her aunt. Damon could not decipher her mood, but occasionally she met his gaze with a faint smile on her lips, as if she held a secret she didn't wish to share. He couldn't shake the suspicion that she was up to something.

On the other hand, her relative's haughty displeasure with him was perfectly clear; the viscountess displayed a bare minimum of polite manners and otherwise ignored him.

All in all, however, the journey through Essex was pleasant enough. Rosemont was Lady Beldon's country home purchased from her private fortune, since her late husband's family seat was entailed on a nephew in the male line. The property was situated a few miles to the north and west of Brighton, in the grassy hills of the South Downs.

Damon could smell the fresh scent of the sea as they neared their destination, and knew that if they traveled a few miles further south, they would reach the English Channel and the chalk cliffs overlooking fine shingle beaches.

He was glad when they finally swept through the great iron gates of Rosemont and bowled up the long, curving drive before halting before a splendid Palladian manor. Just as Damon remembered, the interior was rich and luxuriously appointed, as befitted a wealthy noblewoman with superior taste.

Lady Beldon took charge as soon as they entered, directing her large staff to carry the luggage upstairs before suggesting to the bridal couple that they retire to their chambers to wash off their travel dust and change into evening attire so they could dine formally at seven o'clock.

Then she spoke directly to Damon. "I have allotted you adjoining bedchambers for the sake of appearances, my lord, even though it goes sorely against the grain. But I will not have it said that there is anything havey-cavey about your marriage."

Two years ago, his rooms had been in an entirely different wing from Eleanor, so this would be a significant improvement, Damon reflected. Thus, he didn't contest the accommodations.

Neither did Eleanor. Instead, she merely smiled and accompanied him upstairs, preceded by Rosemont's majordomo. She stopped at a door halfway down the corridor, while Damon was shown to the next suite of rooms. His bedchamber had a magnificent view of the park, but he was more interested in access to his wife's rooms.

When he opened the adjacent door, he found Elle in a similar bedchamber, taking off her bonnet.

The first thing she did—surprisingly—was to apologize. "I am very sorry my aunt is being so difficult, Damon. I imagine she merely needs a period to adjust to our marriage."

"I am willing to let her adjust," he replied rather dryly, "although I don't fancy having to battle her the entire time we are here."

Eleanor returned a coquettish smile. "It might take longer than a fortnight for her to come around. She views you with considerable disfavor, you know. She is even angrier with you for precipitating this debacle than for our broken betrothal two years ago. Nor has she forgotten your libertine ways then—how you flaunted your mistress in public. Aunt Beatrix is determined to protect me from falling for your wicked charms again."

"I gather that is why she assigned us separate bedchambers?"

"That, and because she thinks we will have a marriage in name only."

Damon regarded her narrowly. "You are not of the same mind, I trust."

"Why, yes." When he frowned, Eleanor's eyes widened innocently. "You were the one who wanted a mere marriage of convenience, Damon. Surely you don't expect that to include carnal relations like a real married couple."

"Of course I expect us to share a marital bed."

"Well, we shall just have to see. . . ."

There was a spark of laughter in her eyes that belied her guileless look.

Damon suspected that Eleanor was flirting with him—and he was convinced of it when she crossed to him and placed an imploring hand on his arm. "My maid is not yet here. Will you be so kind as to unfasten the hooks of my gown?"

Without waiting, she gave him her back, and when he had obliged, she thanked him sweetly and turned to face him again.

Gazing up at him, Eleanor started to lower her bodice, then stopped just as the edge of her corset came into view. "Modesty prevents me from undressing in front of you."

Her absurd statement sent his eyebrow shooting up. But the swells of creamy skin already exposed to his avid gaze made Damon recall the lushness of her bare breasts and the potent sensuality of her body when they'd made love yesterday.

Then Eleanor wet her lips with her tongue, and he realized that she was deliberately trying to arouse him. She was definitely succeeding, Damon acknowledged, feeling his loins harden.

Her mouth looked soft and ripe, her skin infinitely touchable. He stepped closer, the need to kiss her as strong as any desire he'd ever felt. And from the telltale pulse flickering at the base of her throat, he knew Eleanor was fighting her own desire for him. Her blue eyes were luminous with heat—

It gave Damon little consolation when she shook her head with a regretful smile. "You had best change your attire, my lord husband. We don't wish to keep my aunt waiting. She becomes exceedingly crotchety when her will is crossed."

When he made no reply, Eleanor pushed gently against his chest, guiding him backward toward their connecting door.

When he had crossed the threshold to his own chamber, her smile turned almost sad. "I think it best to lock this door so we will not be tempted to transgress."

Then stepping back, Eleanor shut the door firmly between them.

Damon heard the bolt settling in place and stared at the panel, torn between exasperation and disbelief. He was married to Elle now, but she intended to deny him her bed. Moreover, she'd made it clear that he would have to battle her resistance as well as contend with her overprotective aunt.

Registering the painful tightness in his pantaloons, Damon grimaced. For a fleeting moment, he had actually started to anticipate this house party with pleasure, yet now it looked as if all he could expect was a fortnight of frustrated desire.

Thinking of the torment in store for him, he let out a long breath.

It would, he suspected, be a very long fortnight indeed.

Chapter Fourteen

You would be wise to appear elusive upon occasion. If you are always easily attainable, the challenge will fade for him and he may turn to more exciting quarry.

—An Anonymous Lady, *Advice . . .*

Finding a private moment with his wife proved as difficult as Damon expected. Lady Beldon kept Eleanor by her side that entire evening and again at breakfast the next morning. Afterward, Elle professed herself too busy to go riding with him, since she would be engaged in reading the manuscript of a novel a friend had written.

Damon enjoyed a solitary ride and sequestered himself in the Rosemont library. Then shortly after one o'clock, the first houseguests began arriving.

He'd known he would dislike having Prince Lazzara in close proximity to his new bride, but he hadn't counted on having his jealousy aroused from another quarter: Rayne Kenyon, the new Earl of Haviland, who'd escorted his grandmother the dowager countess down from London.

Or more precisely, Damon was not happy that Eleanor seemed to be on such easy terms with Lord Haviland and even appeared to flirt with him. Damon overheard them jesting together when they all gathered in the drawing room at four o'clock for tea.

"A pity I was not swift enough to snare your hand in marriage before Wrexham did," the earl told Eleanor with a smile. "My grandmother would have been enraptured had you chosen to wed me, since she thinks you the ideal young lady."

Eleanor smiled back at him. "It is common knowledge that Lady Haviland is pressing you to marry."

"A vast understatement," Haviland said dryly. "She wants an heir to her family bloodlines before she goes to meet her Maker, which she insists will come any day now. But since you are no longer available, I will have to search elsewhere for a suitable bride."

"I regret disappointing your grandmother, my lord. But my husband"—she sent Damon a playful glance, her eyes dancing—"proved impossible for me to resist. I have no doubt, however, that you will easily attract scores of eligible young ladies."

"Eligible, yes . . . but unfortunately not as appealing as I would wish."

"I suppose they are all too tame for you."

"Or they consider me a trifle too uncivilized, since I'm not enamored of London society as a peer should be."

Eleanor laughed lightly with Haviland, which sent a shaft of jealousy straight to Damon's loins.

There was far more substance to the earl, however, than the typical nobleman possessed, Damon knew from their university days together. He was reminded again that evening upon witnessing Haviland's keen powers of observation. The company had repaired to the drawing room after dinner to hear Eleanor perform on the pianoforte. While Prince Lazzara turned the sheet music for her, Haviland crossed to where Damon stood by the French doors taking in a breath of cool air as a respite from the stuffy, overheated formality of the gathering.

"I am curious, Wrexham, as to why two Bow Street Runners would be harboring on the premises."

Damon eyed the earl with amused admiration. "So you noticed that, did you? What gave them away? Neither is wearing his usual red-breasted coat."

"I have had some experience with Bow Street before. What is their purpose? They seem to be hovering near Lazzara whenever possible."

"It is rather a long story."

Haviland shrugged. "I have ample time to listen— and hearing the tale will be far more intriguing than making polite drawing room conversation."

Thus, Damon found himself recounting the frequent accidents that had befallen the prince, beginning with the wheel coming off his phaeton in the park and culminating in the sabotaging of the balloon flight.

Haviland looked thoughtful at the conclusion of Damon's narrative. "You said the pickpocket at the Pantheon Bazaar appeared to be foreign?"

"Yes. He had the olive complexion of the Italians, in fact."

"It would be no surprise if his highness had developed enemies among his countrymen. Royalty often arouses malcontents with grievances." Haviland paused. "It might be interesting to try to set a trap for his assailant."

Damon raised an eyebrow at the earl's proposition

for intrigue, although such unconventionality from him was not entirely unexpected, given Haviland's purported experience with British intelligence.

"Meaning," Damon questioned, "that we should use Lazzara as bait? Could it be done without endangering him too greatly?"

"I expect something could be arranged. Let me think on it. Meanwhile you should have the Runners pay close attention to his servants and compatriots."

"I already have done so," Damon responded. "Lazzara brought his usual retinue of attendants with him, against my advice, and I thought they bore extra scrutiny from Bow Street. I also asked my valet to watch for any suspicious activity in the servants' quarters. But, Haviland, the prince would likely be safer if you agreed to keep an eye on him."

The earl grinned. "I would be happy to oblige. It will be a relief to have something constructive to occupy me for the next fortnight. Frankly, I find these large house parties to be excruciatingly dull."

Damon once had been of the same opinion—until he'd met Elle at this very same event two years ago. From the first moment he'd laid eyes on the raven-haired charmer, he was bowled over. That first time Eleanor had been surrounded by a coterie of admirers, and he'd been hard-pressed to lure her away from her beaux so he could have her to himself.

His challenge was similar now, Damon reflected, only now his adversary was her aunt. At least, however, Signor Vecchi served to distract Lady Beldon somewhat. Evidently Eleanor was right: Her aunt was becoming enamored of the distinguished Italian diplomat.

To Damon's gratification, Lady Beldon's attention was further diverted when nearly two dozen more guests began arriving the next day and her house party began in earnest. She had invited the cream of the ton, and by now they'd all heard about her niece's hasty wedding.

Many of them offered guarded felicitations, but her ladyship set about annihilating their reservations with the resolution of a field general. It amused Damon to hear the viscountess sing his praises and pretend delight at the union when he knew she was lying through her teeth.

Eleanor, too, did her part to tamp down any whiff of scandal—playing the role of the beautiful, vivacious heiress who had made a splendid match with an extremely eligible nobleman.

Damon couldn't help but admire her as she charmed and enchanted her arbiters. Yet Elle would have captured his attention, even had he not been newly married to her. She was so vital and alive, she seemed to raise the spirits of everyone around her. Damon was constantly aware of her and found himself listening for her sparkling laugh, watching for her warm smile.

But while he always knew where Eleanor was at any given moment, his bride continued to keep her distance from him and always found inventive excuses to avoid being alone with him.

His cousin, Tess Blanchard, was the only one who appeared to note their lack of intimacy. Damon was pleased to see Tess in the throng of guests, but when she congratulated him on his marriage and hinted that she would like to know more about the details, he merely thanked her and changed the subject to her favorite topic: her charities.

Tess knew all about his endeavors in Italy and had actually discovered several cases of consumption in the course of her work with the impoverished families of fallen soldiers. She'd brought the sufferers to Otto Geary's notice, who had then arranged for them to become patients at Damon's sanitorium.

Thankfully, Tess was clever and intuitive enough not to press him further, saying merely when they parted, "I truly hope you and Eleanor will be happy together."

Elle's elder brother, on the other hand, was clearly not so hopeful or optimistic—or forgiving. Marcus Pierce, Lord Danvers, and his new wife, Arabella, appeared at the house party two full days before they were expected, having heard of the sudden marriage upon returning from their trip to the Continent.

They arrived on Saturday morning, when the guests were entertaining themselves by playing Pall Mall on the lawn or trying their hands at archery. Eleanor seemed overjoyed to see her brother, judging by her alacrity at setting down her bow and arrow to give Marcus an effusive embrace.

When he quizzed her about what the devil she had been up too, marrying the moment his back was turned, she laughed and gave him an abbreviated recount of the balloon ascension.

Watching brother and sister together, Damon found himself rather envious of the close camaraderie they plainly shared, even if he had purposely avoided that closeness in his own relationship with Eleanor.

Marcus called her Nell, the more common diminutive of her name, as well as "minx" and a few other teasing endearments, but his intense protectiveness was obvious when he skewered Damon with a glance, although he was polite enough when he shook hands and introduced his own new wife, Arabella.

But Marcus took the first opportunity to pull Damon aside from the company and offer a warning. "I'll cut out your liver if you hurt my sister again, Wrexham."

Damon returned a faint smile. "If I hurt her again, you won't have to cut out my liver. I will do it myself."

Marcus regarded him for a long, grim moment, before finally giving a brusque nod. Apparently he was willing to adopt a wait-and-see attitude and allow Damon to prove himself.

His restraint was, in part, a testament to their former friendship. The two of them had known each other since their boarding school days. Damon had regretted losing Marcus's high regard after his broken engagement to Eleanor. He had few close friends, and the ones he did have, he cherished.

Arabella, Lady Danvers, was a bit more welcoming than her new husband, although still reserved in her greeting, making it clear that she was privy to Damon's history with the family.

Her fondness for Eleanor, however, was evident, her manner warm and engaging when she commiserated with Elle about the strangeness of finding oneself married.

"Oh, I so agree," Eleanor heartily assented, sending Damon a provocative glance. "I have yet to become accustomed to the novelty."

"There must be something in the air," Arabella jested, "that is causing this current epidemic of matrimony. I certainly never expected that I and my sisters would succumb all at once, or that you would follow so closely in our footsteps, Eleanor. A pity that Roslyn and Lily cannot be here. We could have had a celebration to commemorate the extraordinary circumstances."

Both Arabella's sisters, Damon knew, were still away on their wedding journeys and so would not be attending the house party.

Arabella was also far warmer to Tess. Over the course of the afternoon, he came to realize that the two women shared a close friendship. They laughed and chatted together with Eleanor all during luncheon, and continued during the drive to the beach afterward.

Despite the overcast sky and brisk breeze, Eleanor's aunt had refused to change her plans and postpone the arranged excursion, evidently expecting the weather to obey her will. Thus, a half dozen carriages were soon making their way south toward the sea, with the viscountess, of course, chaperoning the newlyweds in her equipage.

When Tess expressed a desire to go sea-bathing, saying it would be invigorating, Eleanor agreed but Arabella objected, so a spirited discussion ensued about the wisdom of swimming when a storm threatened.

Damon was exceedingly glad, however, to see Tess coming out of her shell after the loss of her betrothed two years ago. In truth, he hadn't seen her this animated in all that time.

Eleanor, he noted, was her usual lively self, although she ignored him for the most part—except when he handed her down from the carriage. Then she smiled at him with such entrancing warmth that he felt sunstruck.

Yet she refused his help negotiating the rocky cliff path down to the sea. Damon was left to offer his assistance to the other ladies of the party. By the time he reached the shingle beach, Eleanor, Tess, and Arabella were far ahead, strolling arm in arm beside the water.

They made a picturesque sight, Damon thought, with the fresh sea-breeze catching their skirts and rifling the ribbons of their bonnets. It was a pleasure to watch the three beauties enjoying themselves so avidly, and to hear their musical laughter as they danced out of reach of the surging waves to avoid getting their half-boots wet.

Prince Lazzara was apparently of the same opinion, for he gave an appreciative sigh when he caught up with Damon.

Yet the prince's expression soon turned quizzical. "I am holding to my promise to keep away from your ladywife, milord, but you have no such reason to avoid her. Or is Lady Wrexham the one who is avoiding *you*?"

The question, although voiced with humor, was mildly taunting, and Damon had to bite back a retort. "My wife is relishing the company of her friends, your highness, and I mean to allow her the freedom to continue."

"Hmmm," was all Lazzara said. A moment later, he added slyly, "In truth, I confess myself astonished. With your reputed skills as a lover, I expected you to know the first commandment of *amore*."

"And what is that, your highness?"

"Females wish to be wooed. You will never win her favor if you hold back in this detached way."

"So you are suggesting that I woo my wife."

"But yes. It seems a seduction is very much in order."

Damon was only faintly amused at the irony of Lazzara giving *him* advice on seduction. Yet the man was right; he needed to take action if he hoped to end his enforced celibacy any time in the near future. And he very much wished to end it.

Celibacy, Damon thought with a wry grin, was a painful condition indeed when one had an exquisitely beautiful wife sleeping alone in the adjacent bed-chamber every night.

His opportunity to change his circumstances came some half hour later. Damon had kept an eye on the storm clouds accumulating overhead, but the rain came up suddenly, bursting from the skies in shock-ingly cold gusts.

By the time the revellers had hurriedly ascended to the top of the chalk cliff and piled into the waiting carriages, they were all hopelessly drenched, their clothes plastered to their bodies.

Damon remained outside until all the passengers were accounted for. When he settled beside Eleanor, she murmured a breathless "thank you," then leaned closer to whisper in his ear.

"You are soaked to the skin," she added, her voice

quivering with suppressed laughter, "just like the time I pushed you in the fountain."

"If I remember correctly," Damon whispered back, "that incident was far more pleasurable because of what preceded it."

At his reference to their first kiss, Elle smiled again at him, the kind of smile that could stop a man's heartbeat.

When she promptly shivered, Damon badly wanted to pull her against him and warm her with his body heat, but her aunt was watching them with an eagle eye, so he settled for accepting a woolen blanket from the coachman and draping it around Eleanor's shoulders.

The drive home took longer in the downpour. And even though an army of Rosemont footmen hurried out with umbrellas in a futile effort to provide shelter for the guests, they were chilled to the bone.

Eleanor hastened upstairs to change out of her wet attire. Damon followed her more slowly, but it was only when he entered his bedchamber that he struck upon an idea to alter the sleeping arrangements that Elle had insisted upon.

Cornby, bless his heart, had lit a fire in the hearth, and the room was pleasantly warm.

His valet was also dutifully awaiting him, but once Cornby had helped him to remove his wet coat, Damon dismissed him, saying, "I can manage from here. I would rather you perform a small commission for me instead."

Damon strode to the small writing desk in one corner of the room and scribbled a note, folding it once.

"Here," he said, handing the missive to Cornby,

"pray take this to Lady Wrexham and then make yourself scarce."

"Very good, my lord."

The valet's expression never changed, but somehow he looked pleased, as if he approved of his master's plan to woo his new ladywife.

Chapter Fifteen

When plotting a gentleman's seduction, make judicious use of all the feminine weapons in your arsenal . . . a soft word, a careless touch, a kiss. . . .

—An Anonymous Lady, *Advice . . .*

With the help of her abigail, Eleanor had removed her soaked gown and damp corset by the time a polite knock sounded on her bedchamber door. While Jenny went to answer, Eleanor peeled off her clammy garters and stockings and muttered an invective at herself, lamenting her foolishness in taking a seaside jaunt with a storm brewing. She might as well have dunked herself in the Channel; her bare feet were ice-cold, her skin covered in gooseflesh.

She had just reached for a towel to dry her hair when Jenny murmured over her shoulder, "His lordship's valet has a missive for you, milady."

Eleanor hesitated, shivering, then drew on a dressing gown over her shift and went to the door.

"My lady," the valet said with a courteous bow as he held out a folded note. "Lord Wrexham asked me to deliver this to you personally."

She felt her heart rate suddenly quicken at the mention of her husband. "You are Cornby, are you not?" she asked, accepting the note.

"I am, my lady, although I confess surprise that you remember."

Eleanor recalled the elderly servant from two years ago. Cornby had seemed devoted to Damon then—and apparently he was just as devoted now, judging from his watchful regard as she opened the note and read.

The message in Damon's bold scrawl was an invitation to her to share his fire.

Eleanor couldn't help but smile to herself. It was imaginative of him to hit on this way to secure her company. And she wouldn't dream of refusing.

She was freezing, since Jenny hadn't known she would return from her outing sopping wet, and a cheery fire sounded wonderful. Moreover, this would be the perfect opportunity to advance her scheme to increase Damon's ardor. The past several days of teasing had likely been enough to whet his appetite for her. Fanny had warned her not to draw out her elusiveness to the point where Damon became so frustrated that he lost interest entirely. It was time, Eleanor realized, to move to the next stage.

She had to take care, of course. She couldn't let her seduction go too far—no more than a kiss or two—or she would be in danger of succumbing to her own desire for Damon. No, she intended to hold her own against him this time, she promised, and faithfully execute her plan to win his heart.

"Please tell his lordship I will join him in a moment," she told the valet.

Cornby's intent expression seemed to relax. "Very well, my lady. As you wish."

When he had retreated down the corridor, Eleanor

shut the door and went directly to her cheval glass and played with the folds and ribbons of her dressing gown so that she looked artfully disheveled.

"Do you require any further service, milady?" Jenny asked.

"Will you bring me my blue slippers, please? And then take my wet gown downstairs to the kitchens and have it pressed. Then you may have the next hour to yourself, Jenny. I expect I won't be needing you until teatime."

Curtsying, the maid flashed a delighted smile, not only as if happy for a respite from her duties, but as if she, too, was pleased her mistress would spend some time with her new lord. "Thank you, milady. I will not return until you ring for me."

When Eleanor had donned her slippers, she unlocked the connecting door to Damon's bedchamber. The room was dim, she noticed at once, since he had drawn the draperies to shut out the stormy day. A lamp had been turned down low so that it barely glowed, but a fire burned brightly in the grate, throwing out a generous heat.

The effect was warm and welcoming, especially with the steady patter of rain drumming against the windowpanes.

Then Eleanor caught sight of Damon, and her heart skipped a beat. He was standing near the high, four-poster bed, looking supremely handsome in a dressing gown of burgundy brocade. His feet were bare against the Aubusson carpet, and so were his lower legs below the hem of his robe—as if he might be naked underneath.

Awareness tightened her skin and made her shiver

as she stepped into the room and closed the door behind her.

"You look chilled," her husband said, surveying her. "Why don't you warm yourself before the fire?"

"Thank you, I will," Eleanor replied, crossing to the hearth.

There were two wing chairs set invitingly before the fire, but she ignored them and instead gladly held out her frozen hands to the flames while Damon moved to a side table and poured a glass of wine from a decanter.

"I suppose Cornby started your fire some time ago?" she commented.

"Yes. He looks after me very well."

"It was considerate of you to invite me here."

Damon turned toward her. "I am glad for the opportunity to see you without a score of houseguests competing for your attention. It is sad," he added lightly, "that I must resort to clandestine trysts to be alone with my new bride."

Joining her before the hearth, he handed her the wineglass. Eleanor brought it to her lips, looking up at him provocatively as she was supposed to do—which perhaps was a mistake. Damon's dark gaze swept over her in return, almost a physical caress.

And then he turned his scrutiny into an *actual* caress by raising his hand and combing his fingers through her damp hair, which had become a riot of ebony curls.

"I liked your hair long, but this style becomes you. Of course, you are beautiful, no matter how you wear your hair."

Eleanor had tensed at his gesture, bracing herself

against his arousing touch. But she forced herself to relax and return a smile. "My, aren't you complimentary today?"

"I am only stating the truth."

Even so, she was prepared to keep her guard up. She knew firsthand that Damon could be the very essence of devilish seduction, often to her detriment. And from the looks of it, he was bent on seducing her into his bed just now, to end any thoughts she had of having a marriage in name only. She intended to prolong the inevitable moment, however, until the right time. And she was determined to maintain control of this encounter.

Eleanor made no demur when Damon took her free hand between his larger, warm ones and gently chaffed her icy fingers. But then he turned her hand over and lifted it to his lips in a gesture that was warm, enticing, seductive. His breath fanned her palm before he pressed a light kiss on the sensitive flesh of her inner wrist.

Her own breath turned uneven as her nerves tingled under the surface of her skin. Quickly withdrawing her hand, Eleanor stepped back, away from his evocative touch. Casually, she sat in one of the chairs, eager to maintain a minimum distance from Damon.

To her relief, he settled in the wing chair adjacent to hers. Yet his gaze remained fixed on her. And when she took a drink of wine, she realized he was watching her mouth.

"Wine tastes better sipped from a lover's lips, did you know?"

At his suggestive intimation, Eleanor swallowed hard, wondering if by coming here to Damon's bedchamber, she might have taken on more than she could handle. "No, I didn't know."

"Seeing that wine on your lips makes me want to kiss you."

She manufactured a light laugh. "I am afraid you are destined for disappointment, my lord. There won't be any kissing between us just now. I don't want you touching me, either."

"That pains me greatly, sweeting, for I sure as the devil want to touch you. You look wildly desirable, lounging there in your dressing gown."

So do you, Eleanor thought, casting him a sideways glance. The firelight played in his midnight eyes, revealing a tender, teasing glint that caused havoc with her determination to keep the upper hand with Damon.

The boldness of his regard, too, was stirring wanton sensations in her body. Her nipples had tightened against the chill and were so keenly sensitive, she felt the mere brush of his gaze on her breasts.

Eleanor mentally shook herself. Damon could tempt a woman to sin with just a look—and admittedly she was incredibly tempted. But sinning with him would defeat her purpose entirely.

"Pray, will you stop looking at me that way?" she finally requested.

One eyebrow lifted innocently. "How am I looking at you?"

"As if you mean to undress me with your eyes."

"I would much rather undress you with my hands."

His claim was delivered in a soft, throaty drawl that stroked Eleanor's nerve-endings.

She kept her own tone light and amused, however,

when she chastised him. "Damon, behave yourself, or I will return to my own rooms."

He gave a heavy sigh. "That's a fine way to depress a man's carnal fantasies."

Recalling the role she was supposed to be playing, Eleanor sent him a slow, flirtatious smile. "You are allowed to have fantasies, just not act on them."

"Very well, I shall endeavor to keep myself under control, although it will be difficult."

Clasping his hands over his abdomen, Damon leaned back in his chair and stretched his long, bare legs out in front of him, which had the result of parting the folds of his dressing gown to reveal a length of powerful thighs. Eleanor was very certain now that he was naked except for his robe.

She inhaled a ragged breath and drank more wine.

But Damon had seen the focus of her gaze and smiled. "Surely you can't fault me for taking off my wet clothing."

"You could have donned some dry breeches."

"Whatever for? You are my wife now. It's permitted for us to see each other unclothed." He paused. "Regrettably, I have yet to see *you* fully undressed. But I have thought about nothing else since you walked into the room. What are you wearing beneath your robe, Elle? Are you naked?"

A heated tremor eddied deep inside her. Eleanor took another sip of wine for fortitude before replying indirectly, "I know what you are doing, Damon."

"Just what am I doing, love?"

"You are trying to draw me under your spell."

"And you are doing your best to tease me, just as you have during our entire time here. I wonder why?

If I were to guess, I would say you have been employing your advice manual on me."

It seemed foolish to deny the charge, so Eleanor responded with a careless shrug. "Actually I am."

"Why? You no longer need help in capturing a husband. You have already captured me."

She gave him a considering look, debating how honest she should be. "But I have *not* really captured you, Damon. Our marriage lines are little more than a legal contract."

He seemed to give that some thought. "Then what is your objective? To drive me mad with frustrated desire so that I will be eager to do your bidding?"

"In part."

The corner of Damon's mouth twisted. "Perhaps I should read that manual of yours to better understand your methods of seduction."

Eleanor flashed him a genuine smile. "You most certainly don't need an instruction manual to learn about seduction. You are a renowned expert on the subject."

"I will take that as a compliment, love. And I will point out that you don't need a fire to warm you when you have me. I could make you hotter than any fire."

His voice had become a husky murmur, which seriously began to worry Eleanor.

"I expect you could," she said with a shivery little laugh. "But if this is your attempt to lure me to your bed, I must warn you, you won't succeed."

His own smile turned lazy. "You would enjoy my bed, Elle, I promise you. Our lovemaking from now on will be far more pleasurable than your first time."

She had no doubt whatsoever that he could pleasure her. The crackling fire, the potent wine, the sensual sound of rain, had all combined to chase away her chill, but it was Damon himself who had the most profound impact on her. His eyes looked seductive and drowsy in the firelight, which sent a warm ache surging through her body.

With effort, Eleanor tore her gaze away from him and stared into the flickering flames. Damon had awakened her sexuality, had led her to experience her first feelings of power as a woman, and he was rousing those same intense, lustful feelings now. But that was the trouble. Their lust was purely physical. She wanted more from him. Much, much more.

He leaned closer, drawing her attention back to him. "Trust me, Elle. All I care about right now is giving you pleasure."

Eleanor felt her mouth go dry. *She* was the one who was supposed to do the seducing, but Damon was taking over her role completely. His smile tantalized, while his voice dropped another octave.

"You have the most glorious eyes. That vivid shade of blue is entrancing."

His own eyes were dark and wicked, she thought distractedly.

"You have the most luscious body. I would very much like to feel it against me."

"Damon . . . that won't happen."

"No matter," he said easily. "I can imagine how it would be. I can picture making love to you in every exquisite detail. Would you like to know what I would do, sweetheart? How I would pleasure you?"

Eleanor couldn't reply; she was bereft of words just now.

Damon evidently took her silence for agreement, for lazy passion glowed in his eyes as he continued.

"If I were to make love to you, it would be in a soft bed, unlike our hasty coupling in a balloon gondola. That was remarkable, certainly, but not the ideal setting. First, I would undress you slowly and kiss every inch of your lovely body, starting with your breasts. I would begin by caressing them, coddling them. Then I would lift them to my mouth and suckle your nipples."

Her toes curled in her slippers at the very thought. She could almost feel the lush pressure of his mouth on her already hard nipples.

"I would make your breasts ache, Elle. They would feel heavy and hot in my hands. . . . And I can envision your response . . . the soft sounds you make when I suck them."

So could she. Yet it was a mistake to listen to him, Eleanor warned herself. She knew how persuasive, how sensual Damon could be. But she didn't stop him as his voice went on describing how it would be for them.

"Next I would slide my hand between your thighs and find you wet and ready for me. I would stroke your center with my fingers, till you were whimpering with hunger for me. And then I would set my mouth on you and use my tongue to arouse you even further."

Eleanor's stomach clenched as she imagined Damon stroking her with his tongue as he'd done before.

"I can hear your gasps of pleasure as I savor your

taste. Then when you are half mad with need, I would enter you slowly, prolonging the moment. I would fill you with my cock, Elle, so that we moved together, as if we were one person, so that you couldn't tell when I end and you begin. . . ."

Heat flushed her body, while between her legs desire throbbed. Damon was spinning a web of fascination around her, captivating her with his voice, his eyes. Those dark eyes held a memory of their first time together four days ago, reminding her how incredible it had been between them.

And his recitation was having a similar effect on Damon, Eleanor realized when he parted the folds of his dressing gown. "See what you have done to me, love. . . . My loins are full and aching for you."

Rising from his groin was the bold evidence of his sexual arousal, long and huge and swollen. She couldn't help staring at that rigid male flesh, remembering how it had felt moving inside her.

Then Damon untied the sash at his waist and shrugged off his dressing gown. When he rose, something hot and molten unfurled in her belly. It was the first time she had seen him entirely naked, and she looked her fill. Firelight sculpted his sensual, strong-boned body . . . his broad shoulders, his finely muscled chest and taut stomach, his narrow hips, his long, powerful legs.

Damon stood very still, letting her take in every detail, his gaze heated and compelling as he observed her helpless fascination.

If any man could be called beautiful, it was Damon. His chiseled body was perfect, hard and vital, rawly masculine. Eleanor felt a fierce urge to touch him, to caress him. Then her gaze dropped, fixing again on the swirl of dark hair that cradled his hardness. The evidence of his desire stood rigid, flushed, thickly engorged. . . .

Her breath caught in her throat even before he reached out to take her wineglass from her. Setting it on the mantel, he gently grasped her wrists and drew her to her feet.

"D-Damon," she stammered, her protest husky and uneven.

"Touch me, Elle," he coaxed, pressing her palms against his bare chest, inviting her hands to explore the hard expanse. "Touching is allowed, sweeting. I am your husband and you are my wife."

His flesh was smooth and hot; sleek muscles rippled and played beneath satiny skin, and Eleanor couldn't resist doing his bidding.

He was an unholy temptation, she thought, feeling dazed.

Then he bent close, so that his breath ruffled her hair. "You smell like sin, wife," he murmured, nuzzling her temple. "Like rain and sweet, warm woman . . ."

His scent was sinful, too. A hint of musky desire rose between them, while heat radiated upward from his body, enveloping her and holding her spellbound.

When he drew back, the look she saw in his eyes made her heart thud erratically. Then Damon untied the ribbons of her dressing gown and parted the lapels, exposing her chemise. Her nipples were excruciatingly hard and blatantly outlined beneath the fine cambric.

"If I were to make love to you, this is how I would start. . . ."

Lifting a suggestive finger, he found her parted lips and traced slowly downward along her throat. His touch was light, delicate . . . searing. Then raising both hands to fondle her breasts, he traced her shape through the fabric, rubbing his palms with teasing pressure over the mounds.

An intense surge of pleasure rippled through Eleanor as he lightly squeezed each nipple, but she couldn't bring herself to object. She wanted to feel his hands all over her body.

"Let me keep you warm, Elle."

Her heart was pounding wildly when he shifted his hands. Sliding them around her hips to cup her buttocks, he pulled her firmly against his tightly muscled frame, into the cradle of his thighs. "Feel how much I want you."

One of his knees separating hers, he pressed his arousal against her stomach, and Eleanor forgot to breathe. She could feel the rigid, heated length of his sex branding her like hot steel. And the thought of him moving inside her, completing her, made her heart labor even harder. She was overwhelmed with longing, the burning need in her loins to feel him driving deep into her, to feel his thick shaft filling her, plunging rhythmically. . . . Which was precisely what he wanted her to feel, a protective voice warned in her head.

Damon knew how desperately she longed for him, how she craved his passion.

Yet she was stronger than that, Eleanor scolded herself. She wouldn't give in to his enchantment this time. She wouldn't let him win, wouldn't let herself get lost in the fire in his eyes.

On the contrary, she had to turn the tables on him. She had to make Damon feel the same unquenchable yearning for her, so that someday he would come to love her.

"Perhaps you are right," she whispered, her voice an unsteady rasp. "We need a bed."

Her apparent change of heart seemed to take him by surprise, but he didn't question her when she took his hand and led him to the bed.

"Lie down, my lord husband."

Damon obeyed, climbing onto the high bed and stretching out on his back.

He looked starkly beautiful, sprawled there on the dark gold counterpane. Shadow and light roamed over him, accentuating the strong, sleek lines of his body.

Eleanor felt a fresh surge of primitive arousal just looking at him—and so did he, judging by the heat in his eyes.

She took a deep breath, though, bracing herself against her yearning, and placed a palm on his broad chest.

Feeling the firm resilient muscle beneath the warm velvet of his skin, she stroked him for a moment, her touch light and caressing, but then her hand stilled.

"Damon, do you recall how you always manage to fluster me by kissing me to distraction?"

"Yes, love."

"This time I mean to do the same to you."

Bending down to him, she took his lips in a long, sweet, lingering kiss.

Then despite her own yearning to continue, she tore herself away.

"That is all for now, husband. I told you, I am not interested in a marriage of convenience. However, if you ever think you can give me more—if you come to want a true marriage as I do—pray, let me know."

With that she turned and fled to the safety of her own bedchamber.

She had violated Fanny's precepts with a vengeance, Eleanor knew, by declaring her objective so boldly, but she couldn't bring herself to regret her blunder.

It was time Damon learned just how serious she was about wanting him as a true husband and not merely a lover. About wanting his heart and not only his body.

Dismayingly, however, the choice was entirely his to make.

Chapter Sixteen

Sometimes, however, it is best simply to follow your instincts.

—An Anonymous Lady, *Advice . . .*

The shout woke her from a restless sleep.

Her heart thudding in alarm, Eleanor sat up in bed and searched the darkness, wondering what had startled her awake.

The hoarse shout came again from Damon's bedchamber, muffled by the closed door between their rooms. Springing out of bed, Eleanor quickly lit a candle and hurried to unlock their connecting door.

By the time she reached Damon's bedside, his shouts had turned to a low, moaning sound. He was thrashing in his sleep, obviously in the throes of a nightmare.

The tangled covers had lowered to his waist, leaving his torso bare. His skin was damp and chilled with perspiration, Eleanor realized when she put a gentle hand on his shoulder and shook him.

He didn't respond, even when she called his name softly, so she shook him more forcefully. "Damon, wake up!"

At her order, his eyes flew open.

He lay there rigidly, his expression dazed, confused, raw. In the glow of candlelight, she could see his pulse pounding in his throat, could feel the coiled tension in his body beneath her palm.

"You were having a nightmare," she said in a low voice.

The eyes he turned to her were tortured. He stared at her, looking almost lost. Wild locks of mahogany hair framed his face, while a shadow of stubble darkened his jaw.

His shoulders shuddered. Then, brushing off her touch, he sat up and rubbed a hand raggedly down his face.

"What is troubling you, Damon?" Eleanor asked quietly.

"Nothing."

His tone was harsh, abrupt, dismissive. Just as abruptly, he seemed to notice her attire—that she was standing there in her nightshift and bare feet.

"I am fine," he added tersely. "Go back to bed, Elle."

She wasn't proof against his utter vulnerability, though. She ached to smooth away the lines of pain from his features, to hold him until that desolate look had faded from his eyes.

Raising a soothing hand, she cupped the side of his face. "I wish I could help," she murmured.

At her gentle touch, Damon froze for a handful of heartbeats. Then he pulled back sharply, away from her offer of comfort.

His lashes swept down to hide his eyes, shuttering his expression, shutting her out. "I don't need your help."

Eleanor hesitated. "Would you at least like me to stay with you a while?"

"No. I don't want you here."

Lifting his gaze, he stared back at her, his eyes as dark as a moonless midnight. His voice was brittle when he repeated, "Go back to sleep, Eleanor."

Reluctantly she obeyed at least part of his command; she returned to her own bed. Yet she definitely did not feel like sleeping.

A tightness welled in Eleanor's chest, in part because Damon had professed not to want her, but mainly because his emotional state dismayed and disturbed her.

What was causing him such pain that he suffered nightmares from it?

It was a long, long time before Eleanor felt herself drifting off to sleep. And when finally she did, her last thought was that Damon was not only shutting her out of his heart. He was shutting her out of his life.

Sunday dawned wet and miserable, which dampened the spirits of all the houseguests. Most of the company stayed indoors and played parlor games, and Eleanor made an effort to join in with her usual enthusiasm.

Damon, however, remained aloof and withdrawn the entire day. And on Monday she saw nothing of him at all. He never appeared at breakfast, and when there was no sign of him at luncheon, Eleanor decided to search for him.

When she went upstairs and tapped on the connecting door between their rooms, she discovered his manservant in Damon's bedchamber.

"I believe he is out riding, milady," Cornby responded in answer to her question about Lord Wrexham's whereabouts.

Eleanor glanced out the windows where a steady stream of rain was drizzling down. "In *this* weather?"

"He prefers to be alone sometimes. Especially today."

"What is today?"

"The anniversary of his brother's death, my lady."

That intelligence jolted her. ""Oh," she said rather inadequately. "I didn't realize."

"His lordship does not like to speak of it."

Eleanor frowned as a thought occurred to her. "Cornby, Lord Wrexham had a severe nightmare the other night. Would that have anything to do with his brother's death?"

"I expect so, my lady. He always has bad dreams at this time of year."

"Dreams of his brother dying?"

"Regrettably, yes." The valet hesitated before adding with some reluctance, "His lordship usually spends a great deal of time riding, driving himself physically— I believe in order to make himself weary enough to keep away the nightmares. Although that does not always suffice."

Cornby's revelation greatly dismayed Eleanor. "Did he give you any indication of when he might return?"

"No, my lady. Sometimes it is before dark, but sometimes it is late into the night."

"So this has happened before?"

"Regularly, my lady. It is a yearly ritual with him."

Her dismay only increased. Was Damon still punishing himself for being unable to save his brother? Eleanor wondered with a heavy heart.

It was then that Cornby's occupation caught her attention. He had paused respectfully when she entered the room, but now she realized he'd been occupied in tapping a small wooden cask and filling a crystal decanter with a dark amber liquid that looked and smelled like brandy.

"I suppose he plans to drink that when he returns?" she asked.

"Yes, my lady. I have standing orders to have a sufficient quantity of brandy on hand each year for the sad occasion."

It concerned Eleanor that Damon hoped to find solace in an alcoholic stupor, but the reason for his nightmares distressed her more.

She waved a hand at the cask. "It is alarming that he is still tormented by memories. His brother died many years ago."

"Yes, but I believe his lordship's grief was greater than normal, considering how close they were. Sometimes, apparently, there is a bond between twins that is not present between most siblings. It was difficult for Lord Wrexham to watch his twin waste away, suffering such terrible pain. I suppose you could say it devastated him."

Eleanor winced inwardly, imagining how agonizing it must have been for both brothers. Of course Damon was still haunted by his twin's death. And he was enduring his grief all alone. She hated to think of it.

"I wish there was something I could do to help," she said, her voice low and earnest.

"Perhaps there is, my lady." Cornby was not immediately forthcoming, however. When Eleanor gave him a searching glance, he added quietly, "I dislike betraying Lord Wrexham's trust in me by speaking of him out of turn."

"Please tell me, Cornby," she urged, badly wanting to understand her husband better. "I am his wife now, but you know him better than anyone."

The elderly manservant nodded yet still looked uncomfortable when he spoke. "I think perhaps it might do his lordship immeasurable good if he could unburden himself to a confidant. Of course it is not my position to advise you, but perhaps if you could speak to him. . . ."

Eleanor was extremely glad to see that Cornby had his lord's best interests at heart. "I will indeed speak to him, Cornby. Thank you for suggesting it."

The valet hesitated again. "My lady . . . perhaps . . . that is, you should not feel slighted if his lordship rebuffs any attempts at discourse. He is not one to let others close."

Which was an immense understatement, Eleanor reflected, recalling how Damon had abruptly ordered her from his room the other night, despite the torment of his nightmares.

"You are extremely loyal to him, are you not, Cornby?"

"Yes, my lady. I am devoted to him. But he has earned my devotion. He is a fine master . . . and a fine man."

She smiled faintly. "I agree with you—and I thank you for serving him so well."

The valet bowed low. "It is my duty, my lady, but my pleasure also."

Cornby had given her a good deal to think about, Eleanor mused as she returned to her own bedchamber, and she was very grateful to him.

It was crystal clear to her now why Damon was determined to let no one in, even her. Especially her, perhaps. Because the loss of his brother had affected him so profoundly, he was bent on shunning any future intimacy for fear of enduring that devastating grief again.

The thought made her heart hurt.

She also couldn't help thinking of their broken betrothal two years ago. Had Damon turned to his mistress so as to purposely drive *her* away? Because he didn't want to let her get close enough to have the power to hurt him?

It was possible.

But the past concerned her less than what to do now. What happened to a man when all his grief was bottled up inside him? The pain escaped in nightmares, that was what. Unless it had another outlet.

She needed to speak to Damon about his feelings, Eleanor decided as she left her own room and moved down the corridor to return downstairs. But would he allow her to? He'd spurned her recent efforts to console him and might very well do so again if she attempted to make him talk about his brother.

In fact, now that she considered it, Damon had never shared any of his real feelings with her in all the time she'd known him. He'd buried his emotions grave-deep and doubtless wanted to keep them buried.

Well, she would just have to change his mind, Eleanor resolved—and she could not use Fanny's tactics to do it, either. Until now she had relied on the courtesan's counsel for guidance, but this was a time when she needed to follow her own instincts. There had been enough of mating games between them. What Damon needed was a friend.

Strengthening their friendship would go farther than trying to arouse his desire for her, Eleanor concluded. She was still determined to make Damon fall in love with her—and to make certain he had no reason to want a mistress when he had her for his wife—but she intended to rely on her own intuition rather than an instruction manual.

Still stewing, she rejoined the company, but she felt almost hopeful as she spent the next several hours forming a plan.

Damon didn't make an appearance at dinner, although Eleanor knew he had returned to Rosemont; the stables had informed her, as she'd requested.

If anyone noticed his empty place at the table, they didn't question her about it. But Eleanor couldn't forget. Even with Marcus and Arabella and Tess there to distract her, without Damon present, the evening seemed rather interminable. She kept watching the ormolu clock on the hearth mantel, wondering if he was drinking himself into oblivion to keep the haunting memories at bay.

After the tea tray had been brought into the drawing room later that night, Eleanor slipped away and went upstairs. Damon didn't answer her quiet knock on his bedchamber door, but she entered anyway.

She found him sitting alone before a fire that had nearly burned out, wearing merely a shirt and breeches and riding boots. The room was dim except for the fading glow of embers, but there was enough light to see his features. His expression was dark and brooding when he met her gaze.

"What are *you* doing here, Elle?"

His words were only slightly slurred, but she suspected he had drunk a great deal.

"I wanted to see you," she answered, keeping her tone light.

Damon averted his gaze to stare at the floor. "Well, you can just go away again. I am in no mood to suffer your teasing."

"I imagine not." Her tone was wry. "But I am not here to tease you or lead you on."

"Then why the devil *are* you here?"

"To bear you company. I assumed you wouldn't want to sleep for fear your nightmare would return."

He scowled at that and lifted his head. "I don't want your damned pity, Elle."

"Of course you don't. But I mean to stay. Any friend would do the same. You shouldn't be alone just now. You need someone to share your sorrow."

"What do you know about it?" Damon demanded harshly.

"I think I can understand how important your brother was in your life."

His gaze narrowed on her. "Has Cornby been talking out of turn?"

"He happened to mention that this was the anniversary of Joshua's death."

Muttering a low oath, Damon drained his snifter in one long swallow. "If you came to offer solace, I don't want it," he repeated.

"Very well, then I will just watch while you drink yourself into a stupor. May I pour you more brandy?"

Although his expression never softened, he considered her offer for a moment before holding out his glass. "Yes. I fear I am not in the best condition to manage it myself."

Taking his glass, Eleanor poured him a generous measure and handed it to him. "May I have some of your brandy for myself?"

Damon shrugged. "Help yourself." Then he paused to peer up at her. "The Dragon would say that ladies don't drink brandy."

She ignored his provoking reference to her aunt. "I don't want to be a lady tonight, Damon. I just want to be your friend."

"Bloody hell . . . I don't *want* a friend, Elle."

"Well, perhaps *I* want one. I have always enjoyed your company far more than my aunt's illustrious friends, and just now I have had my fill of them."

Damon stared at her a long moment before his mouth curled in agreement. "So have I."

Glad that she'd managed to wipe that dark scowl off his face for the time being, Eleanor fetched her own fingerful of brandy and sat in the wing chair beside him.

For several moments Damon maintained a morose silence—a silence Eleanor was determined not to break until he was willing.

Fortunately he spoke first. "You impress me, Elle. Most females would be upset finding their husbands three sheets to the wind."

She could have made a quip in response, but she kept her tone solemn. "But you have a good reason for getting soused. You want to remember Joshua, and this is your way of keeping his memory alive."

"You *do* understand," Damon mumbled, sounding a bit surprised.

"I am trying to, at least." Eleanor held up her glass. "Shall we toast Joshua's memory?"

Damon didn't answer at first. She glimpsed the shadow of his sadness before the thick fringe of black lashes swept down to hide his eyes.

Still without answering, he drank a long gulp of brandy and then drew a deep, shuddering breath.

"I am terribly sorry you lost your brother, Damon," she said softly. "Especially in that horrible way."

At her quiet condolences, he cast her a sideways glance, yet the aggressiveness had faded from his countenance. Instead, one dark lock had fallen over his brow, giving Eleanor a hint of the young boy Damon had once been. He looked vulnerable, at a loss for words.

When he remained mute, Eleanor added just as quietly, "Mr. Geary told me what a special boy Joshua was."

Averting his gaze, Damon stared down at his glass. "What a waste of a life." She could hear the anger in his voice, an anger that turned to bleakness when he muttered a curse. "It should have been *me*, not Joshua."

"I think I would have felt the same way if Marcus had died."

The raw vulnerability in Damon's face made her heart ache for him. His handsome features were twisted in a merger of desolation and anguish.

She would give anything to be able to take away his

pain, his grief. She wanted to hold and protect him, to find some way to heal him, to chase the shadows from his eyes.

Setting down her glass on the small table between them, Eleanor rose to stir the fire and added another log. Then she turned back to Damon and began to undress, starting with her slippers and stockings.

When she reached behind her to unfasten the hooks of her evening gown, Damon speared her with his glance. "What in hell's name are you doing, Elle?"

"Comforting you."

She thought he might object, but he said nothing. Instead he stared at her broodingly, his eyes dark and watchful.

She finished removing her gown and then her corset. Finally proceeding to her chemise, she slipped the bodice down and let the garment fall to the floor in a whisper of cambric, leaving her completely nude to his view.

She heard Damon inhale a ragged breath, but he didn't stir a muscle when she moved to stand before him. He merely sat there tensely as she took his brandy glass and set it aside, then bent down and pulled out the hem of his shirt from his breeches.

She was heartened that he allowed her to draw his shirt over his head, exposing a smooth expanse of chest. Then she knelt at his feet to remove his boots.

A muscle flexed in his jaw when she reached for the placket of his breeches, and he pushed her hands away. But he himself unfastened his breeches and drawers and took them off, following with his stockings.

When Damon rose in all his naked splendor, Eleanor's breath caught in her throat at the picture he made, illuminated by the glow of firelight. He looked rather disreputable with his tousled hair and shadow of stubble on his face, but he was still the most sinfully beautiful man she had ever known, with his virile strength and muscular grace.

Yet his expression remained enigmatic, as if he was waiting for her to make the next move. She obliged by stepping toward him. In the quiet hush of the room, she could almost hear her heart thudding in rhythm with the soft hiss and crackle of the hearth fire as she cupped his face in her hands and raised her lips to his.

Her kiss started out gentle. The taste of brandy was potent and rich to her senses, and so was the flavor of Damon's mouth . . . the scent of his skin, the heat of his body. But the gentleness vanished when she stirred an unwilling response in him.

Lifting her close to his body, he held her with crushing tightness and kissed as if he needed her, as if he craved her.

His hunger only served to heighten Eleanor's desire, but this moment was not about her. It was all about succoring Damon.

Pressing her palms against his shoulders, she broke off their fervent kiss and stepped back. Then moving to the bed, she turned back the counterpane and drew down the linen sheets.

"Will you join me, Damon?" she asked softly.

His gaze was wary, cautious. "It depends. Do you plan to leave me aching this time?"

"No. I mean to make love to you."

This time she meant to carry through on her implied promise of pleasure.

Damon evidently believed her, for when she climbed onto the bed and stretched out on her side, he lay down beside her, on his back. But he remained rigid, as if he still didn't trust her.

Eleanor knew she would have to win back his trust. She wanted his arms around her, flesh on flesh, touching, but she settled for moving closer and pressing light kisses against the side of his throat, his bare shoulder, his collarbone, his chest.

Finally, when it seemed right, she rose up on her knees and began a tender exploration of his body with her hands, sculpting the hard lines of bone and muscle and burning skin with her palms, her fingertips, until she reached his loins.

He tensed even more when she closed her fingers over his thick arousal, and she could see his jaw tighten, but he lay still while she teased the heavy sacs beneath his erection, pulling lightly. When she took him into her warm hand again, his eyes turned even darker. Then bending, she pressed her lips against the swollen head of his shaft. He sucked in a breath at the first touch of her mouth.

Eleanor continued her tender ministrations, though, plying him with delicate caresses of her tongue. Damon squeezed his eyes shut, while his hands clenched at his sides, his features taut with desire and pain as she softly ran her tongue around the swollen head . . . the sensitive ridge below . . . the pulsing, velvet-smooth length. . . .

Following her instincts then, she closed her lips

around his engorged member to take him more fully in her mouth, enveloping him, welcoming him.

His whole body began to tremble, making her feel both precious and powerful, so she drew him even deeper, suckling, absorbing his scent and taste.

When her lips slowly slid down over his fullness once more, his hands moved to curl in her hair and he strained against her mouth, his breathing harsh and ragged. She heard her name hoarsely whispered, felt him shaking.

Then abruptly he grasped her shoulders and compelled Eleanor to raise her head.

His jaw was knotted tightly, his voice hoarse when he ground out one word: *"Enough."*

Still clutching her shoulders, he rolled her onto her back and mounted her, encountering no resistance. She kept her thighs spread, soft and welcoming, and threaded her fingers in his dark hair.

His face was hard with need, his eyes alight with dark fire as he sank into the cradle she made for him. The desire she saw there made her chest feel tight . . . and then he buried his face in the curve of her neck as he buried his flesh in her wet warmth.

Eleanor arched her back in response and rocked against him, which made Damon drive upward again, and then again with more urgency.

Not protesting his ferocity, Eleanor wrapped herself around him. She felt surrounded by him, invaded by him, fulfilled by him as he ignited a burst of fire inside her. Her hips rose up to meet him as he went on withdrawing, then sinking deep, plunging his hardness into the recesses of her body until he couldn't get any closer.

Her moan turned to a sob of need, a plea that seemed to inflame him. When he grated out her name, the hoarse sound reverberated through her and sent her spiraling over the edge of passion. Every part of her clenched; her inner muscles clutched at him, holding him fast, as shuddering tremors began to ripple remorselessly through her.

At her fierce climax, Damon let himself surrender. His strong body arched helplessly above her as he reached his own harsh explosion deep within her. He threw back his head as he shattered, his teeth bared in primal pleasure while guttural groans of release ripped from his throat.

Afterward, his arms came around her as he collapsed upon her. His breathing ragged, he lay there, hot and heavy, still joined to her, and held her close, almost desperately so.

When Eleanor eventually recovered her own fragmented senses, her hands slid up his back, stroking gently, soothing him. In response, Damon buried his face in the curve of her neck, as if absorbing the warmth and strength of her.

Eleanor had to swallow against the tender rush of feeling his need evoked. When finally he eased his weight off her, onto his side, she searched his face in the dim light. He looked exhausted, vulnerable, but his eyes were not as haunted as they had been before.

Feeling hopeful, she caught his hand and laced her fingers with his. "Go to sleep, Damon. I will stay with you tonight."

To her relief, he didn't argue but merely closed his eyes, his lashes forming black crescents on his cheeks.

Her heart full of emotions, Eleanor kept their

fingers entwined. She intended to watch over him through the night, to keep the tormenting nightmares away.

Yet it was the privilege of a wife to hold and comfort her husband, she reflected. And for the first time since their hasty marriage, she actually felt as if she truly was his wife.

Damon's wife.

The words felt strange and yet wonderful at the same time. She cherished that feeling of belonging to him.

And while Damon might not want to be her true husband, she knew he felt *something* for her. She hadn't mistaken the fierce intensity of his caresses just now.

Nor had she misjudged his exhaustion. From the sound of his slow even breathing, Eleanor realized he had fallen asleep.

She smiled faintly as she lay there in the darkness and gently placed a palm against his chest, measuring the beat of his heart with her fingertips.

Her own heart warmed when unconsciously he moved closer to her, seeking comfort and heat.

She had comforted tonight. He was still gravely reluctant to talk about his brother, but at least she had made a start.

She knew why Damon was guarding his heart so closely, why he refused to let love into his life. He couldn't bear to lose anyone else. She wondered how far his fear would drive him.

Of course *she* was guilty of her own fear. That he would break her heart again.

Could she believe Damon's promises? Could she

trust the devil lure of precious happiness? He could easily betray her as he had two years ago.

And yet for the first time since their betrothal ended, she was beginning to hope that her dreams of true love with Damon might someday become a reality.

Still, if he was going to lower his defenses, it best happen soon, a warning voice prodded Eleanor. She had hoped to protect herself from being hurt, but the more she learned about Damon, the more she loved him.

Chapter Seventeen

Once you are his wife, you should strive to encourage his physical desire for you. And happily, you may take your own pleasure as well.

—An Anonymous Lady, *Advice . . .*

Damon woke to bright sunlight streaming into his bedchamber. Evidently Cornby had decided it was time he arose and so had drawn the draperies wide open.

Damon winced at the bright light and rolled over to bury his beard-stubbled face in the pillows. His head was throbbing from his overindulgence of potent brandy and from his even more potent memories.

He didn't want to remember last night—how raw and exposed he'd felt with Elle, what he'd said to her, how he had made love to her like a frenzied savage, the tender way she had held him through the night. . . . But the sheets smelled of her, and with her scent, vivid images of Elle floated into his mind.

Despite his fierce reluctance to admit it, he had needed her comforting last night. And despite his determination to drive her away, Eleanor had refused to give up. She had stayed beside him, determined to help him battle his demons.

How many women would have done the same for their drunken husbands—?

A familiar masculine throat being cleared told Damon he wasn't alone. When he pried one eye open, he saw that Cornby stood respectfully at one side of the room, waiting for acknowledgment.

A further perusal of his bedchamber showed Damon that his wife was no longer there.

"I have brought your breakfast, my lord," Cornby said with far too much cheer.

"Not hungry," Damon mumbled, wishing the servant would go away.

"Even so, I beg you to eat. Her ladyship asked me to see that you had proper sustenance, and I feel obliged to follow her wishes."

That hint of sedition compelled Damon to rouse himself. Gingerly, he sat up with the pillows propped behind him and the covers drawn up to his waist, concealing the lower half of his nude body.

"Do I need to remind you that I pay your salary, Cornby?" he asked as the valet set a breakfast tray on his lap.

"No, my lord. But I have hopes of ingratiating myself with the new mistress. I have learned from long experience that a household runs much more smoothly if the lady is happy."

Damon bit back a smile, since smiling made his head hurt, and surveyed the contents of the tray. In addition to an ample breakfast of crumpets, eggs, bacon, and coffee, there was a thick greenish-gray liquid in a tall glass. "Pray what is *that*, may I ask?"

"*That* is a concoction that her ladyship says her brother, Lord Danvers, swears by. It is supposed to counter the debilitating effects of liquor. Lady Wrexham claims it will work wonders on your aching head."

Picking up the glass cautiously, Damon took a tentative sip and discovered the taste somewhat more appealing than its appearance, which was not saying much. "What is in this?"

"I am not certain, my lord. Her ladyship mixed it herself in the kitchens. But she promised she would share the recipe with me in anticipation of future occurrences. Oh, and I was supposed to convey a message to you. She hopes you will escort her on a ride in an hour's time, if you feel up to the exertion."

Damon grunted noncommittally, not certain he wanted to face Eleanor so soon after his follies of last night. Keeping his distance from her seemed wise after lowering his defenses so thoroughly in front of her.

Still, that didn't stop him from asking Cornby about the wedding gift he planned to give her. "Has the delivery for Lady Wrexham come yet?"

"Not yet, my lord, but it should arrive from London sometime today. As soon as it does, I will personally supervise its planting as you directed."

"Good."

"Also," Cornby added, "your cousin, Miss Blanchard, asked after you. She expressed a wish to speak to you when you have a free moment."

"Did she say why?"

"No, my lord, but I would venture to guess she was concerned by your disappearance yesterday."

Damon sighed. He would likely be unable to escape Tess's concern if she was set on seeing him. But he supposed she had the right to be worried, since she cared for him—and since she was one of very few people who knew what yesterday had meant to him.

Admittedly he felt somewhat better after drinking the potion Eleanor had concocted and fortifying his empty stomach with nearly half the breakfast. Within the hour he had bathed and shaved and dressed in riding clothes.

He was tying his cravat before the cheval glass when a knock sounded on his bedchamber door. Damon tensed, thinking it might be Eleanor, but instead it was his cousin Tess, he saw over his shoulder.

After greeting Cornby pleasantly, Tess swept past the valet and moved toward Damon, offering him a bright smile when she noted his attire. "Good, you mean to get out. It is a glorious morning—much warmer now that the storm has passed."

When Damon turned to face her fully, she stretched up to kiss him lightly on the cheek, then searched his features. "You look a little the worse for wear, but not as terrible as I feared."

Tess herself looked fresh and lovely in a pale green kerseymere morning dress, Damon noted, but there was a certain glint in her eye that belied her usual serenity—and that boded ill for him, he decided.

Resigning himself to the interview, he dismissed Cornby, who bowed and retrieved the breakfast tray to carry it out.

As the manservant passed her, Tess plucked an uneaten crumpet from the plate. Rather to Damon's surprise then, she perched on the bed Cornby had just made. It was not like Tess to be so oblivious to propriety, although at least the door had been left wide open for the sake of appearances.

Damon kept the observation to himself, however, and turned back to the mirror to finish tying his cravat.

"You have raised my curiosity, cousin," Tess said, nibbling on the crumpet. "I expected you to be a grouch today, but you didn't order me from your bedchamber as I anticipated."

"I should have done so," Damon returned dryly. "It is hardly proper for you to be in a gentleman's bedchamber, even if you *are* my blood relation."

"I know. But you have been purposely avoiding me, and this is my way of foiling your design. I have come to prod you, dear cousin. Granted, you deserve a time to mourn each year, Damon, but enough is enough."

Glancing over his shoulder again at Tess, Damon raised a quelling eyebrow. "Is this a lecture, love? I thought you of all people would understand."

"Oh, I do. Be grateful that I didn't pester you yesterday when you were wallowing in sadness."

Her statement took Damon aback. Tess understood better than most the shock and grief he'd felt at his brother's death, since she had experienced untimely death herself.

"*Wallowing?*" he repeated.

"Yes, wallowing. I know the sentiment quite well, Damon, since I have done the same for the past two years. But you consoled me when I lost my betrothed, and I want to return the favor . . . although now that you have Eleanor, perhaps you don't require my sympathetic ear?"

Damon disregarded her leading question and said instead, "I am perfectly fine, Tess."

She gave a faint nod. "That is precisely what I always told myself, even if it was a patent falsehood." Tess's expression grew solemn. "I understand what you are feeling, Damon. Death of a loved one affects you, even though you pretend it doesn't."

"I am not pretending anything."

"Perhaps not, but I suspect you are indulging in self-flagellation. No matter how illogical it is, you cannot help but blame yourself for living when Joshua died. If he cannot be alive and happy and well, then you don't deserve to be, either. Isn't that true?"

He kept his lips pressed together, not answering, which only encouraged Tess to continue.

"You wish with all your heart that you could have saved him, and you feel a terrible guilt that you failed."

Damon didn't argue her point. His most profound regret in his entire life was being unable to save his dying brother.

His muteness, however, only seemed to frustrate Tess. "But Damon, would Joshua have wanted for you to stop living?" She answered her own question. "Of course not. I was only a child when he died, but from what I remember of him, Joshua loved a lark. He loved *life*. And he would have been distressed to know you have continued to grieve for him so acutely. He would want you to move on with your life, Damon. That is what I am determined to do. I have finally come to the realization that we need to live and love now, in the moment. To make the most of our time on earth."

"So you have become a sage philosopher in your old age?" he drawled.

"Not entirely. But at least I have acknowledged the futility of mourning a tragedy I cannot change."

Rather than replying, Damon completed the last intricate fold of his linen cravat and picked up his riding coat that Cornby had laid out for him.

Watching as he donned the coat, Tess swallowed the remaining morsel of crumpet before commenting again. "I am glad that you have someone to turn to. You did turn to Eleanor and explain your feelings to her, I hope?"

Not willingly, Damon thought to himself. He hadn't wanted to share his feelings with Elle because they were still too raw. Yet admittedly, the pain he'd felt last night had diminished somehow. Her comfort had made something ease inside him.

He owed Eleanor for that, he knew.

He couldn't deny, either, that something had changed between them last night. He just wasn't certain what to do about it. Eleanor filled a need in him that he'd determinedly refused to recognize until now. A need that inwardly he was still fighting. He didn't want to need her.

Tess frowned at his continued silence. "Your marriage was not a love match, I take it, judging from the haste of the ceremony and the distance you and Eleanor have maintained from each other these past few days."

Her prodding comment about love made him uneasy. "No, it was not a love match," Damon responded in a bland tone. "Not that it is any of your concern, darling."

"Of course it is my concern," she retorted sweetly. "You are my nearest family. You are the closest thing

I have to a brother. I had the Loring sisters to help me through my worst days, but you have no one."

She paused. "I *do* know how you feel, Damon. The thought of intimacy, of making yourself vulnerable to pain again, frightens the devil out of you. So you build a protective shell around you. You shun all emotion. You hold your feelings close to yourself. But you pay a price for such isolation. For the past two years, I have felt only half alive while the world moved on around me."

So had he, Damon had to admit.

"It is a dreadfully lonely way to exist," Tess added wistfully. "True, you experience less sorrow, but you also never feel joy, never know love. And love is what makes us whole, Damon."

He mentally shrank from her observation, instinctively resisting her advice. Eschewing love and intimacy was indeed a lonely existence, yet if he needed a reminder of the danger in loving, Tess was it. He intended to spare himself the pain and grief she'd endured upon losing her betrothed.

He and Eleanor were lovers now, but he didn't want any further closeness than that—did he? He certainly didn't want to lead her on and then hurt her when he failed to reciprocate her feelings, as he'd done during their betrothal.

Tess seemed to sense that she had pressed him too intently, however, for her tone lightened and she changed to focus to herself.

"I hope to love again someday. In the meantime, I plan to live my life more fully. I am done worrying about appearances, fretting over what is proper and what is not. I mean to let down my hair a little. You have been wicked all your life, Damon. Now it is my turn."

Damon's gaze narrowed on her as he buttoned his coat. "Should I be worried about *you*, Tess?"

She flashed him a smile that accented her astonishing beauty. "No, you needn't worry. I don't mean to become *too* wicked, merely a dash. No matter the temptation, I cannot turn into a Jezebel since I have my charities to consider. But I have swathed myself in widow's weeds long enough, especially since I never actually *was* a widow."

Crossing to her, Damon took her hand. "If I promise to throw off *my* widow's weeds for now, will you leave me in peace?"

Tess dimpled up at him. "Possibly. What did you have in mind?"

"You will be glad to know I intend to take my wife riding this morning, just the two of us."

Tess's smile was beautiful to behold. "Excellent," she exclaimed as she withdrew her hand and slid down from the bed. "Then you don't need any more prodding from me. I will leave it to Eleanor to try and dissolve that wall you have built around your heart."

With that, Tess exited his room, leaving Damon to grapple with the totally discomfiting thoughts both she and Eleanor had kindled in him.

Eleanor was far from certain that Damon would accept her invitation to ride, but her hopes soared when a servant brought her word from Lord Wrexham, asking her to meet him in the stables at eleven o'clock.

She eagerly went upstairs to change into a stylish,

dark blue riding habit and matching shako hat, and was fairly pleased with the image reflected in her mirror.

Their horses were waiting when she arrived at the stables, as was Damon. He looked supremely handsome, Eleanor thought, searching his face, although his enigmatic expression was no more revealing than it had been last night.

Apparently he preferred to forget that experience altogether, for after a brief greeting, Damon was silent as he lifted her into her sidesaddle and then swung up on his own horse.

Together they guided their mounts along the long sweeping drive flanked by chestnut trees and banks of rhododendrons, and then left the formal grounds of Rosemont behind to ride out into the countryside.

Admittedly, Eleanor felt a little fatigued, since she had stayed awake long into the night watching Damon sleep, and yet her spirits were higher than at any time since before her aunt's house party began.

It was a splendid day, fresh and clean after the rain, and golden with sunshine, with a sweet hint of autumn in the air. She could see for miles over the grassy hills and green valleys of the downs, which stretched off toward the horizon and the English Channel.

After a time, Eleanor began searching her mind for something to say. She was keenly aware of Damon and wanted very much to know what he was thinking, what he was feeling. But she decided she would be wise to stick to mundane topics.

"So, was Marcus's tonic effective in soothing your aching head?" she asked. "I have never had need to use it myself, fortunately."

The wry curve of his mouth raised her spirits even further. "Yes, it was effective. I am in your debt."

"I am glad. I am also glad that you wanted to ride with me. It has been frustrating, being cooped up in the house for so many days."

"Yes," Damon agreed. "I thought it best that we spend some time together. Our distance is beginning to be noticed by the guests."

Eleanor winced inwardly at his casual comment, a little hurt that the only reason Damon gave for accepting her invitation was for appearances' sake.

She couldn't say the same about him. She relished being with him, relished the pleasure of simply sharing his company. She always had.

Indeed, this moment brought back memories of two years ago when their courtship was brand new—the excitement, the anticipation, the feverish delight of having his attention all to herself, the thrill of his kisses. . . . They had spent a good deal of time riding over these same lands together.

It had been a special time in her life, Eleanor remembered, and she would give a great deal to recapture that magic—which was in part why she had proposed this outing with Damon.

He did not seem particularly willing to cooperate, but she set her jaw, determined to persevere and prod him out of his dour mood.

"Did I mention that I was reading a Gothic novel penned by a friend?" Eleanor remarked. "She will be pleased to know that I enjoyed it immensely. I promised that I would give her a critique of the story and characters, so I must write her a letter this afternoon. *That* is how I have been spending my early morning hours, immersed in a good book . . . if you care to know, that is."

Damon sent her an intent glance. "Shall we ride, Elle? It isn't like you to prefer idle chatter to a good gallop."

Eleanor regarded him somberly, wondering if Damon was attempting to push her away once more, or if he was still dwelling on his dark memories, or merely recovering from his overindulgence of spirits. Probably all three, she suspected.

She decided to not to press him at the moment, and instead, opted for a response that at least might help shake him out of his dark thoughts and clear his throbbing head.

"Very well, Lord Wrexham, you want to ride? Then let us ride!"

Without waiting for him to reply, Eleanor spurred her horse into a canter, leaving him to follow if he chose.

Damon took up her challenge, as she'd hoped he would. In barely a heartbeat, she heard him riding after her in hot pursuit.

The competition she initiated *was* invigorating. He gained on her rather easily, and when he caught up to her and started to pass, she urged her horse into a gallop. Soon they were racing neck-or-nothing over hill and dale.

When Damon threatened to inch ahead, Eleanor bent lower over her sidesaddle and urged her mount even faster, her pulse hammering in rhythm with the thud of hoofbeats.

By the time they pulled up, her heart was pounding

with exhilaration and she was two lengths ahead, although she suspected Damon might have let her win.

"That was splendid!" she exclaimed, laughing with pure joy as she turned her horse back toward him.

Damon, didn't reply. Instead, he sat unmoving, watching her intently, his gaze riveted on her face.

At his continued silence, Eleanor's laughter faded while her pique reached its limit. "It is an incredibly beautiful day, Damon, but your dour mood is threatening to spoil any enjoyment of it."

To her surprise, he acknowledged her complaint with a slow nod. "You are right, of course. I apologize."

She eyed him suspiciously. "I can understand if you are in no mood for conversation, considering how much you imbibed last night, but you might make an effort to be pleasant."

His slow smile was completely disarming. "I agree, Elle. And I sincerely beg your pardon. But actually, my mood has little to do with the aftereffects of inebriation. You are much more to blame."

Her chin rose. "Pray, how am *I* to blame?"

"I was struggling to keep my mind off my other condition."

"*What* other condition?" Eleanor demanded, close to losing patience with him.

"The physical pain you are causing me."

That took her aback. Had she hurt Damon somehow? Her gaze swept over him worriedly, yet he didn't look to be in pain. Instead, he sat his horse easily, while a lazy glint of humor entered his eyes that was almost sensual.

"I did not mean to cause you pain," Eleanor said tentatively.

"You can't help it, sweetheart. You have aroused me unbearably. Now that I've had a taste of you, it only makes me want you more."

Eleanor blinked at the change in his demeanor. *This* was more like the charming rogue she knew.

When she remained mute, Damon cocked his head, surveying her. "During our rides two years ago, I used to fantasize about pulling you down to the ground and tearing off your clothes and ravishing you, did you know that, love? Honor prevented me from indulging my fantasy then, but now that we are wed, there is nothing stopping us."

Eleanor's heart skipped a beat. Damon's suggestion that he ravish her here and now was outrageously wicked, even if it held great appeal. No doubt he was trying to distract her from any deeper conversation, but at least his dark mood seemed to have dissipated.

"We are supposed to be repairing my reputation after our hasty marriage, must I remind you?" Eleanor said. "Frolicking naked in a meadow could lead to even more scandal."

"You weren't concerned about scandal the first time we made love out-of-doors."

"But we were sheltered by a balloon. You don't really expect us to take off our clothing out here in the open?" She waved her hand, gesturing at the sun-lit meadow that surrounded them.

"There is no one here but the sheep, and they won't object."

He was truly serious, Eleanor realized, feeling a thrilling little shock course through her. Yet it shouldn't surprise her that Damon seemed unconcerned by the prospect of a fresh scandal. He was a wicked devil who broke all the rules and relished doing so.

"So now you are on intimate terms with sheep?" she parried.

His smile was swift and brilliant. "No. But I would very much like to be on intimate terms with you."

The tender amusement glimmering in Damon's eyes warmed Eleanor down to her soul, yet from Fanny's counsel, she knew better than to surrender too easily.

"Someone could come," she contended, keeping her tone light.

"We will be able to see anyone from a long way away."

"The grass is still wet from the storm."

"Trust me, I can handle the challenge."

"How?"

"By taking you standing up."

She sent Damon a deliberately teasing glance. "That sounds rather uncomfortable."

"I promise it won't be uncomfortable in the least, darling."

When she offered no more arguments, he swung down from his horse and came around to assist her. Eleanor was transfixed by the look in his eyes when he reached up to grasp her by the waist and lift her from her saddle.

Letting her slide down his body, Damon bent close. His voice was an amused rumble against her ear as he murmured, "If you insist on being missish, we can make use of that copse of beeches at the top of the hill to provide a measure of concealment. I will even let you keep your clothing on."

Clearly he was back to his usual provocative self—the same irresistible suitor who had swept her off her feet in the early days of their courtship. The transformation was very welcome, especially compared to the dark, brooding, anguished man he had been last evening. Eleanor was hard-pressed to deny him.

When she hesitated, he nipped at her earlobe. "You wanted to succor me last night. I still need succoring, sweet Eleanor."

Strangely, beneath the seductiveness of his voice there was a serious undertone that suggested complete honesty. And when she drew back to search his face, his expression held a hint of that same vulnerability she had glimpsed last night.

Her heart melting, Eleanor smiled up at him. "How can I possibly refuse such an enticing offer?"

A spark kindled in his eyes at her reply. Leaving their horses to graze, Damon took her hand and led her up the slope of the grassy hillock, stopping just short of the copse.

When he began to remove the pins that held her shako hat in place, Eleanor raised her eyebrows. "I thought you said we would remain dressed."

"We will, but I want to see your hair loose."

Tossing her hat down, he wove his fingers through her curls and held her head still as he gazed down at her.

His face was filling the sky above her, blotting out the bright sun, but she could clearly see his eyes. The possessive hunger in the dark depths made heat uncoil inside her.

"What are you waiting for, my lord husband?" Eleanor queried, the question almost taunting.

He smiled, a promise, and answered by kissing her. Capturing her head between his hands, Damon slanted his mouth over hers and took her lips in a searing assault.

The very rawness of his male desire stole Eleanor's breath and set her heart racing. And that was before he guided her backward until she was pressed up against the trunk of a very large beech tree.

Those fervent kisses kept on coming while his hands dropped to her riding jacket and made short work of the buttons there. Then lifting her skirts, he pulled them up to bare her naked thighs.

When his fingers searched out the heart of her, he found her feminine entrance slick with the liquid evidence of her own need. Eleanor gasped as he slid his fingers into her ready wetness, scarcely believing how damp and swollen she already was for him. Her state of arousal evidently satisfied Damon, for when he broke off his kisses and drew back, his eyes smoldered darkly.

Something deep inside her flared in response to that primal look, and she fumbled for the front buttons of his breeches, fighting the reckless urge to rip them away. When she managed to open the front placket, his rigid phallus sprang free.

He was rock hard, magnificently long, Eleanor thought dazedly, curling her hand around him. Damon groaned as her fingers cupped his sex, and when she raised her face to his again, searching blindly for that clever mouth, he gave a growl of approval and took her lips hard.

His mouth was hot and fevered, devouring hers while he pushed aside the lapels of her jacket. His hands roamed her bodice, covering the swells of her breasts, as if all he cared about was touching her, exploring her.

Eleanor moaned, arching into his possessive caresses. Damon was stirring an aching pool of want inside her, making her long for him with a kind of primitive ferocity. But she needed more, craved more from him.

As if sensing her unspoken entreaty, he obliged her, moving his hands lower, gliding over her hips to grasp her buttocks. Bending his legs slightly, he lifted her up and slowly slid the engorged crest of his erection into her pulsing cleft.

The sensation of his claiming her was exquisite. Shuddering, Eleanor whimpered against his mouth and opened to him fully, desperate to take him deeper, to fill herself with his essence.

When he buried himself all the way inside her, she melted into him with a seizure of need. Her arms tightening around him, she wrapped her legs around Damon's hips hungrily, clutching him to her as he thrust into her.

His whole body was hard with demand, commanding her passion and giving his own in return. Yet Eleanor met him with the same sweet fierceness, her hips moving in an elemental, primitive, needful rhythm as he drove his powerful length deep within her hot, throbbing flesh.

Another keening whimper escaped her throat. Damon was possessing her so completely that she felt mindless, lost. There was so much heat and need and pleasure that her whole body was shaking.

And then the heat between them became too much to bear. The blaze erupted into a firestorm, violent, fierce, raging. An instant later, Eleanor cried out, convulsing wildly as wave after wave of ecstasy buffeted her.

Damon captured the muffled screams of bliss tearing from her throat, but then a hoarse groan ripped from him as he rode his own explosive climax. Shuddering, his body contracting savagely, he spilled his seed deep within her.

She was still pulsating around him when he slumped weakly against her, letting the tree at her back support them both. Eleanor clung to him, her legs wrapped around his thighs, her face buried in his throat. They remained there for a long while, their ragged breaths mingling, their frantic heartbeats slowing.

Eleanor began to recover her shattered senses moments before Damon did. His passion had been devastating, shaking her to her very soul. And when finally she managed to draw back and look up at him, she discovered his eyes glazed with spent desire as he stared back at her.

She felt him move then. Still joined intimately to her, still holding her tightly, he turned and carried her from the protective shelter of the trees, into the sunlight.

When they reached a flat slab of rock on the hillside, he eased her down gently and stretched out beside her, then gathered her close.

As they lay there, tangled in each other's arms, a peace stole over Eleanor. She breathed a contented sigh of exhaustion and satisfaction, wishing she could stay this way forever, lost in the pleasure of Damon's embrace on this beautiful, joyful morning.

Damon, however, did not feel quite the same peace as he watched her. Twice now he had made fierce demands on her body even though she was unaccustomed to such harsh usage.

Yet Eleanor seemed utterly content—in sharp contrast to the agitation stirring inside him. His need to claim her, to possess her, was overpowering, overwhelming, *threatening*.

He wished he could draw back from her allure. If the fire between them continued to burn this hotly, this fiercely, he would be in grave peril.

And yet . . . this was exactly what he craved just now. What he *needed*. This tenderness. This quiet intimacy.

His fingertips tracing the length of her spine, Damon savored the feel of them lying together as he tried to make sense of his warring inclinations.

Part of him hungered fiercely for Eleanor. Part of him wanted desperately to run. And still another part—an intensely insistent part—was beginning to question his long-held convictions. He'd sworn never to let himself love anyone, to let himself become so vulnerable to pain again.

But was loving Eleanor something he needed to run from any longer?

If so, then why did it feel so good just to watch her? Her face was soft, lazy, sleepy; her mouth evocative and passion-bruised. Her hair was a wild, curly tangle, glistening ebony in the sunlight, the heavy fringe of her lashes brushing her cheeks.

Almost without volition, Damon moved his hand upward over her shoulder to stroke the delicate curve of her cheekbone.

Without even opening her eyes, she smiled softly.

Her response touched him, warmed him . . . unnerved him.

Wanting Eleanor, desiring her, needing her as he did, was precariously close to love.

Love.

Flinching, Damon clenched his jaw as he fought the unwanted emotions swelling inside him. He ached to be inside her again, to bury himself so deep he could never break free; to absorb her healing power and let it renew him. In truth, the feeling was so intense, it shocked him. But so were the voices clamoring in his head, warning him to beware.

The same warning signals he'd heeded two years ago.

Circumstances now were not the same as then, however. Eleanor was not merely the beautiful, spirited heiress he'd become obsessed with two years ago. She was his wife now. Their marriage alone changed the stakes.

Damon grimaced as the battle inside him escalated. He'd known from the first that there was something special between them. Eleanor was his perfect match in so many ways. She was all woman. A woman he admired and respected.

Any man fortunate enough to win her would be a fool to let her slip away. Which was precisely what he had done the first time.

Was he so consumed with the risk of pain that he would ruin his future with her? Damon wondered.

Certainly he knew Tess was right: He'd built a protective shell around himself. Held too much inside. Walled himself off too completely. He feared caring too much, losing too much.

He wanted to flee back into that protective shell right now.

Yet he'd acknowledged another important truth without any help from his cousin: When Eleanor was not in his life, he felt only half alive.

Was it also time to finally admit that he'd made a grave mistake when he drove Eleanor away two years ago? He'd been ruthlessly determined not to fall in love with her, but he'd lost something very precious that day.

Perhaps it wasn't too late to rectify his mistake. For both their sakes.

He greatly missed the camaraderie and friendship he'd had with his twin brother. That bond had been shattered by death, yet he'd been set on destroying the fragile bond he shared with Eleanor himself.

She could end his emptiness, though, if he could bring himself to lower his defenses. She could be his friend and companion as well as lover and wife. She could banish the cold loneliness he'd let fill his life. Elle was the essence of what was absent in his existence: joy, friendship, laughter, feeling. He hadn't let himself feel in so long.

Did he dare to reach for more than a cold, emotionless union of convenience with Eleanor?

Did he have a choice any longer?

It was becoming clear that there was no defending himself against her, no denying his need.

No, the simple truth was, he wanted a genuine

marriage with Elle. He wanted to watch her laugh in joyful exuberance as she'd done at the end of their race. To hear her cry his name as he satisfied her desire, just as she had a short while ago when he'd made love to her. He wanted to give her the family she yearned for. He wanted her happiness, her love.

Damon shut his eyes, breathing her in, absorbing the warmth and fragrance of her, finding a rich pleasure in no more than holding her close.

He could imagine himself loving Elle . . . always, forever.

A soft, incredulous laugh whispered from his throat as he realized how far he'd come in a few short weeks. He'd always vowed never to let anyone close enough to put his emotions, much less his heart, at risk. This time, however, he intended to take a chance on making a real marriage with Eleanor.

He would have to earn her trust, though. He had to prove himself deserving of her before she would entrust her heart to him.

But for the first time since he'd stood over his brother's grave, railing against fate, he was resolved to overcome his trepidation.

To seek a real future with Eleanor.

To share his life fully with her.

To let himself love her as she deserved to be loved.

Chapter Eighteen

Damon had every intention of spending the entire
afternoon with Eleanor, and the evening as well.
When he'd informed her that she would sleep in his
bed tonight, she made no demur. Yet when they returned home to Rosemont, outside events conspired
to interfere with his plans to romance his wife and
make a real marriage with her.

After leaving Elle at her bedchamber door to
change out of her riding habit, Damon went to his
own rooms, only to find Cornby eyeing him with a
look of severe disapproval.

"This was delivered by messenger an hour ago, my
lord," the valet said stiffly, handing him a folded note
of lavender-scented vellum with the words "Viscount
Wrexham" neatly penned across the front.

Damon frowned upon recognizing the familiar
handwriting and form of communiqué.

What the devil? Why would Lydia Newling be
writing him just now? And why would his former
mistress come back into his life just when he had resolved to build a future with Eleanor?

My dearest Wrexham, the inside message read. *I truly do not want to interrupt your house party but I desperately need your help. Please, I beg you to spare me a half hour of your time and meet me at the Boar's Head Inn in Brighton. No doubt you would prefer to grant me an interview there, as you do not want me to thrust myself upon Lady Beldon's distinguished gathering.*

Your fond servant, Lydia.

Damon felt his gut clench. Was Lydia's last sentence a veiled threat to barge in on him at the house party if he refused to comply with her request? Or merely her attempt to be considerate of the social consequences? A Cyprian knocking on the door of a noble estate searching for her former patron would horrify the company and create fodder for scandal.

But scandal be damned, it was Elle's response that concerned Damon. At the very least she would be shamed and hurt if his former paramour made such a brazen appearance.

Ordinarily he wouldn't suspect Lydia of resorting to blackmail, since she was kindhearted and generous and not the scheming sort. Yet he couldn't take the chance of destroying Eleanor's fragile trust so soon after vowing to win it.

Cornby, however, clearly did not approve when Damon said he would be going out again for an hour and would change when he returned.

"Are you certain you wish to take this step, my lord?" the valet asked unhappily as Damon turned to leave.

"What step?"

"Visiting Miss Newling. Is that not what you intend?

If so, I feel compelled to observe that Lady Wrexham could take your assignation as an insult. I should not like to see a repeat of two years ago when she terminated her betrothal to you because of Miss Newling."

"Neither would I," Damon said emphatically.

The age lines in the valet's face deepened with his frown. "Then why would you risk incurring her ladyship's wrath? Particularly now so shortly after your nuptials? You have not been in the petticoat line since returning from Italy."

Cornby was well aware that Damon had spent all his nights since at home, alone, in strict celibacy. He also knew that Lydia had been the catalyst in Eleanor's explosion two years ago, and he was evidently worried that a similar furor would result if Damon chose to visit his former mistress now.

But explaining the delicate state of his marriage to his valet was not something he wished to be drawn into just now. "You are being irritatingly close to avuncular, Cornby."

"Perhaps, my lord, but I see it as my duty to champion Lady Wrexham's interests. Also, I confess, I do not wish anything to bring her pain or sorrow."

"Nor do I. But better that I meet Miss Newling elsewhere than have her show up here uninvited."

"I do see your point, my lord."

In truth, Damon was pleased that his longtime manservant felt protective of Eleanor. But he meant to meet Lydia as she'd requested to forestall any visit here. Moreover, he couldn't just glibly dismiss her request for help. After their long relationship, he probably owed it to Lydia to at least determine why she needed him, in her words, so "desperately."

"Tell Lady Wrexham I will be delayed in joining the company for a while since I must see to a business matter."

"Very well, even though it is unlikely to be a *business* matter," the valet returned pointedly.

"It will be," Damon assured him. "I mean to keep my visit strictly business."

Seeming slightly comforted, Cornby remained silent as Damon let himself out and headed back out to the stables.

He had just reached the stableyard when he encountered the Earl of Haviland.

"Well met, Wrexham," Haviland said at once. "You saved me the trouble of searching for you. We need a moment of your time."

Damon noted both the seriousness of the earl's expression and that he was accompanied by Horace Linch, one of the Bow Street Runners hired to see to Prince Lazzara's welfare.

"Yes, of course," Damon replied.

"There has been an interesting development in the case," Haviland said quietly as he led the way along one stable block. "Mr. Linch believes he has identified a possible suspect in the accidents that befell the prince. I shall let him explain."

When they halted at the far end of the stables, Damon regarded the Runner with a quizzical look.

Linch kept his voice low as he spoke. "Milord, you asked me to keep an eye out for any suspicious characters. I think per'aps I found one. See that Italian cove over there?" Surreptitiously, Linch pointed around the corner of the building to where an ebony-haired, wiry-looking fellow with an olive complexion was grooming a pair of carriage horses.

Damon's gaze narrowed as a spark of recognition struck him. He was almost certain he'd seen the man before—on a crowded street outside the Pantheon Bazaar. After staring another moment, Damon drew back, out of sight, so he wouldn't be recognized in turn.

"That chap is Paolo Giacomo," the Runner murmured. "This morning I caught him skulking about the grounds, there is no other word for it. But when I confronted him, he demanded to speak to Signor Vecchi—claimed to be in his employ. The signor was not happy to see him, that much was clear. I couldn't get close enough to overhear since I'd been dismissed, but they looked to be arguing. So naturally I thought it odd when Signor Vecchi arranged for Giacomo to be lodged in the grooms' quarters here above the stables."

Giacomo could very well be the pickpocket who'd assaulted Lazzara and pushed him into the street before fleeing from sight, Damon decided.

When he said as much to his colleagues, Haviland eyed him sharply. "It's doubtful Giacomo acted on his own."

Damon nodded slowly. "Vecchi is likely behind the attacks. Even before this I wondered if he might be the culprit. He was nearest the prince when his highness took a tumble down the stairs of the Opera. And he was present the night the prince's punch was drugged. Vecchi could easily have relied on his minions to execute the other incidents such as sabotaging Lazzara's carriage wheel."

"You will need to find proof of his guilt," Haviland said. "It wouldn't be politic to accuse a high-ranking diplomat of nefarious deeds without evidence, let alone of attempting to murder his cousin."

Damon couldn't dispute the observation. At the moment it was sheer speculation to suspect Vecchi of masterminding the mishaps. Yet all of Damon's instincts told him he wasn't mistaken.

"Any suggestions on how to find proof?" he asked Haviland.

"An obvious one. We should begin by searching the signor's rooms."

Linch spoke up then. "Begging your pardons, milords, but I wouldn't care to attempt such a search. If I was caught out, it could go very ill for me. I could be taken for a thief and sent to prison or worse."

"I will be happy to do it," Haviland volunteered.

Damon considered the earl's offer briefly before declining. "Thank you, but I don't want you to risk discovery either. I won't ask you to become involved in skulduggery."

Haviland's mouth curved in a half smile. "Actually I am no stranger to skulduggery. And I'm eager for a diversion from drawing room intrigues."

Damon felt a twinge of sympathetic amusement. After years of directing spy networks and plotting international political intrigues for British intelligence, Haviland must be champing at the bit, being trapped at a house party for so long merely to oblige his elderly grandmother.

"I am reluctant to disappoint you, Haviland, but I would prefer to conduct any search myself. If I am discovered, Lady Beldon will have a harder time booting me off the premises since I am married to her niece."

Just then Damon remembered where he'd been headed when he was interrupted. "Unfortunately, the investigation will have to wait. I have another matter I must attend to first. I should be gone for less than an hour, however. I can search Vecchi's rooms once I return . . . during luncheon perhaps."

"That should suffice," Haviland conceded. "I will see that Vecchi is occupied while you inspect his possessions."

"And I," Linch chimed in, "will make certain Giacomo keeps away also."

With their plans settled, Damon parted ways with his new partners in crime and ordered his horse saddled so he could meet his former mistress. But he was impatient to return and solve the mystery of Prince Lazzara's assailants, and even more important, to resume courting his wife.

To Damon's surprise, he encountered the prince the moment he walked into the Boar's Head Inn. Lazzara was exiting the taproom with one arm draped around a pretty blond barmaid, his wandering hand groping her ample breast as he whispered something in her ear that made her giggle.

Upon seeing Damon, the prince halted and stood swaying on his feet while blinking owlishly. Lazzara, it seemed, was more than a trifle jugbitten. Apparently he had grown tired of the august company at Rosemont and come raking at the local tavern.

The other Bow Street Runner entrusted with guarding Lazzara was not far behind, Damon noted. The

Runner rolled his eyes at the ceiling as if asking forgiveness for letting his charge become so sotted, although there was probably nothing he could have done to stop it.

Just then Damon's attention was diverted when a sweet, feminine voice hailed him. Lydia Newling had evidently been watching out for him, for she came hurrying down the inn's front staircase, a smile of relief on her beautiful features.

"My lord, I was not certain you would come. I do so want to thank you—Oh . . . your *highness* . . . I never expected to find *you* here."

Lazzara and Lydia had evidently met before, Damon realized, seeing the royal's glance widen. And judging from the smirk Lazzara offered, he knew of Damon's own former relationship with the lovely auburn-haired Cyprian.

"Are you not a sly one, m'lord?" the prince mumbled, slurring his words. "But my lips are sealed."

Loosing his grip on the barmaid's bosom, he sketched an unsteady bow and then sauntered out the front door, leaving his bodyguard to hastily follow.

Damon bit back an oath, regretting the ill luck that had brought him here at the same time as the prince—although Lazzara was unlikely to bandy the news about and therefore broadcast his own visit here. Still, Damon quickly turned to his former mistress, wanting to conclude this interview as soon as possible so he could get back to Rosemont.

"Lydia, what may I do for you? Your message sounded urgent."

"It *is* urgent, Damon. I need your help. Please, may we speak in private? Upstairs would be best," she added with a glance toward the door of the noisy tap-room. "I have bespoken a parlor."

Despite the imploring note in her voice, Damon hesitated to be alone with Lydia. "How did you know where to find me?"

"It is common knowledge that you came here to Lady Beldon's house party—the news was all over the society pages, along with the announcement of your unexpected marriage to Lady Eleanor. But since Mr. Geary refused to write you and intrude on your nuptials, I felt I had to come and implore you myself. You see, time is running out for my sister."

Eleanor was highly disappointed when Damon sent word that he would be delayed. Reminding herself, however, that she would have him all to herself tonight, she joined the other house guests and contributed to the lively discussion of which play to choose for the amateur theatrical to be performed next week.

When Prince Lazzara approached her and invited her to stroll in the gardens with him, she accepted with some pleasure but more out of a sense of obligation. She had not spent much time in his company since her hasty marriage, and she felt a bit guilty that she had led him on so purposefully for several weeks, encouraging his advances and angling for a proposal of marriage from him before wedding Damon in such an abrupt about-face.

It was only when they were strolling along the gravel paths of the beautifully cultivated gardens that Eleanor began to wonder if the prince was in his cups, for his careful speech deteriorated to the point of being almost slurred at times.

Then, when they were out of sight of the manor, Prince Lazzara startled her by taking her hand and pressing an ardent kiss on her knuckles.

"Your highness!" Eleanor exclaimed rather breathlessly, jerking her hand back. "You forget yourself. I am a married woman now."

"I have forgotten nothing, *mia signorina*," he replied in a low, passionate voice. "I have bided my time patiently, but now I see there is no reason to wait. I want you for my lover."

Eleanor pressed her lips together, biting back a sharp reprimand. The prince had evidently mistaken her continued friendliness for something deeper. "I will pretend I did not hear that, your highness."

His brow furrowed. "Why should you pretend? I am all that is serious."

"Because I find it offensive that you are proposing an affair."

Lazzara looked truly puzzled. "But why would you deem my supplication offensive? I should think you would be honored."

Making a valiant effort to hide her disgust, Eleanor forced a smile. "You are sadly mistaken, I fear. I am not honored in the least. You are suggesting that I commit adultery."

The prince shrugged. "But I understand it is the custom in England. Here, many noble marriages are ones of convenience where husband and wife are free to take lovers as long as the lady provides heirs and is discreet."

"Perhaps in some noble marriages that is true, but

not in *mine.*" Turning, she resumed walking along the garden path, leaving the prince to follow.

"Why? What is so different about your marriage?" he asked as if truly wanting to know.

What *was* different about her marriage, Eleanor wondered, when Damon was insisting a union of convenience between them? Frowning, she avoided a direct answer. "I would never betray my husband that way. Certainly not a man I loved."

"Love?" Lazzara looked startled. "Is that what you feel for your husband?"

"Yes, indeed." She had never stopped loving Damon, even after ending their betrothal. When he had forced his way back into her life a few short weeks ago, meddling in her affairs and driving her half mad with his infuriating interference, she'd futilely fought her feelings for him. But in truth, she had never stood a chance against the fierce yearnings of her heart.

Lazzara was regarding her with skepticism, evidently not convinced that she would turn down his unsavory proposition. "So is that your answer, Donna Eleanora?"

"Yes, your highness. And I do not wish to discuss it further. Pray, may we speak of other things?"

"As you wish," the prince muttered. "But Wrexham clearly does not have the same scruples as you."

She cast him a sideways glance. "I beg your pardon?"

"Just this afternoon I was in Brighton and saw him with Miss Newling."

Miss Newling? Miss Lydia Newling?

Eleanor abruptly halted, which required the prince

to follow suit. "*What* did you say?" she demanded in a breathless voice.

"I saw Lord Wrexham with his inamorata. Miss Newling was once his lover, was she not? Or am I not supposed to speak of such things either?"

Eleanor stared at him, not wanting to believe. "You must be mistaken," she rasped.

"I assure you, I am not." The prince smiled faintly. "I confess sometimes I do not understand the English. I cannot fathom why Wrexham would wish to seek his pleasure elsewhere when he has you in his bed."

But Damon had not had her in his bed until last night, Eleanor thought wildly. She had purposely kept her distance in order to taunt and tease him into wanting her more.

A feeling of dread crawled over her. Dear heaven, could it be true? Had Damon returned to his former mistress to fill his carnal needs, all the while swearing fidelity to *her*? Surely it wasn't possible. . . .

"If you do not believe me, Donna, you should see for yourself. The Boar's Head in Brighton is where you will find him. Wrexham is there even as we speak. I left him there only a short time ago."

She knew the place. The Boar's Head was a busy posting inn on the main road leading north to London.

Her hand crept to her heart in response to the sharp pain she felt there. Was Damon betraying her before their marriage lines were barely dry? Dear God.

Her knees suddenly felt like pudding. Her head spun dizzily, as if she might faint.

"Are you ill, Donna Eleanora?" the prince asked. "You look pale."

No doubt she was whitefaced with hurt and shock. She shook her head mutely; her throat had become too tight and arid to speak. She had to get away from the prince before she broke down completely.

With great effort, Eleanor managed to dredge up a denial. "No, I am not ill, your highness. But I believe I will return to the house, if you will excuse me."

Turning, she hurried back down the path until she was almost running. History was repeating itself. Damon had betrayed her again with the same beautiful courtesan who had been his mistress for years.

Eleanor's hand fisted at her breastbone in an effort to stem the terrible ache inside her.

Did he love Lydia Newling? Was that why he kept returning to her? The thought was sharp, painful, overwhelming.

Eleanor let herself in by way of a side door and then halted blindly, not knowing where she was headed or even where she was. Suddenly paralyzed, she bent over at the waist as she tried to draw breath into her lungs. She felt as if she were suffocating.

To think that Damon had been deceiving her this past week, perhaps the entire time since his return to England.

How *could* he? After all his tenderness and passion this morning, she had begun to think they might have a true marriage after all. What a witless fool she was!

The cold desolation that squeezed around her heart threatened to strangle her, yet she felt a kernel of fury forming inside her as well. How *dare* he? Damon had made her love him and then callously proved himself unfaithful at the first opportunity, heedless of her feelings.

Well, she wouldn't stand for it! But what choice did she have? Eleanor wondered in desperation. She couldn't end her marriage the way she had terminated her engagement two years ago; it was far too late for that. But she never wanted to see Damon again, to speak to him.

Her only course was to banish him from her life. He had wanted a marriage of convenience, so she would give him one! She would live independently of him when they returned to London after the house party concluded.

Meanwhile, Eleanor vowed, she wouldn't let on that she knew about his mistress. She had her pride after all.

No, she thought with a surge of panic, that would never work. She couldn't face Damon. Not now, with this awful despair clawing at her heart. She had to return to London at once. . . .

Straightening, Eleanor forced herself to move down the corridor and then mount the rear service stairs. She had nearly reached her bedchamber when, to her dismay, her aunt appeared at the far end of the hall.

Spinning abruptly, Eleanor hurried the opposite way, knowing she was in no condition to encounter her relative.

At first she pretended not to hear when Beatrix called after her. But when the viscountess spoke her name more forcefully, she turned slowly and retraced her footsteps.

"I confess disappointment," Beatrix stated as Eleanor approached, "to find you here instead of entertaining our guests."

"I am sorry, Aunt," Eleanor murmured, "but I beg you to make my excuses. I mean to return to London tonight, and I must pack."

"Good heavens, what is wrong?" Beatrix demanded, examining Eleanor's face more closely.

"Nothing is wrong." Her voice was calm, even though her heart was breaking. "It is just that I cannot stay here a moment longer."

"Whyever not? Come now, Eleanor, I insist that you tell me what is amiss."

She hesitated a long moment before confessing in a low voice. "It is Damon. Prince Lazzara saw him this afternoon at a public inn. He was with the same woman who was his mistress two years ago."

Beatrix stared at her for a long moment, a progression of different emotions crossing her elegant features: anger, distaste, sympathy, and finally dismissal.

"Well, it is not the end of the world," she said brusquely. "Gentlemen frequently keep mistresses. What is important is that your union is sealed. You will always be Lady Wrexham. If you ask me, you must swallow your pride, my dear, and ignore his peccadilloes."

Eleanor could scarcely believe what she was hearing. "You think I should ignore the fact that Damon is keeping a mistress?"

"Yes, indeed. Most genteel wives do. I myself did before I was widowed. It is unfortunate that Wrexham chooses to consort with females of that type, but in my experience, it is wisest to turn a blind eye to your husband's failings."

She didn't want to turn a blind eye to her husband's failings! Eleanor thought scornfully. But there was clearly no point in arguing. Her aunt had clearly been won over by Damon with the mere act of marriage.

When she remained silent, Beatrix reached out and patted her shoulder. "Trust me, Eleanor, you should not let this overset you. Wives have been dealing with this troublesome matter since time began. Now, why don't you go to your room and lie down for a bit? You will feel better after you think on it a while. Have Jenny put a damp cloth on your brow."

A thousand damp cloths would not help, Eleanor knew very well, but she did as her aunt bid and made her way to her room. Once there, however, she rang for Jenny to help her pack, not to comfort her.

Then suddenly losing all her defiance, Eleanor climbed onto her bed where she lay on her side, staring at nothing.

The bright glare shining through the windows, however, reminded her how hopeful she had been this morning. She did not feel hopeful now. One moment she felt hollow, numb. The next, agony tightened her chest, and so did fury.

She hurt so much she wanted to die. She wanted to murder. She wanted to scream, to cry, to stamp her feet hysterically. She wanted to curl up into a little ball of pain and have the world go away.

Worst of all, a significant part of her wanted to go to Damon and plead with him to reconsider.

Furiously Eleanor dashed a hand over her burning eyes. She would *not* cry over that wicked Lothario! She had known Damon was a heartless rake, and he had proved it once again. She would simply have to come to terms with that painful truth and establish a new life for herself, separate and apart from him.

And yet she didn't want to leave him, didn't want to live without him. Without Damon, her life would be empty. He brightened her day. He filled her with wild excitement. He thrilled her with passion. He banished the loneliness.

With him, she felt more complete.

Eleanor swallowed hard as defiance struck her anew. Hadn't she vowed to make Damon give up his rakish ways? Then why was she lying here in this pathetic fashion?

She didn't want to accept that Damon wanted another woman more than her. She would *not* accept it.

She loved him enough to fight for him.

Gritting her teeth, Eleanor sat up abruptly. She intended to do whatever it took to pry him away from that hussy's clutches.

Angry tears scalded the backs of her eyes, but she refused to let them fall as she leapt off the bed and marched from the room. Instead of packing to return to London, she would order the Beldon carriage made ready.

She intended to go straight to the Boar's Head Inn and confront Damon face-to-face!

Chapter Nineteen

✦

Fortitude and mettle are required if you hope to influence Fate to your benefit.

—An Anonymous Lady, *Advice . . .*

When Damon arrived back at Rosemont, Horace Linch was still in the stableyard, keeping watch on Vecchi's lackey, Paolo Giacomo. And luncheon, Damon learned from the majordomo, was already underway in the smaller dining room.

Stifling his impatience to join Eleanor there, Damon instead took the opportunity to search Vecchi's quarters while the diplomat was thus occupied.

It proved an easy matter to discover from an upstairs maid which rooms had been allotted to the Italian guests. And it was not much harder to find the evidence needed to implicate the signor.

Inside a bureau drawer Damon discovered a powdered tin of ipecac. Even more damning was a silk pouch containing two small arrows and a tiny vial of amber liquid—clearly the same curare arrows that had incapacitated Prince Lazzara and caused him to fall headfirst into the Thames and nearly drown.

Carrying the items with him, Damon made his way downstairs to the dining room. Upon entering, he spied Haviland and gave a brief nod, conveying with a glance that his mission had been successful.

Eleanor was not there, Damon noted with a stab of disquiet, but he forced himself to concentrate on the task of exposing Vecchi for his villainy.

Approaching the diplomat at the dining table, Damon bent down to murmur in his ear. "I require a moment of your time, sir."

When Vecchi glanced up, Damon held out the tin and the pouch of arrows.

Unmistakably, the signor paled.

Without protest, he rose from his seat and waited while Damon spoke quietly to Prince Lazzara.

"Will you join us, your highness? I believe this concerns you also."

Lord Haviland followed them all from the dining room, down the corridor to a nearby parlor.

Once there, Damon displayed his treasures to the three men and explained his suspicions that the poisoned arrows and medicinal drug had been used to harm Prince Lazzara—all the while keeping his gaze trained on the prince's elder cousin.

"What do you have to say for yourself, Signor Vecchi?" Damon concluded.

Vecchi frowned. "Say? Why should I say anything? I have never seen those before."

"I found these in your room, sir."

The Italian's countenance darkened. "You pried into my personal belongings? What gentleman would do such at thing?"

Before Damon could reply, Lady Beldon swept into the room. "What is the meaning of this, Wrexham?"

she demanded. "Are you purposely intent on spoiling my luncheon by dragging my guests away?"

Damon held up a hand, not wanting to be distracted. "Allow us a moment, if you please, my lady."

Looking taken aback by his command, the viscountess started to sputter in indignation, but Damon ignored her and kept his gaze pinned on Signor Vecchi.

"What will your servant say if we confront him with this evidence, sir? I myself saw Giacomo assault Prince Lazzara outside a London bazaar and steal his purse. My guess is that Giacomo also shot the curare arrow that day at the Royal Gardens and sabotaged the prince's carriage wheel in the Park. You, however, drugged the prince's cup at the ball and shoved him down the stairs at the opera."

Vecchi's scowl merely deepened. "How dare you, sir! What right have you to accuse me? Perhaps this servant you speak of perpetrated such foul deeds, but I had naught to do with any of it."

"You never attempted to murder your own cousin?"

"Certainly not!" Vecchi exclaimed, attempting to bluster his way out. "This is preposterous! And you can prove none of it!"

"Can I not?" Damon retorted smoothly. "Will Giacomo deny being your accomplice, or will he confess to save his own skin?"

Vecchi abruptly fell mute, evidently not trusting in his minion's loyalty. In the tense silence, Lady Beldon looked bewildered, while the prince's features were growing ever more grim.

"It seems we are at a momentary impasse," Damon

observed after a moment. "Haviland, will you be so kind as to summon Mr. Giacomo to us?"

"I would be delighted," the earl responded lightly.

"*Wait!*"

Vecchi visibly gritted his teeth before hunching his shoulders, as if warding off a blow. Then exhaling a long breath, he bowed his head in surrender, all his defiance gone.

"A gentleman of honor would admit his mistakes," Damon urged quietly. "Were you intent on murder or something less violent, Signor?"

Wincing, Vecchi shook his head. "It was never murder. I never intended his highness real harm."

Prince Lazzara spoke for the first time, his tone edged with fury. "Then what *did* you intend, Cousin?"

Raising his head, Vecchi gazed at the prince imploringly. "Don Antonio, I merely wanted to impede your courtship of Lady Eleanora. I did not wish you to marry an Englishwoman, but your romance was proceeding at an alarming pace."

The prince scowled. "You hoped to prevent me from wooing and winning Lady Eleanora?"

"Yes."

"But *why*?"

"Because I have always wished you to wed Isabella. From the moment my daughter was in her cradle, her mother and I dreamed of your union."

Lazzara looked astounded.

The confession surprised Damon as well. Vecchi had caused the various accidents because he wanted Lazzara to marry his daughter instead of Eleanor?

"Why would a series of mishaps thwart the prince's courtship?" Damon asked.

Vecchi shrugged. "Lady Eleanora is a spirited and capable young lady. I judged that if his highness were made to look ineffectual and effeminate in her eyes, she would be less likely to wed him."

Lazzara voiced an expletive in Italian, but his tone held an edge of bitterness when he muttered, "For my own flesh and blood to betray me this way is beyond belief!"

Damon stiffened as another thought occurred to him. "What about the balloon ascension?" he demanded. "Was Giacomo responsible for releasing the moorings as well as the other incidents?"

The signor shifted his gaze to Damon. "No, I paid an attendant of Signor Pucinelli to loosen the ropes. When you entered the gondola with her, Lord Wrexham, I saw the opportunity to further your own courtship of her."

An attendant who had immediately disappeared afterward, Damon remembered, while he and Eleanor had faced peril with the pilotless flight of the balloon.

He'd played right into Vecchi's hands, Damon thought, cursing the bloody irony of it. They had both harbored similar purposes—to prevent an unwanted marriage between Eleanor and Lazzara. But *he* had also been intent on keeping her away from the prince for the sake of her safety. Unlike Vecchi.

The larger crime was that Eleanor had been seriously endangered, more than once.

Damon set his jaw, finding it difficult to control his own fury. "You are aware, Signor, that you risked Lady Eleanor's life several times over? She could have been hurt badly, even killed."

"Yes, and I regret that sincerely."

As if sensing that Damon was very close to wrapping his hands around the diplomat's throat, Lord Haviland stepped in to diffuse the tension. "I am curious, Signor Vecchi. We might never have identified you as the perpetrator had your servant not arrived at Rosemont. What brought Giacomo here?"

Vecchi grimaced. "He demanded immediate payment for his services."

"So you hired him to contrive these various accidents but then neglected to compensate him?"

"I had every intention of paying him as soon as I came into the funds."

It was like so many of the upper class, treating their servants and tradesmen like cattle, Damon thought, uncurling his fists in an effort to calm his urge for retribution. The question of what to do with Signor Vecchi and his lackey, however, still remained.

Turning, Damon addressed Prince Lazzara. "I am inclined to let you mete out justice for your cousin, your highness. We could perhaps press charges against him for assault, but as he is a high-ranking diplomat, it might create difficulties for our government. And I suspect the punishment you choose will be more severe."

"You may count on it, my lord," the prince agreed grimly.

"You will, of course, see that he leaves the country immediately?"

"Yes, most assuredly."

Moving to kneel before the prince, Vecchi clutched his hand in supplication. "Don Antonio . . . I truly beg your forgiveness!"

Lazzara's expression was one of revulsion. "At this

moment I cannot contain my disgust of you. You are a disgrace to our family and to our country." Pulling his hand away, the prince spoke in a lower, more humble voice to Damon. "I must thank you, Lord Wrexham. You have opened my eyes to my cousin's treachery." He sent Vecchi a glance of loathing. "I could perhaps comprehend his perfidy toward me, but his heinous acts against Lady Eleanora are unforgivable."

"*Indeed.*" The single harsh word had been uttered by Lady Beldon, who had understood enough of the conversation to be enraged.

"This is outrageous, sir!" she exclaimed to Signor Vecchi, her voice trembling with fury. "I never realized what a dastardly blackguard you are. You will understand when I say that you are no longer welcome in my home. I demand that you take your leave at once."

His expression bleak, Vecchi slowly rose to his feet and exited the parlor. Prince Lazzara, after offering profuse apologies to her ladyship, marched determinedly after his cousin.

Lord Haviland caught Damon's eye. "I will make certain Giacomo doesn't decide to flee the premises."

Damon nodded in agreement. But once the earl had left, his attention returned to Lady Beldon.

She was still trembling, although he suspected her ire had ebbed a measure, only to be replaced by despair.

Taking her elbow, Damon helped the viscountess over to the sofa, where she sank down heavily and lifted her hand to her forehead. Clearly she was shaken enough that she scarcely noticed him.

"May I fetch you something, my lady?" Damon asked. "Wine, perhaps? Or smelling salts?"

Lady Beldon stiffened at the question, then grimaced as if berating herself for showing weakness in front of him.

Drawing a long, shuddering breath then, she eyed Damon haughtily. "I want nothing from you, Wrexham. You are in my ill graces once again for bringing pain to my niece."

Damon leveled a cool look at her. "Pray, just how did I cause your niece pain, Lady Beldon?"

"With your philandering ways, that is how. Eleanor was highly aggrieved to discover you are still consorting with your ladybird."

A cold chill ran up Damon's spine. Lazzara must have informed Eleanor about his meeting with Lydia immediately after arriving back at Rosemont.

At his reaction, the viscountess's mouth twisted with disdain. "You might at least have had the decency to wait until returning to London instead of carrying on in this wicked fashion. I sincerely hope you will conduct your affairs with more discretion in the future."

"Where is Eleanor now?" he asked, his voice hoarse.

"Her bedchamber. She meant to leave you this very afternoon and return to London on her own, but I think I persuaded her to hold off for the time being. Her departure in the middle of my house party would only give rise to scandal. I also told her that she would be wise to overlook your dissolution— Wrexham! Where are you going?"

Damon had spun abruptly on his heel and headed for the door.

"I need to speak to her at once," he threw over his shoulder.

A sinking feeling tightened his gut as Damon strode down the corridor toward the front entrance hall. Eleanor would be hurt and furious if she thought he had betrayed her once again—enough that she might very well leave him.

The thought of losing her made his stomach recoil. He couldn't allow her to leave. Not now, when he finally realized how much she meant to him. How dear she was to him.

His breath seized, forming a hard knot in his throat. He loved Eleanor, deeply and irrevocably. He'd vowed to keep his distance from her, to guard his heart from the pain she could cause him. Then he'd ignored his own warnings. He'd let himself dance with fire, telling himself he wouldn't burn when the flames touched him. Yet all this time he had only deceived himself.

He couldn't be with Eleanor and *not* love her.

If he told her of his feelings now, though, she was unlikely to believe him. On the contrary, she would think he was merely trying to make up for his sins.

Damon hurried his pace, mounting the sweeping staircase three steps at a time. Dread drove him, while one thought kept churning over and over in his mind.

Eleanor would never trust him again. Not when she believed he had broken all his ardent promises of fidelity.

Eleanor's stomach was tied in knots by the time her carriage reached the Boar's Head Inn. When she went inside and inquired after Lord Wrexham, however, the proprietor informed her that his lordship was no longer there.

Relief joined the emptiness and despair and anger warring inside her. She'd desperately hoped she wouldn't find Damon making love to his beautiful mistress. But fortunately or unfortunately, she must have missed him, perhaps because he had ridden cross-country on horseback while she had taken the roads in a carriage.

Eleanor stood for a long moment debating what to do before she finally asked to see Miss Newling. As she followed the innkeep up the wooden stairs to the upper rooms, a dozen chaotic thoughts whirled in her mind. How could she possibly approach the courtesan? With threats? With pleas to keep away from her husband? Or could bribery work to persuade Lydia Newling to leave the district?

And what if she couldn't convince the woman to give up her claim to Damon? Eleanor asked herself with a feeling of panic. Even worse, what if Damon insisted on continuing their liaison?

The very thought was too painful to bear.

She still had not settled on a plan when the proprietor halted before a door to what he said was a private parlor. When Eleanor nodded in dismissal, he bowed and left.

Clammy nerves churned in the pit of her stomach as she hesitated, trying to gather her courage. Deciding it wiser not to show her fear, however, Eleanor took a steadying breath and rapped sharply on the door panel.

When a soft, melodious voice bid entrance, she stepped inside.

Miss Newling had lifted her head, but upon seeing her visitor, her eyes widened in recognition and she sprang to her feet.

"L-Lady Wrexham . . ." she stammered. "What brings you here?"

Eleanor's heart twisted when she saw the courtesan up close, understanding clearly why Damon would be attracted to the remarkably striking auburn-haired beauty. But she forced herself to offer a cool smile. "I should like to ask the very same of you, Miss Newling."

"Th-This is not what you think, my lady."

"No? How do you know what I think?

"Damon said you would not be happy to learn . . . I m-mean . . ." Miss Newling stammered to a halt. Then her gloved hands reached out imploringly. "This is all quite innocent, no matter how it looks. In fact, I was just leaving Brighton—I am waiting for the stage to take me back to London."

For the first time, Eleanor discerned that Lydia wore a traveling dress, yet the realization did nothing to relieve the pain and dread in her heart. "But you don't deny that you had a rendezvous with my husband?"

"No . . . I mean, it was not a rendezvous. Not a romantic one, at any event."

Eleanor's mouth tightened. "Do you honestly think me so gullible?"

"It is true—there is no relationship between us, I swear it. I have not even seen Lord Wrexham in two years, not until today. You see, I came to plead for his help. My sister was recently struck ill with consumption, and her best chance for survival is for her to attend his hospital for consumptives in Italy. I cannot afford the enormous expense to send her there, however. And Mr. Geary didn't wish his lordship to be reminded of our . . . past alliance and so refused to ask him for me. So I had no choice but to come here and beg Damon . . . Lord Wrexham to help me."

Eleanor stared at the courtesan, taken aback by her wholly unexpected revelation.

"Damon has agreed to send my sister there," the beauty said quietly. "You cannot know how grateful I am for the chance to cure her. She is my only flesh and blood, the sole family I have left, and I could not just allow her to die without doing everything in my power to save her."

"I think I can imagine," Eleanor murmured after a long hesitation.

"*Please,* my lady," Lydia added. "I beg your understanding. I would never have come here if there had been any choice. Lord Wrexham is all that is kind and generous, and I had nowhere else to turn."

She couldn't fault Damon for his compassion, Eleanor thought distractedly. Indeed, she had to praise him. But even so, she couldn't forgive him for concealing the truth from her and causing her such anguish.

"If he had such a simple explanation, Miss Newling, why did he meet with you in this clandestine fashion and allow me to think he was carrying on an affair?"

"He feared you might misconstrue my presence and wished to spare you any pain. Please believe me, my lady, you needn't worry. I would never purposely cause any harm to your union. There is nothing between us now. Nor was there any affair two years ago when you ended your betrothal to him."

"No affair?" Eleanor repeated sharply.

"No, none. I know Damon . . . Lord Wrexham wanted you to think so, but it was completely over between us by then. He broke off our liaison practically the first moment he met you."

Eleanor stiffened at that obvious falsehood. The Cyprian was trying to defend Damon, but it was no use. "I have little patience for lies, Miss Newling. I saw you together in the park that day, and when I confronted Damon, he never denied that he still had you in keeping."

"Yes, but it was all a ruse to make you break off your betrothal."

Eleanor continued to stare.

"It is the God's honest truth, my lady," Lydia insisted. "I swear on my life."

"You are saying . . ." Eleanor tried to swallow past the dryness in her throat. "You mean that he fabricated the entire contretemps so he would not have to marry me?"

"Yes, my lady. He got cold feet about the wedding, you might say." Lydia suddenly grimaced. "I suspect he would not thank me for telling you, though. I promised him then I would say nary a word to anyone."

Eleanor took another step into the room. "You have already begun, Miss Newling. And it will be no more incriminating to continue. Pray tell me everything you know about what happened two years ago. I am waiting with bated breath."

*　　　*　　　*

As Eleanor entered her carriage to return to Rose-mont half an hour later, her heart felt the battering of so many conflicting emotions: amazement, relief, contrition, sympathy, gladness, vexation, wonder, anger.

She was overwhelmingly relieved that she'd been wrong about Damon. He had *not* betrayed her with his beautiful former mistress as she'd feared.

She regretted having thought the worst of him just now and was willing to admit that she should have trusted him more.

Yet he was chiefly to blame for her lack of trust, Eleanor thought defiantly. Two years ago Damon had deliberately goaded her into ending their engagement.

Even though she understood why, that galled her the most. All that wasted time when they could have been together.

She had always known that he was her ideal mate, even if, infuriatingly, he couldn't see it. For a man as clever and quick-witted as Damon was, he could be awfully thick-headed!

She was touched that he could be so caring, though. She had actually liked Lydia and found herself glad that Damon had agreed to help her sister.

Eleanor was also heartened a small measure. The empty, hopeless feeling inside her had diminished. And yet she couldn't be easy. Simply because Damon hadn't broken his vow of fidelity didn't mean he could let himself love her.

When the conversation had turned to his late brother, the courtesan had confessed that in past years she had consoled Damon during his yearly ritual mourning of his twin's loss.

Eleanor was glad that he'd had someone to comfort him. Yet enough was enough. She had to make Damon see that his fears, while understandable, threatened his entire future, and her own as well.

The moment she reached Rosemont, she would face him and lay all her cards on the table. She would tell Damon of her love and demand that he at least acknowledge his fears. If he could lance the festering wound inside him, perhaps he could finally begin to heal.

Only then, Eleanor knew, could Damon give her what she wanted most in all the world: his heart.

She had no immediate chance to be alone with her husband, however, for she arrived home to an unexpected uproar.

Strangely, the stableyard was bustling with activity, Eleanor saw upon alighting from her carriage, with servants rushing to and fro, carrying trunks and baggage to various equipages. It seemed that the prince's entourage was preparing to depart.

Puzzled, she entered the house and was immediately greeted by the Rosemont majordomo, who was overseeing the activity.

"What is happening, Mollet?" Eleanor inquired as she handed over her bonnet and gloves to him.

"I do not have all the particulars, my lady, but Lady Beldon has ordered that Signor Vecchi take his leave."

Her aunt had sent the diplomat packing? Eleanor wondered.

"Her ladyship has been asking for you," Mollet added, "if you will be so kind as to go to her."

"Where may I find her?"

"In her rooms. She has taken to her bed with orders not to be disturbed by anyone but you."

Eleanor frowned in concern. "Is she ill?"

"I am not certain, my lady."

Turning, Eleanor made her way down the corridor only to encounter Prince Lazzara, who was dressed for traveling.

"You are leaving, your highness?" she asked in surprise.

Halting before her, the prince bowed stiffly. "I must, Donna Eleanora. The shame to my family honor will not permit me to trespass on your aunt's hospitality a moment longer."

"I fear I don't understand," she murmured.

"My cousin was the perpetrator of the mishaps all along."

Eleanor's eyebrows snapped together. "*Signor Vecchi* was behind your mishaps?"

"Yes, to my immense regret and mortification."

"How did you find out?"

"Lord Wrexham discovered the evidence and presented it to my cousin, who was compelled to admit his treachery."

Lazzara briefly explained about Damon finding the pouch of arrows and the tin containing the powdered medication that had been used to drug him.

"I beg you to accept my deepest apologies, Donna Eleanora, for having endangered you, although I know what my cousin did was unforgivable. I mean to return with him to my country at once, so I will importune you no longer."

As he gallantly kissed her fingers, the prince gave her a long, smoldering look. Then with another low bow, he continued on his way down the corridor, heading for the stableyard.

Watching his retreating figure, Eleanor realized that she would not be sorry in the least to see the last of Prince Lazzara. His highness had taken shameful advantage of Damon's supposed transgression, proposing an adulterous affair right under her husband's nose.

How, Eleanor wondered, had she ever thought the prince could love her as she wanted to be loved? More bewilderingly, why had she ever wanted to fall in love with him in the first place? He was not a fraction of the man Damon was. There would never be any man for her but Damon, she knew that now—

Her heart leapt just then when she spied the very object of her reflections. Damon was moving down the corridor toward her, his gaze trained intently on her.

"I saw your arrival from an upstairs window," he said when he reached her.

When Eleanor made no reply, they regarded each other wordlessly, their eyes locked.

Damon's expression was wary, worried even, Eleanor realized. Undoubtedly he was concerned that she had learned about his former mistress's presence in Brighton.

She was worried as well, although for different reasons. The tight emotion in her chest was a tangle of love and nerves. Yet she was of two minds about how to react to Damon just now.

On the one hand, she wanted to throw her arms around him and reassure him of her love. At the same time she wanted to let him stew in his own remorse for a little while.

She settled for saying coolly, "My aunt may be ill, my lord. I must go to her now, but I should like a word with you afterward."

Searching her face, Damon looked as if he might argue. But in the end, he nodded briefly and stood back to allow her to pass.

Her heart beating wildly, Eleanor retreated, aware that his keen gaze was following her all the while.

When Eleanor knocked softly on her aunt's bedchamber door, she received no reply, so she entered quietly. The draperies had been drawn shut, but in the dim light she could see Beatrix lying curled on the bed, a handkerchief pressed to her mouth.

Moving closer, Eleanor was shocked to realize that the viscountess's face was wet with tears.

"Dearest Aunt," she murmured in alarm, "what is the matter? Are you ill?"

Beatrix gave a shuddering sob yet shook her head.

Greatly concerned, Eleanor sat beside her on the bed and took her hand. "Please tell me, what is wrong?"

"I am not ill," she replied, her voice quavering. "It is just that I have been such a fool. To think I actually entertained the notion of marrying that villain."

Eleanor gazed down at her in sympathy, comprehending why she was so distressed. "You could not have known about Signor Vecchi's machinations, Aunt. He deceived us all."

"But I was eager to think the best of him." Beatrix's lower lip trembled. "That is what rankles the most, knowing how blind I was to his true character. He was so distinguished, so courteous. He paid me such pretty compliments. . . ."

Her voice breaking then, she buried her face in her pillow and gave way to sobs.

Eleanor felt her aunt's anguish, her vulnerability. The imperious Lady Beldon had always seemed indomitable, invincible, but now she seemed heartbroken.

When Beatrix continued weeping, Eleanor rubbed her shoulder soothingly, trying to console her.

It was quite some time, however, before her sobs quieted to mere sniffles.

"Look at me, carrying on this way," she finally muttered in a disgusted voice.

"I understand perfectly how you feel," Eleanor murmured. "Men can cause a great deal of pain."

"*Indeed,*" her ladyship agreed before wiping inelegantly at her nose. "But it is more than that. I was lured by Umberto's charming manner, in part because he was so different from my late husband. Beldon was such a stick-in-the-mud by comparison. I let myself be bowled over by that blackguard's charisma as much as his Italian flourishes." She held her niece's gaze. "I felt lovely and alive, Eleanor. For the first time in memory, I felt as if I were a real woman and not merely a gentlewoman. But I am not the first person to be taken in by the promise of an exciting lover."

Eleanor's heart hurt at that bruised look in her aunt's eyes. "I feel wretched myself, dear Aunt. I was the one who encouraged you to entertain the notion of a romance with Signor Vecchi. I thought it would make you happy."

Beatrix sniffed. "I am far from happy—I am utterly miserable. But *you* certainly are not to blame."

Eleanor was not so certain. "You would never have been thrown into his company so often had you not wanted to advance my matrimonial prospects with Prince Lazzara."

"True, but it is my duty as your aunt and guardian to see you well-married." Curiously, Beatrix's aristocrat features softened as she gazed up at Eleanor. "I do not wish to make you feel indebted, dear girl. You mean much more to me than duty."

Her voice lowered even further. "I never wanted children of my own, Eleanor, and in truth, I was appalled when I was suddenly handed the responsibility of raising you. You always were such a lively, rambunctious child. But my scoldings and insistence on proper behavior never dampened your spirit, and in time I came to cherish that quality about you. I am grateful you came into my life, Eleanor. I know I have never told you how precious you are to me, how much joy you have given me these many years. And I may not show it often. But I love you dearly."

Her aunt's humble, heartfelt admission brought tears to Eleanor's eyes. In her own exacting way, Beatrix's love was deep and abiding. "I know, darling Aunt. And I love you dearly as well."

Beatrix dashed angrily at her damp eyes. "I suppose *that* was partly why I was so eager to bestow my affections on Umberto. I realized that when you married, I would be alone. I will miss you greatly, Eleanor, when you leave me to live with Wrexham."

"I will never leave you entirely, Aunt."

"Yes, but you belong with him. You were meant to be together, as much as it galls me to admit it." Beatrix grimaced. "I abhorred what Wrexham did to you two years ago, causing a scandal and nearly ruining your reputation. But I cannot deny how he affects you—it is the same way Umberto affected me. You come even more alive in Wrexham's presence. There is a special glow about you that makes you even more beautiful. You love him, do you not?"

"Yes, I do, Aunt," Eleanor admitted. "Very much."

She nodded sagely. "I can see it in your eyes every time you look at him."

Eleanor dredged up a humorless smile. "Are my feelings for him so obvious?"

"I fear so. It was evident from the very first." Beatrix hesitated. "Honestly, my dear, that is a prime reason I insisted on your marriage to Wrexham this time. If you had truly despised him, I would never have insisted that you wed him. We would have weathered the scandal together, no matter how painful."

Eleanor's throat tightened at this proof of her aunt's love.

"I realize," Beatrix added slowly, "that I counseled you to ignore Wrexham's inamoratas, but I believe I was wrong. You should not settle for less than his full devotion."

She swallowed. "I don't intend to."

"You cannot permit him to break your heart."

"I won't," Eleanor promised with more conviction than she felt.

Beatrix searched her features intently. "I know there is serious trouble between you, my dear. You should go to Wrexham at once and attempt to make him see reason."

"I will, but I don't like to leave you like this, Aunt."

"Pah, I will be fine. You know I am not one to be defeated by a little setback." As if to prove the point, Beatrix sat up and propped the pillows behind her back. "On the positive side, I now realize I may eventually find a husband who will suit me instead of eschewing marriage forever. You needn't worry about me, Eleanor. I will indulge in a few more moments of self-pity, berating myself for my foolishness. But then I must return to my houseguests. It is the height of rudeness to leave one's company to their own devices."

Eleanor smiled again faintly, knowing that her aunt would recover eventually since she was already fretting more about the value of proper deportment than the pain in her wounded heart.

Eleanor was not as sanguine about her own future, however, as she gave her aunt's hand one final squeeze and slid down from the bed. But as she let herself out of the room, she felt as if she was girding herself for battle.

Even her aunt could see that she and Damon were meant for each other, and she had every intention of making Damon see it also.

Chapter Twenty

In the end, men are not so very different from women. Both long to be appreciated, desired, loved.

—An Anonymous Lady, *Advice . . .*

Damon spent the next quarter hour with Lady Beldon's houseguests, explaining the sudden unexpected departure of Prince Lazzara and Signor Vecchi by saying they were returning to their own country on a personal matter of importance.

Having difficulty repressing his agitation, however, Damon was on the verge of going in search of Eleanor when his valet brought him a message from her.

"Lady Wrexham commissioned me to find you, my lord," Cornby murmured in a low voice. "She asks that you meet her at the fountain in the south gardens. She said you would know which one."

Indeed, Damon knew. It was the same fountain Eleanor had used to cool his overheated intentions during their first kiss.

He couldn't decide if her choice was a positive sign or an ominous one, but unease gnawed at his gut as he made his way out to the south gardens.

She was waiting for him at the fountain as promised, sitting on the low ledge, her face turned up to the sun, her eyes closed as she listened to the musical splash of water spouting from a stone statue of Poseidon. The bright afternoon rays bathed her perfect complexion in golden light and turned her raven curls to black fire.

As usual, her uncommon beauty struck Damon hard in his chest, but he shoved aside his enchantment. The conflict between them was far too serious for him to be distracted by his physical attraction for her.

"Do you mean to push me in the fountain again?" he asked as he settled beside her on the ledge.

Opening her eyes, Eleanor cast him a sideways glance, yet her expression was unreadable. "That depends."

"On what?"

"On what you have to say for yourself."

"I haven't betrayed you, Elle," Damon said quietly.

Eleanor waved an impatient hand. "I beg to differ. You kept your assignation with your former mistress a secret from me. Imagine my delight when Prince Lazzara gleefully related the news of your tryst."

Damon grimaced at the stinging sarcasm in her tone. "I did not want to hurt you—or to have you jump to the wrong conclusion. I knew what you would think."

Her lips clamped together in an obvious struggle to bite back a retort, before she said tartly, "If you truly didn't wish to hurt me, then why did you meet with her at all?"

"Chiefly because I hoped to prevent her from coming here and causing a scene. But also because at one time Lydia was a friend. When she implored me for help, I didn't feel I could turn my back on her."

Still gritting her teeth, Eleanor took a long time to respond. "It is highly admirable of you to stand by Lydia Newling, Damon," she said at last. "And so is your generosity in aiding her ill sister. But she is not the main reason I am so furious with you."

Damon inhaled a slow breath. There was only one way Eleanor could have known about Lydia's ill sister. "You spoke to Lydia?"

"Yes, I spoke to her!" Eleanor's eyes were sparking now as she glared at him. "It was no accident that I saw you with her in the park two years ago. You purposely flaunted your mistress to my face because you wanted me to call off our engagement."

Evidently Lydia had also told Eleanor about his motivations, Damon realized. Yet he couldn't regret it since he had intended to come clean anyway. "Yes, I purposely flaunted her in front of you," he admitted.

"*Why,* Damon?"

"Because I was becoming too enamored of you, Elle, and I wanted to break free. As a gentleman, however, I could not be the one to end our betrothal."

"You were afraid to wed me, so you took the craven way out."

Damon winced at her accusation, knowing it was partly true. He had also wanted to keep Eleanor from falling any more deeply in love with him when he couldn't return her love. "You might put it that way."

"I would indeed put it that way!" Eleanor made a sound of disgust. "And that is *precisely* what you are doing now. You fear loving me because you can't bear the thought of losing someone else you cherish. So you have closed your heart to me entirely."

Not allowing him to answer, Eleanor jumped to her

feet and began pacing in front of him while she ranted. "It *infuriates* me that you are wasting your life this way, Damon! What happened to your brother and your parents was tragic, but you cannot let tragedy ruin your life forever!"

"I realize that," Damon acknowledged.

But Eleanor did not seem to hear him. "You are *not* to blame for Joshua's death or for being unable to save him. You are not a deity, Damon. You cannot control who lives and who dies!"

She was practically shouting, so his quiet "I know" was lost on her.

"I won't let you shut me out of your life, either!" Eleanor exclaimed.

"I don't intend to shut you out, Elle."

That at last seemed to get her attention. She whirled on him, still glowering, her hands on her hips.

Damon cocked his head as he gazed up at her. "Now that you have gotten that off your chest, will you allow me to get in a word edgewise?"

"No, I will not! I am not finished berating you yet."

Even though her fury was clearly not over, however, she returned to sit beside him, and her voice softened to something resembling a plea. "You *have* to talk about your brother sometime, Damon. You cannot continue to keep all your pain inside you. An unhealed wound will only fester."

He knew what she was asking. He needed to bare his soul to her. More crucially, he had to open his heart to her.

"What do you want me to say, Elle?"

"I want you to tell me how you *feel* instead of always denying your hurt. I want you to be able to talk about Joshua with me. I want to know all about him. What is the best thing you remember about him from when you were boys?"

Damon frowned. It wasn't easy to speak of his brother, or to deal with the grief that still festered inside him. But he found he wanted to share this with Eleanor.

"Joshua was my closest friend," Damon finally said in a low, rough voice. "Losing him was like losing a limb. But it was the way he died that was most painful. Watching him suffer as he wasted away to a pale skeleton . . . I would rather have died myself."

"That is why your nightmares are so tormenting, isn't it? You relive his suffering and are helpless to save him."

"Yes."

Her brows drew together in compassion. "Mr. Geary said he tended Joshua's sickbed. Was there nothing that could be done to relieve his suffering?"

"The best we could do was to drug him with laudanum so he could find oblivion from the pain for a few hours at a time."

Eleanor fell quiet for a moment before she reached over and slipped her hand into Damon's. "You and Joshua must have had good times together before he fell ill."

Damon nodded, remembering. "Our boyhood was everything a boyhood should be."

"Would it help if you tried to think of the happy times instead of his last days?"

"Perhaps."

"What if you had something to remind you? Do you have a portrait of Joshua when he was still healthy?"

He shrugged. "There is one of the both of us when we were fourteen, hanging in the gallery at Oak Hill."

"Your family seat in Suffolk? I would like very much to see it."

Damon felt himself stiffen. "That would entail visiting. I haven't spent much time there except for duty calls. I have an excellent factor who manages the estate so I am not obliged to."

"Let me guess. You have avoided your home all these years because Joshua died there."

There was no need for him to reply since she had hit on the truth.

"Perhaps," Eleanor suggested, "you *should* spend some time there. It would give you a chance to summon back the good memories."

He didn't respond, although he knew she had a point.

"Was Joshua much like you?" Eleanor asked. "Did you look exactly alike?"

"We were spitting images."

"Was he a vexing rogue like you?"

Damon gave a soft huff of laughter. "He could be. Joshua was far from a saint. The pranks he used to play on me were devilishly wicked."

"And I'll wager you played similar pranks on him. You must have been a double terror to your parents."

His mouth curved faintly. Then his smile slipped as sadness washed over him. "He was so full of life, so vital."

"Just like you," Eleanor murmured. Startling Damon, she turned to him and flung her arms around his neck, pulling him into a tight, fierce hug.

She held him that way for a long while, and Damon allowed it, pressing his face into her hair. The pain started to ease a small measure as he accepted—no, *welcomed*—the solace Elle offered him.

Yet it soon became clear that she was not only set on comforting him but on exhorting him.

"You *must* forgive yourself, Damon," she murmured in his ear. "You have to let go if you are ever to begin healing. Isn't that what Joshua would have wished for you? Do you honestly think he would have wanted you to punish yourself all these years?"

He knew the answer to that question, Damon realized as a forgotten memory pushed its way into his mind: that final day of his brother's life, when he'd bent down to hear Joshua's last words to him.

"Live . . . for . . . me," he rasped through his cracked lips.

Damon swallowed against the constriction in his throat. He had buried that painful memory along with all his other emotions.

"No," Damon responded in a raw voice. "My brother would not want me to keep punishing myself. He would have wanted me to live life to the fullest."

"Of course he would," Eleanor said with conviction. "Still, *you* are the only one who can grant yourself absolution, Damon. Until then you will continue denying yourself any chance for real happiness, and me as well. *That* is why I want to throttle you," she whispered fiercely even as she clung to him.

Grasping her arms in a gentle grip, Damon extricated himself from her embrace and held her away. "My throat is entirely at your disposal, Elle, but I would rather you delay your craving for violence for a moment. I have something to say to you. A confession, if you will."

When she eyed him warily, Damon held her gaze steadily in return. "You asked me why I kept my recent meeting with Lydia a secret from you. It's because I didn't want to drive you away again, as I foolishly did two years ago."

"Foolishly?" Eleanor said slowly. "You think inciting me to end our betrothal was foolish?"

Damon responded with a wry twist of his lips. "Foolish, imbecilic, idiotic, dimwitted—and yes, craven. And I regret it more than I can ever say."

She drew a shaky breath. "I was so afraid you intended to return to Lydia, Damon."

"I am sorry, sweetheart." Seeing the bruises in the depths of her eyes, the vulnerability, Damon damned himself for causing Eleanor pain. He'd cherished her, but he'd deliberately hurt her, both then and now. He would make it up to her, he swore silently.

As she stared at him, he clasped her hand more tightly, entwining their fingers. "You had me dead to rights, Elle. I never wanted to care that much for anyone again, to allow myself to hurt that way. So when I realized how close I was growing to you during our betrothal, I reacted out of fear. These past two weeks, however, I've experienced a revelation. Not having you in my life is far more painful than the risk of losing you."

It was Eleanor's turn to swallow. "Damon, it isn't

possible to have a future with no pain, no regrets, no unhappiness."

"I know, but with you, my odds of happiness are infinitely greater. You are my happiness. I love you, Elle."

Biting her lower lip, she searched his face as if not daring to believe. "You love me? Are you certain?"

Damon reached up to stroke her cheek. "Utterly absolutely certain. I fought against it, God knows. The entire time I was in Italy, I tried to dismiss you from my mind. I wanted to forget all about you, but it was hopeless. And when I returned to find you being courted by that Lothario . . . I couldn't let you wed him and walk out of my life forever. I couldn't lose you again when you were the only woman I could ever hope to love."

Tears sprang to her eyes. "I think I must be dreaming. You truly love me?"

He smiled. "I never had any other choice, Elle. You made me feel again, whether I wanted to or not . . . joy, hope, passion, love."

The knowledge burned inside him with searing power. After the many numb years, he had opened his heart again. Because of Eleanor he felt whole again.

"You fill the emptiness in my heart," he said softly. "I know that now. Without you, Elle, I was simply existing. I don't want to live like that, merely surviving day to day."

"Oh, Damon . . ." she breathed.

He cupped her cheek. "I am sorry it took me so long to recognize my feelings for you. I'm sorry to have let you think I betrayed you. I lost something precious when I lost your trust, but I hope to earn it back someday."

Her lower lip quivered. "I feared you wanted Lydia for your mistress again," she repeated.

"I don't want Lydia, Elle—not in the slightest. She doesn't make my heart pound as you do. She doesn't make me look forward to each new day. She doesn't provoke and challenge me and kindle a jealous rage in me when she merely looks at another man. She doesn't intrigue me or constantly make me guess what unconventional thing she will say or do next. She doesn't own my heart the way you do, my lovely Eleanor."

The sheer relief in her beautiful face humbled him.

"You are every man's dream," Damon murmured. "You are *my* dream. You have been since the moment you shoved me in this fountain. How could I *not* want you?"

She smiled, truly smiled, the kind of smile that made his heart turn over. And some of her lively spirit reappeared in her tone when she quizzed him. "Did you honestly think I would allow you to return to Lydia without a fight, Damon? I am warning you, you will keep a mistress over my dead body—and yours, too."

"You needn't worry on that score. I will never look at another woman again. I am too afraid of losing you."

Eleanor gazed back at him solemnly. "You will never lose me, Damon. I love you too much. I have since the moment I met you. Even my aunt noticed. Do you know what she just told me? That I glow when I am with you."

It was true that she was glowing, Damon thought, gazing at her beautiful face. What he saw there tightened his chest with emotion.

When he started to speak, however, Eleanor pressed a hand against his lips. "But, Damon . . . if we are to have a true marriage, you cannot keep secrets from me and hide your feelings. You have to trust me and tell me what is troubling you."

"I will."

"I will always be there with you when you have nightmares."

"I am glad."

Her expression turned somber. "No one can ever replace your brother in your heart, but I would love to be your dearest friend as well as your wife."

"You already are, Elle."

"Good."

"Then you will forgive me?" Damon asked quietly.

Another moment passed before her mouth took on a teasing tilt. "I first have to decide if you have groveled properly enough."

His own mouth curved. "You won't make this easy, will you?"

"Certainly not. I have endured two years of pent-up fury and frustration. You have a great deal to atone for, my lord husband."

"Amazingly enough, I am looking forward to the prospect. I will even throw myself into the water behind us if it will help get me back into your good graces."

The laughter that tumbled from her lips made him crave to kiss her. He wanted to hear that sparkling laugh every day of his life. He ached to see Eleanor smile, to touch her, to hold her in his arms. To wake with her beside him. To love her for the rest of their days. She was warmth and laughter, and she was his. Damon could scarcely believe his good fortune.

His features gentling with tenderness, he rose and held out his hand to her. "Come with me, Elle."

She didn't hesitate to oblige, yet she was curious what he intended.

"Where are we going?" she asked as he led her along the graveled path toward the south end of Rosemont's beautifully landscaped gardens.

"I want to show you my wedding gift to you."

"What is it?"

"You will have to wait and see, love."

Eleanor fell silent when Damon refused to reveal anything more. After a while, she realized they were nearing her own special rose garden, the one her brother had created for her when she was ten in order to ease her loneliness. Marcus had given her a rose-bush each year afterward on her birthday, as a remembrance of his love.

She wondered why Damon had chosen to bring her here . . . until they reached her special place. There, adjacent to her own garden, was a patch of newly tilled ground adorned with a similar spiral path. At the very heart of the new spiral, a single rosebush, lush with rich red blooms, had been planted.

Eleanor came to halt, a little stunned. "You are giving me a rosebush as a wedding gift?" she asked Damon.

"Yes. This one is to mark the start of our years together. I thought we would plant another on each anniversary, to mark the passage of time."

Eleanor's eyes filled with tears. Damon had remembered how precious her garden was to her, and he had duplicated it for her. The knowledge melted her heart.

"You *do* love me," she said, turning to gaze up at him reverently.

"Certainly, I do. I told you so, Elle."

She bent to pluck one perfect rose and brought it to her lips, breathing in its delicious scent. "This is worth more to me than rubies and diamonds, Damon."

He reached up to wipe away a tear with a gentle forefinger. "I will be giving you rubies and diamonds, as well, love. The Wrexham jewels are safely stored in a bank vault in London. But meanwhile, I wanted you to know that I consider our union much more than a mere marriage of convenience."

"Thank you, Damon," she whispered, smiling with joy.

He took the rose from her and tucked it behind her ear. "I'll make you another vow, Elle. There will never be a day you won't know how much I love you."

"I mean to hold you to that vow," Eleanor said softly.

She had longed for love, for a cherished husband to grow old with, for children. And she knew Damon would fulfill her yearning. She saw a thousand sensual promises in his dark eyes as he gazed back at her.

Turning to gaze down at her new rose garden, she gave a dreamy sigh and rested her head against Damon's shoulder. "Aunt Beatrix will be relieved that we have made up," Eleanor murmured. "She thinks you are the key to my happiness. I only regret that her own hopes for happiness have been crushed. She was greatly hurt to learn that Signor Vecchi was behind the threats against Prince Lazzara. But I suppose it is better for her to learn his true nature now, before her affections became even more deeply engaged."

"No doubt. I was surprised that Vecchi would go to such lengths to keep you from wedding Lazzara, but I have no regrets that he succeeded."

"You were clever to have divined the signor as the perpetrator."

"I had help—from the Runners and from Haviland. There is a great deal more to Haviland than meets the eye."

Eleanor laughed to herself. "I would imagine so. A woman can sense these things, you know."

"Is that so?" Placing his finger under her chin, Damon made her look at him. "You don't have a partiality for Haviland, do you?"

"No, of course not."

"Good. I don't ever want to see you flirting with him again, wife."

"You won't. I only did so to make you jealous."

"It worked—although I was far more jealous of Lazzara. I am glad to be rid of him, I must say."

"In truth, so am I. He offered to make me his mistress a short while ago."

"Did he now." Damon's eyes glittered dangerously, gratifying Eleanor with his possessiveness. "He's fortunate then to have left the premises before I learned of it."

"He thought that since you were consorting with

your mistress, I would be at liberty to take lovers outside our marriage."

"You will never be free, love. I am your husband for now and always."

Eleanor smiled with happiness. "Fanny will be pleased to know her advice succeeded."

"Fanny?"

Realizing her slip, Eleanor hesitated, debating how much she could honorably reveal about Fanny. But she wanted Damon to know about their friendship since she had every intention of continuing it. Besides, Damon could be trusted to keep Fanny's identity a secret.

"Fanny Irwin wrote the book on capturing a husband, in addition to offering me private counsel on how to win your heart."

Damon's eyebrows shot up. "A notorious Cyprian is the anonymous lady author?"

"Yes. She obviously could not publish it under her own name, but who better to advise women on how to deal with men than a noted expert? She also penned the manuscript I have been reading. Fanny is attempting to turn over a new leaf by entering a less disreputable profession. There is a certain gentleman she hopes to marry, so she is aspiring to earn her living as a novelist." Eleanor sighed again, this time with fondness. "I am exceedingly grateful to Fanny. She helped me capture the husband of my dreams."

"I am not so grateful to her," Damon remarked. "Because of her book, you nearly landed Lazzara."

Eleanor shook her head. "I don't believe there was ever any real danger of that. I could never have loved

Prince Lazzara because I had already given my heart to you." Raising Damon's hand, she held it against her cheek. "I love you, Damon. I love you so much that it frightens me."

"Then we are well matched."

Staring back into his eyes, she saw her own love reflected there—and heard it in Damon's tone when he added in a low voice, "I know Joshua would be happy for us."

She smiled mistily, acknowledging his concession. "I hope with all my heart that he would be." She paused. "Marcus will certainly be happy for us."

"I trust so," Damon said, his tone turning dry. "Perhaps now he won't cut out my liver as he threatened."

"Marcus threatened you?"

"Yes, but his protectiveness of you is one of his most sterling qualities."

Suddenly Eleanor found herself being drawn into Damon's arms. "Enough talking, wife. We should be kissing instead. I expect you to show me your love with deeds, not words."

"You realize that we could be seen by the gardeners?" she asked, amused.

His smile pierced her heart. "Do you want to stop?"

"Certainly not."

His eyes, bright with laughter, gazed into hers. Then his lips came down to meet hers with a poignant passion.

His kiss was tender, ardent, yet it felt different somehow. This kiss was richer, deeper, sweeter because they loved.

It was a good beginning, Eleanor thought as she

wrapped her arms tightly around Damon and surrendered fully to his embrace. Together they would vanquish the fears and doubts and pain and instead forge a bond built on trust and love and devotion that would last the rest of their lives.

Epilogue

If you find true love with your gentleman, count yourself blessed. Shared love is the rarest of treasures.

—An Anonymous Lady, *Advice . . .*

Oak Hill, Suffolk: October 1817

Damon woke slowly, the remnants of a dream teasing his consciousness. Early morning sunlight streamed into the bedchamber he shared with Elle, warming him just as his dream had done.

The dream had centered around a fond memory from his childhood when his twin brother was still alive: he and Joshua watching a foal being born, experiencing the awe of a new life coming into the world, laughing together as the spindly legged colt struggled to stand and root for its mother's nourishing milk.

Eleanor had been right, Damon reflected drowsily. Coming home to Oak Hill had finally allowed him to lay his grief to rest. After a fortnight here, the pain had lessened to a faint, bittersweet ache, and so had his regrets, while his nightmares had disappeared entirely.

And yet Eleanor was the chief reason he felt a sense

of peace. She had wrapped him in her caring embrace, giving him solace with her love.

She had set his heart free so that she could claim it.

Damon lay there with her sweet body curled against him, savoring his contentment as fragmented thoughts mingled with the lingering images from his dream.

His cousin Tess had also been right. He needed to live life for the moment, to make the most of his time on earth. The whims of Fate were so uncertain, he could not entirely control his future. He could lose Eleanor the way he'd lost his brother, his parents. Yet he would not have given up this chance to be with her for all the world.

And in truth, because of his knowledge of sorrow, he was more able to fully appreciate the joy Eleanor brought him.

Easing onto his side, Damon slid his arm around her, absorbing her sleeping body into his.

My wife, he thought as happiness reached deep inside him.

Elle's love was fierce and intense and healing. Her lovemaking was the same. She welcomed his passion with a joyous delight that only compounded his own.

After another moment, though, he brushed a tender kiss on her bare shoulder, then pulled the covers up to keep her warm. Sliding out of bed, Damon shrugged on a dressing gown over his nude body and quietly opened the French door that lead to an outer balcony.

Stepping outside into the coolness, Damon looked out over the dew-drenched morning, drinking in the last of the sunrise. He'd done this often during their time here. He and Eleanor had remained at Rosemont through the final week of the house party, since she wouldn't abandon her aunt when Lady Beldon's sensibilities were so wounded. But once they arrived at his family seat, Eleanor had set out with single-minded resolve to banish his demons.

She understood how important his brother had been in his life, so they'd spent long hours tramping through the woods and riding all over Wrexham lands, exploring the forgotten hideaways where he and Joshua had played as boys, swimming and fishing and frolicking. Not surprisingly, Damon felt much the same camaraderie with Eleanor that he'd known with his brother.

The most painful moment had come when they visited his family's graves in the village cemetery. But Eleanor had helped him say farewell at last.

She had also accompanied him when he called at his tenant farms and made himself known to his tenants. For the most part, they forgave him for being an absentee landlord, since their cottages and parcels of land had always been well tended and they wanted for little. But Damon was determined to take a stronger interest in the management of Oak Hill.

Additionally, he had tried his utmost to make up for the pain he'd caused Eleanor. They'd spent long nights tangled in each other's bodies, sharing the whispers and secrets of lovers. They fit together so perfectly, like two halves of a whole. His greatest pleasure was in pleasing her, and she was easily pleased—

It was no surprise to Damon when Elle quietly crept up behind him and wrapped her arms around his waist. His body knew hers instantly. She stood with her cheek pressed against his back for a long moment.

When eventually she stepped back, Damon turned to face her, taking in the lovely picture she made: her raven curls tousled, her vivid blue eyes soft and hazy with sleep, her luscious body barely concealed by her cambric night rail.

She smiled at him with such entrancing warmth that his heart turned over. Then, her eyes dancing with sudden mischief, she reached up and slipped something over his head.

"You should wear your medal with pride, my lord," Eleanor said, laughter in her voice.

Damon chuckled softly as he fingered the gold medallion, which dangled from a red satin ribbon. Prince Lazzara had awarded him a medal for extraordinary service to his royal house, as well as sending a crate of oranges and several casks of excellent Marsala wine in gratitude for their efforts to keep him safe.

His highness had also invited them to visit his principality when they made their wedding trip to Italy next week, after Damon took Eleanor to see his sanitorium. But they had jointly decided that they'd had their fill of the prince for now.

As for the prince's perfidious cousin, Signor Vecchi had been banished to India, to a diplomatic post there, although reportedly Lazzara was showing interest in the signor's beautiful daughter, Isabella, who had been the motivation for Vecchi's machinations in the first place.

Shaking his head, Damon drew the medal from

around his neck and consigned it to his pocket. "I trust you'll understand, darling, why I don't wish to wear a reminder of a rival when I am making love to my beautiful wife."

Eleanor tilted her head to one side, her tone teasing when she asked, "*Do* you intend to make love to me?"

She had no doubt what his answer would be, Damon knew. She'd become so attuned to him that she could sense his feelings, his thoughts, his desires.

Even so, he replied, "But of course."

The smile Elle gave him in response was so sweetly pure—so sensual, so womanly, so beautiful—that need slammed into his chest. He felt as if the sun was warming him from the inside. And when she eagerly turned her face up to his and took his lips, he felt his desire soar even higher.

Kissing her was like coming home after being too long away . . . infinitely satisfying. Yet it was still not enough. He wanted more.

And so did Eleanor, apparently, for she broke off with a shiver. "I wish you would hurry and make good on your intentions, Damon," she prodded, though her tone still held amusement. "And no, that is not an invitation for you to take me here standing on a balcony, in view of the world. It is chilly out here, and we shouldn't scandalize your servants any more than we have already done these past two weeks."

"Your complaint is duly noted, wife," Damon asserted, sweeping her up into his arms. Then carrying her inside, he closed the door with his heel, shutting out the cool morning mists.

Clinging to his neck, Eleanor returned his intent regard. His eyes had softened with laughter and something far more powerful: Love.

The depth of love she saw in Damon's eyes was a constant reassurance, she reflected as he laid her on their bed and divested her of her nightdress. And she knew his feelings were mirrored in her own eyes as she watched him shrug off his dressing gown.

Her admiring gaze riveted on the broad expanse of his bare chest, on the sinewed torso sculpted by sunlight. His body was strong and vital and even more breathtaking than any woman could hope for in a lover. His skin was tinted a deeper golden hue now after all the hours they had spent swimming together—as was hers.

His reciprocal perusal warmed Eleanor, his bold, seductive gaze searing her wherever it touched. Yet she yearned for Damon to hold her, for the touch of skin against warm skin.

She sighed with pleasure when he joined her in their marriage bed and proceeded to fulfill his promise to make love to her.

His hands were gentle on her body, yet urgent as well. Damon kissed his way along her jaw and downward, his stubble abrading her sensitized skin while his fingers played over her feminine curves. He made a feast of her throat and breasts, showering her with tender touches and arousing kisses as he searched out the secrets between her thighs. And when she was trembling uncontrollably, he positioned himself at the heart of her and slid his hands under her hips, guiding her sweetly up to meet him as his hardness slowly thrust into her.

She was slick and eager for him, so he slid home easily. Then Damon stilled, his eyes hazed with a possessive look as he stared down at her.

When Eleanor contracted her inner muscles around him, though, he shuddered and his lips came down upon hers with hot, wet heat.

His searching kiss reached deep, as did his flesh. Her breath grew ragged as he went on kissing and stroking and moving, controlling their rhythm with his mouth, his hands, his body. But soon her whimpers turned to soft, helpless moans.

She was near the breaking point when he ended his kisses and lifted his head again so he could watch her climax.

"Elle," he rasped. His voice was soft, thick with passion, his eyes fierce and vulnerable with love.

Eleanor found herself caught in the magnetic heat of his gaze—those beautiful eyes that were rich and dark and deep enough to drown in. Then Damon drove into her once more, hard, setting off a firestorm between them.

"Elle," he ground out again, the single word an oath, a prayer, a plea, even as she cried out his name.

They shattered together, erupting into bright sparks of bliss.

In the aftermath, Damon made no effort to unbury himself from deep inside her. Instead they lay there holding on to each other, boneless, sated, content.

Eleanor closed her eyes, relishing the incredible elation she felt, the sheer happiness, and counted herself blessed for her tremendous good fortune. She knew in her heart that she and Damon had always been meant for each other. But they had fulfilled their destiny only after a long separation, overcoming their fears and hurts to find true love. She'd helped to banish the bleak emptiness inside him, while he had healed parts of her that had always felt cold and lonely.

She could not ask for more.

When she pressed a grateful kiss against his bare shoulder, Damon stirred enough to ease his weight onto the bed beside her, then gathered her close again. Her eyelids growing even heavier, Eleanor dozed off in his arms.

When she awoke, she judged it was at least two hours later. Damon was lying on his side, his head propped on one hand.

He had been watching her sleep, Eleanor realized.

Stifling a yawn, she offered him a sheepish glance. "I suppose we should not be lazing abed this slothful way," she murmured. "Cornby will be eager to perform his valet duties for you."

"Cornby will forgive you for making me so indolent," Damon observed. "He adores you almost as much as I do. But he takes your side far too often," he added in an aggrieved tone.

Eleanor smiled. At every opportunity the elderly manservant had abetted her efforts in persuading Damon to relinquish the pain and sorrow of his past. "Cornby is simply concerned for your welfare."

"That is not the half of it. He highly approves of you, you know very well." Damon's mouth quirked. "I cannot say that your aunt holds a similar lofty opinion of me, although she does appear to be granting me grudging acceptance these days."

"Aunt Beatrix will grow quite fond of you in time," Eleanor predicted with conviction.

"I think perhaps her experience with Vecchi softened her."

"That, and the prospect of being presented with a great niece or nephew next year. You read her latest letter. She is in alt that Marcus and Arabella are expecting their first child. And Marcus is overjoyed that he is to be a father."

"Your aunt seemed none too pleased for her friend, the Countess Haviland."

"No. Lady Haviland is livid at her grandson's choice of a bride. Arabella and her sisters were aiding Lord Haviland in his search, but he surprised them all by preferring a lady whom his grandmother greatly disapproves of."

Damon brushed back a curl from Eleanor's temple. "I trust you don't intend to involve yourself in any matchmaking schemes, sweetheart."

"I won't have the opportunity to become involved since we won't even be here in England." Eleanor paused. "I think it unfortunate that Roslyn and Lily have returned from their wedding journeys to the Continent just as we are about to embark on ours. But I am glad Mr. Geary will be accompanying us on our voyage. It is only fitting. Didn't you say he has only visited your sanitorium once, when you first began construction?"

"Yes. But he deserves acclaim for making the entire endeavor possible."

"It is remarkable that Lydia Newling's sister is already reported to be making some progress toward recovery." Eleanor sighed with contentment. "Now it only remains for Fanny Irwin to find happiness. I hope she will be able to earn a sufficient living as an author so that she can wed her childhood sweet-heart."

"I think she stands a good chance," Damon mused. "Her novel was intriguing enough to hold my complete attention."

Eleanor nodded in agreement, pleased that after reading the manuscript, Damon held a view similar to hers: Fanny's Gothic novel was sure to be a success.

"And the sales," Eleanor added, "of her manual on capturing a husband are still brisk since it contains so much valuable advice. Even my aunt is making use of my copy, since I no longer need it. 'Tether him tightly but not too tightly,' " she quoted from Fanny's book.

Damon gazed back at her tenderly. "You may tether me as tightly as you wish, love."

Reaching up, Eleanor looped her arms around his neck. "I am in favor of disappointing Cornby a while longer, my lord. What do you say?"

As she hoped, Damon laughed softly and bent to take her mouth in a heart-stirring kiss.

A kiss which, Eleanor knew, was only a prelude to the soul-deep passion to come.